Dark in the Forest

Another Modern Fairytale

Books by Connie A. Walker

Young Reader

Timmy and the K'nick K'nocker Ring

Teen Fantasy

Echoes: A Modern Fairytale
Dark in the Forest: Another Modern Fairytale
Sunshine and Shadows: Another Modern Fairytale

Fantasy

THE WOLKAREAN INSCRIPTION
The Spire of Kylet
The Eyes of Landor
Triumph at Serpent's Head

THE WOLKAREAN ENIGMA – Available Soon
Revelations of Riddles
Sorcerers in Shokareen
Temple of Rulianthabah

Dark in the Forest

Another Modern Fairytale

Connie A. Walker

Press Forward Press
Fiction Division
5060 S 710 West
Salt Lake City, UT 84123

ISBN: 978-1-940802-16-9

LIBRARY OF CONGRESS CONTROL NUMBER: 2017941557

Cover Design by Bud Spencer, SUMO Graphics

First Edition: April 2017
Second Printing: October 2021

Printed in the United States of America

This book is dedicated to my friend Alberta Blue.
I miss you.

Chapter One

"Hellie, get up," Angel says, giving my shoulder a shake.

I take a look at the clock on my bed stand. It's 7:45 on the first Monday morning of summer vacation. My junior year in high school has just ended, and my senior year is three months away.

Now what?

My twin, being the good sister, had a job all lined up at the local newspaper an entire month before school let out. She did it by winning a journalism contest that had a three-month internship as part of the prize.

Me? I submitted employment applications all over town.

Nothing.

I don't know if it's because we live in Shawon, Colorado, which houses a small state university, putting teenagers in competition with college students for part-time and summertime employment, or if it's because Angel has so much good luck that there's nothing left for me except the bad.

For the next several weeks, I won't even have anyone to hang out with. Over the weekend, my two best friends left town for opposite coasts. Nadine went to Boston to spend two months with her grandparents while her folks go to Europe, and Karen went to Los Angeles to spend six weeks with her father and his new wife.

It's going to be a long summer.

"Go away," I grumble at Angel as I roll over to face the wall.

"Mom has already called you twice."

Angel sits down on the edge of my bed and starts bouncing up and down. My stomach lurches and begs me to make her stop before it turns inside out.

We're identical twins, so why do I get motion sickness and she doesn't?

"If you make me puke," I threaten her, "I'll do it in the middle of your bed."

Giving the springs another good bounce, she says, "You'll never make it that far."

She's probably right.

Angel and I shared a bedroom until we started seventh grade, but then our folks decided we needed our own space.

Dark in the Forest: Another Modern Fairytale

They had to do a little remodeling, but now we each have our own room and in between them a large bathroom to share, complete with double sinks and a separate bathtub and shower.

Angel stops bouncing, and I elbow her off of my bed and onto the floor. She lands hard on her fanny, but the floor is carpeted so I know she's not hurt.

"Grouch," she mutters as she gets up and leaves.

Reluctantly, I slip on some flip-flops and trudge out of my room to the head of the stairs.

"Mom," I call, "did you want me?"

She appears at the bottom of the steps. She's all ready for work in a tailored white blouse and a baby blue linen pantsuit, which really sets off her auburn hair, blue eyes, and creamy complexion. She's a tiny person, barely 5' 2" tall and weighs less than a hundred pounds. (Angel and I were taller than Mom before we even got out of elementary school). She's the public information specialist for the mayor.

"I don't want you to stay in bed all day. Remember, you have chores to do."

"I won't forget."

Dad comes out of the kitchen and joins Mom.

"Angel," he hollers. "Hurry up. We've got to go."

He mumbles something to Mom before he bends down and plants a kiss on her. He's over a foot taller than she is and almost seven years older.

Although Dad is kind of pudgy around the middle now, he was lean and had well-articulated muscles when he played basketball in high school and college. (He calls those years his "glory days," and he has two albums full of photographs and newspaper clippings, plus a trunk full of memorabilia, to prove it). He has dark hair with a few strands of gray and a really magnificent moustache, which make him look distinguished. He teaches English at the university.

Angel bounds out of her room. "Bye, Hellie," she says as she darts past me and rushes down the stairs.

Dad throws a kiss in my direction. "Have a good day, kitten." Then he follows Angel out.

A moment later I hear the garage door open.

"I've got to go, too," Mom says. "Make sure you have your cellphone with you when you go outside."

"I will."

"Call me if you need anything. See you around 5:30."

Then Mom's gone.

I want to go back to bed, but I make myself get dressed.

Then I head for the kitchen.

After I fix myself a bowl of cereal with fresh strawberries, I stand in front of the refrigerator, eating and staring at my To Do list.

2

Inside	Outside
Laundry—sheets and towels	Weed peas in vegetable garden
Dinner—pot roast, carrots, potatoes, and onions in crockpot by 8:30 a.m.	Water flowers in decorative pots
	Deadhead petunias
Living room—vacuum & dust	Pick wild raspberries

Because I couldn't find summer employment, my parents decided that taking care of the house and the yard would be my job.

Every weekday morning for the next three months, I'll find a To Do list on the refrigerator door.

At the end of the week, if I complete the assigned tasks, I'll receive a stipend. (My parents call it a stipend instead of a paycheck because [1] I can control my work hours, [2] I don't have to pay taxes, and [3] I won't get minimum wage.)

I don't look forward to the work, but I do look forward to the money. I want to buy a class ring, and Mom and Dad said I have to pay for it myself. Angel has to pay for hers, too, but it should be easy for her since she has a real job.

I look out the kitchen window.

It's a beautiful day: clear without a single cloud in the sky.

A slight breeze stirs the leaves on the trees.

I want to be out there.

I put the vegetables, meat, and a cup of water in the crockpot and turn it on low.

I throw the light colored towels and sheets into the washer.

Using a feather duster, I do a quick sweep over all of the non-fabric surfaces in the living room. I don't bother moving magazines, books, or knick-knacks. I dust over them or around their bases. Then I do a nice cosmetic job on the carpet, making sure the vacuum picks up any loose debris and fluffs up the pile, but not worrying about deep-down dirt. The room looks good when I'm done. I can do a more thorough job on another day—preferably a rainy, windy, stormy, yucky day.

I set the timer on my cellphone for thirty minutes, put it in the front pocket of my jeans, grab my basketball, and go out to shoot a few hoops while the first load of laundry finishes going through the wash cycle.

At 5' 7" tall, I'm not the tallest girl on my intramural team at school, but I'm the best. I play shooting guard because I'm fast on my feet, can dribble circles around everyone else, and can shoot and pass equally well from anywhere on the court.

I love it, and it's the only thing I can do that Angel can't. She's not the least bit interested in sports—or anything else that might make her perspire or mess up her hair. Her favorite activity is reading.

People are always comparing us, and 95% of the time Angel comes out on

Dark in the Forest: Another Modern Fairytale

top. She's only fifteen minutes older than I am, but that fifteen minutes has had a significant bearing on both of our lives, especially when it comes to our names.

In my psychology class last year, the teacher said that our names contribute to the way people perceive us. For example, are you going to expect the same things from a guy named Winston and a guy named Bubba or from a girl named Agatha and a girl named Bambi?

The answer is no.

It's not right and it's not fair, but it's true.

Give a boy an intellectual name, and he'll grow up to be smart. It's not because the name increases his IQ, but because unconsciously his parents, teachers, and acquaintances will treat him as if he's smart, and he will grow into their expectations.

The same thing happens to girls. If you give a girl a serious, dignified name, she's more likely to become a high achiever than if you give her a silly "girly" name. That's because, if people treat her like a frivolous shallow airhead, she'll start to act like one.

An article I read on the Internet said that most people spend more time choosing a name for the family pet than they spend on choosing names for their children.

Tragic.

I am the unhappy victim of how a name affects a person's life.

Like most things with my parents, I suppose it started out innocently enough. When they learned they were going to have twin daughters, they decided to avoid the cutesy names (Lonnie and Bonnie, Cindy and Suzie, Jana and Jena, Carolyn and Marilyn). Their solution was to name us after our great-grandmothers.

It might have worked out fine if the women had had ordinary names like Susan, Judith, or Mary, but they didn't.

My father's grandmothers' names were Angelica and Prudence. Since my sister was born first, she was named after Dad's side of the family.

As soon as her christening was over, everyone automatically shortened Angelica to Angel. Angel Prudence Powers. With a name like that, how could she grow up to be anything but good?

My name didn't turn out so favorably.

It's not that the names themselves were bad. It was what my parents did with them that created problems.

Mom's grandmothers were named Helena and Aura.

But my parents didn't like the sound of a first name that ended in "a" being followed by a middle name that began with an "a," so they decided to combine the names into a single word.

I could have lived with that if they had stopped there.

They didn't.

They thought the name looked odd with more vowels than consonants, so they doubled the "L" in Helena and created H E L L E N A U R A, making the number of vowels and consonants equal. It's kind of pretty when it's pronounced correctly: (HEL-LE-nor-ruh).

Even though it was cumbersome when I was five years old and just learning how to write, it was totally doable.

All I needed was the right nickname. I could have gone by Helen (disregarding the spelling on the birth certificates) or one of its derivatives like Ellen or Ellie. Since Helen means "light" or "bright being," those names would have been good omens.

But my parents weren't finished yet.

Although they gave me a made-up name that has four syllables, they were determined that I have a middle name as well.

But how does a person choose a name to follow Hellenaura?

The simplest solution was to use my mother's maiden name.

Lots of families do that for at least one of their children.

Mom's maiden name is Dark.

So I got christened Hellenaura Dark Powers.

Try saying that five times real fast.

It comes out sounding like Hell and Her Dark Powers.

When people compare my name with Angelica Prudence, they assume she's the good twin and I'm the bad one, especially since the nickname my parents chose for me is Hellie.

Angel and Hellie.

Perfect!

Chapter Two

When my cellphone's alarm goes off, I go into the house, put my basketball away, wash my hands, and then take the laundry out of the washer and put it into the dryer.

I pop in the next load.

I snatch a bottle of water from the fridge and my sunglasses from the counter and head outside again.

Standing on the back porch, I take a deep breath.

I notice half a dozen delicious aromas that I missed earlier. Bacon, someone nearby is frying bacon. I can also smell newly mowed grass, fabric softener, and flowers—lots of flowers.

I get my gardening gloves, plastic kneeling pad, bucket, trowel, and dandelion digger from the shed.

At this time of day, the garden is still in the shade.

I kind of enjoy weeding if I don't have to work in the hot sun.

I like the smell of moist dirt.

Mom says I'm a natural born farmer.

Of the different kinds of weeds I have to pull, the only one that I know the name of is morning glory. It has long roots that can branch out in several directions. I use the dandelion digger and try to reach the deepest roots, but I know I can't get them all, which means I'll have to dig up a new generation of morning glory next week when this chore rolls around again.

Even working in the shade, I'm hot and sticky by the time I've completed the job.

My bucket is full of wilting weeds. I dump them in the big garbage can and return my tools to the shed.

Sitting on the back steps, I take a break and sip from my bottle of water, relaxing and enjoying the view.

Behind our house is a forest that my father's family has owned for five generations.

My great-great-great-grandfather Eugene Powers purchased almost this entire valley and halfway up the foothills with money he inherited when his father died. Eugene established Shawon's first mercantile store, its first bank, and its first boarding house. That's how the town was born.

After I finish my break, I toss the empty water bottle into the recycle bin and then go back to the chores on my list.

I can't help but smile as I water the pots of flowers that are spaced around the patio.

When Angel and I were little, Grandma Powers gave us each a child sized watering can. She said whenever we watered the flowers we made it rain for the fairies that lived among the blossoms. She said they would come out to splash in the droplets as soon as we left.

Sprinkling the flowers by hand became one of our favorite activities.

As soon as we were finished, Angel and I would take a few steps and then spin around so we could see the fairies. For old time's sake, as soon as I'm done today, I do the same thing—I act like I'm walking away and then I whirl around.

As always, there are no little people playing in the water.

Sighing, I attack my most disliked job of all time: deadheading the petunias. (Deadheading means you cut or pluck off all the wilted flower heads.) Deadheading petunias is a messy, never-ending task. The wilting petals are sticky, and it's hard to tell the dying from the just-opening blossoms.

The frustrating part is that I really like petunias, and I know if I want the plants to grow thick and full instead of long and spindly, they have to be deadheaded regularly. Besides, a plant covered with a bunch of dry, brown flowers is just plain ugly.

I only wish someone else had the job.

Today I'm not as thorough as I've been in the past, but since I have to do this every second day, I doubt a single lapse will be too critical.

I go inside and wash my face and hands before I take the first load of laundry from the dryer and dump it into a basket. After I pull the other load from the washer and stuff it into dryer, I carry the basket into the family room and plunk it down on the couch.

I turn on the television and flip through channels until I come across the 1956 version of *Invasion of the Body Snatchers* on one of the retro channels. (I love classic science fiction movies.) I watch the tail end of the show while I fold towels, washcloths, sheets, and pillowcases. We finish at about the same time. I put the folded articles in the linen closet and the basket back in the laundry room.

With that done, I'm ready to go pick raspberries.

Almost.

First, though, following in Grandma's traditions, I must make certain preparations.

I run up to my room and grab my box of miniatures.

When I get back to the kitchen, I make a cup of tea, which I sweeten with five teaspoons of sugar before pouring it into an empty jelly jar with a tight-

Dark in the Forest: Another Modern Fairytale

fitting lid.

I open a package of chocolate, crème-filled cupcakes. I put one in a plastic sandwich bag and set it aside for my lunch.

I lift the frosting off of the other one, place two miniature serving-trays upside down on it, and carefully cut around them with the tip of a sharp knife. I cut two quarter-inch thick slices off of the top of the cupcake. Using the platters as a guide again, I cut the cake to match the frosting. Now I have four pieces of cake and two of frosting.

I scoop out the crème-filling.

I spread a thin layer of crème on one platter, put on a layer of cake, cover it with crème, put on a second layer of cake, spread on more crème, and top it with the frosting. I repeat the process with the other platter. I fill my biggest miniature bowl with the remaining crème and crumble up enough cake to fill the miniature Dutch oven. I put the treats in a shallow plastic container and snap on the lid.

Since there's a little pile of leftover bits of cake and icing, I go ahead and eat them.

I have one of those insulated canvas lunch totes. I put two bottles of water in one section and the box of miniatures, the plastic container full of tiny treats, and the jelly jar of tea in the other. I quickly throw together a tuna fish sandwich with lettuce and tomato for my lunch, grab an individual sized bag of chips and the cupcake I'd set aside earlier, put them on top of the other stuff, and zip the bag shut.

The tote has a pocket on the front, and I stuff a couple of napkins and some wet-wipes inside. It's a tight fit because the pocket is already half-full of junk. I never know what I might need, and I like to be prepared.

I make sure my cellphone is still in my pocket.

Hanging the tote's strap on my shoulder, I go to the pantry to get my favorite blue plastic berry-picking pail.

I'm all set to go.

My house key is on a chain that has a clip on top. I lock the back door, hook the clip to the waistband of my jeans, and drop the key into a pocket. I cut across the backyard.

A tall hedge marks the boundary between our yard and the forest. There's a narrow break in the foliage on the left side.

I push my way through and emerge in my favorite place on the planet.

Even though the forest and our backyard are separated by a mere three-foot-wide band of hedge, they feel completely different.

The forest floods my soul with peace, harmony, and joy.

It isn't because of all the trees and flowers. We have lots of those in our yard: front, back, and sides.

It's not because of the many streams and their cascading little waterfalls. We have a beautiful fountain in our backyard. The water flows down a series of steps into a large artificial pond that's filled with water lilies and fish and surrounded by decorative grasses and clusters of flowers.

Our yard is beautiful, but it doesn't have the same magical atmosphere that the forest does.

That's because our forest is enchanted.

Really.

Chapter Three

When Grandpa Powers died nearly twenty years ago, Grandma invited my about-to-be-married parents to move in with her. Dad had just gotten his doctorate in English and Mom had graduated with her BA in communications. At the same time, Dad's youngest sibling, Aunt Mary Ellen, was preparing to leave home to attend college in Connecticut.

Grandma had diabetes, high blood pressure, and osteoarthritis, which made it difficult for her to keep up the house and yard work all by herself.

My parents moved in right after their honeymoon and have lived here all of their married life. Some people thought it was strange. Maybe a situation like that wouldn't work for most young couples, but Grandma was a kind and loving person who minded her own business.

When she died three years ago, she left the house and the forest, free and clear, to my dad. My aunts and uncles weren't too happy, but Dad is the eldest son, and there wasn't anything they could do about it. The rest of Grandma's estate was divided equally among the five siblings.

One of the ways that I know my luck isn't totally bad is that I got to spend the first fourteen years of my life in the same house with Grandma Powers. Some days I miss her so much that I have an actual ache in my chest.

While I was growing up, Grandma had good days and bad days. Often when she was feeling well, she and I would wander through the woods together. Sometimes Angel would come with us. Sometimes she wouldn't.

Grandma Powers said that she recognized the forest's magic the first time she walked among its trees. She said at one time there were enchanted forests all over the world, but slowly they've disappeared because of wars and civil unrest.

"You see," Grandma told me, "it's magical creatures that make a forest enchanted. If they can't live in peace and harmony in a particular area, they must leave it or die. That's why your great-great-great-grandfather Eugene Powers was determined to keep our forest safe.

"In one of his diaries, he wrote that during the Civil War an enchanted forest in the Appalachian Mountains was abandoned when the fighting got too close. He was afraid that eventually this forest might be the only enchanted one left in the world."

Grandma loved to talk about her husband's heritage. The Powers clan produced avid storytellers long before the first family members came to this country from Ireland in the late eighteenth century. Although many of them kept personal journals, no one was more obsessive about it than Great-great-great-grandfather Eugene and his son Michael.

Feeling nostalgic, I follow a wide trail created by the feet of the Powers children over the past one hundred and fifty years. When I come to a large rock that sparkles when the sunlight hits it, I turn left onto a narrower, less used, path.

I hear a stream splashing over rocks several minutes before I can see it. Later in the summer, the creek will dry up and stay that way until the autumn rains start.

Going around a thick clump of trees, I come to a glade that would feel magical even if it weren't in an enchanted forest. The stream burbles along one side of the clearing.

Here, the grass is lush, there are wildflowers everywhere, and vivid green moss decorates the shady sides of the trees.

I follow the stream until I come to a rock outcrop near the water's edge. The configuration of stones makes a small cave that's about three feet wide, a foot and a half high, and two feet deep. Grandma called it *the grotto*. This was where she sat down for the first time to ponder over the implications of her husband owning a magical forest.

I set my lunch tote on a rock and go gather a few wildflowers, which I tie together with a long blade of grass.

Then I sit cross-legged on the ground at the mouth of the little cave and place the bouquet inside, about a foot back from the opening. I get out the cakes and tea. I arrange the platters of cake, the extra crème, and the pan full of cake crumbs in a line in front of the flowers.

From my box of miniatures, I take out a stack of little plates and put them beside the cake crumbs. Next I get two teapots and eight pencil-eraser-sized matching teacups. I fill them all with sweet tea from the jelly jar. I line up the cups in front of the other stuff, and put the teapots at the ends. I leave the lid off of the jelly jar in case the extra tea is needed.

Before Grandma bought me the miniature dishes, we used thimbles for cups and buttons for plates.

"Enjoy your tea party," I say softly to the air.

It might sound stupid that someone as old as I am believes in fairies, or elves, or pixies, or whatever the magical beings are that live here. But Grandma believed until the day she died, and she was significantly older than I am.

With my offering made to the forest people, I return to the glade.

I hang my lunch tote from the branch of a tree and leave it there while I go

11

berry picking.

The bushes aren't very far away.

Because they need sunshine and water, they tend to grow along the edges of open spaces that are near streams, like here in the glade. But the berries in our forest are atypical. They blossom and ripen earlier than ones grown in the mundane world, and they produce fruit for longer periods of time.

Grandma wasn't sure if it was because the plants were magical themselves or if the little people did something to them. Whatever the cause, we can usually have berries from the end of May until the middle of September.

As I pick raspberries, I occasionally pop one into my mouth.

Yummy!

My mom makes the best raspberry jam in the world. Last year during the spring, we had a sudden late frost that killed many berry blossoms even here in our forest. As a result, we only got one batch of raspberry jam, and we ate the last of it on Thanksgiving Day. It's really hard to go back to store-bought preserves when you've been eating the homemade variety.

Luckily, this doesn't happen very often.

I work with my back to the stream in case any of the little people are following the water to the grotto. Grandma always said they wouldn't accept gifts if humans were watching.

I strain my ears to listen.

Grandma told me that when she and her children were young, she occasionally heard the forest people's tinkling little voices squealing with delight when they saw the treats that she brought them. (She learned by listening that they preferred sweets—the sweeter the better. That's why I put five teaspoons of sugar in the tea.)

Grandma said she heard the little people talking, singing, and laughing on various occasions, but she never caught a glimpse of one.

Sadly, none of her children believed her when she talked about the forest's enchantment. She was so happy when Angel and I did.

A few tears roll down my cheeks and drip off my chin.

Now Grandma's gone, and Angel might as well be.

Bringing treats for the residents of the forest used to be a special summertime ritual for the three of us.

When Grandma died, Angel and I continued to do it together.

Then suddenly last year, after Angel won her first journalism contest, she decided she was too mature and too busy for such foolishness.

Now, it's just me.

Brushing the tears away with the backs of my hands—since my fingers are sticky—I tell myself that everything is progressing just as it should.

Angel and I had to go our separate ways eventually.

After all, we're twins, not artificially created clones.

With a sad sigh I realize I'm not in the mood to pick berries anymore even though I'm only halfway around the patch. If I eat lunch, maybe I will feel better and will be able to continue later.

I take my lunch bag from the tree branch, lifting the strap with my wrist and trying not to stain the fabric with raspberry juice from my fingers.

I set the bag on a rock, slide the zipper to the pocket open with a knuckle, and then fish out a handy-wipe.

I use the towelette to clean my fingers, but I don't want to eat lunch with that chemical smell on my skin.

I kneel at the water's edge and lean forward so I can swish my hands in the stream.

My reflection stares back at me.

I don't see myself.

I see Angel.

We have the same light brown hair and hazel eyes. We both have pretty heart shaped faces, straight narrow noses, and well-shaped mouths. We're the same height and have nice slender figures. We probably weigh within two ounces of each other.

But we're not at all like those twins you see on television, the ones who were separated at birth but end up pursuing the same careers, marrying spouses with the same names, buying the same make, model, and color of cars, and owning the same breed of dogs, which they just happened to purchase on the same day during a rainstorm after eating grilled chicken sandwiches from the same fast food chain.

Yuck!

Angel would rather stay indoors glued to her computer, scanning the Internet for stories that might make good articles for the school newspaper or that might make interesting research papers someday. She has two 3" three-ring binders full of intriguing facts that she's printed for possible future use.

Although she doesn't like sports, she likes to dance, as long as it's the freestyle gyrating, which features shuffling feet and arms swaying above the head instead of predetermined steps and movements.

I would rather be outside almost any day, even when it's hot enough to fry eggs on the sidewalk or snowing so hard you can't see your hand in front of your face.

There are only two occasions when I prefer being indoors.

The first is when I'm playing on the basketball court.

The second is when we're having lightning storms—I'd just as soon not get electrocuted, thank you very much. Every year we have some pretty spectacular lightning displays. I can thoroughly enjoy them as long as I'm safely inside the house.

Academically, Angel and I do equally well, and we both like to write, but we go about it in different ways.

Angel is analytical. She is fascinated by everything that is real, factual, and provable. Her favorite classes are math and science, with language arts taking the third spot. She reads a lot, mostly scientific magazines, historical novels,

Dark in the Forest: Another Modern Fairytale

and biographies. She is an excellent journalistic writer.

I'm creative. My favorite class has always been English composition. I don't care if we're writing essays, book reports, stories, or poetry because I can always put my own spin on the assignments. I'm fascinated by the supernatural and the paranormal. Although I read just as much as Angel does, I prefer fantasy and science fiction. I'm an imaginative writer.

Angel is interested in reality.

I'm interest in possibilities.

I suppose it was those basic differences between us that caused Angel to decide she was too mature to believe in magic anymore and to leave me behind last year after she had her first big journalistic successes.

Knowing that doesn't make me feel any better.

I go to slap my reflection to make it disappear, but just before my hand makes contact with the water, I see another face—a masculine face—right behind me.

Chapter Four

I jerk around.

My heart tries to pound its way out of my chest.

My hands tremble.

This is the first time I've ever been afraid in these woods.

I search the area behind me with my eyes.

No one is there.

I concentrate on breathing.

This is an enchanted forest, I tell myself, *and I am its keeper. Nothing will ever harm me here. It was merely a trick of the light.*

I repeat it several times.

Although my impulse is to jump up and sprint for home, I won't let myself. If I run away now, I might become too afraid to come back here alone. That would break my heart.

Leaving my lunch tote on the rock beside the stream, I pick up my blue bucket and resume berry picking.

I stay on alert, but I don't see or hear anything unusual.

A breeze whispers among the leaves. Birds trill joyfully. Bees buzz from flower to flower. A squirrel darts through the undergrowth and then scampers up the trunk of a tree.

Nice normal sights and sounds.

Even though I'm getting hungry, I force myself to work my way around the entire raspberry patch.

Before eating lunch, I decide to see if the forest people have accepted my offerings in the grotto. I'll admit part of the reason for checking right now is that I'm not quite ready to sit down and try relaxing in the glade. I'm still a little spooked by the reflection I thought I saw behind me.

I take the blue pail with me. It is full to the brim with berries. If I leave it behind, birds or other little beasties will surely get into it.

At the grotto, the food is gone. The little plates are scattered around and covered with cake crumbs and smears of crème. The cups, teapots, and jelly jar are all empty.

Dark in the Forest: Another Modern Fairytale

If Angel were here, she'd say animals consumed everything. Two years ago, she wouldn't have said it, but she has changed a lot since then.

I gather up the tea set, plates, etc. and put them on top of the raspberries. I will wash the dishes when I get home and then put them away until next time.

When I return to the glade, my pulse and respiration have returned to normal. Walking to the grotto and back without seeing or hearing anything amiss has restored my sense of security.

I lie on my side, reach for my lunch tote, and watch the stream flow serenely past while I eat.

The tomatoes have made my sandwich a little soggy, but I like it that way. Angel insists on putting her sliced tomatoes in a separate plastic bag so she can place them on her sandwiches immediately before she eats them. She doesn't like mushy bread. That's another difference between us.

After I finish my chips, I get out a napkin and wipe my fingers.

I fumble in the bag for my cupcake.

It's not there.

I know I put it in the tote.

I sit up and check again.

It's still gone.

Could it have fallen out while I was digging through the bag for the miniatures and the container of treats before I laid out my offerings?

Seems like I would've noticed.

I go back to the grotto and look around.

The cupcake isn't there.

As I return to the glade, I check both sides of the path. Still no cupcake!

I sit down beside the stream.

When I went to finish picking berries, after I had my fright, I left my lunch bag on a rock near the water.

Could a raccoon have gotten into it and taken the cupcake? I don't think so. Even though their little paws are pretty dexterous, almost like human hands, I think raccoons usually feed at night.

What else? A cat? A crow?

Do they like sweets? Wouldn't they have more naturally gone for the meat and veggies in the sandwich?

Maybe the thief was one of the forest people. They're all sugar addicts according to Grandma. They'd only be interested in the dessert.

I smile at the thought of a six-inch tall supernatural creature struggling to open a zippered sandwich bag. Of course I don't know how big they are, or even what they are. Grandma called them the little people because she didn't know if they were elves, sprites, pixies, fairies, or something else entirely. She assumed they were small because of their high, chirping voices.

I've always pictured them about hand sized. That's how elves and sprites are portrayed in all of my illustrated fairytale books.

Well, I just hope whatever creature took the cupcake enjoyed it.

I climb to my feet, grab the lunch tote, and slip the strap over my shoulder. I pick up the bucket of raspberries and head back to the trail.

I've gone maybe ten yards when I spy an empty plastic sandwich bag on the ground.

I bend over to get it. There appear to be chocolate crumbs visible in the bottom, but the zippered seal is closed tight.

As clever as some animals are, I don't think they can open a sealed bag, remove the contents, and then reseal it.

I don't think the little people would even try.

Nervously I glance around, thinking about the face I saw reflected on the water earlier. Maybe it wasn't the light after all.

I stuff the plastic bag into my pocket. Even though I'm suddenly scared again, I can't—won't—leave litter in the forest.

I don't run, but I walk very quickly down the trail and through the opening in the hedge.

I don't feel safe until I'm in the house with the door locked.

I flop down on the couch in the living room.

Someone besides me was in the woods this afternoon.

Although there is a barbed wire fence around the forest and there are signs at regular intervals that read "No trespassing/Private property," people still get in. Every now and then we'll find a pile of beer cans and rubbish left behind from someone's illicit party.

Obviously, I tell myself, *whoever was in the woods with me today didn't mean me any harm. I didn't have a clue that anyone was nearby. He could have sneaked up behind me and strangled me if he'd wanted.*

Maybe that's true, I respond to myself, *but it is still really creepy to imagine a stranger pawing through my lunch bag.*

I don't want to think about it anymore.

I go get my laptop and turn on Spotify.

My favorite playlists all feature the violin.

For the past two years at Millard Fillmore High School's Spring Concert (at this year's Christmas Pageant too), a boy played a solo on the violin. Each time he just about broke my heart with the beauty of his music. Before seeing him, I'd never heard a teenager play an instrument like that, so full of energy and passion and perfection.

It stunned me.

Ever since Angel and I were babies, Mom has insisted that we support the cultural events at the high school and the college. We've seen nearly every play, concert, and dance review performed locally for the past fifteen or sixteen years.

Of all those presentations, the guy with the violin made the biggest impression on me. I don't even remember his name, but he inspired my appreciation of that particular musical instrument.

The first violin video I ever watched on YouTube was David Garrett

Dark in the Forest: Another Modern Fairytale

playing "Viva La Vida." I found it by typing in *"who is the best and most popular contemporary violinist."* David Garrett wasn't at the top of the list, but when I scrolled through the results, I noticed his videos had a lot more views than the others. In fact the top two videos, ranking them by the number of views, were both his.

While watching them, I fell hopelessly in love with David Garrett. You can tell that playing the violin makes him happy. His facial expressions are sublime. He is as beautiful as his music.

When I put together my first violin playlist on Spotify, I alternated music from his albums with ones by other violinists.

Now I have two playlists that are entirely David Garrett. One is classical and the other is his crossover rock music.

Since I need something to help calm my nerves right now, I decide on classical. This list starts with David Garrett playing "Air" by Johann Sebastian Bach. I take my laptop into the kitchen so David and Johann can keep me company while I make a fruit salad to go with this evening's dinner.

I check to make sure there's a tub of Cool Whip in the fridge.

There is.

I wash my hands and get to work.

As soon as the salad is chilling in the refrigerator, I dig through the linen closet until I find a white tablecloth with a border of bright yellow flowers, and then I set the table.

What can I do now?

I don't want to think about the stranger in our woods.

Then I remember I left the dark load of laundry in the dryer. I pull it out, fold it, and put it away.

Now what?

Before I have to answer that question I hear the garage door open.

Mom is home.

She always beats Dad by ten or fifteen minutes. It'll probably be more today since he has to stop by the newspaper office to pick up Angel.

Chapter Five

While Mom changes out of her work clothes, I fill the glasses on the table with iced water. I set out the butter dish and the salt and pepper shakers.

By the time Dad and Angel get home and changed into something comfortable, Mom and I have dinner on the table.

"How was the job today?" Mom asks Angel as she passes her the potatoes.

"Not exactly what I expected," Angel says with a frown. "I had to take a vocabulary test, a spelling test, a writing test, and a general knowledge test."

"Why?" I ask. "Don't people usually take tests before they get a job? Not after?"

"I suppose so," Angel says, "but my internship is part of the grand prize I got for taking first place in this year's journalism contest. I didn't interview for the job."

"Are the people nice?" Mom inquires.

"So far," Angel answers. "But it's just the first day."

"Do you know what you're going to be doing?" I ask.

"Mostly looking things up on the Internet for the reporters. You know, researching background information and statistics for their stories."

"Aren't you going to get to write anything?" Dad asks.

"I don't know. Maybe if I come across something interesting while I'm on the net, something that'll make a good story." She sighs and picks up her fork. "Someone mentioned that I might get to write obituaries, but I don't know if he was being serious. A couple of people who were listening laughed. I guess I'll just have to wait and see what happens."

"Well," Mom says, "it's still a good opportunity. If we lived in a big city, you'd never get a chance like this. Make the most of it."

"I will."

"How'd your day go, Hellie?" Mom asks. "Looks like you hit a bonanza with the raspberries."

"I did, and there are more that aren't quite ripe yet. We'll have plenty of jam this year."

For just a moment, I want to tell her that someone was in our woods today, but I stop myself. Trespassers seldom come as near to our house as the glade. They usually stay closer to the road that runs along the far side of the property.

I don't want to scare my parents.

They might tell me I have to stay out of the forest unless someone is with me.

I'm not willing to let that happen.

After dinner, as I get ready for bed, I review the incident in the forest. I'll admit I had a momentary fright, but I wasn't hurt, and the trespasser had plenty of opportunities to harm me if he had been so inclined.

I'm brushing my teeth when Angel comes into the bathroom.

"What happened today?" she asks me.

"What do you mean what happened?"

"Come on, Hellie," Angel says. "When Mom mentioned raspberries at the table, your face went completely blank. I know that look. It means you're hiding something."

"You're imagining things," I tell her.

"No, I'm not."

"If my face went blank," I say, "it was probably because I was thinking about Grandma while I was picking berries." Tears well up in my eyes. "I miss her a lot."

"I miss her too." Angel puts her arm around me. "She loved to go berry picking with you. I understand how that could bring back memories."

"It always upsets Mom and Dad when I get tearful over Grandma," I say. "They don't realize how close we were."

"I think maybe they're a bit jealous. I was sometimes."

"Oh, Angel," I cry. "We never meant to leave you out. You've got to believe that."

"I do." Angel laughs. "I never could understand the fascination you two had for the woods—especially since that's where bugs and spiders and snakes hang out."

"Well," I say, "I've seen a few bugs, but personally I've never seen spiders or snakes in the forest, although I know they're there. If I ever catch sight of some, I'll give them your regards."

"Don't go to any trouble on my account," Angel says.

In the morning, I do my regular thirty minutes of basketball practice and then rush through my chores. I feel the need to return to the forest and prove to myself that I can be as relaxed and as calm as I was before.

I make a lunch to eat in the glade, but I don't go to a lot of trouble making a fancy offering for the little people this time.

I get half a dozen Oreo cookies, put them in a sandwich bag, and smack them with the bowl of a spoon.

When I shake the bag I have a nice collection of cookie crumbs and chunks of frosting. I find a plastic lid that doesn't fit anything anymore that I can use as a big serving platter. I fill a jelly jar with wild cherry soda pop. The only miniatures I include are the cups.

I hang my earbuds around my neck and carry my Kindle with me instead of the plastic berry-picking bucket. I intend to listen to David Garrett's violin while I lie in the shade and read. His album *Garrett vs. Paganini* is the first one I ever bought and downloaded.

After I enter the forest, I go straight to the grotto, dump the smashed Oreos onto the plastic lid and fill the cups with pop. I place the offering inside the little cave.

Now I can go to the glade, relax, watch the water, listen to music, and read until I'm hungry enough to eat.

When I get there, though, I'm confronted with a mystery.

Hanging from the same branch where I hung my lunch bag yesterday is a glossy round red object that looks a lot like a large plastic Christmas tree ornament. It is tied to the branch with a loop of black velvet ribbon. At the top of the ornament is a rolled up piece of paper tied inside the big bowknot.

I look around curiously.

No one from my family, except for me, has been in the forest for months. I wonder if the letter and ornament are meant for me or for the unknown person who was here yesterday.

Maybe it isn't for either of us.

There might be dozens of people I don't know anything about who are wandering around in our woods.

Even so, what are the odds that they would chose my favorite place in the entire forest to exchange their communications?

I pull the paper free.

It is sealed with a circle of deep purple wax about the size of a nickel. There is no name written on the outside of the letter.

Letter?

Hmm?

Why do I assume it's a letter?

For all I know, it could be the recipe for cinnamon rolls, or an advertisement for a movie, or the announcement of a new sporting goods store opening in downtown Shawon.

I rub the edge of the paper between my thumb and index finger. It's thick like velum, but it looks like parchment.

I slide my finger over the sealing wax.

The top is smooth except for a slightly depressed area. I hold the paper sideways in the sunlight and move it around until I get enough contrast between light and shadow that I can identify the subtle pattern. It's a flower with six overlapping lobes, three large and three small.

I decide I might as well open the paper and find out what it is.

Since I don't want to ruin the seal—it is very pretty—I carefully pry the wax away from the edge with my fingernails.

A secondary reason for not breaking the seal is that if the note is addressed

Dark in the Forest: Another Modern Fairytale

to someone else, I might be able to heat the bottom of the wax and reseal it.

Happily, that's not necessary.

The letter is meant for me.

> *Dear Minder of the Woods,*
>
> *It was not my intention to frighten you yesterday, and I offer you my sincere apology for any discomfort I unintentionally caused.*
>
> *I was in the forest seeking items that were stolen from my friends and possibly concealed here. Unfortunately, not knowing where to look, or even if the items had indeed ever been at this location, my search was prolonged.*
>
> *As I wandered fruitlessly through the forest, I detected an enticing aroma coming from a fabric bag that was dangling from the branch of a tree.*
>
> *To my embarrassment and profound regret, this served to set my stomach a-rumbling, reminding me that I had not brought any kind of sustenance with me.*
>
> *Surrendering to my hunger, I momentarily set aside the constraints of courtesy and good upbringing and indulged my appetite with something to which I had no rights.*
>
> *Again, I offer you my apology.*
>
> *In hopes of making recompense, I have brought you a delicacy from my home to replace the one that I took.*
>
> *In order to easily open the container, you need to place your thumbs on the sides of the engraving, press slightly, and then slide your thumbs apart.*
>
> *I did not find the items I sought. I hope I will be allowed to return to continue the search. If that be so, it is my fervent desire that we might meet and speak.*
>
>
>
> *Your devoted servant,*
> *Kaden Deke Katsenevas*
>
>

I sit down cross-legged on the grass and read through the letter again. Having been raised by a mother who is a public information specialist and a father who is an English professor, I have been exposed to a great deal of classical and contemporary literature.

Kaden's letter doesn't feel like it belongs in modern America. First, the language is awfully stilted and formal. Second, there is a total lack of contractions. Third, there is not a single word of slang.

His letter makes me think of *Gulliver's Travels* and *Alice's Adventures in Wonderland*. I don't know why. Maybe there is some similarity of style that my unconscious mind recognizes. To figure out what, though, would require a great deal of research, and I don't care that much.

I'm tempted to open the "Christmas tree ornament" right now, but just in case there is something really luscious and decadent inside, I decide I'd better wait until after I've eaten my lunch.

I check the time on my cellphone.

It's only 11:15.

I plug in my earbuds, open my Kindle to Music, select *Garrett vs. Paganini*, and tap on the first number. I listen to the music for several seconds before I go to Books and choose *Selected Poetry of Lord Byron.*

Lying on my stomach, I read Byron's "The Prisoner of Chillon." It's a long poem and one of my favorites.

Every now and then, I glance at the red ball and wonder what's inside.

I probably should have chosen something else to read, something that would have forced my eyes to stay on the page.

I've read "The Prisoner of Chillon" so often that I almost have the entire thing memorized. When I get to the last line, "—even I / Regained my freedom with a sigh," I reach for my lunch tote.

I take out a sandwich made from some of last night's leftover roast beef. Munching on it, I read through Kaden's letter again.

I doubt we'll ever meet.

If it were Angel, their meeting would be a foregone conclusion, but my luck just doesn't work that way—unless he's a serial killer or something.

However, since he regrets having stolen my cupcake and has tried to repay me by providing a substitute, I doubt he's a sociopath or a hardened criminal. He's probably a nice normal guy, which puts him out of my league.

I wonder what he's like.

He must be educated, although not necessarily in this country. The stilted writing style and the wordiness might be explained if English weren't his first language. Taking that into account, his letter is well written with only one grammatical error that I , daughter of an English professor, spotted. (In the second to the last paragraph, he split the infinitive *to open* with the world *easily.* The phrase should read *In order to open the container easily,* but it's still a sweet letter, so I'm willing to cut him some slack).

I wonder how old Kaden is.

Could he possibly be my age?

I shake my head.

As noted earlier, my luck just doesn't work that way.

Now that I think about it, though, I'll bet he's not too much older than I am. Here's my reasoning:

Obviously, someone considers him a responsible person since he was given the task of coming here by himself to search for the missing items, and the objects must be valuable—or why bother?

Since he doesn't know if he'll be allowed to come back and continue looking, he didn't come here by choice but was under someone else's direction, maybe a parent or an employer. Whichever, their trust in him implies that he has a certain level of maturity, so I would guess he's beyond high school age.

Next, he refers to the constraints of courtesy and good upbringing. That sounds as if he's still young enough to hear those silent, and not so silent, rules about manners that our parents plant and cultivate in our brains. To me, that indicates he hasn't been out on his own very long.

Thus, he's probably in his late teens or early twenties.

I think his upbringing must have been fairly strict for him to feel guilty about swiping a cupcake.

Heck, kids from my school have been stealing treats from each other's lunch trays, lockers, desks, and lunchboxes ever since kindergarten. (Not me, of course. If I tried, I'd be the only person in the history of the world who got caught and expelled for it.)

The part of Kaden's letter that puzzles me the most is his desire that we meet and speak.

Granting that he caught glimpses of me while he was wandering around yesterday, I'm no raving beauty.

Angel and I are attractive. I look at her and I look at my reflection in a mirror, and I can't deny that. But we're not the drop-dead gorgeous types that guys fall in love (or in lust) with at first sight.

Maybe he saw me and thought I looked like a nice person, someone who might share his enjoyment of being in the woods—if he enjoys being in the woods. Or maybe he thought that I looked like a sad, lonely girl who was performing strange rituals in the forest all by herself. Maybe he felt sorry for me and wanted to give me something positive to anticipate.

Dang!

I sure know how to ruin my own good mood, don't I?

I sit up.

Refocusing my attention, I pick up the ornament. I haven't finished my lunch yet, but suddenly I feel a little depressed and could do with some unhealthy comfort food.

The engraving is a six-lobed flower that matches the one in the sealing wax on the letter. But the ball doesn't have seams anywhere—or any upside or downside. How am I supposed to know how to hold it so the contents don't spill out?

I ponder.

Probably the engraving goes on the top.

I put my thumbs on it, but quickly remove them.

Should I be nervous?

My parents always warned Angel and me not to accept gifts from strangers.

What if this is some kind of trick?

Some kind of booby trap?

I think about it a moment and then start to laugh.

Don't be paranoid, I tell myself. *You're not that important. No one's going to go to this kind of elaborate bother to harm some unknown girl in backwater*

Colorado.

Amused at my arrogance, I place my thumbs on the flower, apply a little pressure, and slide my thumbs away from each other.

The ball unfolds like a blossom.

Its upper half splits into six sections that curl back like arched and pointed petals.

Centered in the middle is a cube.

The top and sides fold away, revealing a confection that looks a bit like cake and a bit like candy. It's square and slightly smaller than the cupcake he took.

It appears to be frosted with fondant or covered with a thin candy shell. Whatever the coating is, it's translucent. I can see a soft peachy-colored interior. On top are tiny six-lobed candy flowers in a dozen bright colors.

It's almost too pretty to eat.

Almost.

I nibble at the top edge.

My mouth experiences an explosion of fantastic flavors.

The inside texture is similar to cake, but maybe a little moister than the average. The coating is lighter than fondant. It's almost a glaze, but creamier, although it's not regular icing.

I take another bite, a real bite this time.

I chew slowly, encouraging my tongue to sort through the various tastes.

They can't be identified, only savored.

I have no idea what this confectionary marvel is called, but it deserves something like—uhm—like Transcendental Delight, maybe.

Regardless of the name, this extraordinary treat obviously originated in a foreign country.

How in the world has its existence been kept secret?

In the USA we enjoy lots of desserts from other countries: baklava, tiramisu, biscotti, apple strudel, marzipan, crème brûlée, Swiss chocolates, and Danish pastries. I'm sure there are others, but those are the ones I can pull off the top of my head.

Where has this wonder been all my life?

And where can I get more?

Before I took my first bite, I had intended to eat only half.

In case it was poisoned, I figured maybe I'd only get halfway sick.

Alas, I don't have enough willpower.

Transcendental Delight (I have to call it something) might be the only food in the world that's worth dying for.

I take small bites in order to prolong the pleasure.

When the entire thing is gone, I lie back on the grass feeling satisfied and contented.

I need to write Kaden a thank you note.

In the pocket at the front of my lunch bag, besides a lot of miscellaneous junk, I always have a pen and a small notepad.

I roll over so I can grab the bag and pull it to me.

I dig out the pen and paper.

I write:

> *Dear Kaden,*
>
> *I accept your apology.*
>
> *You didn't need to give me anything in return, but I'm glad you did. I don't know the name of the sweet treat you provided, but it was scrumptious. I've never tasted anything like it. You've more than repaid me for the cupcake you took.*
>
> *Thank you very much.*
>
> *I don't know if our paths will cross in the future, but if they do, please introduce yourself.*
>
> > *Sincerely yours,*
> > *Hellenaura Dark Powers*

My thank you note isn't as formal as his letter, but I simply don't write that way and I don't see any reason to try.

However, since he signed his full name, I feel obligated to do the same. I hope he doesn't turn around and run when he sees it.

I take the sandwich bag that the Oreo cookie crumbs were in, turn it inside out, and wipe it clean on my jeans. After I turn it right again, I slip the note inside, smooth the bag from bottom to top in order to press out the excess air, and zip the bag closed.

For a moment I consider tying it to the branch with the black velvet ribbon, but I'm too selfish.

I want to keep the ribbon, the letter, and the red ball (which surprised me by closing as soon as I removed the cake) as mementoes. I don't think I'll even tell Angel about them.

I dig around in the pocket of my tote and pull out a piece of pink yarn. I use the pen to poke a hole in the top of the sandwich bag, right below the seal. Then I thread the yarn through.

I tie my thank you note to the same branch he used.

If Kaden doesn't return before the next summer storm, he'll probably never find my note. The wind and the rain will destroy it.

Regardless of how I was feeling earlier about my generally bad luck, for some reason, I'm not worried.

I believe he'll come back.

We're destined to meet each other face to face eventually.

I'm sure of it, and the knowledge frightens and excites me at the same time.

Chapter Six

Once again, I'm wakened by someone shaking me, but it's not Angel.
It's Dad.

"Hellie," he says. "I need a favor."

I sit up in bed.

"How would you like to earn a little extra money today?"

"Doing what?" I ask, not wanting to commit to anything too quickly since I'm still half asleep.

"You've met Margie, my secretary, haven't you?"

I nod.

"Her sister, Joan Bennett, owns Happy Hands Daycare Center. One of her employees went to Las Vegas to get married last week. She was due back to work this morning, but apparently she and her husband missed their flight last night and can't get another one until later today.

"That leaves Joan shorthanded. She called Margie and asked if she knew any young girls who might be available to help out today. Margie called me. Are you interested?"

"Sure," I say. "How much do I get paid?"

"I'm afraid it's just minimum wage, but you'll work seven hours and get paid for eight to compensate you for having to eat lunch with the children."

I glance at the clock. "When do I need to be there?"

"You'll work from 8:30 to 3:30. Mom said she'd go in a little late today so she can drop you off on her way downtown. Then if you don't mind, you can take the bus home. The daycare center is on Sycamore Drive, and there's a bus stop half a block away on the corner of Sycamore and Eighth Avenue."

"All right," I say. "I'll do it."

My heart is pounding excitedly.

Eight hours at minimum wage will help pay for my class ring.

Dad gives me a kiss on the forehead. "I'll go call Joan and let her know."

What does a daycare worker wear on the job?

After staring dumbly in my closet for several minutes, I decide on jeans, light blue t-shirt, white socks, and black runners.

Dark in the Forest: Another Modern Fairytale

I decide not to carry a purse.

I put my driver's license, a five-dollar bill, and some loose change in a small credit card holder. (Actually it was supposed to be a wallet. I made it at girls' camp when I was ten, but I read the instructions wrong and cut my piece of leather too small. Typical.)

I put the holder in my back pocket, clip my key chain to my waistband, and slide the key into a front pocket.

I figure my light brown hair is just about the right length to get blown into my eyes and hamper my vision, or droop in the soup, or get tangled up in some child's fist. Bending at the waist, I brush my hair forward and catch it with a white scrunchie, creating a high ponytail. I tuck the ends under and use a couple of hairpins to fasten them in place.

I eat a light breakfast, just whole-wheat toast and milk, so my stomach doesn't act up like it does sometimes when I'm jittery.

Over the years I've passed Happy Hands dozens of times, but I've never paid any attention to it. As Mom pulls up in front this morning, I take a good look.

The building appears to be a nice, one-story, middle-aged house (not too new, not too old) with a basement. The outside is painted white, but the trim, front door, and shutters are sky blue. "Happy Hands Daycare Center" is printed inside a rainbow that makes an arc over the top of the door.

The front yard is small and outlined with flowerbeds full of brightly colored blossoms.

Through a high chain-link fence that surrounds the backyard, I see one of those fancy, hard plastic contraptions that looks like a tall, multilayered castle with slides, monkey bars, rope bridges, and various other gizmos attached to the outer walls.

The house next door to Happy Hands on the left is similar except that the trim, door, and shutters are apple green. Above the door is some kind of printing (no rainbow), but I can't read it from this angle.

As I walk up the sidewalk, I wonder if I'm supposed to knock, ring the doorbell, or barge right in. This place looks more like a home than a business. When I get to the door, though, the question is answered for me.

There is a small sign that reads: "Please come in."

Mrs. Bennett isn't anything like I imagined.

I don't know where I got the idea that a daycare matron should be plump, gray-haired, over fifty years old, and wearing a flowered dress with a white apron. Dumb, I know, but that's what I expected.

Holy cow! Was I wrong!

Mrs. Bennett is probably in her early thirties and has a slender, athletic figure. Her dark hair is short and curly. Like me, she's dressed in jeans, t-shirt, and running shoes. She doesn't appear to be wearing makeup, but she has that "all-American-girl-next-door" look that doesn't require any.

"You must be Hellie," she says warmly. "Let's step into my office."

Connie A. Walker

There are half a dozen kids, aged two to five, sitting on the floor watching a "Thomas the Train" show on television. Another group is in a corner playing with various toys. A girl about my age is sitting on the floor helping a couple of boys build a tower out of old-fashioned wooden blocks.

Mrs. Bennett notices me glancing around.

"We don't start structured activities until 9:00," she says. "Before then, as long as the children are behaving, they have free time."

She leads me into a small room that has windows on all four sides. The one regular window faces the white and green house next door. The other windows provide interior views: the room we just left, the kitchen, and another activity/classroom. It looks as if most of the rooms in this building have interior windows—maybe for security or liability reasons.

"Tell me a little bit about yourself," Mrs. Bennett says.

After we talk about me and my interests and goals, she asks about my experiences with children.

"I don't have any younger siblings," I tell her, "but I have several younger cousins that I babysit occasionally, and every other week I assist with one of the younger Sunday School classes at my church. I like kids."

Joan (Mrs. Bennett) shows me around and presents me to the rest of the staff. Everyone is on a first name basis. The girl who looks about my age is named Missy (and I thought my name was demeaning).

Joan explains that I will be working in Helping Hands Junior, which takes care of children from two to six years old, including kindergarteners who go to school for half-days. They are bussed to and from school in the daycare center's van even though the elementary school is just a couple of blocks away.

The house next door (the one with green trim) is Helping Hands Senior. It has a before and after school program for children from first grade through fifth whose parents work. They walk to and from school in a group.

The staff at Happy Hands works in pairs and I'm partnered with Missy. Joan says she'll be joining us off and on. We have the youngest kids, many of whom aren't potty trained.

Their activities are short and simple.

At 9:00, I help Missy gather the two- and three-year-olds in a semicircle on the floor. There are nine of them. She introduces me and then tells me all of their names.

The older children (ages four to six) are herded into the other activity room.

Missy tells a simple story about farm animals. Every time she names an animal she holds up its picture and has the children make the appropriate sound effects. She holds a picture of a cow, and the kids all moo. She holds up a dog, and they bark.

Of course, it's not easy to hold the attention of all nine kids when they're this young. Not everyone can sit still long enough for even a five-minute story. As kids wander off, I redirect them to the circle.

I also change a couple of diapers.

29

Dark in the Forest: Another Modern Fairytale

After the story, we "exercise."

Missy has the kids jump up and down, touch their shoulders, their waists, and the floor, and then skip around the room. Watching two and three-year-olds trying to skip is great fun.

We count numbers and then sing the alphabet song. At least, Missy, Joan, and I do. Some of the kids follow along. Then we have another playtime.

Before we have snacks, the kids are lined up according to gender and taken to bathrooms with the smallest toilets I've ever seen (girls on the right, boys on the left). Each is allowed to sit on the toilet. If they use it appropriately, they get to put a sticker on a chart that's divided into rows and tacked to the wall. At the front of each row is the name and photo of a child. Some of the rows are crowded with stickers. Some don't have any.

There's no pressure. If the child doesn't "go" within about half a minute, it's no big deal. They wash their hands and can sit at the table and have apple juice and animal crackers.

Joan and Missy take toilet duty.

I get to pass out the snacks.

Then we go outside to play. We're out there about ten minutes before the other class joins us.

Along the left side of the backyard is a paved strip as wide as a double driveway and a long as the yard is deep. There are various sizes of trikes and plastic vehicles with wheels that can be ridden on the concrete surface.

In addition to the castle that I saw when Mom pulled up in front of the Center, there is a swing set, a sandbox, and heaps of toys: wagons, balls, cars, trucks, dolls, blocks, plastic and stuffed animals.

Dinosaurs seem particularly popular, especially in the sandbox.

I spend a lot of time watching Missy and Joan mediating when two or more kids want the same toy.

Sharing and/or playing together are emphasized.

Missy gets a couple of girls engaged in playing "Ring around the Rosie." Her little group enlarges with every "We all fall down."

She is really good with the kids, and I learn a lot just watching her interact with them.

I have a great day, though I have to admit, by the time lunch is over I'm as ready for "quiet time" as the kids are. Missy puts on soft music and both groups of children lie down on mats that are spread on the floor. Within minutes they're all asleep.

The staff gathers around a table in the dining room. The older women have coffee, but there are soft drinks, iced tea, and bottled water in the refrigerator. Missy opts for a Diet Coke.

All I want is water and a few minutes to relax.

It's been a fun morning, but it's been taxing.

Joan and Missy both tell me I've been doing a good job.

Then Joan goes over the schedule and activities for next week.

Wednesday, a children's theatre group from the university is going to come over in the morning to put on a couple of puppet plays: one with hand puppets and the other with marionettes. They'll set up at 9:00 and it'll take them about half an hour. As the daycare team plans outdoor games to fill the 30 minutes, I almost wish I could be here.

By the end of staff meeting, the kids are beginning to wake up. They are taken to the bathroom and then allowed to play. They can stay inside, or they can go outside.

Ronda, a part-time university student, and I are assigned to supervise on the playground. I guess it's to broaden my experiences.

Ronda isn't as good with the kids as Missy is.

No, I guess that's not fair. She interacts with them appropriately, but she doesn't reach out and try to engage them the way Missy does. Ronda lets them do their own thing without interference unless they get too rowdy or start trying to hurt each other.

I roam around, smiling as I observe the children.

At the same time, I try to keep my eyes moving, hoping to spot potential problems before they turn nasty. Joan, Missy, and Ronda have all warned me that we have a couple of "biters" that have to be watched carefully.

I'm beside the concrete strip as some of the kids have a tricycle race. One little boy tips over and scrapes his elbow. While I comfort him, Ronda dashes inside for the first aid kit.

She washes the wound and then puts some antibiotic ointment on a star spangled bandage and carefully applies it. While she's doing that, my attention is drawn to the castle and to the top of the spiral slide.

Three of the older kids are scuffling up there.

I think they're fighting to see who gets to go down first. Although there is a guardrail, a girl falls (or is pushed) sideways beyond it. She scrambles to grab hold of something, and for a split second she dangles in the air.

If she hits the ground, she's going to be hurt, maybe seriously.

The whole area is cluttered with toys that should have been put away.

Oh, please, no, I pray silently, *not on my shift.*

But I know the curse of Hellenaura is about to strike again.

31

Chapter Seven

I run.

All the while I'm running, I'm praying I'll reach the little girl before she hits the ground.

I know it's impossible.

But suddenly I'm the only person moving.

Everyone and everything around me has slowed down and stopped.

I jump over a wagon, zigzag around a couple of plastic dinosaurs, and barely miss landing on Barbie and Ken in her pink convertible.

I've heard people talk about time standing still, but I always assumed it was a metaphor. Maybe it's not.

As I lunge toward the castle, I open my arms.

Time returns to normal.

I slide under the little girl and snatch her mid-air.

At the same time, the kids in the castle start yelling and screaming.

The little girl and I burst into tears.

We're both scared: her because of the fall, me because I don't understand what just happened. I was 40 or 50 feet away when I realized she was going over the side.

How did I get from one place to the other?

A moment later Joan rushes over and shushes the children, reassuring them that everything is all right. Ronda is a second behind her. I manage to wipe my eyes and get control of myself before anyone notices.

"What happened?" Joan and Ronda ask at the same time. From the expressions on their faces and the tones of their voices, I know that neither one of them saw my miraculous dash across the yard.

They just want to know what is upsetting the children.

"I'm not sure," I answer. "Three of the kids were on the platform," I glance upward. "I think they were arguing over who was going to have the first turn going down the slide. This one," I nod at the child I'm holding, "fell over the edge. She held onto the side for a few seconds—giving me just enough time to catch her."

Neither Joan nor Ronda asks for more information than that. They call the kids to order and usher them back to the house for another structured activity, stopping for a bathroom break along the way.

Before I know it, it's almost 3:30. The part-time girl who works from 3:00 to 7:00 has already arrived to relieve me.

"Do I need to do anything else before I go?" I ask Joan.

"No," she answers with a smile. "You did great today. How would you like to be our backup for the rest of the summer?"

"Backup?" I repeat.

"In case of an emergency, could I call you at the last minute and have you fill in?"

"Sure," I say. I don't even have to think about it. Any extra money I can pick up will be welcome. "Call me anytime."

"Thanks, Hellie. Your paycheck will be in the mail next week. I hope that's all right."

"It's fine. Bye."

I head for the bus stop.

During the ride home, I watch the scenery pass, checking out the flower gardens in people's yards. I don't want to think about my mad dash across the playground while everyone else was imitating statues. If I think about it, I'll end up wondering if I made it all up—or if maybe I'm losing my mind.

When I get home, of course, the house is empty.

I feel jumpy. I don't know why.

I've been home alone often enough.

Maybe I feel the emptiness more acutely this afternoon because I miss my grandmother, as I always do when something perplexing happens to me. (This isn't the first weirdness I've experienced. The Hellenaura curse comes in many varieties).

If Grandma were here, she would calmly listen to my story. She'd try to understand, and if she didn't, she'd still mange to say something that made me feel better until we could figure out an explanation.

I feel as if I've been thrust into one of those paranormal television shows that's based on "the experiences and observations of real people." No one believes those tales, and I don't believe I covered 50 feet in less time than it should have taken a little girl to fall 10 feet.

But I did it!

How?

It boggles my mind.

I check the refrigerator to see if I have a To Do list for this afternoon.

Just a note from Mom:

Congratulations on surviving daycare. Relax and enjoy the rest of your day. I'll pick up something for dinner on my way home.

33

Dark in the Forest: Another Modern Fairytale

Figures! On the one day that I need some chores to take my mind off of things, Mom tells me to relax.

If she stops someplace to pick up dinner, she won't be home until shortly before 6:00. Dad and Angel won't be home much before that.

I grab a red Sharpie and scribble a sentence below Mom's note:

I've gone to see if I can find any more berries worth picking.

Within minutes I've crushed up some chocolate covered graham crackers, filled a jelly jar with orange soda, grabbed two bottles of water, put it all into my lunch tote, and gotten the blue pail from the pantry.

Then I'm out the backdoor.

I take a shortcut to the grotto, leave my offerings, and then head for the glade. My note to Kaden has been replaced:

Dear Hellenaura:
    Thank you for your letter. I am glad you enjoyed the
fauvenell. It is my favorite dessert. I was here this morning
but was called home unexpectedly. I'll return sometime
this afternoon.
                    Your servant,
                    Kaden

I read through his note a second time. I feel a little shiver of excitement snake up and down my spine.

I'm not used to having guys pay attention to me. Even though Angel and I look alike, boys flock around her and pretty much ignore me. For just a moment I consider running home instead of hanging around to meet a stranger who will probably just reject me.

Nevertheless, I find the situation I'm in too tantalizing.

I know that logically I should be afraid, and maybe I am just a little, but my curiosity is greater than my fear.

I wish his time schedule was a little less ambiguous.

What am I supposed to do in the meantime?

I don't want him to think I have nothing to do except wait around for him.

In the note I left for my folks, I said I was going berry picking.

That's as good a way to spend my time as any.

I take a look around. The raspberry bushes that border the glade won't be ready for me to harvest again for another day or two.

Oh well. I know where there are lots of other bushes.

While I'm walking through the woods, I figure I might as well look for rubbish in some of the more popular partying spots. I always carry a few plastic garbage bags in the front pocket of my tote in case I come across a pile of litter somewhere.

As I wander among the trees, I have a brief flash of a recurring nightmare that I sometimes have. In it, I'm walking through these woods and I'm lost, which is impossible. My grandmother and I spent hours strolling all around here. She introduced me to the trees, the rocks, the foliage, and as many animals as we could find. I'm as familiar with this forest as I am with my bedroom. How could I get lost here, even in a dream?

I start to repeat that it's impossible—but then I think of covering 50 feet in a split second and suddenly I'm not sure what's possible and what's not.

I step past a boulder, stop, and shake my head in disgust.

The debris of another party is scattered all over the ground. It even spills into a little creek. A lump of trash has caught on a rock in the water and has partially dammed up the stream.

At least the idiots made sure to contain their campfire; they dug down a couple of inches and lined the pit with rocks.

That must have been before they started drinking.

There is a pile of beer cans, hamburger wrappers, potato chip bags, plastic cups, and other junk next to the fire pit. At least they threw their cigarette butts into the pit. Remnants of the scorched filters are still visible among the charcoal, ash, and partially burned sticks.

I pull a garbage bag from my tote and then dig for a set of disposable latex gloves. There aren't any. After I used the last ones, I must have forgotten to replace them.

Ick! I hate picking up other people's garbage with my bare hands.

At least I have some antiseptic towelettes I can use to clean my fingers when I'm finished. I start shoving trash into the plastic bag.

I hear a faint hum.

From the corner of my eye, I see a brief flash of light. I glance up and feel my mouth drop open.

A guy emerges from a beam of sunlight that has somehow penetrated the forest canopy. The scene looks like one of those supernatural shots you sometimes see in the movies where a god or goddess (sometimes an alien) descends to earth on a ray of light.

He smiles as he walks toward me.

I can hardly breathe.

He is tall, as tall as my father, and athletically slender.

His artificially blond hair has been parted down the middle, exposing two inches of dark roots, and then pulled loosely back from his face in a man bun. A few loose strands dangle in front of his ears, framing his face.

His lips are beautifully bowed, and the lower one is slightly fuller than the upper, which I've always found to be sexy. His teeth are gleaming white. His nose is straight, his jaw line gracefully curved, his eyebrows delicately arched, and his lashes thick and black.

His eyes are light brown, but the irises are outlined in black and the pupils with a narrow band of gold, making them mysterious and unique.

I could stare into them forever.

I can't begin to guess his age.

There is something timeless about him—the same way that Renaissance art feels timeless. He could be my age or a couple dozen years older. I know he can't be younger.

His facial features, the proportions of his body, his stance, and his movements are all perfect.

He is too beautiful to call handsome.

"I'm Kaden," he tells me as he offers me his hand.

"I'm Hellenaura." When I place my hand in his, he lifts it and gives it a light kiss. His lips are satiny soft.

"I know," he says.

He holds onto my hand for several seconds longer than required for courtesy. I don't mind.

When eye contact is broken, it is because he looks away.

I couldn't.

He glances around the littered campsite. "I don't understand how anyone could leave such a lovely place in such a deplorable state. Let me help you."

I nod.

I haven't been able to say a word since I introduced myself. My brain feels as if it's been scrambled and then fried.

"If you'll hold the sack open," he says. "I'll do the bending and picking up."

Again I nod.

I'm unable to think of anything to say.

Part of me wants to fall down on my knees and worship him.

Thunderstruck is what my grandmother would call it.

When he drops a handful of rubbish into the trash bag, he looks at me and grins as if he recognizes the effect he's having on me.

It's exactly the wrong thing to do.

Suddenly I'm on guard.

It must show on my face because he turns off the charm like a light bulb and simply helps me finish cleaning up. He breaks up the fire pit by tossing most of the stones among the foliage. Somehow he does it gently enough that the rocks don't damage the plant life or send the forest creatures scampering.

He scoops up the unburned wood and drops it into the sack with the rest of the trash.

Using a stick, he stirs the remaining ashes into the dirt. He smooths the ground with his hands, places a few rocks in a random pattern, and gathers up some twigs and leaves and tosses them into the air. When they drift down and land among the stones, there are no remaining signs of the former pit.

"That's remarkable," I say. "If whoever made the mess expects to come back and party in the same spot some night, they're going to be disappointed.

The area looks untouched now. Maybe they'll get spooked when they can't find the campsite and leave and not come back."

"That might be a little too optimistic," Kaden says, "but at least they will probably build their fire somewhere else, which will allow the life in this area to recover from past abuses."

"Thank you for your help," I tell him.

"You're welcome."

He looks at me tentatively and then quickly glances away. He takes a handkerchief from the front pocket of his jeans and scrubs at the ashes on his hands. I hand him a towelette, which he accepts. After using it, he drops it in the garbage bag and then focuses his attention on the blue pail.

"You are going berry picking again?"

"I'm going to try. People don't sneak into the woods just to have parties and make messes. They also sneak in to pick berries. By the time I get to the bushes that are very far from my house, often the branches are bare."

"May I accompany you?" he asks.

I like it that he doesn't assume that he's automatically welcome just because he's drop-dead gorgeous. Maybe I misinterpreted the grin that looked so cocky, arrogant, and entitled.

"If you want to," I say.

"Thank you." He takes the trash bag from me, and I pick up my lunch tote and pail. I take the lead since I know where all the berry bushes are.

He walks beside me at a comfortable distance. He doesn't lag behind or crowd me. We don't speak, and for some reason I find it natural and pleasant. Our companionable silence is like I used to have when walking through the woods with Grandma.

I suppose I should be nervous.

He's a stranger and much bigger than I am. He could easily overpower me if he wanted.

I'm not afraid.

Chapter Eight

We come to a blackberry bush that is just begging to be plucked.

Without saying anything, I hand Kaden the blue bucket.

The inside of my tote bag is waterproofed with plastic. Except for the two bottles of water in the narrow section, the tote is empty. In the past I've used it to hold berries when I've unexpectedly stumbled across particularly plump ones.

We've been picking berries for a couple of minutes when Kaden says, "Your name is quite beautiful. Can you tell me about it? How did your parents happen to choose it?"

He's the first person to say anything nice about my name, and the first one to show the slightest curiosity about how I got it. When my teachers at school see my name for the first time, they only worry about how to pronounce it. When kids see or hear it, they just make fun of me.

Kaden is looking at me with interest.

Why not?

"I was named after two of my great-grandmothers: Helena and Aura. My parents combined them into one word."

"I assume they were your maternal great-grandmothers."

"What makes you say that?" I ask.

I take a break from berry picking to stare at him.

He stops also and meets my gaze. "Simple deduction. I figured your parents must have combined the two names into one so they could use your mother's maiden name as your middle name."

"Why do you think Dark is my mother's maiden name?"

Kaden shrugs. "Dark is not a name that parents would usually give a baby girl unless the name had special meaning. A maiden name was the logical presumption. Have I offended you?"

"Not really," I answer. "It's just that people are seldom interested in my name except as an excuse to tease me."

"They mock you for having a unique, beautiful, and musical name?"

You'd think I'd be used to snide remarks and ridicule by now.

But I'm not. It hurts.

As a result, I become defensive.

"Why does it matter to you?" I demand antagonistically.

"I'm just curious," he answers softly. "I think your name is lovely. It troubles me that something that's so beautiful to me makes you unhappy."

I don't know how to respond.

He sounds sincere, as if my pain hurts him.

I don't understand.

I decide to change the subject.

"How has your search for the lost items been going?"

His face becomes sober.

"Not too well," he says. "I'm usually very good at finding things, but these have eluded me. I am fairly sure, however, that they have been here and probably still are. I will keep looking."

"If you describe the objects to me, maybe I can help you look."

He glances over at me. "You are very sweet to suggest it, but I would not want to impose on your kindness. Tell me about yourself. What kinds of things do you like to do when you are not picking berries?"

"I like to read a lot, mostly fantasy and science fiction. I also like to listen to music."

"What kind?"

"All kinds, as long as it's melodic and played well. Just recently I've developed an appreciation of stringed instruments, and I've been almost exclusively listening to instrumentals that feature the violin. How about you? What type of things do you enjoy?"

"I'm also fond of all kinds of music, although I prefer the piano to the violin as a solo instrument."

He pauses. I think he expects me to say something about the piano, so I do. "I suppose, if I had to choose an instrument to learn how to play, I'd take the piano over the violin."

"Are you familiar with panpipes?"

"I think so," I tell him. "They're those narrow vertical tubes that are all different lengths and are hooked together side by side in a row. They sort of sound like flutes."

"That's a fair description," Kaden says with a laugh. "I play the panpipes."

"Really?" I exclaim. "I've heard them in recordings and I've seen them on television a few times, but I've never known anyone who actually played them. I wish—" I stop abruptly.

Kaden raises his eyebrows. "What do you wish?" he prompts.

I can feel myself blushing.

What I wish is that I hadn't started to say what I wish.

"Perhaps," Kaden says, "you would let me play the panpipes for you sometime."

Before I stop to think, I respond, "I would like that." It's as if I actually believe we'll see each other again.

Once we start sharing our likes and dislikes, however, our conversation flows as if we've been friends forever.

It feels strange, but I enjoy it.

I don't know how long we've been talking, but we're taking a break from berry picking when my cellphone rings. I'm sitting on the ground across from Kaden. I'm so startled by the unexpected sound that I probably levitate a foot in the air.

I pull my phone out of my pocket.

Caller ID says it's my mother.

"Hi, Mom, are you home already?"

"Yes. The mayor was feeling guilty about all the overtime I put in last month so he sent me home early. Have any luck berry picking?"

"I found a great blackberry bush where the berries are just perfect."

"Do you have enough for a pie?"

I glance in the blue bucket and my tote. There might be enough for two pies, but I don't want to tell Mom. If she thinks I'm still picking, I'll have an excuse to stay out a little longer and get better acquainted with Kaden.

"I will have by the time I head back."

"All right. I'll make the crust now so it can chill while we eat dinner. Think you can finish in half an hour?"

"I think so."

"See you then."

"Bye, Mom."

I turn to Kaden. "I have to leave."

"Can you meet me here tomorrow?"

I feel heat rush to my face and realize I am probably turning bright red.

"I'll have to do my chores first," I tell him despite my nervousness. "Why don't you give me your phone number? I'll call you and let you know when."

Kaden glances at his shoes and brushes away a couple of leaves that are stuck to the bottom of one sole.

"I won't be available by phone, but I can be here shortly after the noon hour. I can meet you in the clearing where we exchanged notes, or we can meet here. Do you have a preference?"

I think about it a moment. "How flexible are you?"

He gives me a startled look. "I beg your pardon!"

Now I'm sure he's foreign. Any American would realize I am referring to flexibility in terms of scheduling, not flexibility in terms of body movement, but I can tell by the expression on Kaden's face that he is confused.

"What I mean is do you mind if we leave that decision a little vague? If I get done with my chores early, I'll probably want to come here and pick berries until you arrive. If I'm late getting my chores done, then the glade is closer to my home, and it would be quicker for me to go there."

"Oh," Kaden says, "I understand. I will come here first. If you are not here,

I will go to the glade and meet you there."

"Thanks. I'll see you tomorrow."

He gets to his feet and extends a hand to me to help me up. For a moment I hesitate but then I put my hand in his. He doesn't exactly pull me up, anyway I don't feel a tug, but I'm upright before I consciously think of standing.

He grins at me. "I'll bring you another fauvenell."

I grin back. "I'll get here as close to noon as I can."

I dump the blackberries from my tote into the bucket. After I hang the tote's strap on my shoulder and pick up the blue pail, I reach for the trash bag.

Kaden gets to it first. "I'll dispose of that for you. I was happy to see you functioning so well as the keeper of the forest. This is a beautiful place, very much like my home. You treasure it, don't you?"

"I love it. I feel closest to my grandmother when I'm here in the woods." I sigh as my loneliness for her returns. Suddenly I feel like crying. "Well, I'd better go. I'll see you tomorrow."

Before I can turn to leave, Kaden takes my hand and kisses it again. "I am so glad we got to meet. I look forward to seeing you again. Have a pleasant evening."

I watch him walk away.

I suppose his car is parked on the far side of woods, which means he has quite a trek ahead of him. I wonder if I should invite him to park in front of the house next time and cut through the yard with me.

With my head in the clouds, daydreaming as I head for home, I catch my foot on a protruding root and almost drop the blackberries as I stumble.

I put thinking on hold and concentrate on walking.

When I enter through the back door, Angel and Dad are just coming into the kitchen. They've both already changed out of their work clothes.

Instead of stopping to buy something for dinner as she'd planned, Mom ordered in because she got home early.

Spread out on the bar that's between the kitchen and the dining room is an assortment of Asian dishes including cashew chicken (my favorite), beef and broccoli (Angel's favorite), and sweet and sour pork (Dad's favorite). Of course, we have all the popular side dishes too: fried rice, egg rolls, wontons, and fortune cookies.

Paper plates, napkins, and plastic forks are piled at the front.

This is a real treat for our family. The restaurant that delivers is so popular that you have to place your orders really early if you want to get them before bedtime.

I hand Mom the pail of blackberries.

"I'll just run upstairs and wash my hands," I say as I pass.

When I rejoin the family, they are already filling their plates. I fall in at the end of the line. I take a little bit of everything.

As I'm sitting down, Dad asks me how things went at the daycare center.

"It was a lot of fun," I tell him. "I got to work with the youngest kids, the two- and three-year-olds. They kept us jumping, so the time passed really fast. I was surprised when 3:30 came around."

"Anything special?" Dad asks as I fork some cashew chicken into my mouth.

I chew and swallow.

For a moment I'm tempted to mention the incident with the falling girl, but how can I explain it to my family if I don't understand it myself.

"Mrs. Bennett insists that everyone call her Joan. Oh, and there's a girl who has a first name that's even worse than mine. Her name is Missy. It's actually on her birth certificate. I asked her. Can you imagine that?"

Angel and I laugh together.

"If she wants to be a doctor or a politician—" Angel says.

"—or anything serious—" I insert.

"—she'll have to change her name—" Angel continues.

"—or use her initials," I finish.

"That wasn't what I was thinking about," Dad says. "Actually, Joan called my office and left a message for me to call her, which I did as soon as I finished my last class."

I swallow hard.

Chapter Nine

I run the day through my mind.

Joan told me I did a good job.

After I left, could she have discovered some terrible mistake I made earlier in the day?

No, I don't think so. Everything went well as far as I can remember.

"Did I do something wrong?" I ask Dad.

"No, Joan called it heroic."

"Oh," I say.

Mom looks back and forth between Dad and me.

"Well, tell her," Dad says to me.

"It wasn't any big deal," I say, glancing around the table. "Some kids were messing around at the top of the slippery slide and one got pushed off. She grabbed onto the side and held on just long enough for me to get under her and catch her when she fell."

"Wow," exclaims Angel. "You're a hero."

I feel myself blush. I look over at Dad. "Why did Joan call and tell you?"

"She said it didn't occur to her until after you had gone, but she worried that you might have injured your arms without realizing it. Catching thirty pounds falling from a height of ten feet is no small thing."

I hold out my arms. "Not even a bruise," I say. "And she didn't fall ten feet. She was dangling from one arm, and I probably caught her three feet from the ground. At the most she fell four feet."

"Even so," Mom says, "you deserve credit for thinking fast enough to act. Lots of people would have just covered their eyes and done nothing."

"Except pick up the pieces afterward," Dad says, agreeing with Mom. "Well done, Hellie. I'm proud of you."

"Me too," exclaims Angel.

"That makes it unanimous," Mom says.

"We need to have a celebration." Dad tells Mom. "Why don't you see how fast you can get that pie in the oven? I'll get the ice cream maker and rock salt from the basement."

"I can run to the store and buy the cream," Angel offers. "Do we have enough milk for ice cream tonight and breakfast tomorrow?"

Mom checks the fridge. "It wouldn't hurt to pick up a gallon while you're at the store." She goes to get her wallet.

"Mind if I come along?" I ask Angel.

She throws her arm around my shoulders and we climb the stairs side by side. "You're the guest of honor. You do whatever you want. You can come with me or go sit in Dad's recliner with your feet up and bask in your glory."

"I'll risk riding in the car with you—despite your tendency to sing while you drive—rather than risk having to deal with Dad if I try to usurp his chair."

She dashes into her room to get her purse.

I go get mine at the same time. My driver's license is still in the cardholder in my back pocket. I take it out and put it in my billfold.

When Angel and I get back downstairs, Mom hands Angel some money and the car keys.

I snatch the keys right out of Angel's hand. "You said I could do whatever I want, so I'll drive."

The grocery store's only a few blocks away. When we get back, Dad has the electric ice cream maker set up on the kitchen counter and Mom is putting the pie in the oven.

While Dad prepares the mixture to go into the ice cream freezer and Mom puts her pie-making utensils in the dishwasher, Angel and I dump the leftover food into plastic containers and stack them in the refrigerator. We put the unused paper plates and plastic forks in the pantry with other picnic supplies.

Dad gets the ice cream maker going.

We all hang out in the kitchen, getting in each other's way.

The pie finishes cooking about fifteen minutes before the ice cream is ready. Mom sets it on a cooling rack.

Angel gets dessert bowls from the cupboard while I take forks and spoons from the silverware drawer. Usually, we start eating pie and ice cream with forks, but as the ice cream melts, it makes a wonderfully gooey mess in the bottom of the bowls, and we switch to spoons to make sure we can get it all.

It's a fun evening.

We watch a DVD while we eat dessert.

Since we're celebrating me, I get to choose.

I'd prefer to pick a classic sci-fi or old paranormal thriller, like *It Came From Outer Space* (1953) or *The Uninvited* (1944), but I know Angel doesn't like black and white movies. I choose *Jurassic World* because I know it's something all four of us can enjoy.

Later, after the movie, as Angel and I get ready for bed, I tell her I need to talk to her. She comes into my room and sits on my bed beside me.

"Something strange happened to me this afternoon," I tell her. "When the little girl started to fall, I was clear across the yard from her. I shouldn't have been able to reach her before she hit the ground. Not even an Olympic runner could have crossed that much distance in those few seconds."

Angel's brows pinch together. "That doesn't make any sense. You must have been closer than you realized."

I shake my head. "There's a paved strip on the west side of the yard and the slide is along the fence on the east side. In between there is grass and a sandbox and piles of toys. I was standing by the paved strip. When I started running, everyone else seemed to freeze in place. They didn't move again until I was in a position to catch the little girl. It was as if time stood still for everyone but me."

"Hellie," Angel says, cocking her head to one side, "you've done something truly heroic. You don't need to embellish anything to make it sound more dramatic."

My throat tightens up like it always does when Angel patronizes me. "I thought at least you'd try to understand." Tears form in my eyes. "I wish Grandma was here."

Angel reaches out and strokes my arm. "Hellie, I'm trying to understand. It's just that what you're saying is impossible. There has to be a logical explanation."

"Like what?" I demand. "I told you exactly what happened. Come up with a logical explanation if you can."

"Well, what do you think happened? Did you suddenly become a superhero who can teleport from one place to another in a split second? Have you mastered the mysteries of the fourth dimension so you can manipulate time?" She rolls her eyes up so only the whites show, holds her arms out, and waves her hands. "Or are you secretly a witch with magical powers?" She drops her silly pose. "Be real!"

When she sees the tears dripping down my cheeks, she scoots over and puts her arms around me. "I'm sorry. I didn't mean to make you cry. But, Hellie, even if it was superpowers or magic, it still has to work within the realms of known physics, and it doesn't. The only explanation is that you remember it wrong. It was a tense, scary moment, and your mind was playing tricks on you. The little girl must have held on longer than you thought, giving you time to get to her."

"Sure," I say. I pull a tissue out of a box on my bedside table and wipe my eyes. "You're right. That must have been it."

Angel kisses me on the cheek before she leaves.

"Good night," I tell her. "Switch off the light on your way out."

When she's gone and the room is dark, I flip over onto my stomach, bury my face in my pillow, and cry.

I am so alone since Grandma died.

No one else has ever really understood me.

I tell myself to think about something pleasant, something positive.

Usually when I'm unhappy, I focus on the fun that Grandma and I had together, but tonight Kaden pops into my mind instead.

Dark in the Forest: Another Modern Fairytale

He told me he plays the panpipes.

My friend Nadine has a couple of DVDs of some man playing them, except he called them pan flutes. I can't recall his name, but I remember that the videos are full of beautiful mountain scenery.

I get out of bed, sit down at my desk, and turn on my computer.

When I get to YouTube, I type *panpipe instrumentals*.

I watch three different men and two women perform.

They're all wonderful. One of the men plays a solo, and one plays with a guitarist. One of the women has an entire orchestra behind her, and the other plays with a four-piece band.

My favorite video, however, shows a man playing a duet with a violinist.

I picture Kaden playing with David Garrett.

I go to bed with a smile on my face.

Chapter Ten

Well-rested and surprisingly happy, I wake up at 6:00. I know I can't go back to sleep when I feel like this, so I get up and put on raggedy sweatpants and an old, long sleeved t-shirt. I saw today's To Do list when I got up during the night and went downstairs to get a bottle of water from the fridge.

My #1 outdoor task this morning is to trim the roses.

No matter how careful I am when I work on the rose bushes, if I'm not wearing long pants and long sleeves, I'll end up with scratches on my arms and legs that are deep enough to bleed.

I don't hear anyone moving around yet, but it won't be long.

I have a bowl of cereal with a handful of blackberries on top. Mom has already frozen the raspberries. She always does that until the season ends. When she knows that we've picked the last of them, she'll spend an entire Saturday making jam.

After I put my bowl and spoon in the dishwasher, I leave a note on the refrigerator door.

> *Woke up early and am getting a jumpstart on my chores.*
> *I'm out front pruning roses. H*

Like just about everything else in life, deadheading the roses and cutting out the cross canes is more fun when someone works with you.

This is another activity that Grandma Powers and I usually did together. When her arthritis was acting up, she'd sit in a lawn chair and show me where to cut by tapping the right spot with her cane. While I worked, she would tell me stories about Eugene and Michael Powers and our enchanted forest.

After I get a big plastic tub, my heavy canvas gardening gloves, and my pruning shears from the shed, I start on the roses in the front yard by cutting out the cross canes. As I work, I mentally replay some of the stories Grandma told me. I can actually hear her voice in my head.

The first time my great-great-great-grandfather Eugene Powers reined in his horse and looked out over this valley, he fell in love with the land. There wasn't a city here back then, just a few deserted shacks near the river.

Rolling foothills covered with pine and fir trees surrounded the entire valley and then climbed up to meet the Rocky Mountains.

In his journal Eugene wrote that not even the Garden of Eden could have been more beautiful.

His father had recently died and left him a hefty inheritance. As the only son, he was expected to use part of the legacy to support his mother and his unmarried sister who lived together somewhere back east. With his father's attorney as administrator, Eugene set up a trust and arranged for his mother and sister each to receive a monthly allowance from it.

Then he headed west until he reached this part of Colorado.

I don't know how many acres of the valley and the western foothills he purchased, but it was substantial. He cleared enough land to build a large cabin, married a young woman he met in Kansas, and fathered three children. He farmed and raised cattle to support his family. When his children were old enough, he sent them one by one to his mother so she could introduce them to city life and could teach them social graces. She found good husbands for the two daughters and made sure his son was well educated.

The boy, Michael, was the only one of Eugene's children to return home.

In the meantime, Eugene increased his fortune by selling off small tracts of his land to people who had been drawn to the state during the Pikes Peak gold rush. Some people had struck it rich and wanted to stay in the area, hoping to discover new veins of gold as the existing mines played out. Other people, the ones who hadn't struck it rich, couldn't afford to move on and had settled here by default.

By establishing a bank, a mercantile store, and a boarding house, Eugene provided the foundation for a growing community.

According to Eugene's journal, when Michael came home, Eugene took him on a tour of their remaining property.

There was one huge parcel of land that Eugene told Michael needed to remain intact and unsullied. In his journal he wrote that he carefully explained the reasons to Michael. Unfortunately, Eugene never wrote his explanation down, or if he did, it somehow got separated from his other papers and was subsequently lost, creating a frustrating mystery for many of his descendants.

Before Eugene died, he gave all his property to Michael, instructing him to guard and protect that one special section.

Michael promised, and Eugene signed over the deed.

Like his father, Michael Powers loved the land.

Unlike his father, however, Michael did not trust his children.

He had sent them back east for education and refinement, as his father had done, but by that time Eugene's mother had died and Michael sent his children to live with Eugene's sister, Aunt Adeline, and her well-to-do new husband.

From his time back east, Michael remembered Adeline as a quiet, simple young woman who had a moderate social life and who enjoyed reading, painting, and embroidery. She had married late, after Michael had returned to Colorado, and had no offspring of her own. She took in Michael's children and proceeded to give them the life she had wanted for herself.

She introduced them to society. She took them to parties, to balls, and to the theatre. She taught them about fashion and the proper attire for all occasions. She showered them with gifts.

Although Michael was a wealthy man, his children had grown up modestly in Shawon, which was still more frontier than settlement. He had tried to raise them to be hardworking, honest, and ethical people.

After a few years under Aunt Adeline's tutelage, however, they became materialistic and acquisitive. Although they came back to Colorado to visit, as long as Michael paid for their transportation, they all settled in the east except for Michael's eldest son, Samuel, who moved as far west as St. Louis, Missouri.

Michael feared, as soon as he died, that his children would look at the reserved property as a source of income, either as collateral for loans or as a commodity to be sold.

He could not allow that to happen.

He had promised his father.

So Michael hired a surveyor and a cartographer to make a detailed map of his land, clearly delineating the property that was to remain pristine. Then he spent a small fortune having that specific parcel fenced all the way around.

When that was completed, he retained the best lawyer in the state to compose his will, specifying that the designated property could never be sold, developed, or despoiled in any form in perpetuity.

No one remembers the lawyer's name, but he must have been brilliant and exceptionally well versed in his craft.

Sometime in the 1940s or 50s, a couple of Michael's grandchildren (the children of Samuel, Michael's eldest son) tried to take control of the protected property so it could be sold to a logging company.

What happened instead was that they lost all rights to the land.

Ownership passed to my father's father, who was the second son.

When Grandpa Powers inherited the property from his father, the first thing he did was build this house as close to the protected portion of the forest as possible. Grandpa Powers didn't know why these woods were so important, but he was determined to keep them safe.

It took Grandma Powers to recognize the magic.

Daydreaming, I snag my sweatpants on a couple of thorns.

I'm freeing myself when the front door opens and Mom comes out.

"Did you take time for breakfast?" she asks.

I grin at her. "When do I ever miss a meal?"

Mom is wearing a white, lightweight, skirted suit with a red silk blouse. She looks great in it, and she only wears it when she wants to be noticed and acknowledged. A black suit with a white shirt or blouse might be the power combination, but for attention it's hard to beat the high contrast of white and red.

"Something special going on at the mayor's office today?" I ask.

"Luncheon meeting with some uppity-ups from the University."

"Have fun."

She winks at me. "I'm going in early to prepare, but that doesn't mean I'll be able to take off before 5:00. In fact, I might have to work late. Since we have an abundance of leftovers in the fridge, we'll have potluck for dinner tonight. I've already told your father and Angel."

"Sounds good," I say. "Have a nice lunch."

"See you later."

Mom gets into her car and drives away.

I have finished with the roses and am raking up the loose leaves and bits of stem when Dad and Angel pull out of the driveway. They both wave at me, and I wave back.

After I dump the rose clippings into the large garbage bin, I put away the tub, shears, and heavy gloves. I get out my weed digging tools and attack the unwanted growth around the recently sprouted corn.

I'm really glad I got started so early this morning.

Fresh-from-the-garden corn is a treat that our family really enjoys, but whereas my parents plant two rows of peas, two rows of string beans, two rows of beets, two rows of potatoes, and one row each of carrots and onions, they plant ten rows of corn.

Weeding it feels like a never-ending task.

The only consolation I have is that there are no indoor chores on my To Do list. After I weed the corn, I need to deadhead the petunias, but then I'll be done for the day.

When I finish the fifth row of corn, I take a break. I go inside to cool down and drink a bottle of water. As I toss the bottle into the recycle bin, I notice it's almost 9:30. I'll have to scurry if I want to meet Kaden at noon.

I work as fast as I can.

It's 10:15 when I put my tools back in the shed and head for the bathroom and a quick shower.

I set speed records.

I towel dry my hair, part it down the middle, pull the sides up and back, and fasten them in place with barrettes. By noon my hair will have air-dried. I choose a yellow t-shirt to wear with my jeans because my white tennis shoes have yellow laces.

Now that I've showered and dressed, I cut a piece of blackberry pie for the forest people. I put it in a plastic container, but I place it on the inside surface of the lid and fit the bottom part on top like on a cake carrier. This way the lid will become a serving tray when I remove the top. I put milk in a jelly jar and then add five teaspoons of sugar. (Since I can't conveniently take ice cream with me, I figure sweetened milk is the next best thing. I can't picture drinking anything but milk with blackberry pie.) I put it all in my tote and place a fork on top.

Quickly I throw together a sandwich. I grab an apple from the fruit bowl and a small bag of chips from the pantry. I get the blue bucket at the same time.

If Kaden remembers to bring me one of those dessert things (what did he call it? I can't remember, but it sounded French), I don't need to add anything sweet. All I need now are a couple of bottles of water.

I write a note just in case anyone comes home for some reason before I'm back.

I've gone for a walk in the woods. I might pick berries
for a while. P.S. My chores are done.
                              H

I don't say when I'll be back. No one will worry about me while I'm gone as long as they know where I am and what I'm doing. I've wandered around the forest from dawn till dusk often enough that the folks are used to it. If they need me back earlier, they'll call or text me on my cellphone.

I leave by the backdoor, sprint across the yard, and slip through the hedge. I take my phone out of the pocket of my tote. It's only 11:25. I didn't realize I'd made such good time. Maybe I can fill the pail with blackberries before Kaden gets here.

As always, I go to the grotto first. I take out the container that holds the pie and carefully remove the top. I use the fork I brought to cut the pie into little pieces. Before I put the fork back into the tote, I lick it clean. I pour milk into the teapots and cups and leave the jar open next to them. I don't need to worry about the milk going sour. It will be gone before it even has time to get warm.

I take off through the trees and head straight for the blackberry patch. Like every thing else in the forest, I know how to get there from any direction.

It's wonderfully cool in here, and the air smells delicious. Water tumbles over rocks in the streams. A breeze brushes across my face and stirs the leaves on the bushes and trees.

When I get to the berry patch, Kaden isn't here yet.

I didn't expect him to be. He said he'd be here shortly after noon.

Since I've been rushing since 6:00 this morning, I decide to lie on the grass and let the forest feed my spirit for a few minutes. Grandma used to come out here to do the same.

I guess I doze.

I wake up when I hear a musical hum.

I roll onto my side, prop myself up with one arm, and glance around.

There's a flash of light.

For a moment I look directly into it, and it's like I'm looking through window glare. Although what I see on the other side is blurry, it is clear enough that I can tell it isn't my forest anymore. The trees are huge, dripping with long streamers of moss, and shrouded in a foggy mist.

Half a dozen twinkling lights float through the haze close to the ground.

A bird that is colored like a rainbow swoops down from a branch and flies straight at me, but then it banks sharply and soars away in the opposite direction.

The light flares up brightly one more time, and then it goes out as if someone has flipped a switch.

I lie back down.

Obviously I'm dreaming even though I don't feel like I'm asleep.

Vaguely I recall something my psychology teacher mentioned last year. Sometimes people think they're having true experiences while in fact they are dreaming in that halfway state between wakefulness and sleep. What did he call it? It sounded kind of like hypnosis.

Hypnotic something? No.

Come on, Hellie, you can remember. What was it?

Wait a minute.

There are two kinds: one happens when you're falling asleep and the other when you're waking up. Hypnopompic hallucinations? Hypnagogic dreams? Yeah, I think that's what they are, but which is which? I can't remember. Oh well, that's what the Internet is for. I can look them up when I get home if I still care.

Now comes the real question.

Am I currently awake?

I sit up and then stand. It feels real.

Bending, I pick up the blue pail.

I'm pretty sure I'm awake.

I stare at the blackberry bush. Visions of my grandmother wrap around me like a soft quilt. I can almost feel her arms hugging me.

I remember times when we would lie on the grass in the glade and watch the clouds drift by. We'd try to find formations that looked like animals or vehicles or people. Once we saw a cloud that Grandma said looked like Grandpa. He died before my parents were married, so I never got to know him, but the cloud resembled photographs I'd seen of him. He had a kind, gentle face.

Occasionally Grandma made up stories that coordinated with the shifting shapes in the sky. I especially like the ones she told when a storm was rolling in and the clouds were getting dark. Then the tales were full of conflict and drama, often reaching the climax just seconds before the first flash of lightning. Then we'd hold hands and run for the house. Sometimes we beat the rain and sometimes we didn't. Either way, when we got home, Grandma would finish the story, tying everything together to make a happy ending.

I loved being with her, listening to her, watching her.

I wish Angel had been willing to come with us more often. If she had, she and I could reminisce about Grandma, sharing our memories of her, remembering her stories together.

But Angel didn't enjoy wandering through the woods. She missed out on so much of what Grandma and I shared.

My throat tightens and I want to cry.

I miss them both.

Tears are starting to well up in my eyes when, all of a sudden, I'm distracted.

I hear that same strange humming sound that I heard earlier.

I turn toward it.

A beam of light forms.

Through it, I see the same hazy trees and hanging moss.

Kaden walks between the trees.

He parts the light with his hands, as if opening a curtain, and then steps through.

The light goes out.

Chapter Eleven

For a moment Kaden and I just stare at each other.

I don't know what to say.

My brain has ceased functioning.

"You got here earlier than I expected," Kaden says casually. "I had hoped to arrive first."

I am still totally tongue-tied.

My mind is running around in circles, trying to figure out what I just saw. It looked as if Kaden stepped out of somewhere else into the here and now by way of a helpful sunbeam.

I close my eyes.

Could I still be dreaming?

I purposely reach over to the blackberry bush and fumble among the leaves and fruit until I prick my finger on a thorn. I squeeze the puncture to make sure there's no residue in the wound and then stick the finger in my mouth.

I can taste the metallic tang of my blood.

My psychology teacher said that taste was the sense that we experienced the least often when dreaming. We see, hear, touch/feel, and sometimes smell, but seldom taste.

"You appear puzzled," Kaden says.

"Who are you?" I demand. I wave my hand at the place where he stepped out of the sunbeam. "How did you get here?" I feel a bubble of panic forming in my chest. My next questions come out in a breathy whisper. "Are you real? Are you human?"

"I can explain everything," he says softly. "Do you want to do it here? Or would you prefer to go to the clearing, which seems to be where you're the most comfortable within the forest?"

"Here is just fine," I say.

"Well, let's at least sit down." He lowers himself to the ground, never taking his eyes off of me. He sits cross-legged.

I sit directly across from him.

When he starts talking, his voice is soft. "You know there is something special about this forest, don't you? Every time you come here you make an offering of food in the same location. Do you know why you do that?"

"My grandmother taught me."

"But why? Did she not give you any reasons?"

I pause to think.

Although I've always accepted as absolute truth everything my grandmother told me, now, suddenly being put in the position of needing to explain it to someone else, I'm not so sure.

I search my inner self.

Do I secretly doubt my grandmother's stories?

Or am I just afraid to repeat them?

Grandma had a favorite quote from Robert Louis Stevenson. She recited it so often while I was growing up that I will probably never forget it, even if I live to be a couple hundred years old: *You cannot run away from a weakness; you must sometime fight it out or perish. If that be so, why not now, and where you stand?*

In this moment, I feel uncommonly weak-willed.

Why?

I'm almost too ashamed to acknowledge the answer to myself.

But, in fairness to Grandma, I must.

I'm afraid if I tell Kaden the things Grandma said that he will make fun of me, and I'd almost rather deny my grandmother than to face his ridicule. I've been hurt so many times.

Or, on second thought, maybe I'm just stalling.

I saw him walk out of a ray of light.

Maybe I don't want to hear what he has to say. Maybe what I'm actually afraid of is having him confirm everything Grandma taught me, taking away the tantalizing mystery.

What a coward I am!

I take a deep breath.

I will not accept such fearfulness in myself.

"My grandmother said this forest is enchanted, and although our family holds the deed to the property, it really belongs to the magical beings who live here. She taught me that it is polite to bring a gift to your hosts when they allow you to enter their home."

I glare at Kaden defiantly.

He smiles sweetly at me.

No one has ever smiled at me like that before. It's as if I've done something that has made him very happy. I think my heart will break from the sheer unexpected glory of it.

"Your grandmother was right," Kaden says. "The forest is enchanted. Do you know if she ever saw them—the ones who live here?"

I shake my head. "She never did, although she said she heard their voices talking and singing and laughing a few times. She said they had high chirping voices, which is why our tributes have always been small in scale. She assumed the beings were little people, like fairies or elves or pixies."

"Your grandmother was a most insightful woman. The creatures that migrated from my world to yours are quite small. That's why they wanted to come here, so they could hide from the predators who hunt them in our forests. They are very vulnerable there."

"What do you mean they migrated from your world to mine?"

"There are many worlds," Kaden says, "all moving within their own time and space. Sometimes the worlds come so close to each other that passageways open up between them. It happens to our worlds, yours and mine, frequently. In fact it has occurred so often that some of the openings have become fixed, making it possible for beings to travel from one world to the other."

"You mean I could step through a sunbeam into your world?"

"Indeed, yes, if you had a key that would unlock the passageway."

I can't tell if he is serious or if he is mocking me.

"It's easier to open from my side," Kaden continues, "because magic is more active in my world, and we have developed objects that help us control it." He glances around. "Of course your world is awash with untapped enchantment. If those magical forces weren't here, the little people, as you call them, would never have immigrated to your woods."

I'm struggling.

Grandma told me this was an enchanted forest and I believed her, but Kaden's telling me that he comes from a magical world is harder for me to accept.

Why?

Why can I accept Grandma's word on faith, but I can't accept Kaden's word even though it confirms what I saw with my own eyes just a few moments ago?

"Can you do magic?" I suddenly ask Kaden.

"It depends on what you mean by magic," he answers.

"Well, what do you mean by magic?" I ask. "I'm a non-magical person from a non-magical world, so I don't know what it is. You tell me."

Kaden gets to his feet and paces around. "Magic is being able to do something without using your normal five senses." He recites it as if it's a school lesson.

"Show me," I suggest.

"My magic isn't the kind you can see," he mumbles. He shakes his head ruefully as he looks down at me.

"This isn't going the way I planned. I wasn't prepped for you to see me arrive, and I don't know the best way to answer your questions in order to give you information without overwhelming you. I haven't been trained in diplomacy. I wonder if the prince could explain this to you better than I can."

"Oh, pullleeeaazzzzze," I say, drawing out the word sarcastically. "Now, on top of all the magic mumbo jumbo, you're going to add a prince. What comes next? A fairy godmother? My credulity can only be pushed so far. I'm taking my empty pail and going home."

"Please." He steps in front of me. "Don't go, please. I know this must all sound strange to you. When my father told me I needed to come here to look for the three lost items, I had no idea I would stumble across someone who could entrance me as you have. There are things you need to know. It's very important. I realize I'm not deporting myself as befits my position and my training, but please give me another chance."

His voice portrays such a mixture of pleading and hopelessness that it wrings at my heart.

Many times in my life, when I've made a mess of things, I would have liked to make that same kind of plea, begging someone to give me another chance. I lacked the courage. Maybe I owe Kaden another chance simply because he was brave enough to ask for it.

"There is someone here," he continues, "someone nearby at least, who can probably explain all of this to you better than I can. Will you let me call him to see if he is available?"

"What makes you think he will be more believable than you are?"

Kaden glances down and shuffles his feet awkwardly, as if he's afraid to say anything else that might come out wrong.

Finally he looks at me. "He has been here longer than I have and has more experience with your people. Also, throughout his training, he has been taught to be gentle and tactful and more gracious than I have been. May I call him? Will you stay long enough to hear him out?"

"All right," I say.

He glances around a moment, and I realize he doesn't have a cellphone.

I hand him mine.

He stares at it as if he's never seen one before. Then he takes it and presses some numbers. To me it looks as if he hasn't tapped enough pads for a phone number, but I must have been wrong. He begins speaking.

"Your Highness, this is Kaden Deke Katsenevas, son of Trevor, your father's chronicler."

I hear a voice responding but I can't understand the words. It doesn't matter. I'm stuck on Kaden's first two words: *Your Highness.* After that, nothing makes any sense to me. I stop listening. What good would it do for me to hear a nonsensical conversation?

"Thank you," Kaden says. "You're most kind. I am here at the request of my father and yours. Because of information my father provided, your father asked me to locate three items brought here many years ago by a member of the Dark family. I have just met a human girl whose name is Hellenaura Dark Powers."

More mumbling comments from whoever is on the other side of the call.

"That was my thought also. We met for the first time yesterday, and I had hoped to broach the subject with her today. I used my family's key to get here, but unfortunately she saw me come through the portal. Now she is frightened and doesn't know what to believe."

More unintelligible sounds.

"Yes, if you would, I'd appreciate it. She is willing to listen to what you have to say."

Mumble, mumble.

"I will ask her." He turns to me. "He wants to know how to get here. Is there an address?"

I am feeling overwhelmed, but I try to remain calm.

"The easiest way to get here would be to go to my house and cut through the backyard, but that's probably not a good plan since he'd have to climb over a fence and the neighbors might notice. He'll have to come around to the other side like everyone else does. Tell him to drive west out of town on Highway 50. About ten miles out he'll come—"

More cellphone noise.

Kaden says, "He told me to tell you that he doesn't have a car. Please just focus on where we are in relationship to the town hall."

"What? I don't understand."

"Do you know where the town hall is?"

"Of course," I answer.

"Picture in your mind that you are there and then picture yourself traveling from there to here. Can you do that?"

"Yes, but how—"

"Please," Kaden says, "will you just please do it."

My feelings of overwhelm are beginning to feel a little bit more like panic. What Kaden is implying is that, if I imagine the route, the person on the other end of the line will be able to see it and use it to find his way here. I am beginning to think that Kaden is probably crazy and is engaged in some kind of plot with another lunatic.

I wonder if I shouldn't make a break for it and run home.

Suddenly Kaden starts to laugh, but he tries to hide it by coughing. When he finishes with the phony coughing fit, he says, "He said to tell you that neither of us is crazy and you will be perfectly safe with us. He will bring his human girlfriend with him to help put you at ease."

I feel the blood draining from my face. I imagine I'm as white as a sheet. How did he know what I was thinking? Can someone really read my mind? Now I'm truly afraid.

"You have nothing to fear from us, Hellenaura," Kaden says. "Yes, he can see into your mind. No, I cannot. Will you show him the way here?"

I close my eyes and picture the route from the town hall. I imagine the road out of town to the far side of the forest and then along the paths through the trees to this spot.

"How long?" Kaden asks. "Yes. Thank you." Kaden hands me my cellphone. "He will be here as soon as possible. His girlfriend is occupied right now, but they should arrive in approximately an hour."

"All right," I say automatically.

I'm committed to seeing this mess through. I don't think I could force myself to leave even if I wanted to, but in fact, even though I'm scared half to death, I don't want to go.

I want to stay until things make sense again.

Otherwise, I might become the lunatic.

Kaden and I sit on the grass, trying not to stare at each other.

I wish I had checked the time when Kaden handed my cellphone back to me. I would like to keep track of how much longer we have to wait. I just might develop an ulcer or have a heart attack if it's too long.

Well, there is one thing I can suggest that might help me relax.

Food.

"I'm hungry," I say. "I'll share my lunch with you."

His eyes light up.

"I brought us each a fauvenell," he exclaims.

"Why didn't you say so?" I reply, grinning despite myself.

Until that moment, I hadn't noticed the pouch hanging from his belt. It looks a little bit like a fanny pack, but it's worn on the side and appears to be constructed of simple, brown, unadorned leather.

Much of my fear disappears in anticipation of enjoying another of those delicious cakes.

We sit in the shade and I open my lunch tote.

"I hope you like tuna fish." I hand him half a sandwich.

"I like all seafood," Kaden says.

I open the bag of chips and place it between us. Then I use the edge of the fork to cut the apple in half. I don't tell him I've licked the fork. I don't think I have any deadly germs that we need to worry about.

After Kaden takes a bite of the sandwich, he opens it and looks at the tuna salad, the lettuce, and the tomato. He puts it back together and takes another bite.

"This is really good," he says. "It's more than just fish inside two pieces of bread. How is it made? Do you have a recipe?"

"I doubt there's an actual recipe anywhere. That's one of the nice things about tuna salad: you can make it any way you want in an infinite number of variations. I'll demonstrate some of the more popular combinations for you sometime."

He finishes the sandwich and then starts on the apple.

He eats the core, seeds and all. I've only seen a few other people do that. Assuming this is customary where he's from—whether it's a foreign country, a different world, or an insane asylum—I decide to do the same thing. It's not bad.

He takes a potato chip from the bag, smells it, holds it up to the light, and turns it this way and that.

Dark in the Forest: Another Modern Fairytale

He takes a nibble.

He must have swallowed wrong.

He stops breathing and his face goes sort of green.

I grab a bottle of water, twist off the cap, and hand it to him.

He takes it, gets to his knees, and turns his back on me. I see him lift the bottle and then I hear him swishing water around in his mouth. A second later, he spits it out. Then he does it again.

When he turns around and sits back down, the coloring in his face is blotchy. He takes a couple of swallows from the bottle and clears his throat before he begins speaking.

"I knew I shouldn't eat it," he says, "but it smelled so tantalizing I just wanted to know if it tasted as good as it smelled. So many things don't. I apologize for my coarse behavior."

"No need to apologize." I shove the potato chips back into my tote bag. "Are you allergic? Do you need medication?"

"I'll be fine, but I'd like to eat the fauvenell to get rid of the residual taste." He opens his bag and takes out a container that holds two fauvenell. "It is a tradition in Auravale that when two friends share fauvenell for the first time that they feed each other. Would you be offended if we did that?"

"Not at all," I say, although it reminds me a little bit of a bride and groom sharing the first bites of their wedding cake. I put the emotional brakes on the thought. Kaden is a stranger, and I shouldn't be putting him and wedding in the same sentence—not even in my mind.

With a smile on his face, he hands me a fauvenell.

"If you wouldn't mind," he says, leaning forward and opening his mouth. I hold my fauvenell out to him, and he takes a small bite.

As if he is savoring the taste, he chews slowly.

After he swallows, he extends his hand and holds his cake out to me.

I'm leaning forward and am just about to take a bite when an angry voice interrupts.

"Kaden, what are you doing!"

I turn around and see a guy holding a girl in his arms.

He is tall, slender, and handsome. The top and sides of his pale blond hair have been pulled back and braided. The braid dangles over hair that hangs halfway down his back. His eyes are startlingly green. He's wearing jeans and a black t-shirt.

The girl he's carrying has one arm hooked around his neck.

She also has blond hair, but it's more a golden color, and her eyes are dark blue. She's cute and pert. She's the type that would usually be head cheerleader or class secretary. On her lower half she's wearing what looks like navy blue sweatpants made of a lightweight fabric. She's got on a pink t-shirt.

With a start, I recognize them.

Chapter Twelve

Kaden jumps to his feet. "Your Highness," he says, making a small bow from the waist. Then he bends over, takes the fauvenell from me, and hands me the one without a bite in it.

I don't know what's going on.

Because I'm feeling befuddled, I'm slow getting up, but I don't feel right about staying seated. With the heated atmosphere, I'm almost afraid I'll have to step between the guys to prevent a fight, even if the newcomer has his arms full.

No one speaks for a long second.

Then Kaden says formally, "Your Highness, may I present Hellenaura Dark Powers?"

"Cut it out, Kaden," the boy snaps.

"Everyone calls me Hellie," I say, trying to pretend I didn't hear the anger in the guy's voice and totally ignoring the fact that Kaden addressed him as *Your Highness* twice.

Nodding at the boy, I add, "I've heard you play the violin. When you played at the Spring Concert two years ago, that was the first time I'd heard the violin played as a solo instrument, not just as part of an orchestra. I really enjoyed it, and I was glad to hear you play again at this year's Christmas and Spring Concerts. You're very good."

"Thank you. I'm Neeve Maynard, and this is Karissa Day."

I smile at the girl.

Usually, she's in a wheelchair. However, at graduation this month, when her name was called, Neeve helped her walk across the stage to get her diploma. There was a lot of clapping and whistling and whooping from the audience. I clapped myself even though I only knew her by sight.

Neeve sets her gently on her feet.

I don't realize she's holding a cane until I see her use it to gain her balance.

"I'm pleased to meet you, Karissa," I say.

She smiles. "I've watched you play basketball. You're remarkable. I was disappointed that Millard Fillmore doesn't belong to a girls' league and just

61

has intramurals. If you'd gone to my high school in Chicago, you'd have been captain of the team."

"Thanks," I say, feeling a blush creep up my cheeks. "I'm flattered that you noticed me."

"The way you fly around the court," Karissa says, "you're hard to miss. But your sister doesn't do sports, does she?"

"No," I stammer. "How did you know?"

Usually, until people know us well, they don't realize that Angel and I have any differences. Angel and I make a habit of not hanging out together at school. We're together so much at home, Mom and Dad have always encouraged each of us to find interests and friends of our own. Lots of people who are only casually acquainted with our family haven't even figured out that there are two of us yet.

"The first time I saw you together," Karissa says, "I thought I was seeing double. It was after the game when you made that three pointer at the last moment. When the final buzzer went off, your sister ran onto the court and hugged you. You and your sister look alike, but you move like an athlete and she doesn't." She smiles a little wanly. "Having spent so much time in a wheelchair, I tend to notice how other people use their bodies. Your twin has the gait of a scholar not an athlete."

"Most people can't even tell us apart," I say.

"You have a twin?" Kaden and Neeve exclaim at the same time.

"Yes, I do."

Neeve glances over at Karissa. "How is it that you spotted them, and I didn't?"

Karissa pokes him in the chest with her finger. "Because you know if I catch you staring at other girls, I'd smack you."

He takes her hand and kisses the palm. "Why would I look at anyone else when I have you?"

"Obviously you don't," she says, "or you'd have noticed the twins." She smiles tenderly at him as if they are the only two people in the world.

"I don't suppose your sister's middle name is Dark also," Kaden asks.

When he speaks, he draws Neeve and Karissa's attention back to us.

"No," I answer. "Her middle name is Prudence. Angelica Prudence Powers."

"Well, that's a relief," Neeve mumbles.

I don't know what he's implying, but I bristle at his tone because he sounds as if he is somehow insulting my sister.

"She's a very nice person," I insist defensively.

"With a name like that," he says, "how could she be anything else?"

"Neeve," Karissa says, poking him in the chest again, "you're going all enigmatic. You've got to stop doing that."

He smiles at her sheepishly and then looks at me. "My apologies. I didn't mean to sound cryptic. I simply believe some names can influence behaviors, and your sister has three strong names—as you do."

While I'm trying to figure out how to ask him to go into more detail about my name, he turns away from me.

His voice becomes serious and authoritative. "Kaden, I need to speak with you privately."

"Of course," Kaden responds.

For a moment I get a glimpse of the person that Kaden must see when he uses the term *Your Highness*. I think Neeve might actually be a prince somewhere, and it gives me a shiver.

Before the guys leave, Neeve sets up a chair for Karissa. Its one of those folding canvas affairs—field chairs I think they're called—that people take to outdoor concerts and little league baseball games, things like that, where there are no bleachers.

"Thank you." Karissa sits down, looking grateful to be off her feet.

"We'll be back in a few minutes," Neeve says. He motions for Kaden to follow him, and they leave together.

After they are out of sight, I sit on the ground across from Karissa.

"I still can't stand for very long," she explains, "but I'm getting better. I hope to be able to walk unassisted down the aisle next year when Neeve and I get married."

I notice the engagement ring she's wearing. It would ransom a small country, I think, or maybe two.

She notices me looking at it. "I'm not used to wearing it yet. He gave it to me last week for graduation."

"Congratulations," I tell her.

"Thank you, but I don't think we should waste our time talking about me. You look like you're about to burst with questions. Go ahead and ask."

"Why did Kaden call Neeve *Your Highness*?"

"Before I answer that," she says, "I need to ask you a question. Has Kaden told you anything about where he comes from?"

"A little," I admit. "He said he's from a magical country that comes in contact with our world often enough that passageways exist between them. He said people can pass through if they have the right key."

"That's one way to put it," Karissa says, "and at least it's a starting point. Neeve and Kaden come from a place called Auravale, and Neeve actually is a prince there."

"Why did he come here then?"

"It's complicated," she answers. "It's easiest just to think of him as a foreign exchange student. That's what I do most of the time."

"Do you know why he was so angry with Kaden when you guys first got here? I listened to Kaden's side of the conversation when they talked earlier, and he sounded perfectly fine. But you two hadn't been here more than a second before Neeve yelled at him."

I don't know if she'll answer me.

Dark in the Forest: Another Modern Fairytale

She stares off into the distance.

I can't tell if she's shutting me out or merely stalling. Maybe she's embarrassed. I know there are people who are always trying to take responsibility for their partner's feelings and behaviors.

I guess she was just thinking because she starts speaking slowly. "There were two reasons for Neeve's reaction. First, their world is much more steeped in rituals and traditions than ours is and fauvenell is used in some of their ceremonies.

"The other thing is that Kaden kept calling Neeve *Your Highness.* Although Neeve's father is the king of Auravale, Neeve is here and not there. He has been passing as a U.S. citizen for two years and needs to continue doing so while we attend college. If Kaden is going to be visiting, he needs to be careful not to expose Neeve's true nature, either intentionally or unintentionally. Calling him *Your Highness* while he's here is a bad habit to get into."

I squirm around for a moment trying to get comfortable. I reach under my left hip and pull out a rock that's been trying to bore its way into my flesh. I scowl at it and toss it aside.

"I guess I can understand," I say, "how Neeve might get irritated about Kaden calling him *Your Highness* if his presence is supposed to be a secret." Then I have a terrible thought, and I stare open-mouthed at Karissa. "He's not a spy, is he? Tell me his father isn't planning to invade us or something."

She laughs. "I promise you, we have nothing that they want."

"How do you know?" I demand. "Neeve could be deceiving you, trying to get you to betray your country—our whole world maybe."

"No he couldn't," she says. "He's taken me to Auravale several times, and I've met his family. I'll admit I don't understand half of what goes on in their culture, but I do know that traveling to other worlds is a rare and unusual occurrence. Invading and occupying an alien world is a concept they wouldn't even be able to understand."

"All right." I can't help but believe her. She's one of those people who just exudes honesty. "Tell me why Neeve was upset about the fauvenell."

"I will, but first tell me what Kaden told you."

"He said that when friends share fauvenell together for the first time that it's usual for them to feed each other a bite. Is that wrong?"

"It depends. Do you mind telling me how long you've known each other and how you met?"

"Not at all," I say. I tell her about Kaden's stealing my cupcake, his apologizing in a letter, and his leaving me a fauvenell as repayment. I finish with: "We met face to face for the first time yesterday."

Nodding, she says, "That's why Neeve was angry."

Before I can ask what she means, she goes on.

"In Auravale they have all kinds of little customs and ceremonies regarding relationships. Here, if a guy likes a girl, he might ask her to wear his school sweater or he might give her his class ring. Going steady could be considered one of our rituals that bind a guy and a girl together. But in our world going steady is usually a pretty flimsy bond. Either party can break up at any time for any reason. Am I making sense?"

"Sure," I tell her, "but what does it have to do with fauvenell?" Then it hits me. "Are you saying that feeding each other bites of cake means we're going steady?"

"Close," she says, "but not quite." She takes some deep breaths. "Give me a moment." She closes her eyes, and I guess she's thinking really hard. Her lips move slightly as if she's talking silently to herself. When she opens her eyes, she gives me a little smile.

"I wish I knew you well enough to know how to word this," she says. "My dad's a shrink, and he always says the better you know someone the greater the odds are that you can tell them something difficult without having them freak out."

"I don't freak out easily," I assert. I don't know if that's exactly true, but I want to hear what she has to say so I try to reassure her.

"It has to do with the magic," she says. "A guy here might give a girl his class ring just because he wants to have sex with her. When he gets bored, he can always break up and move on to another girl."

I nod. It's sad, but it happens often enough. Guys can be so fickle.

"Neeve's people can't afford to be that casual about romance," Karissa says. "First of all, the magic is always present to make words or thoughts or promises become reality."

When I took psychology, we talked a little bit about self-fulfilling prophecy and magical thinking. Is Karissa implying that in Auravale desires come true just by thinking about them? If they do, what about all those malicious, spur-of-the-moment, unhealthy things that pop into our minds when we're emotionally overwrought and then disappear when we become rational again?

I don't ask because I want Karissa to continue.

She does.

"The other part is that they can only fall in love once. And, Hellie, it looks like Kaden has fallen for you. I don't know how or when, you'll have to ask him, but when he offered to share bites of fauvenell with you, he was trying to bind you to him."

"What does that mean?" I demand. "Bind me to him how?"

"Fauvenell is a wonderful dessert," she says, "and it is served often in Auravale. But it doesn't just taste good, it has a little magic in it, so it makes you feel good too."

"I noticed that," I say.

"When a guy and a girl feed each other fauvenell, the feelings increase into a bond of mutual goodwill. The first time Neeve took me to meet his family, one of his older brothers teased him about when he and I would share fauvenell together."

I guess I look blank.

Dark in the Forest: Another Modern Fairytale

"At engagement parties for arranged marriages, the betrothed couple feed each other fauvenell. Even if they've never met before, the fauvenell makes them sensitive to each other's positive qualities. It doesn't actually make them fall in love, but it makes them susceptible to the possibility."

My mouth falls open.

"Are you saying Kaden was trying to make me susceptible to his charms? To make me want to fall in love with him?"

"Hellie," Karissa says, "I'm sure he felt a powerful compulsion. If he's fallen in love with you, his only hope is to help you fall in love with him."

I feel exploited, abused, wronged.

I'm almost too hurt to be angry.

When I look at Karissa again, I'm about ready to burst with unexpressed and confused emotions, but then I see tears streaking her face.

"I should have let Neeve explain," she says to me. "It's so hard for us earthlings to understand the ways they think and feel. When Neeve described how he felt towards me, I thought my heart would break.

"Before he even reached puberty, he saw my face in a magical pool of water and fell in love with me. He defied his father and went through terrible trials in order to find me.

"If Kaden is going through something similar with you, I ache for him—for you both. Romantic love is treated so tritely in our world. Movies, television shows, and even our literature are full of quick romances that blossom and fade in almost the same moment.

"It's hard for us to sort through all that garbage to realize that love like theirs even exists. I'm not suggesting that you fake feelings for Kaden that you don't have—it wouldn't do any good anyway because they can always tell—but I do encourage you to be kind to him.

"He wasn't trying to seduce you with the fauvenell. It doesn't work that way. If one of them falls in love with someone and the love isn't returned, he can find and marry someone who is compatible and they can live a happy and contented life. But that one true love will always remain there in his heart.

"I'm sure Kaden knew it was too early for him to tell you how he feels. He wouldn't want to scare you off. I think he was just trying to use the fauvenell to influence you so you would be less likely to fall for someone else before he could try to win you."

I grab hold of my head.

"It's all too much," I say. "What you're describing doesn't compute. The system is about to shut down."

"I'm sorry," she says. "I've probably told you too much. But if Kaden is allowed to return here long enough to pursue a relationship with you, which isn't guaranteed, you're likely to go through some tremendous emotional upheavals. However, if the result is that you grow to love him back, it will be worth it a thousand times over."

I study her face and can see she believes what's she's saying.

"I appreciate your trying to explain," I tell her. "My mind will probably sort through it all and begin making sense out of it tonight while I sleep. I don't know why but I do some of my best problem solving in my dreams."

"Do you have your cellphone with you?" she asks.

I nod.

"Why don't you let me enter my phone number? If you ever want to talk, you can call me."

"Thanks." I give her my phone.

"While I'm at it, do you mind if I take your number?"

"I'd like that," I say. "If anything new occurs to you that might help me understand all this magic stuff, I'd like you to call me."

I think Karissa and I are going to be friends, and it's such a relief.

With Grandma gone and Angel unavailable, it would be nice to have someone to talk to.

Karissa is still entering phone numbers when the guys come back.

Kaden looks a little subdued, but the hostility between him and Neeve is gone.

When Kaden's eyes meet mine, they appear apprehensive. I imagine he's worried about what Karissa might have told me. I've got to admit I feel a little nervous about all that *one true love* stuff, but I also have to admit that I want to see Kaden again.

Dang it.

I like him.

Without instructions from my brain, my lips turn upward and I smile at him.

Chapter Thirteen

Neeve sits on the ground next to Karissa, his shoulder against her knee.

As if it's an automatic response, she strokes his hair, and he tips his head to the side and presses his cheek against her hand.

If I had to describe the expression on their faces, I'd say they were almost angelic. No. As I picture all the phony angel figurines, posters, and illustrations I've seen, I realize it's not as if Neeve and Karissa are angelic. It's as if they have looked at the divine and have assimilated it into their lives. Or maybe this is what love looks like in Neeve and Kaden's world.

I feel like a voyeur, observing something I have no right to see.

I avert my gaze and look at the trees instead.

"Kaden has explained as much as he could to me," Neeve says, drawing my attention back to him. "There are still unanswered questions, but the most significant thing right now is to establish his veracity, and mine."

"I told him," Kaden adds, "that your grandmother taught you that this is an enchanted forest and you believed her, but accepting a magical world that exists beyond your reality has stretched your credulity too much. Did I paraphrase it correctly?"

"Yes," I say. "That sums it up pretty much, although I have to admit talking with Karissa has swayed me a little more to your side."

"What would it take to convince you completely?" Neeve asks.

"Seeing a little true magic might help," I answer with a grin. "When I asked Kaden to give me a demonstration, he told me that his magic wasn't the visual kind." I expect Neeve to say that his isn't either.

"Kaden was telling the truth," Neeve says. "There are many different kinds of magic. I have a younger sister who encompasses all of them, and she will begin training as a mage later this year. Most of us can do a few spells, but all of us have at least one magical skill. Kaden has the ability to find anything, anywhere, and not necessarily just lost items although that's how his talent is generally utilized. My magic is a little showier."

He raises his hand above his head and then sweeps it toward his feet. His black t-shirt turns into a red silk poet's shirt. His blue jeans and sneakers become tapered black pants that are tucked into shiny, mid-calf, black boots.

"It doesn't just work on me," Neeve says. A glance at Kaden and Kaden is suddenly wearing a white shirt with a lacy neckpiece, a gold brocade jacket, white knee breeches, white stockings, and black shoes with gold buckles.

Neeve tips his head up so he can look at Karissa.

"Don't you dare," she says. "If you put me in some kind of fancy gown, I'll smack you."

"Green?" he asks.

"As long as it matches your eyes," she says. The next moment her shirt, sweatpants, shoes and socks all turn emerald green.

He looks at me. "Do you have a preference?"

"No farthingales," I say, picturing him outfitting me like someone out of the Elizabethan Era to match Kaden.

The next thing I know, I'm wearing a simple blue gown trimmed with dark blue braid. Maid Marian might have worn something similar in Sherwood Forest when she went to meet with Robin Hood.

I expect it to be merely an illusion.

I finger the fabric.

The dress feels as if it's made of lightweight, brushed wool. The braid has a texture that I don't recognize. The significant thing is that neither of them feels like the denim of my jeans or the cotton knit of my shirt.

Neeve waves his hand and all of our clothing reverts to its previous state. Having watched several television shows featuring street magicians, however, I know that they can create astounding effects even though it's still all trickery.

I ask Karissa, "Do you believe that this magical stuff is real?"

"It's not a matter of belief," she says. "I've seen and experienced so much that I don't have room to doubt. I know it's real. What Neeve has shown you is just a fraction of what his people can do."

I turn to Kaden. "If your magical ability is finding things, why haven't you found the objects that you came here to get?"

"I'm pretty sure I've located one," he answers. "I believe the other two are here, hidden by the ones you call *the forest people*. They can be mischievous, and they sometimes have their own agendas. If the objects are here, I could force them to appear, but I've hesitated because there might be negative consequences in the future. If there is a less aggressive way to obtain them, I will find it."

His gaze settles on me for a moment.

Then he looks down at the ground and then over at Neeve. "I don't know how to do this. I realize it has to be done, but I don't think I can be the one to do it."

"All right," Neeve says. "Hellie, what do you know about your name?"

"My name," I exclaim. "Why do you want to know?"

"As I mentioned before," Neeve says, "names can be powerful. What can you tell me about yours?"

Dark in the Forest: Another Modern Fairytale

I really don't know how to answer. When I consider my name, I have such extreme emotions I can hardly sort them out. All I know is that my name has had a negative impact on me all my life.

"He really needs to know," Karissa inserts into the pause. "He has something to tell you, and he's trying to get enough information about you so he can tell you in the best way."

"So I won't freak out?"

"That's right," Karissa says.

I purse my lips while I try to think of what to say.

I guess I'll just have to plunge in and hope I don't get swept away by my feelings.

"When my parents found out they were having twin daughters, they decided to name us after our great-grandmothers. Whoever was born first would to be named for my father's grandmothers. That was Angel, and that's where she got the names Angelica and Prudence.

"I was named after my mother's grandmothers, but my parents didn't like the way that Helena and Aura sounded together because of the double 'a' created by the end of Helena and the beginning of Aura. You have to pause between the two names or they blend together. So my folks decided to go ahead and combine the names into one word in order to eliminate the problem. But then I didn't have a middle name. They decided to use my mother's maiden name, which is Dark. So I became Hellenaura Dark Powers, which I hate."

"Why do you hate it?" Neeve asks.

"When I told you Angel's name was Angelica Prudence and insisted that she's a good person, you said 'With a name like that how could she be anything else.' That's the way everyone responds. Then, when they consider my name, they don't know what to think."

"I don't understand," Neeve says. "What's wrong with your name?"

"I understand," Karissa says with sympathy. "It's because when they say your name, they say it like *Hell and Her Dark Powers*, don't they?"

When I nod, Neeve exclaims, "You've got to be kidding!"

"I'm not. Unless they've seen it spelled out, that's what most people think my name is. It gives them the creeps."

"I don't understand," Kaden says.

Neeve rattles off a spate of foreign words.

Kaden opens his eyes wide. "No. That can't be right." He turns his horrified gaze at me. "What do they think you're going to do? Sprout horns and start killing people?"

"I don't think they do it consciously," I say, suddenly defensive about the foibles of the human race, "but they can't help it. To the average person my name sounds evil. When I was little, I thought a wicked fiend had tricked my parents into giving me my name so I'd be corrupt from the beginning.

"I decided that I would fool the fiend by growing up to be an exemplary person: good, kind, thoughtful, and helpful. I tried hard, but for some reason things never went very well for me. Good intentions often led to catastrophic consequences.

"Angel has always been better at everything than I am. But even if she's not, people assume that she is. Whenever she got caught making a little mischief, everyone laughed as if she had pulled some cute, innocent prank. If I did the same thing, everyone was sure that I meant to be malicious and was trying to hurt someone.

"If she got caught telling a lie, people forgave her without a second thought and went right on trusting her. I didn't even need to lie to make people distrust me. If ten kids told the teacher that so-and-so broke a window, and then one person said that I did it, I was the one who got into trouble."

"Holy stars," Kaden exclaims, "no wonder you hate your name. I suppose I would too if I were in your position. But your name isn't evil. Hasn't anyone ever explained what your name actually means?"

"Not really," I answer, "but I looked it up on the Internet."

"What did you learn?" asks Neeve.

"The name Helena is a version of Helen and means light or bright being. Aura is complicated because it is both a name and a word, and we have no way of knowing which one her parents meant. As a name it usually means something like soft breeze. As a word it refers to the distinctive atmosphere or radiant emanations that surround everyone. Dark is the absence of light, and Powers refers to strengths and abilities and is sometimes used as a euphemism for supernatural forces."

"What does all of that mean to you?" Neeve asks.

Is there something accusatory in his voice?

Or do I just imagine it?

I automatically replay everything he has said to me, listening for criticism and sarcasm. I watch his face for the widening of the eyes and the little twitches around the mouth that indicate someone is trying to set me up so he can mock me.

I don't see any of the signs, but I'm still hesitant.

After a few minutes, I decide I might as well answer him.

Sitting here with three people staring at me isn't accomplishing anything.

"In my psychology class last year, the teacher told us that our names affect how we develop as children and how we're perceived as adults. It's not because our names actually change us in some way, but because they cause us, and the people around us, to have certain expectations. Unfortunately for me, people expect Angel to be good and they expect me to be bad."

I've kept all of these feeling dammed up inside of me for years, and now that the flood gates have opened, I can't seem to close them again.

I continue with fervor.

"When I hear someone say my name like *Hell and Her Dark Powers,* I feel like I'm being shoved into the role of a demon who only has the power to do evil. I've tried to look at my name from lots of different angles, and I just can't come up with anything that has a positive connotation.

"One day I tried to explain to my parents the ways that Angel and I were being shaped by our names, but they didn't understand. They told me I was jealous or ridiculously superstitious or both. They said all I had to do was to work harder if I wanted to match or exceed Angel's accomplishments. I didn't try explaining a second time."

"Have you given any thought to what your great-grandmothers were like?" Neeve asks me. "They were real people. Don't you think you might have inherited some of their positive qualities along with their names?"

"Of course I've thought about them," I assert. "I think about them all the time, especially my great-grandmother Aura Dark. I've seen pictures of her, and Angel and I actually look a lot like she did at our age. But no one on that side of my family kept journals, or wrote personal histories, or even saved very many mementos, so I don't know much about Aura Dark. My mother said Aura's past was filled with scandal and mystery. My mother figured it was because no one knew who her father was, and no one knew who fathered her mother either. Her daughter became my grandmother Mable Dark."

"Wait a minute," Neeve says. "Let me get this straight. Your mother, your mother's mother, and your mother's grandmother all had the last name of Dark?"

"That's right," I answer, "plus my mother's great-grandmother and her great-great-grandmother. The first Dark in our line was named Bree-Ella Dark. She was foreign, and she insisted that the girls in her direct line keep the surname Dark, even when they married. The boys could take their father's name, but not the girls. There's supposed to be some kind of family curse involved. My mother wanted to follow the tradition, but my father said no. When Angel was born, Dad refused to give her the name Dark. He compromised by giving it to me, but as my middle name, not my last."

"Bree-Ella Dark," Kaden repeats in a whisper.

Neeve nods at him. "This is more complicated than I thought. Kaden, you and I need to talk with my father, and yours as well." Then he turns to me, "I'll be back, but probably not for a few days. Kaden will let you know when. It was nice meeting you."

Neeve's abrupt ending of our conversation startles me, and there is something about his tone and body language that attests that he is not used to explaining himself.

I feel like telling him that if he wants Kaden to stop referring to him as *Your Highness* in this world then he needs to stop acting like royalty. I don't know him well enough to say it, but I might mention it to Karissa some time when I talk with her on the phone.

After Neeve helps Karissa stand, Kaden folds the field chair and slides it back into its case.

Neeve slips the case's strap over his shoulder and then picks Karissa up.

She hooks her arms around his neck.

"Don't be too long," Neeve says to Kaden. He makes a sideward flip with his right index finger.

"Call me," Karissa says, giving me one last glance before Neeve takes a step forward and they disappear.

But it's not like "poof," one moment they're here and the next moment they're gone. It's more like Neeve simply walks behind a screen that's painted to look exactly like the forest, and they disappear as he moves forward.

Kaden sits back down facing me.

"I know we need to talk," he says, "but Neeve won't give me more than a few minutes, and we'll need more time that that. Will you meet me again tomorrow? Please."

When I don't answer right away, he closes his eyes and his shoulders slump in defeat.

I reach over to touch him.

I aim my hand at his arm, but somehow I end up stroking his cheek.

He takes my hand and kisses the palm.

"I can be here by noon," I say.

Chapter Fourteen

Kaden picks up the fauvenells, places them back in the container, and puts the container in his belt pouch. "I'll see you tomorrow," he says.

A beam of light appears. Through it I see the hazy picture of a room with a big desk and walls covered with books. I sense people, but I can't see them. Kaden steps into the light. Then he and the light are both gone.

I feel like screaming hysterically.

Nothing my grandmother told me prepared me for watching people simply vanish. When Neeve altered our clothing, it felt like a parlor trick, but this?

I just saw three people disappear.

That has to be magic—real magic—bona fide, irrefutable, indisputable, genuine magic.

I gather up my things and walk home in a daze.

When Dad and Angel get home, I'm glad I don't have to do anything for dinner. Mom calls and says she'll be home late. She tells us to eat without her. The three of us pull out the leftovers, microwave what we want, and put the rest back in the refrigerator.

Angel and Dad settle down in the family room to watch something on television.

I sit at the dining room table alone and pick at my food. My brain just can't handle everything that happened this afternoon.

I guess I eat. When I look down at my plate later, it's empty.

I go up to my room, put on pajamas, floss and brush my teeth, select a CD, start the player, turn out my lights, and stare into the darkness.

Eventually I fall sleep.

I dream.

Even though I realize I'm asleep, knowing that doesn't decrease the terror. Neither does recognizing that I've had this dream dozens of times since I turned ten years old.

I'm trying to catch my breath, standing with my back pressed into the rough bark of a huge old tree. I've got to rest.

I can't run anymore.

I don't know where I am.

Tears try to form in my eyes, but I blink them away.

Straining my ears, I listen for the howling and growling of pursuit.

I don't hear anything, not even the normal sounds of the forest.

Nevertheless, even though I can't hear them, I know the hellhounds are still out there.

The dim shadows of the forest deepen.

The sun is setting.

I need to find shelter.

In the distance I hear a male voice call. The baying and snapping of the almost-dogs answer. I clear my mind and picture myself surrounded by nothingness.

Turning my head from left to right, I look for a place to hide where the hellhounds can't reach me.

This old lodgepole pine appears to be my only hope.

There are some things that naturally repel magic. Trees are one.

Keeping my mind blank, I circle the trunk and look for a low branch. There is one I might be able to reach if I jump for it.

The bag I'm carrying dangles from my shoulder. I slip the strap over my head so that it slants diagonally across my chest. I shove the pouch part toward my back so it won't get in the way.

I pull the sleeves of my sweatshirt down to cover my hands. Hopefully the fabric will protect them enough that I won't draw blood when I grab the tree branch. No matter how well I shield my mind, I won't be able to hide from the hellhounds if they scent blood.

I visualize myself as light as a feather.

I leap up and grasp the branch. I dangle for a moment before I pull myself up far enough that I can hook one arm around the limb. Then I swing a leg over. I haul myself up the rest of the way and climb as high as I can.

I allow myself a moment to breathe.

I close my eyes, concentrate, and erase my tracks all the way back to where I crossed the stream. Moving water is another elemental force that rejects magic. I finish eliminating my trail not a moment too soon.

I modify my vision so I can see the hellhounds. They are enormous creatures. Solid black in color, they have red glowing eyes.

They terrify me.

I watch as they reach the spot where I crossed the water. They pace back and forth along the bank.

In sharp contrast to the hellhounds, a man who is dressed all in white and is riding a white horse joins them.

He gazes beyond the stream. His eyes dart around for a moment.

Then he holds up a talisman of some kind.

A beam of light from the setting sun shoots through the charm and

Dark in the Forest: Another Modern Fairytale

illuminates the tree I'm hiding in.
The tree bursts into flames. Fire surrounds me.
I hear my skin begin to sizzle and crackle.
Pain.
I scream.

I bolt upright in bed.

Tears stream down my face.

Suddenly the light in the bathroom that separates my room from Angel's switches on. A moment later, Angel climbs into bed with me and puts her arms around me.

"The dream again?" she asks.

I nod.

"I'll stay with you," she says.

I lie back down.

Angel strokes my hair away from my face and dries my tears with a corner of the sheet.

She starts singing a lullaby. She has the sweetest voice.

I feel safe.

I drift off to sleep.

When I wake up in the morning, my first thought is *I've survived another night.*

I glance at the clock.

It's almost 10:00.

Angel must have told Mom and Dad that I had the nightmare again, so they decided to let me sleep in. That was thoughtful.

Then I jump out of bed.

I told Kaden I'd meet him at noon. I'll really have to rush through my chores.

I get dressed in a hurry and dash down to the kitchen.

Mom has written a note in red marker across my To Do list.

> *You've been working hard all week. Take today off and*
> *relax. We won't dock your stipend.* (She ends with a
> smiley face and a heart.)

I heave a sigh and blow a kiss at Mom's note.

Sometimes my parents can be pretty cool.

Opening the refrigerator, I try to decide if I want to have breakfast or if I would just as soon make a lunch I can eat under a tree in the woods.

Actually the decision is easy. Why should I be indoors if I can be out?

I try to remember what I've taken to the forest people so far this week. I hate to take the same things two days in a row, although I've had to a couple of times when I didn't have anything else to offer. I rummage in the pantry

76

until I find an unopened package of chocolate filled Oreos. I smash half a dozen of them to bits and make a jelly jar full of sweet tea. I run upstairs for my miniatures and tote bag. I pack my offerings.

Now I can make my lunch.

I decide to make two sandwiches. Kaden enjoyed the tuna so much that I make one sandwich just for him. I add two bananas and six chocolate filled Oreos. I wish I'd grabbed my fauvenell yesterday before Kaden had a chance to take the two of them away, but I guess in light of what Karissa told me it made sense for him to take them back.

I'm about to open the door and leave when I realize that Kaden and I didn't specify where we'd meet. Since we said goodbye at the blackberry bush, I'll bet he tries there first.

Hmm.

I don't suppose our conversation is going to be an easy one. Having something to do while we talk might make things easier.

I go to the pantry and get my blue plastic berry-picking pail. With all that went on yesterday, I never got around to picking blackberries, and I don't want them to "spoil on the vine," as the saying goes.

While I lock up the house and start across the yard, my heart pounds with nervous anticipation.

I don't have any idea what's going to happen when Kaden and I meet again.

I don't like not knowing what to expect.

In fact, I don't even know what I want to happen.

When I make my offering at the grotto, I don't enjoy the ritual as much as I usually do. Maybe it's because I'm tempted to use it as an excuse to delay meeting Kaden.

Reluctantly, I force myself to get up and get moving.

The closer I am to the blackberry patch, the more afraid I become. As it comes into view, I feel like turning around and going back home.

Too late!

Kaden is already there, waiting for me.

When I look at him, I can tell he's as unsure as I am.

In one hand he is holding the leather pouch that was attached to his belt yesterday. In his other hand is the container he put our uneaten fauvenells in. I can see that the cakes are still inside.

He glances at me and then looks away. "Neeve told me that Karissa explained about the fauvenell to you. Do you hate me?"

There is pain in his voice.

I get a quick flashback of Karissa telling me that Neeve's people can only fall in love once and how sorry she felt for Kaden if that's what he was confronting. I realize her compassion for him touched me deeply.

I respond honestly when I answer his question.

"No," I say. "I don't hate you, but I don't understand what you expected to accomplish by tricking me into trading bites of fauvenell with you. Karissa tried to explain, but she could only talk in generalities. She doesn't know you. She merely knows that you come from the same magical country that Neeve does. Why don't you explain it to me?"

"Will you believe me?"

"I'll try."

Kaden sits down cross-legged, and I sit down across from him.

He sets his leather pouch and the fauvenells between us and then slumps forward with his elbows on his knees. His head drops forward, and his hands cup his eyes. I wish I knew if he was doing that because he doesn't want me to watch his face while he talks or if he is too embarrassed to face me.

"I haven't eaten yet today," I tell him as I open my tote. "I brought you a sandwich too in case you're hungry."

He looks at me with surprise.

When he stretches out his hand to accept the sandwich, he gifts me with a sweet and tentative smile.

After he takes a bite, he exclaims, "It's the same fish, but it's prepared differently this time."

"I added onion and celery to the salad mixture. Do you like it?"

"Very much," he says. "Thank you."

"Can you talk and eat?" I ask him. "I'd like you to explain about the fauvenell and me. I'm especially curious since you brought the cakes back today."

"All right," he says. He takes another bite of sandwich, chews, and swallows. He gazes off in the distance as he begins to speak. "The day I stole your cupcake was not the first time I've been in your woods, nor was it the first time I ever saw you. Three summers ago I was playing around with our family's portal key. It's forbidden, of course, but I am sometimes rebellious— more so then than now—and that day I was angry with my father and my eldest brother. So I—"

"Why?" I interrupt him.

He peers at me quizzically.

"Why were you angry?" I ask again.

"Is it important?" he counters.

"I don't know," I tell him with a shrug. "It might be if I'm going to understand who you are and why you've acted as you have."

He sets down the sandwich and then appears to study it for several seconds. Eventually he looks up and makes eye contact, which is both positive and negative: positive because it's easier to believe someone who can look you in the eyes, negative because looking at him and having him look back at me does strange things to my heartbeat, my respiration, and my body temperature.

He is soooooo beautiful on the outside that he must be beautiful on the inside.

"I was angry with my father and my brother because they were talking about me, planning my future career, evaluating my apprenticeship, and totally ignoring me even though I was sitting right there in the room with them. So I decided to leave. I thought about going to visit friends, or going hunting, or just flying around for a while, but—"

"Flying?" I say. "You have an airplane."

"No. Why would I need a plane?" He twitches slightly and these amazing black, gold, and yellow wings spread out behind him.

Wings!

I pass out.

He revives me by blotting my face with a damp handkerchief. I start to sit up.

I see the wings.

I pass out again.

When he revives me the second time, the wings are gone. That gives me a few seconds to try to convince myself I didn't see them.

He helps me sit up.

"I'm sorry," he says. "I thought Karissa would have told you."

I shake my head.

"Stand up and turn around," I tell him.

When he is on his feet, he extends his hand to me. I take it and he helps me up. Then he turns around.

I feel his back.

Chapter Fifteen

Starting at the base of Kaden's neck, I slide my hands down his spine, and then I spread my fingers and run my hands from his waist up to his shoulders.

I feel his shoulder blades, tracing the curve with my thumbs.

It doesn't occur to me until I feel him shiver that I'm being rather intimate with a guy I don't know.

I drop my hands to my sides.

"Do you wish to see them form?" he asks me.

I start to nod, but then I realize he can't see me.

"Yes," I whisper.

"You'll need to move back a few steps."

I can't seem to make my feet work.

Somehow he knows I'm rooted in place.

He takes three steps forward.

Two translucent lumps that look like small loaves of bread appear on top of his clothing and along the outer edge of the shoulder blades.

The lumps unroll until they are beyond the sides of his body.

Then they unfurl like flags in the wind.

When I saw the wings before I passed out, I didn't realize there were two on each side. Now I can distinguish the upper wings from the lower.

Kaden lifts his arms and holds them parallel to the ground.

His upper wings spread out and sweep upward.

Kaden lifts his arms, so they form a wide "V." The central rib of the upper wing follows the line of his arms, and the tips of his wings extend at least two feet beyond his hands.

Then he lowers his arms and holds them out from his body in an inverted "V." The central rib of the lower wing follows the line of his arms in this position too. The tips extend beyond his hands almost to the ground.

He drops his arms to his sides and slowly turns around.

"Are they repugnant to you?" he asks. "Is that why you fainted?"

"Repugnant!" I exclaim. "They're the most beautiful things I've ever seen. Can you actually fly with them? They look way too fragile."

His smile is dazzling.

With barely a flutter, Kaden is hanging ten feet in the air.

I have no idea how I must look, but I feel my mouth drop open and my eyes bulge out as far as they'll go.

Suddenly, Kaden swoops down, takes me in his arms, and flies me up above the treetops.

I throw my arms around his neck and cling to him in a convulsive spasm of terror.

I feel the quivering of his diaphragm as he laughs at me.

We drift to the ground.

When we land, his wings disappear. He sits cross-legged on the ground with me on his lap.

I scramble off of him.

My emotions are a tangled up mess.

I want to lie down on the ground, kick my feet, and bawl like a baby because I can hardly bear the wonder of what I've just experienced. I want to jump up, laugh, and dance for the same reason.

Neither of us speaks for several minutes.

We just stare at each other.

In an unconscious synchronized motion, we both reach for the remnants of our sandwiches and begin eating again.

Kaden's smile is more uncertain than it was before.

I probably looked perplexed and overwhelmed, which is how I feel.

Finally Kaden speaks softly. "Do you want me to finish telling you about the other times I've come to your woods and what that has to do with fauvenell, or do you want to talk about the shock of discovering I have wings?"

I try to answer, but I can't find my voice.

I get a bottle of water from my tote and take a good long drink. I hand him the other bottle and he does the same.

"Tell me about coming to the woods," I suggest. "Before we discuss your wings, I need a little time to adjust to the idea that you have them."

"As I said, I was angry, and I couldn't find anything I wanted to do to calm myself. I was storming around the house when I found myself in the library. My father has quite a collection of foreign books that he's brought home when his work has taken him to other worlds. Since, when he goes on those journeys, he always leaves from the library, he keeps his portal key in there.

"Impulsively I grabbed it, said the spell that activated it, pictured a magical spot on another world, and stepped forward."

"And you ended up here?"

"Not at first," Kaden says. "There are four enchanted locations on this world. I didn't specify one because I didn't care where I ended up.

"The first place the magic took me was to a very hot jungle—probably to match my hot mood. There, the magical beings live high up in the canopy. I visited with them for a while, but the heat began to bother me, so I used the key to take me to one of the other areas.

"I ended up on the top of a mountain, higher in elevation and latitude than your forest. I found the coolness invigorating and I stayed there for a few of your days."

"My days?" I repeat.

"Your world's days," Kaden explains. "Time runs differently here than in Auravale. Actually every world travels within its own time, some faster than others and some slower. The portal key compensates for it somehow or else a traveler would move too slowly in a world whose time ran faster than his own, or he would move too quickly in a world whose time was slower. Does that make any sense to you?"

"Of course," I say.

I feel as if all the hours I've spent reading science fiction have just paid off. Not that I understand how such an anomaly occurs, but I've had the right kind of background to comprehend it as a possibility.

That's enough for now.

"Your forest was the third place I visited," Kaden continues. "I was letting the forest people show me around when you and an elderly woman appeared. She was very frail, very near to the end of her life."

"She wanted to say goodbye," I mumble.

I can't stop a few tears from trailing down my cheeks. Kaden leans forward and gently wipes them away with his fingertips.

I notice we've both finished our sandwiches.

I hand him a banana.

"We only went to the forest together once the spring that she died," I tell him. "My parents wouldn't let her come here anymore because, as you said, she was very frail. They didn't realize how much she loved being among the trees. So one day I pretended to be sick so I could stay home with her. While Mom and Dad were at work and Angel was at school, I brought Grandma out here for the last time. She died two weeks later."

I peel my banana.

After a moment, Kaden does the same thing. I wonder if he has seen a banana before. They might not exist in his world.

We both take a bite.

Confirming my suspicion that the fruit is new to Kaden, after he swallows, he says, "Very nice. Thank you."

Then he returns to his story.

"It was your love for your grandmother that first stirred my heart. Your devotion and compassion and kindness glowed like a flame. I watched you take your offering of cake and tea to the usual place, and then you and your grandmother walked around for several minutes. You picked a few flowers for her and then plucked a couple of leaves from a tree. After that, you left. You were practically carrying her at the end."

I nod slowly. "That's when I knew she was really going to die. She had lost

Connie A. Walker

so much weight there was hardly anything left of her. I've always been grateful that I have that last special memory of her in these woods. We never told anyone. It was our final secret."

Kaden takes my hand and holds it between both of his.

I let him.

"The forest people told me they loved your grandmother. She always brought them gifts of food and drink when she came here. Sometimes she would sit with her back to them while they ate, and she would talk to them.

"She told them stories about her family: her parents and siblings and her husband and children. She told them how this land had been purchased and protected by her husband's family so the forest people would always have a safe place to live.

"Although they are very shy, and they seldom reveal themselves to humans, they would cluster around her whenever she was here, ducking behind the foliage if she happened to glance in their direction. They told me they sang to her and sometimes told her jokes—although they didn't bother using your language—and even though she didn't understand what they said, whenever they laughed, she smiled."

"Thank you for telling me," I say. "She would have been so happy to know they were aware of her."

"I've strayed from the topic again, I'm afraid," Kaden says. "I was explaining why I kept coming back to your forest."

"Before you go on," I say, "will you tell me the real word for the forest people. Grandma and I called them the forest people, or the little people, or the enchanted people because we didn't know what we should call them. I'd like to know their true name."

He doesn't answer right away, and I sense that he is somehow getting permission to share a well-guarded secret.

"They call themselves the stwethil-thage."

"Can you spell it for me?"

He does, and then he pronounces it again.

"One more time," I say, "slowly."

"Stwethil-thage."

I try to repeat it.

I feel like I'm tying my tongue into a knot.

I exhale loudly.

"That 's, t, w' sound is hard to make." I try again.

Kaden grins. "Don't turn around—they'll just duck and hide if you do—but there are a few stwethil-thage behind you. They're enjoying your struggle to say their name."

I freeze, not daring to twitch. "Are you serious? They're listening?"

"Yes to both questions."

"I want to pronounce it correctly." Although I'm looking at Kaden, I'm addressing the forest people. I close my eyes. The word actually sounds exactly the way it's spelled. I concentrate. "Stwethil-thage, stwethil-thage, stwethil-thage. Did I get it right?"

Behind me I hear some high-pitched chirping followed by the rustling of leaves as the chirping fades away.

"Did I get it right?" I ask Kaden again.

"Yes, and you have just made some friends for life."

Chapter Sixteen

"I guess I'm the one who got us off topic this time," I say. "Please go on. You were explaining about why you kept coming back here."

He stuffs his banana peel in his empty sandwich bag and hands it to me. I put our garbage in my tote to throw away at home.

"How about helping me pick blackberries while you talk?"

He looks relieved as he stands up.

I set the pail on the ground between us. We start picking.

"I was touched by your devotion to your grandmother," Kaden says. "I wanted to get to know you, but I couldn't get access to the portal key very often. I had to sneak into the library when my father and my eldest brother were busy. The first few times I came back you weren't here. Then, several months ago, I saw you, but you were different. I didn't get the same feelings from you. A few minutes later, a young man joined you, and I sensed your pleasure at seeing him. I was crushed."

"No," I protest. "I've never met any boys here."

"I realize that now," Kaden says with half a smile, "but I didn't then. I was confused. I came back several times, and some of the time my feelings for you would almost overwhelm me. Other times, I'd see you and feel absolutely nothing. I didn't understand it until you said you have a twin. I've known about twin births theoretically, but they are unknown in Auravale, so that possibility never occurred to me."

He takes a deep breath.

"Now, I must confess something that I hope will not make you angry." He gets a pleading look on his face. "Will you try to resist judgment until I have finished explaining?"

"I'll try," I say suspiciously, not taking my eyes from the blackberry bush.

"The day I inadvertently let you see my reflection in the water, I was here on business for my father and the king, but I was also looking for you. I hadn't seen you the past few times I'd come, and I was worried. The reason I was close enough for you to see me was that I was trying to get near enough to understand why you were so distressed. Once again I sensed that enormously strong bond you have with your grandmother.

"I stole your cupcake so I'd have an excuse to set up a meeting between us. I placed the little bag that the cupcake had been in on the ground where you would likely be able to spot it."

"Why?" I drop a handful of berries in the pail and then look over at him. He keeps picking.

"Because your unhappiness was strong enough to pull me halfway across the forest that day. Also, because when I saw you, my feelings for you were as strong as ever. While I was trying to sense the cause of your distress, I realized that there was nothing wrong with your mind or your personality. I can't tell you how relieved I was.

"When the king originally gave me the assignment of coming to your world to look for three lost artifacts, I feared I would have to abjure my feelings for you. I thought you suffered from an unstable personality and that was the reason my feelings fluctuated so drastically when I saw you. I thought, when you were having a good day, I was drawn to you, and when you were having a bad day, I was repelled. That day, when I got close enough to you to know you were stable, I wanted to help you stay that way.

"I decided to leave you a fauvenell to see how you'd react. The red ball that I put it in is called a Lover's Embrace."

He takes a quick glance at me from the corner of his eye. I assume he wants to see my reaction.

Too bad!

I just go on picking berries.

He returns to helping me while he continues. "I suppose Neeve would be furious if he knew I gave you one, but a Lover's Embrace supports and comforts the sender as well as the receiver.

"The way you reacted to my letter, to the Lover's Embrace, and to the fauvenell showed an optimistic and healthy mind. You were curious and cautious, but you chose trust rather than fear. I hoped whatever malady plagued you in the past was completely gone.

"When I brought the fauvenells yesterday and suggested we trade bites, I wanted to share my strength with you so you would not lapse into that vacillating personality again. If I could help stabilize you, then I might be able to win your heart someday.

"I am embarrassed that I didn't realize that you and your sister were distinct and separate individuals. The physical resemblance between you is astonishing, but not the personality and the character. You are far superior to your sister in every way."

"You don't know her," I say protectively. "She's—"

"Please, you love your sister and I don't know her, so let's not argue about her."

He dumps a handful of blackberries into the bucket. "Why don't we sit down and take a break."

We sit facing each other.

He reaches for the container the fauvenells are in. "Even if we do not share bites, it is a shame to waste them." He keeps the fauvenell that has his bite mark in it and offers me the other.

Instead of taking it from him, on impulse, I lean forward and take a small bite out of it.

I thought my first bite of fauvenell sent a burst of flavor coursing through my body, filling me with joy, but this time it is a dozen times more intense.

The look on Kaden's face is a study. I suppose mine is no better.

"I hope you don't regret doing that," he tells me softly. "It binds you to me even though my original intension was only to give you strength."

"It binds you to me, too, doesn't it." I don't wait for him to answer. "I'm aware of you in a new way, different from before." I reach over and take the fauvenell that has his bite mark in it. "You said we shouldn't waste them."

Without knowing exactly why, I take a bite that overlaps the one he took. Somehow I sense that's how it should be done. (My guess is that since I exchanged bites of fauvenell with Kaden, I now have access to a portion of his knowledge.)

Keeping his eyes on me, Kaden lifts his fauvenell to his lips and takes a bite that overlaps mine.

The bond between us really snaps into place. Besides the emotional link, I also sense a spiritual or metaphysical connection. He couldn't have tricked me into exchanging bites with him without my knowing that we had just shared a serious and significant experience.

"Neeve's going to know we did this? Isn't he?" I ask.

"Yes," Kaden answers, "the very first time he sees us together."

"Is there anything he can do about it?"

"Besides get angry? No. He can't undo what we've done voluntarily. However, since he knows he interrupted us and he chastised me for the timing, he'll have questions. He will especially want to know if I did something to compel you against your will. Undoubtedly, he will ask you about it. Will you have an answer for him?"

"I don't suppose I could just tell him it's none of his business."

"You could try," Kaden says with a wry grin, "but you know he can take the information directly from your mind. I don't think he would do it without your permission. There are rules of conduct involved, and he has been trained to respect them, but he has the power to do it if he chooses."

I gulp. "But you can't read my mind, can you?"

"No," Kaden says. "I can sense many of your feelings, but if I could go into your mind, I'd have recognized the differences between you and your sister immediately."

"I don't think I'd enjoy spending time around someone who could hear my thoughts. How would you have any privacy? If he —"

Kaden holds up his hand in a typical *stop* position. I think he's getting ready to contradict me about something, but he isn't.

"I have to go. His Majesty is calling me."

When he stands, he extends his hand to me.

I let him help me to my feet, but he doesn't let go of me. He turns my hand over and kisses my palm.

"I'll be back tomorrow as close to noon as possible. Will you meet me? We still have much to talk about."

"I'll try," I say.

"In the meantime, I'd like to point out something that occurred to me last night. You think having Dark as your middle name has added another layer of bad luck to you. But although Dark can mean the absence of light, it can also mean mysterious, hidden, and secret. Think about it."

He releases my hand, steps into a sunbeam, and disappears.

As I watch his afterimage fade, I nibble on my fauvenell. I notice that he took his with him, but he left behind the fanny pack and the container that the fauvenells were in. I wonder what he'll do with his fauvenell while he meets with His Majesty.

Surely he can't eat in front of the king.

What are his other options? Put it in his pocket?

He said his magical talent was finding things. Maybe he has a way of "losing" them too.

After I savor my last bite of fauvenell, I lie on the grass and try to picture how you'd go about losing something on command.

Abracadabra! The fauvenell disappears and reappears somewhere else. Maybe it has to go someplace random so no one else's magic can track it. Then when Kaden is ready, he can turn on his "finding" power and go get it.

Interesting possibility!

I wonder what kind of limitations "finding" has?

Could Kaden find a lost memory?

Or lost innocence?

Or lost time?

If I go crazy by asking myself such stupid questions, could he find my lost mind?

I close my eyes and try to picture it.

I fall asleep.

My nightmare returns.

I'm trying to catch my breath, standing with my back pressed into the rough bark of a huge old pine tree. I've got to rest.

I can't run anymore.

I don't know where I am.

Tears try to form in my eyes, but I blink them away.

Straining my ears, I listen for the howling and growling of pursuit.

I don't hear anything, not even the normal sounds of the forest.

Nevertheless, even though I can't hear them, I know the hellhounds are still out there.

The dim shadows of the forest deepen.

The sun is setting.

I need to find shelter.

"Hellie."

I hear my name being called. That's not part of the recurring dream. I try to make the sound go away.

"Hellie!"

Someone grabs my shoulders and shakes me.

"Hellie, wake up."

I pry my eyes open and see Angel's concerned face.

"Are you all right?" she says. "Mom's been trying to get you on your cellphone for the past hour. She sent me to find you. If I don't call her within the next few minutes and tell her you're all right, she's going to call the sheriff's office and have him arrange a search."

I sit up.

"What's all the fuss about?" I mumble. Then I realize it's getting dark. It must be after 8:00 in the evening. "I guess I dozed off. What a dumb thing for me to do!"

Angel takes her cellphone out of her pocket and then sits down beside me on the grass.

"She's all right," Angel says into her phone. "She fell asleep on the ground. She must have worn herself out picking blackberries. Her bucket is almost overflowing."

She pauses to let Mom get in a word or two.

"We'll be home in a couple of minutes. Bye."

Angel starts helping me gather up my mess: two empty water bottles, a sandwich bag, the container the two fauvenells were in, and Kaden's leather bag.

"What's that?" Angel asks when I pick up the pouch.

"Something someone left behind," I say. "You know how we're always finding strange stuff out here."

"What're you going to do with it?" she asks.

"Well, unless someone comes to the house asking for it, I'm thinking: 'Finders keepers, losers weepers'."

"It looks like real leather."

"I think it is."

"Hmm, I don't suppose you'd give it up, would you?"

"Why?" I ask. "Do you want it?"

"I might. You know how I am about leather."

"Sorry," I say. "I like it. I have an old belt about this color. I was thinking I might cut the ends off the belt and then sew the belt to the pouch as a shoulder strap. It would make a handy-sized purse for when I don't need to take much with me but I have a little too much for my pockets."

"Well," Angel says, "if you change your mind, I wouldn't mind having it for the same reason. It looks just about the right size for a notepad, a couple of pens, my cellphone, and my wallet. It'd be handy for when I have to dash off someplace for the newspaper. A regular purse is so bulky."

I stuff the pouch into my lunch tote. It barely fits with all the other junk already in it, but that's all right. I'm not letting Angel get her hands on it. She is really good at making me change my mind, especially once she takes possession of something.

I am not giving her Kaden's bag, no matter how she wheedles.

With my lunch tote hanging from my shoulder, I pick up the pail of blackberries.

"We'd better get going," I say. "I don't want Mom to call out a search party for both of us."

I expect my parents to be angry when I get home, and they do not disappoint.

"Hellie," my mother starts yelling at me. "How could you be so irresponsible? You never know who might be hanging out in the woods partying—especially in the summer. I don't think you should spend so much time out there. You're becoming as obsessed as Grandma Powers was."

"Now, Bethany," Dad says. "Hellie is perfectly safe in the woods during the day. There has never been any indication that people wander around out there during the daylight hours."

"Except for your daughter!" Mom snaps at him. "Are you defending her?"

"No," Dad answers. "But this is the first time she's been out there this late. I think we might cut her some slack."

"Really?" Mom says. "Or maybe you're confusing Hellie with your mother. It was her influence—always talking about magic and fairies and enchanted forests—that got our daughter infatuated with the woods in the first place."

"There's nothing wrong with children having a fantasy life," Dad argues. "It's called imagination. Every advancement civilization has ever made has come through someone who had enough imagination to see past the status quo."

"I'm not talking about the status quo," Mom asserts, not quite shouting but definitely turning up the volume. "I don't want her out there in the woods by herself so much. It's not healthy."

"Of course not," Dad says sarcastically. "We must protect her from all that unhealthy fresh air."

I glance around the kitchen.

It's clear that part of the reason Mom is angry is because I ruined her routine. The way Mom copes with all the stress that the mayor heaps on her is by keeping things at home simple and on schedule.

The family ate dinner without me, but cleanup had to be postponed until I got home and had a chance to eat too.

My parents' arguing has ruined my appetite.

They don't argue very often, but when they do, it can go on for hours.

Before they finally stop trying to change or punish each other, they'll have brought up everything that's ever bothered them about anything, sometimes going all the way back to when they first met in college by colliding at some cafeteria and spilling their lunches all over each other.

Angel is nowhere in sight. I suppose she's gone to her room.

I put the leftovers in plastic containers, clear off the table, fill the dishwasher, and start it. I dump the blackberries into a glass bowl with a snap on lid, rinse out the bucket, put the bowl in the refrigerator and the pail in the pantry, and take my tote bag up to my room.

Chapter Seventeen

Saturday morning I wake up at 8:15.

Last night, after I cleaned up the kitchen, I felt sort of itchy from sleeping on the ground in the forest.

I took a shower and went to bed.

Now I'm a little apprehensive because I have no idea how the argument between my parents ended. Dad might have convinced Mom to let me come and go as I please, or Mom could have convinced Dad to banish me from the forest for life. My parents can be fairly open-minded about most things, but they tend to be all-or-nothing with Angel and me.

I wash my face and then dress in shorts and a tank top. It's my turn to mow the lawn. Angel and I trade off. When I mow, she does the edging. The next Saturday, we switch.

As I go downstairs, I realize the house is awfully quiet.

I hope my parents didn't decide to get divorced in the middle of night without bothering to wake me up and tell me.

When I get to the kitchen, the first thing I notice is a notepad on the counter.

Dear Nathan and girls,

I need to go to the office for a while. The mayor's son got into some trouble with the law last night, and the mayor wants me to do some damage control with the media.

Don't know how long I'll be.

Love you,
Mom

Written below Mom's note is another one.

Girls,

I went out to wash the car and the right rear tire was flat. I've got a tow truck coming to haul the car over to Smitty's Garage. Since Smitty's is usually closed until noon on Saturdays and I need my car this afternoon, George is opening up just for me. After he fixes the tire, I'm going to take him out for a late breakfast. If you need me, call me on my cell.

Love, Dad

Below Dad's note is still another.

Hellie,

Courtney Bingham's folks had to go out of town, and she invited me to come over and spend the day with her. You were still asleep when she called. Courtney said to tell you that you're welcome to join us if you want. Lunch will be at 1:00 (pizza, breadsticks, salad, and brownies) and then we're going to watch a DVD of "Magic in the Moonlight" starring Colin Firth. I can't remember if you came with us when we saw it at the theater, but it's really cute.

Come on over if you want.

Angel

P.S. I've already checked with Mom and she said we could do the lawn tomorrow.

I look at the clock.

It's not even 8:30.

No reflection on Angel or Courtney, but I'd rather do my chores and get them out of the way. Then I can meet Kaden with a clear conscience. Nowhere in any of the notes is there an indication that I can't go to the woods if I want.

After I bolt down a bowl of cereal with blackberries and sliced banana, I get the lawnmower out. I always mow the backyard first because it's over twice the size of the front. Next I water the flowers in the decorative planters, followed by deadheading the petunias. By the time I'm done with all that, mowing the front yard is almost like taking a break.

When I'm finished, I dash upstairs, take a quick shower, and dress in jeans and t-shirt.

After I get out my miniatures, I snatch up my lunch tote, ready to run to the kitchen and fix lunch. The bag feels too light.

I look inside.

Kaden's leather pouch is gone.

Darn Angel!

I stomp through the connecting bathroom into her room and rummage around. I look in her closet, pull out all the dresser drawers, check under the bed, and search everywhere I can think of, including her desk.

She must have taken it with her.

I wish I knew more about this magic business.

What if the pouch has some kind of magical properties?

What if it automatically fills up with whatever the person holding it wants—things like fauvenell (I wish), money, or jewels? Or what if it takes

93

revenge on thieves and spews out fire ants or spiders or snakes when they open it up—instant karma.

I guess Angel will just have to take her chances.

I don't have time to worry about it.

As I bound down the stairs, I'm wondering what kind of treat I can take to the stwethil-thage. (I love that word now that I can say it without twisting my tongue out of shape. I wish Grandma were here so we could enjoy it together.)

I dig through the cupboards until I find a half-full bag of frosted animal crackers. I put a bunch in a plastic bag and smash them with the rolling pin. There's a gallon jug of chocolate milk in the fridge. I pour some into a jelly jar. Throughout grade school this was my all-time favorite after-school snack: frosted animal crackers and chocolate milk.

I decide to eat lunch before I go. I don't want to get into the habit of feeding Kaden, and I don't want him to come to expect it.

I make a peanut butter and jelly sandwich and pour myself a glass of milk. I sit on the kitchen counter to eat. When I drink the last of the milk, I stretch to the side so I can reach the cold-water faucet. I rinse out the glass and leave it in the sink before I hop off the counter.

After I pack my tote with goodies for the stwethil-thage, I figure I might get hungry again if Kaden is late or fails to show up, so I fill a sandwich bag full of animal crackers for me. I add a couple of bottles of water and a small thermos of chocolate milk, and I'm off.

I'm just about to lock the backdoor behind me when I realize I forgot to leave a note. I sprint back in, grab a sharpie, and write below Angel's message.

To Whom It May Concern:

Since there are no messages directing me to the contrary, I'm going to commune with nature in the forest. I have my cellphone with me and I have set the alarm for 4:30. I will be home shortly after it goes off.

I promise I will not lose track of the time or fall asleep again.

Hellie

As I walk across the yard, I set the alarm on my phone. I stuff it into the pocket on my lunch tote because the pockets on these jeans are small and decorative rather than deep and functional.

After I push through the hedge, I am tempted to stop by the glade to see if Kaden is already there, but I decide not to. Not this time. This is my first trip to the grotto since I learned the forest people's real name. I don't want to share this moment with anyone but them.

I kneel down in front of the little cave in the rocks and set out the cookie crumbs and chocolate milk.

Not daring to look around, I focus my attention on a reddish rock that is near the opening of the cave.

"I've brought you a different kind of treat today, stwethil-thage. This was my favorite snack when I was little girl. I hope you like it. Thank you for letting Kaden tell me who you are. Stwethil-thage is a beautiful name. And thank you for singing and talking to my grandmother. She loved you very much."

I feel my grandmother's spirit all around me as I walk toward the glade. I would die if my parents forbade me to come back.

I hear talking.

I freeze and listen.

I recognize Kaden and Neeve's voices, but there is a third one, deeper and more mature. My first thought is that someone—perhaps Kaden's father or the king—might have magic that is stronger than Neeve's and therefore might not need to see Kaden and me together to realize we've shared bites of fauvenell. Would they end up angry like Neeve did?

I'd just hate it if my impulsivity got Kaden into trouble.

Taking a deep breath, fearing the worst, I walk forward.

I step around the last cluster of trees and look into the glade.

Kaden is sitting cross-legged on the ground.

Although Neeve's back is to me, I can see that he's taken off his shoes and stockings and is sitting at the edge of the stream, letting the water flow over his feet.

About fifteen feet behind Neeve, a third man is lying on his side with his head propped on one hand. He has long blond hair that's a shade or two darker than Neeve's and is tied at the nape of his neck with a black velvet ribbon. He is wearing a white ruffled shirt, a long green vest, and black tapered trousers that are tucked into mid-calf shiny black boots. While I watch, he picks up a pinecone and with perfect aim bounces it off of the back of Neeve's head.

When Neeve spins around, he somehow manages to scoop up a handful of water and splash it all the way across the glade to catch the other guy in the face with it.

I can't help but laugh.

All three guys jerk around in my direction.

Kaden leaps to his feet and stretches out his hand to me.

He is smiling so brightly I know he hasn't gotten into trouble because of the fauvenell incident. I sense, too, that our exchange is no secret.

By the time I finish smiling at Kaden and am ready to acknowledge that the rest of the world exists, Neeve and the other man are standing beside each other and Neeve has his shoes and stockings on. I have no idea how he managed that without having me notice, except I have been sort of busy concentrating on Kaden.

Neeve gestures at the man.

"Hellie, may I present His Highness, Prince Jerrin of Auravale, my elder brother."

I have a brief panic. How does an American acknowledge a prince from a foreign country? Kaden told me Neeve could read minds. Maybe if I ask, he'll answer.

Neeve, I think, *do I bow, offer to shake hands, or turn around and run?*

I can hardly believe it when I hear his voice inside my mind. *After I introduce you, just nod your head and then offer him your hand.*

"Jerrin, it is my honor to present to you Miss Hellenaura Dark Powers."

I drop my head in a little nod, and then I step forward and offer my hand. He meets me halfway. I expect him to take my hand for a quick, half-a-second shake. He astounds me (and surprises Neeve and Kaden, judging by their facial expressions) when he takes my hand and kisses it.

"It is a great pleasure to meet you, Hellenaura."

"I'm honored to meet you, Your Highness," I say.

"Call me Jerrin, please."

"Thank you. My friends call me Hellie."

I let him lead me into the glade.

The four of us sit on the grass in a square.

Jerrin is clearly in charge. Kaden, Neeve, and I automatically look at him and wait for him to speak.

"First," Jerrin says, "just as a matter of record, will you tell me why you exchanged bites of fauvenell with Kaden after Neeve interceded?"

I turn to Kaden, feeling sick at heart. "Did I get you in trouble?"

"No," he says reassuringly.

"You told them?" I ask. "Why didn't you wait for Neeve to figure it out when he saw us together for the first time?"

Kaden shrugs. "I couldn't help it. I was very happy when I went back. Sometimes joy has to be shared, even when you're not sure others will approve or understand."

I smile at him—he is easy to smile at—before I turn my attention back to His Highness, Prince Jerrin. I don't know how to answer him, but my mouth opens and words come out automatically.

"I'm not sure I can explain all of my reasons, but I suppose the most significant one is that Kaden offered me comfort and support without asking for anything in return. Karissa explained that fauvenell couldn't make me fall in love with Kaden. She said it could only promote a sense of mutual goodwill between us.

"I have been so lonely since my grandmother died and my twin sister has moved on to her own friends and interests. I wanted to have someone on my side, someone I could talk to and share things with, someone who wouldn't just dump me when times got rough or when someone better came along."

I glance over at Kaden, but I'm not smiling now. I revealed more than I intended, more than I was even aware of, and I suddenly feel guilty.

"Kaden," I say, "I hope I haven't been unfair to you. I didn't realize how selfish my motives were until I started talking about them."

He has the sweetest expression on his face. "I am honored that you would allow me to fill that role for you, Hellie."

Dang it.

This guy is way too good for me.

I can feel tears forming in my eyes.

"Thank you for your candor, Hellie," Jerrin says. His gaze goes to Kaden. "Congratulations. It looks to bode well for you."

Kaden dips his head in acknowledgement.

I don't understand.

Before I can give it more than a cursory thought, however, Jerrin begins speaking again.

"Hellie, I would like you to think over the past few days. Has anything unexplainable happened to you?" He grins, and it makes him look more like a kid than a prince. "I mean other than the encounters with Kaden, Neeve, and Karissa."

I shake my head. "No, I don't think so."

"Try," Jerrin says. "A ripple of magic from your world has reached ours. My guess is that it is associated with you. Please picture in your mind all of your activities and interactions with people over, say, the past five days."

I am confused.

He obviously thinks something extraordinary has happened, but I have no idea what he's talking about.

Glancing at him, I feel my mind being pulled in his direction. His sky blue eyes trap mine.

When it finally hits me, I stare at him. "How did you know?"

"Would you describe it to us?" he asks quietly.

I have no volition. It is impossible for me to refuse.

"It happened on Wednesday while I was helping out at a children's daycare center. I was at one end of the playground, and a little girl was at the other. She was on top of a slippery slide with two other children. They were scuffling, and she got knocked over the side.

"Even though I knew I was too far away, I ran to catch her. Impossibly, everyone around me froze in place. It was as if time stopped for everyone but me. Time didn't start again until I was right below the little girl. When I caught her, she felt as if she weighed nothing at all. My boss and my father both thought I should have bruises from the impact, but I don't."

I hold my arms out in front of me.

"See, no bruises. No damage to me or to the child. And no one remembers that I was on the opposite side of the playground and that it was impossible for me to cover the distance before the child fell."

"Thank you, Hellie." Jerrin stands up and looks down on Neeve. "I'll go report to our father. I'll send Shiane through."

"Who is Shiane?" I ask.

Jerrin sits back down. "Shiane is Neeve's and my youngest sister. She is coming for two purposes. First, it is improper for you to be alone with two single men, especially when you have so recently shared fauvenell with one of them. Shiane will act as chaperone. Second, Shiane will someday be a mage. She has extraordinary powers, and she will be able to help you understand who you are."

I heave a gigantic sigh.

"Why do I need a mage who has extraordinary powers to help me know who I am?"

Getting to his feet again, Jerrin says, "Because you obviously don't know. Neeve and Kaden, explain to her what you can. Shiane will be here momentarily." He disappears the way that most humans would expect. He is here one moment and gone the next. No sound. No afterimage. No abracadabra.

I shift position so I can see Kaden and Neeve both.

"Explain," I say.

"It's complicated," Neeve replies, "and covers several generations. If you have questions, feel free to interrupt me. If you don't ask immediately, you'll forget what you want to know and end up confused." He shakes his head and smiles wanly. "The story is confusing enough on its own. I'm afraid, for it to make any sense, I'll have to give you a history lesson."

Before he can begin, a beam of light appears between two trees and sliding down it is a young girl.

She appears to be about twelve years old.

Chapter Eighteen

When the girl's feet touch the ground, the light disappears.

Neeve and Kaden both get to their feet, so I do too.

The girl comes straight to me, stands tippy-toes, puts her arms around my neck, and kisses me on the cheek. "No wonder Kaden is drawn to you," she sings in a sweet, high-pitched voice. "I'd almost like to share a fauvenell with you myself."

Although Kaden, Neeve, and Jerrin all wear their hair long, hers is short. It's reddish blond and so curly it sort of bounces all around her face. She's shorter than I am, and tiny. She has narrow shoulders, and her wrists are so small I could probably encircle them with my thumbs and forefingers, and my hands are not particularly large.

She has a narrow face, big green eyes, a button of a nose, and a cute little mouth that looks as if she's never frowned or pouted in her life. If she sprouted wings (which, no doubt, she can do), she would look exactly like my mental picture of a fairy.

She is absolutely adorable.

"You shine so bright," she continues, "you almost hurt my eyes."

"Shiane," Neeve says softly. "This is not the time."

"Oh." She takes a couple of steps backward and puts her hands over her mouth. "You haven't told her yet."

I feel as if I'm in the middle of a stage play where all the performers have memorized their lines except for me.

I refuse to let these people drive me crazy.

I decide to be unpredictable and proactive.

I take a step forward, give Shiane a hug, and return her kiss on the cheek. "Shiane, I'm Hellenaura Dark Powers. Jerrin said you would be able to help me understand who I am."

She takes me by the hand, "I am soooo going to like you. Come on, let's sit down and let Neeve and Kaden try to describe the situation. If you get confused, tell me, and I'll interpret for you."

Shiane and I sit side by side and gaze at Neeve expectantly.

99

Dark in the Forest: Another Modern Fairytale

"As I was saying before Shiane arrived, Hellie, for you to understand what is going on and how it relates to you, I'll need to give you a brief history lesson."

Shiane leans her head on my shoulder. "What he means is that the beginning of all this goes back to the time when our family inherited the throne."

Neeve gives her a little nod, as if to acknowledge that he heard her, but he doesn't comment on her comment.

"Over eight hundred years ago," Neeve says, "the ruling monarch of Auravale was King Kenner VI of the Dursteler dynasty. His wife died while giving birth to their only child, a son who lived for less than a week. Since Kenner VI was a young man when his wife died, everyone assumed he would marry again and produce an heir, but he never had the chance. The Dursteler line ended with him.

"While Kenner was mourning the loss of his wife and son, the king of Woodensley attacked Auravale in an effort to take control of the gold mines in our northern mountains. Kenner spent most of his reign defending the mines and waging war against Woodensley. When he was finally victorious and had slain Woodensley's king, he subjugated the people and annexed the land. By then, he was in his declining years. He chose his cousin Wasner Trudimahn to be his successor. The next year he abdicated in Wasner's favor."

"How sad," I say, "for a king to lose his wife and child and then spend nearly all the rest of his adulthood fighting a war. He must have been a very lonely man."

"It was sad," Shiane tells me, "and he was lonely. But the story of King Kenner VI has a happy ending. After his abdication, he retired to his family's hereditary estates, which he had been using as a restful retreat whenever he had a break from the wars.

"Living in a nearby village was a lovely unmarried woman who was half Kenner's age. A mutual friend introduced them, and they were immediately attracted to each other. Within a year they got married and subsequently had three daughters together. They were very happy raising their little family in the Dursteler country home."

"You can imagine," Neeve says, "how nervous the Trudimahns were each time Kenner's young wife gave birth. If Kenner had sired a son, the kingdom might have been plunged into civil war. Even though Kenner never gave any indication that he regretted his decision to abdicate in favor of his cousin, supporters of the Dursteler line could still have tried to use him and a son in efforts to reestablish the old order."

"Luckily that didn't happen," Kaden adds. "The Trudimahn philosophy has always been to foster peace abroad and to encourage productivity and innovation at home, which has kept the kingdom prosperous and stable."

"Still," Neeve says, taking over the role of teacher again, "there have been wars and internal conflicts during my family's reign, but never one initiated by the Crown."

Without saying anything, Kaden captures my attention by shifting position, rotating his shoulders, and twisting at the waist. I hear a few joints pop. Afterward, he seems to sit up a little straighter.

I smile at him. I can't help it. I wonder if what I'm experiencing is the result of the fauvenell, or if I'd have felt this way without it.

I force my attention to return to Neeve.

"It's an interesting story," I tell him, "but how do the Darks fit in?"

"I'm getting to that," he replies. "Preston Dark had been Wasner Trudimahn's best friend while they were growing up, so when Wasner ascended to the throne, he brought Preston to the palace as one of his advisors. The problems started after Wasner suddenly died and his son became the ruler. Wasner II had grown up with Preston Dark's children, learning to ride, hunt, fight, and fish with the boys.

"One day, two of the Dark brothers realized they had both fallen in love with the same young lady. She seemed to enjoy keeping company with each of them equally well. As one of the queen's companions and as a member of the court, she could not wed without royal consent. Separately the young men entreated the king for her hand. Wasner II did not feel right about favoring one of his friends over the other, so he arranged to meet with the three of them. He put it to the lady. Which brother would she choose to marry? Or did she prefer not to wed either?

"She chose the elder son. Many people thought she was actually in love with the younger but chose the elder for his potential wealth. As the eldest son in the family, he would inherit the bulk of their father's estate when their father died, whereas the younger sons would receive only a pittance to provide for them while they established themselves in a profession or trade that would make them a living.

"Filled with anger and disappointment, the younger of the two brothers left Auravale to seek his fortune within the other kingdoms. He did not return until after his father's death. When he finally came back, he was a rich man. He had changed his name to Darker and brought home with him a foreign wife and a troupe of servants. He purchased an estate adjacent to the one of his childhood.

"In contrast, by the time the younger brother returned, the elder had gone through much of his inheritance trying to appease his wife's extravagant tastes. The elder brother often had cause to regret that he had fought so hard to win her. He felt he had spent his entire married life trying to keep the bill collectors off of his doorstep.

"When the elder brother saw the wealth his younger brother had accumulated, he was filled with jealousy and embarrassment. He immediately sent his wife on a journey to visit her ailing grandmother, a trip she never returned from, and then put all of his time and attention into creating a fortune larger than his brother's.

"That was the beginning of the rivalry and antagonism between the two branches of the clan, the Darks and the Darkers."

I think this story is even sadder than the one about King Kenner. "Didn't Wasner II try to help the brothers reconcile? They were both his friends."

"No," Kaden says. "In fact he encouraged the rivalry."

"Why?" I exclaim.

"Because," Neeve answers, "their competitiveness increased the productivity of both estates. Their farmers produced more crops, their merchants brought new and interesting products into the cities, and their far-reaching enterprises enhanced trade with other kingdoms.

"Through the rivalry of these two brothers, all of Auravale enjoyed new prosperity, including the Crown. The increase in trade caused an increase in the revenues that were collected through tariffs and taxation."

"All right," I say, "now I understand a little of the ancient history. Are you going to move into the present now?"

"Not quite," Neeve says, "there are a couple more bits of our history that you need to understand."

Kaden grins at me. "Have you ever heard the expression: *History tends to repeat itself?*"

I nod.

"Well," Kaden continues, "during the reign of King Justus II, it all happened again."

"What happened again?" I ask.

"Two Dark brothers fell in love with the same girl," Shiane explains. "You'd think they would've learned from the first time, wouldn't you?"

I snicker a little. "Some people never learn."

Neeve asserts his princely position by taking charge again. I almost laugh at him. Once you know he's a prince, it's not hard to notice how often he falls into the role. I wonder if it ever bothers Karissa. But maybe he isn't so peremptory with her.

"Justus II," Neeve says, "was not as sympathetic as Wasner had been with his friends. When the two brothers entreated him for permission to marry the young lady of their desires, the king turned them both down without discussion.

"For one thing, the girl was the companion of his eldest daughter. Finding out that two young nobles were arguing over the favors of a girl who, to the king, was little more than a servant was both astounding and distressing. Also, his daughter was very fond of the girl. They had been inseparable since they were about seven years old. The king did not want his daughter to be deprived of her trusted companion.

"Another reason Justus II refused to consider the brothers' requests was that he did not think it was proper for the servant to wed before her mistress, and Justus was still searching for candidates who were worthy of applying for the position of son-in-law."

At this point Shiane interrupts. "I think Neeve left out the main reason

Justus II was so unsympathetic with the Dark brothers. His own marriage had been arranged strictly for political reasons. Nomadic marauders had been terrorizing the outlying communities of both Auravale and Ladonnya, which is one of Auravale's neighbors to the south. The two kingdoms could not adequately defend their borders separately. By marrying Addelyn of Ladonnya, Justus II united the two kingdoms. Then, by combining their resources, he destroyed the leaders of the nomads and drove the rest of them into the wastelands in the west."

Kaden nods. "Although Justus II acknowledged that his marriage to Addelyn was one of convenience, he thought they had been well-matched. They were united in purpose and had an amicable partnership, if not a loving marriage."

"Besides," Shiane says, "the king thought, if the two Dark brothers were ready to get married, they should marry for the betterment of the kingdom, just as he had. Although Justus II hadn't been able to find a suitable match for his daughter, he knew of several young women who had connections that would have strengthened Auravale politically if they had been wed to the right young men."

I am really impressed by this kind of insight from someone so young.

I stop myself. I wonder how old Shiane is.

"I'm thirteen," she answers. "In a few months I'll turn fourteen. Then I can begin mage training."

"Did I say that out loud?" I ask, embarrassed.

"Well," Shiane begins, "not really, it just because we're—"

Neeve cuts her off sharply. "You owe her an apology not an excuse."

Shiane begins to sniffle.

Since Neeve answered me when I asked him silently how to act when I was introduce to his brother, I know Neeve can hear my thoughts.

I guess Shiane can too. However, I'm sure she did it unintentionally—otherwise she would be justifying or rationalizing her behavior rather than trying not to cry.

I put my arm around Shiane's shoulders. "It's all right," I say. "You didn't mean to do it, did you?"

"No." She leans into me and I feel tears dampen my shirt. "I'm sorry. I won't do it again."

"Maybe we should take a break from all this history," I suggest, "and just deal with the magic for a few minutes. Would that be all right?" I direct my question to Shiane, not to the guys.

"What do you want to know?" she asks me.

"First, how much control do you have over it?"

"Most of the time it's pretty good," Shiane says. "But the major objective of mage-training for the first couple of years is to increase control. As I get stronger, I'll make more mistakes and do more things accidentally. Most people in Auravale try to keep some distance between themselves and me since

103

the closer I am to someone, the more likely it is that I'll do something without thinking."

"Like reading my mind?"

"Not just that," Shiane says. "I might sense that a man wants a drink of water and thoughtlessly fill a bucket at the nearest well and dump it all over him."

"Really!" I exclaim.

Shiane nods with a sad little smile on her face. "I actually did that once when I was ten years old, except I didn't use a bucket. It was just a big glob of water. I don't want to do bad things, but sometimes the magic happens against my will."

"I understand," I say. "Often when I try to do something good, it'll go wrong. I never know why."

Shiane gives my hand a squeeze. "At least I'm surrounded by people who understand what's happening to me. It must be awfully hard on you when your magic goes wild and you don't have anyone to explain it and comfort you."

"What do you mean when my magic goes wild?"

Shiane clasps a hand over her mouth. "I did it again. I forgot they haven't told you, yet."

"Then you tell me."

Shiane's eyes dart over at Neeve.

I put my hand in her line of sight. "You don't need to ask Neeve for permission, or Kaden. You're a big girl. Please tell me."

"Well," she says slowly, "you have so much power that I can see it shining right through your skin."

"Shiane," I say gently, trying not to sound sarcastic, "if I had anything shining through my skin, I'm sure someone would've mentioned it to me before now."

"Not everyone can see it. I doubt that Neeve and Kaden see it very clearly, although they probably sense something. My eldest brothers, Skylar and Jerrin, though, are both sorcerers. They would see it without any trouble. You got your magic from Bree-Ella."

Chapter Nineteen

I fling myself away from Shiane.

I know I asked her to tell me, but I wanted her to tell me something that made things better not worse.

"Is this some kind of conspiracy to drive me crazy?" I cry. I jump to my feet, grabbing my lunch tote on my way up, and prepare to dash for home. Kaden somehow gets in front of me.

He grabs my shoulders.

"How can you believe so much, Hellie," he demands, "and then balk at acknowledging yourself? Doesn't having uncontrolled powers make sense of many of your past experiences?"

"No," I snap at him.

I glance around the glade that my grandmother loved so much.

"I know this is an enchanted forest because my grandmother told me, and I know it's enchanted because the stwethil-thage live here. I know that you and Neeve and Jerrin and Shiane are magical beings. I've seen too much to deny that.

"But I am an average American teenage girl who has an outstanding twin and parents who are as normal as apple pie. I am nothing special except for my unusual bad luck."

"Hellie," Shiane says, coming up to stand next to Kaden. Neeve is already standing at his other side.

I close my eyes and don't say anything.

She continues. "Hellie, you have got to try to believe. If you don't, you're going to do a lot of unintentional harm. You're like me. You have mage-level potential. If you don't want it, the elders can block it for you, but you'll have to acknowledge your power before they'll do it. One of their axioms is that you must understand something before you can forsake it."

"Come back and sit down," Kaden says. "Neeve and I had planned to lead up to your inheriting Bree-Ella's mage-level magic a little more gradually than this. But you asked Shiane to tell you, and since you're stronger than she is, you compelled her."

Dark in the Forest: Another Modern Fairytale

My eyes pop open and I stare at Shiane. "I made you tell me?"

"It was just a little shove," she answers. "I wasn't expecting it, so I didn't have my defenses ready. Don't worry. You won't be able to do it again."

"As long as you were just doing simple magic," Neeve continues, "things like compelling Shiane to respond to your question, you were safe. But now that you've used one of the great powers, the Darkers will sense you. If they recognize you as Bree-Ella's descendant, they'll come for you."

"When did I—?"

I stop myself.

I already know the answer.

I was the one who made everyone on the playground at Happy Hands freeze while I ran the distance from the concrete pad to the slippery slide in order to catch the girl. I was the one who made them think nothing out of the ordinary had happened. Somehow I knew it all the time.

I have magical powers.

I can make things happen.

"I don't want to sound dense," I say, "but if my Bree-Ella and your Bree-Ella are the same person, wouldn't she have passed her abilities on to at least some of her descendants before me?"

"How do you know she didn't?" Shiane asks.

"I don't, but—"

"How well do you know your mother's family?" Kaden asks. He leads me back to our previous position over by the stream.

"Except for Grandmother Dark," I say, "I hardly ever see Mom's family. She grew up in Pullman, Washington, but she and her sisters all moved away after they got married. One of her sisters lives in Hawaii, one lives in Texas, and the other lives in Florida. Grandmother Dark comes to see us at least once a year, usually in the fall. She calls it doing the circuit. She starts in Florida and flies west, visiting each of her daughters for about a week. She rotates Christmas. We had her last year."

"So," Neeve says, "you have no idea if anyone in your mother's family has also inherited Bree-Ella's abilities."

"But wouldn't they naturally—"

My cellphone rings.

I jump and involuntarily utter a word that good girls don't use.

My emotions have been on such a rollercoaster ride that I almost forgot the outside world exists.

When I try to unzip the pocket at the front of my tote, my hand starts shaking so bad I can't make my fingers work.

Kaden unzips it for me. He hands me my phone.

It's my mother.

I take a deep breath and punch the button to accept the call.

"Hi, Mom, are you at home?"

"Yes, and I need you to come back right now."

106

"What's up?" I ask as I walk away from the trio.

When I glance back over my shoulder, they are staring at me.

Mom continues talking. "The mayor was so grateful to me for coming in this morning and handling the media coverage of his son's arrest that he gave me a $250.00 gift card for dinner at the Fleur-de-Lis and then tickets for four to see *Cats* at the new outdoor theater. Tonight. Now hurry home. I need to call your dad and Angel too."

She disconnects.

"I've got to go."

Kaden, Neeve, and Shiane say "NO" at the same time.

"I have to," I say. "My mother doesn't like it that I spend so much time out here by myself. If I want to get banned for life, all I'd have to do is delay going home now."

"Tomorrow then—" Neeve says. "Early."

"I can't guarantee it. Tomorrow is Sunday. We have church in the morning, and then my parents will be home the rest of the day. I can get here by noon on Monday. What difference can one day make?"

Neeve starts to argue with me, but Kaden intervenes on my behalf.

"Even if the Darkers have become aware of Hellie," Kaden says, "it'll take them a while to figure out where she is. Remember, they weren't ever able to find Bree-Ella, and they had decades to look for her. The Darkers have never been able to breed finders or farseers."

"Monday, then," Neeve says. "Please don't forget."

"I won't, but I've got to go now." I wave as I start running.

By the time I get home, Mom has already gone through my closet and set out what I need to wear for such a fancy night out. She cuts through the bathroom to get to Angel's room, presumably to pick out what Angel should wear too.

When I hop out of the shower and start blow-drying my hair, I wonder where Angel is. Courtney Bingham's house is only two blocks from ours. If Mom called Angel right after she called me, Angel should have been home long ago.

I've just finished my hair, when Angel comes into the bathroom.

She's been crying.

I step forward to find out what's wrong.

She steps back.

"Do you have a boyfriend?" she demands. "Do you meet with him in the forest? Is that why you're always going there?"

I don't know what to say.

Kaden isn't my boyfriend.

I've known him for less than a week.

There's no way she could have learned about him.

If she had, though, she would have started the conversation differently, something like: W*ho is that boy you've been meeting in the woods?*

107

Dark in the Forest: Another Modern Fairytale

Besides, I doubt that a human being could sneak up on someone like Kaden. I'm sure he'd sense them or maybe even hear them. I had the distinct impression that Kaden, Neeve, and Shiane could all hear both sides of the conversation I had with my mother even after I was several yards away. Kaden and Neeve were both frowning before Mom ended the call.

No, this isn't about Kaden. It's about something completely different.

I answer Angel in the only way I can.

"You know I don't have a boyfriend, Angel. I haven't gone out on a tenth of the dates you have. You're the popular one."

"Then why did Courtney's brother accuse me of having a secret boyfriend that I meet in the woods?"

Suddenly I see the light.

Kaden told me that he had seen me in the woods, or thought he did, when in actuality it was Angel going there to meet a boy she really liked. Someone has discovered her secret and is spreading it around.

I don't know if she's hoping to find out that I have a boyfriend I meet in the woods so she can blame it on me, or if she wants to convince me that we're both being slandered in hopes that I'll join her to challenge the rumors in a unified front.

I sit down on the edge of the bathtub.

"A little while ago," I say, "I met a guy who told me that he had seen me in the woods with a boy. I told him it wasn't me, and he said, a little sarcastically, then it must have been my twin sister. He was surprised when I told him I actually do have an identical twin."

Angel goes pale. "Did you tell Mom and Dad?"

"Of course not," I say, "but it sounds like someone else has seen you. The guy I met was from out of town, so I doubt he's responsible for the rumors. However, you know what it's like in Shawon. Once a rumor starts flying around, it won't stop until everyone has heard it. You'd better tell Mom and Dad before they hear about it from another source."

Angel gets a washcloth and starts washing the tears off her face.

"I think Sammy's been following me around off and on for weeks. Today he came home while Courtney and I were watching *Magic in the Moonlight* and started chanting 'Angel's got a boyfriend' and making squeaky kissing noises. I wanted to slap him."

"You didn't though," I say confidently.

"I might have if Courtney hadn't chased him out the door. I was almost afraid to go ahead and meet Peter Bradley, but I'd already called him and told him I needed to see him. I thought that bag you found in the woods was his. He had something similar with him the last time we met."

My mouth falls open.

Peter Bradley is Shawon's bad boy.

I think every town must have one: the nonconformist who rides a big motorcycle and wears leather year round.

He's not really a bad person in the stereotypical way.

He graduated from high school and even spent a couple of years at the local university, but then he decided he wanted to be a mechanic fulltime and to work on bikes and, to a lesser degree, on cars, especially classic automobiles.

He recently finished refurbishing a 1963 Aston-Martin for Berton Creed, who is president of the Shawon Board of Realtors and whose father made millions selling commercial properties in Denver.

I think people look down on Peter because he insists on being his own person and because he never seems able to get the grease and grime out from under his fingernails.

The only negatives I've ever heard about him were things like he charges too much, won't drop what he's doing to take care of other people's emergencies, won't work on Sundays no matter how much extra people offer to pay him, and doesn't show the proper respect for his betters.

I've also heard that he doesn't do drugs and has never been arrested.

"You and Peter Bradley," I say. "It'll take a few minutes for that to settle in."

"He's really very nice," Angel says defensively.

"So why were you crying?"

"I told him I thought we should take a break and not see each other for a while. He got angry and accused me of being ashamed of him. He wouldn't believe me when I told him I'm not."

"Then why do you meet with him in the woods?" I ask.

She grimaces and her face turns red. "I know this is going to sound awful, but we meet there because everyone knows I hate the forest."

Understanding is instantaneous.

"You wanted anyone who saw you together to assume it was me!"

"Hellie, it's not that I wanted to get you into trouble. I just wanted to create reasonable doubt. You know, make people unsure of what they'd seen."

I should be angry, but I'm not. Angel is not a brave person. She hates conflict because it makes her feel vulnerable, and she knows she is terrible at defending herself.

I sigh. "You had to know it couldn't go on forever. Someone was bound to spot you eventually, and that kind of clandestine activity always makes things look sleazy. If he picked you up at the house for a real date, even if you went on his motorcycle, your relationship would look less guilty."

Angel plops down on the side of the bathtub. "Do you think for one moment that Mom and Dad would let me go out with him if they knew?"

"Certainly not if the first time Mom hears about it comes from Mandy Brown the next time she goes in for a hair cut."

"Girls," Mom's voice yells, "we need to leave in thirty minutes if we're going to make our reservations at Fleur-de-Lis. Get a move on."

"I'll get dressed and go pacify Mom while you take a quick shower—no time for a bath." I kiss Angel on the cheek. "Tonight at dinner might be a good time to tell the folks. They won't want to make a scene at a place like Fleur-de-Lis."

"You'll have my back?" Angel asks.

"You know it," I answer.

Chapter Twenty

Angel waits until after we have all ordered from the menu and the waitress has brought drinks and appetizers.

She doesn't slide into it or give the folks any warning.

She merely says, "Peter Bradley asked me out for dinner and a movie this coming Friday, and I accepted."

I almost choke on my Diet Coke.

Mom has just taken a bite of stuffed mushroom, and she barely manages not to gag and spit it out. She finishes chewing and swallowing, but she makes such a face that the headwaiter comes over to see if something is wrong.

"No," Mom says, "everything's fine. Thank you for asking."

He waits a few seconds, I think to see if Mom will elucidate, but since she doesn't, he just nods at my parents and goes back to where he belongs.

"Angel," Dad says, "I don't think he's the kind of young man you should encourage. He's at least three or four years older than you are and has probably had a great deal of intimate contact with other young women."

"You should be dating boys your own age who won't have unrealistic expectations about how your evening will end," Mom adds.

Parents are so strange.

They can't just say the S, E, X word.

They have to skirt around the issue.

"Actually," Angel says, "Peter treats me with courtesy and respect, unlike most of the boys I've dated who are my age, who are all hands and who think N, O spells yes."

"You've gone out with him before!" Mom's voice starts out a little loud but she turns down the volume quickly. "You've gone out with him behind our backs?"

"Not really," Angel says. "I met him for the first time early in the spring. You sent me to look for Hellie in the woods because she'd forgotten to take her cellphone with her."

"What was he doing in our forest?" Dad demands in a hoarse whisper.

"Drinking beer with his buddies, no doubt," Mom says.

Dark in the Forest: Another Modern Fairytale

Angel gets angry.

She usually doesn't let contentions grow into confrontations (I'm the one with the temper), but she obviously feels strongly about Peter.

She holds her head up high and speaks in a carefully modulated voice. "Peter has a developmentally delayed sister. She likes to paint, and Peter was taking pictures of the early blooming wildflowers for her. Both of their parents work to pay for Cindy's occupational and physical therapy since it's not all covered by their medical insurance. Peter helps.

"The first time I bumped into Peter we exchanged cellphone numbers, and I offered to show him some of the more beautiful parts of the woods so he could photograph them for Cindy. She painted me a picture in appreciation."

Mom softens her tone. "How many times have you met with him in the woods?"

"Maybe half a dozen," Angel says.

"Why didn't you mention this to us earlier?" Dad asks.

Angel dips her head and closes her eyes, like she does sometimes when she is struggling for words.

I answer for her. "She was probably afraid you'd react just the way that you did."

Angel glances up and gives me a little smile.

Then she adds, "I had no way of knowing that he was interested in dating me. There are lots of kinds of friends, you know, and he might merely have been thinking of me as a friend that he could talk to about his sister without worrying about whether or not he was going to be mocked, or criticized, or judged."

"Frankly," I say, "I've never heard anything bad about him except that he's a nonconformist—and that can be either a positive or a negative."

My parents have one of those silent conversations that married couples sometimes have in which they use facial expressions instead of words.

"He'll have to pick you up at the house so we can meet him," Dad says.

"He will," Angel asserts.

Although Mom looks at Angel a little strangely off and on all night, she doesn't say anything more about it.

When we get home after the show (which was great), while Angel and I get ready for bed, I ask her, "How much of what you told Mom and Dad was true?"

"All of it," she says. Then her voice drops low. "Most of it. We've met a few more times than I led the folks to believe, but Mom asked me specifically how often we've met in the woods, not how often we've met all together. A few times, when he had access to a car, he picked me up at school and we went for a drive up the canyon."

"How long have you two been hanging out?"

"A couple of months. Long enough for him to give me a ride on his motorcycle half a dozen times. Oh, and twice he took me over to see his sister.

She really is a sweetheart, and she just adores Peter."

I wash my face while Angel talks.

"What about the dinner and a movie?" I ask. "Isn't he going to be a little surprised to learn he's asked you out?"

"Every time I see him he asks me out for dinner and a movie on Friday night." She smiles with the dreamiest expression on her face. "He says he'll know he's making progress when I finally tell him yes."

"What about you?" I ask. "How do you feel about him?"

She hitches herself up onto the vanity so she's sitting between the two sinks. She looks me straight in the eyes.

"Oh, Hellie," she says, "I like him a lot. He really is smarter than people give him credit for. He might have dropped out of college but that doesn't mean he stopped using his brain. He reads fast, about 900 words a minute, and he reads all of the time, everything: newspapers, magazines, novels, history, biographies, science, and anything else he can get his hands on. He reads a lot more than I do."

I've started to pick up my toothbrush, but I set it back down and stare at Angel. That's the first time I've heard her admit that it's possible for anyone to read more than she does.

"He is so sweet with his sister," she continues. "He reads children's books to her and makes her laugh. He can do all kinds of voices and accents and sound effects. He's gentle and kind and thoughtful."

"Holy cow, Angel," I say, "you really have it bad."

"I know. I'm sorry I yelled at you and accused you of doing what I was doing. I was just so afraid that Sammy Bingham was going to ruin it all by telling everyone about Peter and me, making it sound nasty."

She reaches over and takes my hand.

"Thank you for encouraging me to tell Mom and Dad. Peter has wanted us to go public, but I've been such a coward. He'll be relieved when I tell him he can come over Friday night to meet my family—and that we can go on a real date afterward."

She hops off the vanity and goes into her room.

She returns a moment later with Kaden's leather pouch.

"I'm sorry I took this from your tote bag without asking you. You were asleep when I left and I planned on seeing Peter after I left Courtney's house. I thought it was his. I didn't know how to ask you if I could show it to him without doing a lot of explaining first.

"I should have trusted you. You've always been supportive, and you've never betrayed me before. I can't imagine any circumstances when you would. I've got the best sister in the world."

She hugs me. "I love you, Hellie."

I'm almost in tears. I've gotten my sister back.

Chapter Twenty-one

I am so happy when I go to bed I expect to sleep soundly with no bad dreams.

Right!

The dream starts as usual with me racing through the forest like a frightened animal. But this time, when I decide to hide in the tree and make a jump for the low branch, hands catch mine and lift me up.

It's Kaden. He pulls me into his embrace.

When I hear the hellhounds, I'm not afraid.

I wake up still feeling Kaden holding me.

I wrap my arms around myself so I can hug him back.

While I get dressed for church, I consider everything Angel shared about her and Peter. I wish I could tell her about Kaden and Auravale and about the stwethil-thage that live in our forest.

But I know I can't.

I'm not even sure I could share it with her if she still believed in magic.

Certainly I'll never be able to tell her about Bree-Ella and her mage-level powers, which she might have passed on to me.

It makes me feel lonely all over again.

It's no easier to have this distance between us when I'm the one who's pulling away instead of her.

When we get to church, I stand just outside the door with Angel to wait for Courtney. We almost always sit together.

When Courtney's father pulls into the parking lot, he spots us and lets Courtney out at the curb before he goes in search of a parking space.

Immediately Angel and Courtney start jabbering at a hundred miles an minute. They have to catch up quickly so they don't have to whisper during church services. I'm strictly a third wheel with them, but that's all right. When my friend Nadine gets back from Boston, she'll hang with us, and that will even things up.

As people pass us on their way into the building, most give us a cheerful "good morning." That's why hearing an angry voice draws my attention.

Three-year-old Tommy Baxter apparently dropped his cute little Batman backpack as he climbed out of the car. A few of his toys fell out.

He scrambles to pick them up and gets no help from Mom.

His two older siblings dart past him as if he's invisible.

"Hurry," Mrs. Baxter snaps. "You're going to make us late."

Mrs. Baxter is known for being an impatient person. True to her nature, she has parked illegally in the handicapped parking spot at the end of the row of cars closest to the church doors.

Tommy picks up the last toy, puts it in his backpack, and struggles to get the straps over his shoulders.

"Get going," his mother says and gives him a little shove. Tommy stumbles, dropping his backpack and spilling the contents again.

"Clumsy brat!" Mrs. Baxter snarls.

I rush over. "I'll take care of Tommy if you want to go on in, Mrs. Baxter." I don't wait for her to answer me. I crouch down and help Tommy pick up his toy cars and books.

Mrs. Baxter doesn't say thank you to me or goodbye to Tommy.

She just stomps off.

I help Tommy get the straps of his backpack onto his shoulders. Then I take his hand and we cross the stretch of parking lot between the first row of cars and the sidewalk.

By the time his mother reaches the church doors, we're about ten feet behind her. She hasn't once turned back to check on Tommy.

I think: *That woman needs a little humbling so she can remember what it's like to feel young and helpless.*

A moment later, I hear a loud crash.

A car has sideswiped Mrs. Baxter's car and then burned rubber out of the church parking lot.

I must be an awfully wicked person at heart because I want to burst out laughing. If Mrs. Baxter had taken just an extra minute or two to park her car in the next row, the handicapped parking spot would have been empty and the other car wouldn't have had anything to hit.

As she angrily digs her cellphone out of her purse, I say, "Shall I go ahead and take Tommy to the nursery for you?"

She glares at me a moment then gives me a curt nod.

Generally I enjoy church. I let my stresses flow away while I surround myself with peacefulness.

Today, however, I can't relax.

I'm surprised at how distressed I feel knowing I won't see Kaden until tomorrow. How can I feel this way about someone I've just met? Perhaps having shared fauvenell is contributing to my unease, but then that brings up the question of why I would choose to go through that little ritual with a stranger.

After the congregation has sung the last song and Pastor Keating has said

Dark in the Forest: Another Modern Fairytale

the benediction, I don't experience the sense of serenity that I usually do.

Monday afternoon seems a long way away.

Angel and Courtney disappear as soon as the service is over.

As I follow my parents to the car I experience déjà vu.

Instead of a bullying mother, this time it's a father.

Mr. Thompson, dragging his six-year-old son, Aaron, by the hand, crowds in between my parents and me. Like the mother this morning, Mr. Thompson is snapping at his son to hurry up.

"I've got to drop you off at your mother's house and then get to work. Why she insists that I to take you to Sunday school on my weekends, I'll never understand. Now, move it."

The angrier the father gets the more Aaron pulls back.

Obviously, Mr. Thompson terrifies his son. While Aaron is looking up at his father, as if expecting to receive a blow, he isn't watching where he puts his feet. He stumbles off the edge of the sidewalk and falls into the two-foot-wide bordering flowerbed.

The nasty father doesn't even help Aaron get up but swears at him instead.

While I rush over to help untangle Aaron from the zinnias, his father pulls a pack of cigarettes and a book of matches from his pocket. As he is lighting up, I think *I wouldn't spit on that moron if he was on fire.*

Suddenly he drops the lighted match, and I watch it slide into the pocket of his light blue dress shirt. At first he glances around his feet, apparently not realizing the match is caught in his clothing. He lights another match just as the first one sets his shirt on fire. The man is so shocked that he drops the second match and it becomes caught in the cuff of his slacks.

While he is screeching and pounding at his burning shirt with his hands, he doesn't notice that his cuff is starting to smoke.

Aaron is crying.

Mr. Thompson is swearing.

The fire is spreading.

People in the parking lot turn to stare, but no one moves a muscle.

I spy a hose attached to a faucet near the corner of the building. Before I can reach it, the pastor rushes out with a pitcher of water and throws it at Mr. Thompson's chest, putting out the fire in his shirt.

However, by now, Mr. Thompson's trousers are on fire, and he is hopping around, shaking his leg, and making the fire worse.

A moment later, I get there with the hose and am able to put out the second blaze.

As Pastor Keating calls 911 on his cellphone, he asks, "What happened?"

No one answers.

One member of the congregation is a nurse, and she fusses over Mr. Thompson while two groups of gawkers form: one in the doorway of the church building and the other in the parking lot.

Parents try to maintain some kind of control over the youngest of the children, all of whom seem to respond to Aaron's distress by crying too.

After Pastor Keating puts away his cellphone, he asks again, "What happened?" He glances around at the crowd. When he gets to me, he looks at my feet and says, "Hellie?"

When I glance down, I realize I've dropped the hose to the ground without turning the nozzle closed tightly enough. I'm standing in a nice little puddle of water.

"I'm not sure," I answer, sidestepping onto the sidewalk while praying I won't get struck by lightning for lying at church. "Aaron tripped and fell into the flowerbed. While I was helping him get up, I saw Mr. Thompson reach for a cigarette. The next thing I knew he was on fire."

"Two accidents in one parking lot in one day," Mrs. Newton, the pastor's secretary, moans. I assume she means Mrs. Baxter's car as well as Mr. Thompson's fire. Suddenly I feel sick to my stomach.

Sirens approach.

Mrs. Newton takes the sniffling Aaron from my arms.

When did I pick him up?

I start trembling.

"I'd better go call his mother," Mrs. Newton tells the pastor.

"Yes, do that," he says. Then he starts shooing the spectators away. "Go on home, people. See if you can't clear the parking lot by the time the paramedics get here. You can call me or Mrs. Newton later in the day to find out how Daniel is doing."

My heart is pounding erratically. My stomach is turning over. I'm on the verge of vomiting. I think I'm going into shock.

I know I made Mr. Thompson drop those matches and then made the fires hard to put out. I probably made that car hit Mrs. Baxter's car too.

The curse of Hellenaura strikes again!

On the ride home, I pray I can keep it together long enough to get to my bedroom. It seems to take forever. I'm fighting tears the whole way.

As soon as Dad unlocks the door, I rush into the house and up the stairs. I'm crying by the time I get to my room.

Mom is right behind me.

"Hellie, honey, what's wrong?"

"Mr. Thompson," I sob. "I tried to get to the hose, but I wasn't fast enough. Now he's going to the hospital, and it's my fault."

Mom puts her arms around me. "Honey, you reacted faster than any of the rest of us. You kept him from getting burned even worse."

I clutch at her and sob. I've tried to tell her about the Hellenaura curse before, but she didn't get it.

She pats my back and coos at me like I'm a little girl. "Maybe you should lie down for a while and take a nap."

I shake my head.

"Can I get you anything to eat, sometimes—"

I shake my head again.

"All right," she says softly, "what do you think will help you feel better?"

I can't meet her eyes.

"Shall I guess?"

I risk glancing down at her. I forget how small she is until something like this happens and reminds me.

"I'll bet a few hours in the forest would help, wouldn't it?"

I wipe my eyes with the backs of my hands.

"Yes," I whisper.

"Because of the magic?"

I shrug.

"Oh, Hellie," Mom says. "It's hard to be a mother who is jealous of a bunch of trees."

"I'm sorry."

"Three hours," she says. "You make sure you're back by then."

"Starting now?" I ask, trying to fake a smile. "Or after I've changed my clothes?"

She shakes her head, as if saying she'll never understand me, and then glances at the clock on my bed stand. It shows 12:45.

"Four o'clock. We're going to barbeque tonight. You get home by 4:00 so you can help make salads and dessert."

I hug her. "Thank you. You're the best mom in the world."

I change my clothes as fast as I can.

I don't take time to hang up my dress or to clean the mud off of my good shoes. I throw on yesterday's jeans and t-shirt. I set my cellphone alarm for 3:45 and start to slip the phone into my pocket.

It doesn't fit. I should never have bought these jeans. The pockets are so small they're useless. (However, they're cute, outlined with red embroidery and studded with rhinestones.)

I cram my phone into the pocket on the front of my lunch tote. I didn't eat the animal crackers I put in it yesterday or drink the chocolate milk. I unfasten the thermos and sniff. The milk hasn't gone sour. It's probably not too cold anymore, but the stwethil-thage can deal with lukewarm milk for once.

I eat a couple of cookies before I put a washcloth over the plastic bag containing the rest and use a shoe to smash them to pieces.

On my way out of the house, I pause in the kitchen long enough to grab two bottles of water. I never go into the woods without water. Then I'm out the back door. I practically run across the yard.

I crash through the hedge.

My arms get snagged and scratched. I don't care. I pause at the grotto long enough to put out the animal crackers and milk, then I seek the comfort and safety of the glade.

At last, I'm free to give vent to my feelings.

I collapse onto the ground and cry for my grandmother. I know the evil

118

created by my treacherous name is coming out, and if Shiane is right, it's coming out with mage-level strength.

I almost killed someone today.

I almost killed three people if I count Aaron and myself. We were close enough to Mr. Thompson to get burned if he'd panicked and turned in our direction.

I don't know what to do.

The only people who would understand what's happening to me live in a completely different world. And the only person who would believe me even if she didn't understand is dead.

I curl up on my side, bury my face in my hands, and sob.

I don't know how I'll ever be able to stop.

I've tried so hard to keep from going bad.

It's all been in vain!

Suddenly, I feel myself being lifted up and cradled in strong arms. For a moment I think it must be my grandmother. I remember her holding me like this when I was little, when Angel said things to me to hurt my feelings. Grandma was the only person who ever noticed Angel's tendency to bully me.

I know it can't be my grandmother.

I open my eyes and look up.

It's Kaden.

He kisses my forehead.

"Your pain called me all the way from Auravale," he whispers tenderly. "I hope you can figure out how to send me back because I don't have a portal key with me."

We're sitting on the ground with me on his lap.

I lay my head on his chest.

I stop crying.

Chapter Twenty-two

"What's happened, Hellie?" he murmurs softly in my ear. His warm breath brushes across my skin.

I tell him.

As his arms constrict around me, I think he might be able to keep the evil from exploding out of me if he can only hold onto me tight enough.

When I finish telling him everything, he kisses my forehead again and then sets me down on the ground. I sit cross-legged, and after he scoots around so he's facing me, he sits the same way. We're so close together that our knees touch. He takes my hands in his.

"Are you ready to accept the fact that you have powers?" he asks.

"I don't have any choice, do I? I don't know how I did what I did, but I do know that I did it." I dip my head and blink a couple of times. Did that sentence make sense?

"Hellie," Kaden asks, "do you remember any of the story that Neeve, Shiane, and I were telling you yesterday?"

I fish a tissue out of my tote bag so I can blot my face and blow my nose.

"Yes. I remember it fairly well, maybe not word for word."

"Good. Now give me a minute while I call Neeve. His father wants him to be here while you decide whether or not you're going to keep your powers and accept mage training."

I start to hand him my cellphone but he shakes his head. I should have guessed. He and Neeve don't need to be in close proximity to communicate mind-to-mind.

While he has his eyes averted and is presumably talking to Neeve, I wonder how they "dial" each other. There must be a way of assuring that they're going to end up talking to the right person. Otherwise, everyone would be listening to everyone else's business all the time.

When Kaden finishes with his communiqué, he tells me that Neeve and Karissa will be here soon. She has been to church and is changing into casual clothing.

"Is she coming so she can act as our chaperone?"

"Not really," Kaden says, smiling. "Neeve just likes having her around."

"So that stuff Jerrin said about us needing a chaperone because we had shared fauvenell wasn't true?"

"Oh, it's quite true. In Auravale it's part of the courtship, and because it intensifies feelings, a couple usually doesn't share it until right before their wedding. Some couples integrate it into the marriage ceremony, sharing fauvenell right before their first kiss."

I'm a bit flustered when he says that, but I don't think he's being literal. I mean, really, how can a couple have a courtship without some passionate kissing, even if that's as far as it goes until the wedding night?

"If Karissa hadn't been available," Kaden continues, "I suppose Neeve would have called on Shiane or one of his other sisters."

"Are you taking a risk by being alone with me now?" I ask.

"No," Kaden says. "No risk. It's only a risk when people aren't absolutely certain what they want in the long run. I know what I want."

"What?"

"Now isn't the proper time to discuss it. Let's talk about something else."

"Like what?"

"I don't think you finished explaining why you think your name predisposes you to being a bad person. You were telling us, but Neeve interrupted when you mentioned Bree-Ella Dark. I had a feeling at the time that there was more. Would you mind finishing now?"

"Why?" I ask.

"So I can understand the compulsion that made you immediately assume something evil inside you caused those accidents today instead of thinking your untrained magic responded to an unintentional wish and it got away from you."

"I don't remember what I've told you and what I haven't."

"Think, Hellie. It could be important."

"All right." I ponder a moment and then say the first things to pop into my head. "My two family names, Powers and Dark, when used together as nouns in a single sentence would generally fight for dominance: power would represent the positive and dark would represent the negative. Since they're both strong words, they would either balance each other or cancel each other out.

"However, the way the two words are arranged in my name Dark changes into an adjective that defines Powers: dark powers. Although *hell* means light in German, we're dealing with English, and in English *hell* is the place where the damned go to be punished for eternity. An aura can indicate either positive or negative forces, but sandwiched there between *hell* and *dark,* I don't think there's a chance that it implies goodness.

"So it's not just the four words that predict and determine my future, it's also their placement in relationship to each other. Hellenaura Dark Powers predestines me to messing up my life and the lives of anyone who gets too close. I call it the Hellenaura Curse."

To my surprise Kaden laughs. "You really are determined to embrace the negative, aren't you?"

"You asked me, and I told you," I say irritably. "It's not funny."

"I suppose not," Kaden says, "certainly not the way you've been looking at it all your life," he abruptly interrupts himself. "By the way, just how old are you?"

"Seventeen," I answer. "I'll be a senior in high school this fall. How old are you?"

"Twenty," he says. "I am unmarried and am in my third year of training in my profession. In two more years, I will be able to support a wife and a family."

I don't know what to make of that last sentence, but it makes my heart race. Two years.

Is this his way of asking me to wait for him? Or is this his way of warning me that in two years he'll be old enough for his father or the king to arrange a marriage for him?

"Will you be expected to marry for the good of the kingdom like the two Dark brothers?" I ask before my brain can take control of my mouth.

"I don't know," he says thoughtfully. "As far as I know, neither the king nor my father has plans to arrange a marriage for me. It never occurred to me to ask. I always assumed I'd be allowed to fall in love, to propose to the young woman of my choice, and to build or to buy an estate where we could raise our children."

"Are you in a position with the court that would lend itself to a marriage of convenience for the king?"

"I don't know." He purses his lips and stares over the top of my head for several seconds. "The Katsenevas clan has always been close to the throne. We have served in a number of different capacities, but always we have been there to support and to advise. Currently, my father is the king's chronicler."

"What does a chronicler do?"

"He keeps a continuous record of significant historical, biographical, and political events for the Crown to make sure knowledge is not lost and is not misunderstood by future generations. Often he is required to decide if a piece of written information is of value."

"What kind of written information?"

"Letters, decrees, manifests, judgments, and the transference of property."

"Except for the letters," I say, "those all sound like legal documents. Don't you have a system where things like that are filed and kept as part of a public record?"

"We do," Kaden answers. "Clerks handle it, but the legal record might simply list the date of a hearing and the final outcome. A chronicler's record would detail why the issue was important within the context of the times. For example, the legal record might indicate that two people disputed a property line and the complaint was resolved by a specific ruling. In contrast, a chronicler's report of the same incident would include who initiated the action, which person benefited and which person was hurt by the ruling, whether there was popular support for the decision, if there were immediate negative consequences, and a projection of what the long-term aftereffects might be.

"A chronicler also does whatever the king asks him to do.

"At the request of Justus IV, my father is currently compiling a record of the social reforms and societal improvements that occurred under each Trudimahn monarch. Although he is including things like wars, treaties, and trade agreements, his main focus is on how the major events affected the daily lives of Auravale's citizenry, especially in terms of civil disputes, domestic unrest, and fluctuating economics.

"My father spends a third of his time studying written histories, a third searching through obscure documents, diaries, archived letters and papers, and the other third writing summaries and/or interpretations of events.

"In fact, it was while my father was looking through some recently discovered documents left by Justus III that he found a letter that led to my being sent here. It described an incident that had previously been unrecorded. He took the matter to the king, and the king recommended that I search the libraries for corroborative information. When I didn't find any, he asked me to check the entire palace."

"How could one person go through an entire library and come out knowing that the information he wanted wasn't there?"

"The average person couldn't. That's why the king wanted me to do it. As a finder, that's what I do."

I don't think I'm ever going to get this magic stuff sorted out.

"Explain the process to me. How do you go about finding something?"

Kaden looks away and gazes at the trees for a while. Then he looks down and notices the corner of his leather pouch sticking out of my tote.

"You found it!"

"Didn't you know? You're the finder. Surely you knew that you left it behind and I picked it up."

"My magic doesn't work that way. I can find things for other people, but my magic doesn't always work for me. I suppose it's because when people ask me to find things, they actually don't know where they are and they want them to be found. After the king sent for me and I realized I didn't have my bag, I wasn't worried. I was fairly sure it would either be here in the forest when I came back or you would have it."

I take the pouch out of my tote and hand it to him. "Now back to the process of finding things."

"In the incident I was talking about, the king wanted confirmation that the event described in the letter had actually happened. Since documents are often stored in libraries, that's where I started. I walked up and down the aisles thinking about the information the king wanted. A few times I got the feeling

Dark in the Forest: Another Modern Fairytale

that something related to the incident was present. After I ran my hand across the spines of the books in question, I knew the specific information wasn't there, but corroborative information was. So I set those books aside for the king to review.

"After the libraries, I wandered through every corridor in the palace. There were two rooms that gave me the sensation of being related to the incident. Neither was currently inhabited so I went in and ran my hand over things. It was in the second of these rooms that I found the residual trail that led to this world. That's why I'm here."

I nod as if I understand.

I don't really, but I have a hunch.

"I'm just guessing," I say, "but, by any chance, was the letter your father found about Bree-Ella Dark?"

"Actually it was from her," Kaden says. "But we can't go into that part of the story until Neeve arrives. I told you the king wants him here while—"

"Sorry we're late," Neeve says as he walks out of nowhere, pushing Karissa in a wheelchair. She is holding a couple of large paper bags on her lap. "Karissa hasn't eaten since breakfast, so we stopped to get some fast food. I hope you're hungry because we bought you some, too."

My phone alarm goes off. "Oh my gosh, I didn't realize it was so late. I'm supposed to be home by 4:00."

Chapter Twenty-three

"Isn't there any way that you can stay?" Kaden asks. "More is involved here than you realize. It is really important that you tell Neeve what happened and then let him decide how best to help you."

I open my mouth, prepared to argue, but the expression on Kaden's face says more than his words.

He is really worried for me.

I get out my cellphone and text my mother:

> I bumped into some friends and they invited
> me out for fast food. I'd like to say yes. Can
> you BBQ without me?

I hold my breath until I get an answer. Our conversation goes like this:

> Mom: How long will u b?
> Me: Is 6:30 ok?
> Mom: Ok. Call if u will b longer.
> Me: Thx.

"Everything all right?" Kaden asks.

"It is now," I say. "She said I could stay. We were going to barbeque tonight, but my mother is in a generous mood because of what happened." I glance over at Neeve and then back at Kaden. "Did you tell him?"

"Yes, he did," Neeve answers. "I haven't had a chance to explain it to Karissa, but it'll wait a while longer. I think we should eat first." He takes food out of the bags. When he hands Kaden a burger, he says, "It's vegetable protein and should be all right on your stomach. I like them myself, but you might want to go slow, just in case. I also got you a salad and a chocolate marshmallow milkshake."

"What's a chocolate marshmallow milkshake?" Kaden asks.

"As close to heaven as you can get without dying," Neeve answers. He hands Kaden a super-sized cup, a long plastic spoon, and a straw. Kaden looks at them, puzzled.

"I'll show you in just a minute," Neeve says. He hands me a hamburger, fries, and a Diet Coke. "I hope this is all right," he says. "Karissa assured me this is what 80% of American teenage girls would order."

I unwrap the burger and lift the top bun: hamburger, cheese, bacon, lettuce, tomato, and pickles.

"Perfect," I say.

Karissa offers me half a dozen packets of ketchup. "I told Neeve that you probably couldn't handle one of those gigantic milkshakes," she says. "I know I can't. But it's hard for me to watch other people enjoying ice cream if I don't have any. We got two sundaes: one chocolate and one strawberry. I like them both. You can choose, and I'll take the other one."

I grin at her. "I like them both too. You want to go halfsies?"

"Absolutely," she says grinning back. "Burgers first? Or dessert?"

I vacillate, rocking my shoulders back and forth. "I like some desserts before dinner, but I really enjoy ice cream after."

"After it is," Karissa says.

As I take a bite of my hamburger, I keep an eye on Kaden.

The first time I shared food with him he about gagged to death on a potato chip. I assume there are things in our diets that their bodies can't handle.

He nibbles on the veggie burger. "Not bad," he says to Neeve.

"Try the milkshake," Neeve suggests. "You'll need to use the spoon until the ice cream melts enough that you can use the straw."

Karissa stops eating, and we watch together.

Neeve takes the lid off of his cup and sets it on a napkin.

Then he drags the spoon around the inner rim of the cup, scooping up the ice cream that is the softest. He closes his eyes in anticipation.

Mimicking Neeve perfectly, Kaden does the same thing. Except when he takes that first bite, his eyes fly open with surprise. He scoops out a bigger spoonful the second time.

"Do you like it?" Karissa asks him.

"It's wonderful," Kaden exclaims. "Do people have access to these all the time or are they reserved for special occasions?"

"All the time," Karissa and I tell him simultaneously.

"Why would you eat anything else if you could have one of these any time you wanted?" he asks.

I answer. "We have a saying here that goes: *Too much of a good thing is still too much.* If you had to eat one of those every day, you'd soon think it was too much, no matter how good."

He rolls his eyes up as he downs another spoonful.

"I suppose," he says, "it's a little bit like fauvenell. You don't want to have it so often that you ruin the specialness."

"Very good analogy," Karissa says.

We all concentrate on eating for a while.

Then Kaden and Neeve start talking about local sports and how some of our games seem to echo ones played on their world.

While the guys are engrossed in their conversation, Karissa leans forward in her chair and speaks to me quietly. "What happened to you today, Hellie? Clearly you had been crying before we got here."

The guys are still intently involved in their conversation, so I tell her.

"How awful for you," Karissa says, "but surely you realize those things didn't happen because you're a bad person. It's what Shiane was trying to explain to you yesterday.

"Magic is a force all its own, like moving water. We humans have probably been trying to control water since we first crawled out of our caves and decided to build communities.

"Over the centuries our ancestors experimented with levees and dikes and dams, and today we're much more successful than they were, but it's because we're always learning more about the way water works.

"Every time we have a hurricane or a tidal wave or a flood, we learn a little bit more. Today you had a tidal wave. The only way to cope with the next one is to learn what you can from this one. That's why Shiane—"

"Wait a minute," I say. "How do you know what Shiane said to me yesterday? You weren't here."

"Oh," she blushes. "I wasn't, was I? I have physical therapy on Saturdays." She hitches her shoulders in a little shrug. "Sometimes Neeve acts like a relay station for me when I wish I were in on something but can't be."

"A relay station?"

"Yes. He sees or hears something and passes it on to me with maybe a second or two delay."

"How can you stand it, having him in your mind all the time? Don't you need privacy?"

Karissa laughs. "If he were in my mind all the time, I'd probably have a nervous breakdown, but he's not. When we're not together, we do most of our communicating by phone or text. The mind reading is for special occasions."

Neither of us speaks for a moment.

"I'm sorry," I tell her. "I interrupted you. You started to say something about Shiane."

"Let me think a minute. Oh, yes. Shiane told you about unintentionally dumping water on someone who was thirsty. I think that's what happened to you today. You were trying to protect the children, but without your conscious control, the magic reacted to what was going on in the environment and tried to meet your inner desire. Considering what might have happened, I think you got off easy."

"What do you mean I got off easy? I wrecked Mrs. Baxter's car and sent Mr. Thompson to the hospital."

"Shiane told you that you have mage-level potential," Karissa says. "That's a lot of power. If you weren't such a kind and caring person, you could have picked up Mrs. Baxter's car and hit her with it and turned Mr. Thompson into a pillar of fire."

"I would never—" I let the sentence fade away.

"Not this time, but if you're ever truly enraged, who knows?"

I sigh, feeling helpless. "You think I should take the mage training."

"You only have three choices: let the magic run wild, ask the elders to block it, or learn how to use it responsibly."

"As a resident of earth, where magic is considered fantasy, those options don't sound particularly appealing to me," I tell her. "How am I supposed to know which one to choose?"

"I'll tell you what my dad tells me: *the more information you have the better decisions you can make.*"

"Your dad sounds like a smart man."

"Oh, he is," Karissa says with a laugh, "and he knows it, which means sometimes he can be a real pain in the butt because he believes he's always right."

I laugh with her. "That's what my mother is like. My dad can be kind of mellow sometimes, but my mom is pretty uptight. It's hard work telling everyone else how to handle their lives."

"Hey," Karissa says, "how about some ice cream before it melts!"

Neeve had set the bags on the ground, and I peer inside them to find the sundaes. I take them out. The cups are filled to the brim and beyond with ice cream and toppings.

"How do you want to do this?" I ask her.

"I don't think we can transfer half of the ice cream from one cup to the other without slopping it all over."

"How about if we just share the chocolate and strawberries?" I suggest. "We can each scoop out half and dribble it over our ice cream."

"Excellent," Karissa says.

I get up on my knees. I hand Karissa the cups so I can spread one of the paper bags across her lap. No matter how careful we are, no matter how close we hold the cups together, I can't imagine being successful without making a heck of a mess.

We make a heck of a mess.

By the time we've divvied up the toppings, the paper bag is covered with various sized splotches of brown and red. Our hands are sticky and so are the outsides of the cups.

I wipe my hands on a napkin and then pull two individually packaged towelettes from my tote. We clean our hands and wrap napkins around the outside of the cups.

"I hope you won't think me rude for asking," I say after we start eating, "but you were walking the other time I saw you. What happened?"

She glares at her legs a moment. "Yesterday at physical therapy, I tripped

128

and pulled a muscle. I have to concentrate on what I'm doing every second I'm on my feet. If I don't, disaster!"

"And when you concentrate—?"

She smiles happily. "I can walk, but I have to be careful. I use the cane for balance."

I look down at her legs and then back up at her face. "What happened?"

"Car accident."

The tone she uses is polite, but it clearly indicates that she doesn't want to talk about it. I wonder—two years ago a couple of girls were in a car accident over by the school. One of them, the head cheerleader, was killed. The other girl was injured. It might have been Karissa. Angel and I were just sophomores then and not part of the upper classmen grapevine.

The story was probably in the newspaper, but that was about the time Angel was getting interested in journalism and was starting to leave me behind. I tried to get back at her by pretending I didn't care about the news. All I accomplished was being out of touch with what was going on locally, nationally, and internationally for about six months.

I change the subject by holding up a spoonful of ice cream dripping with syrup.

"This is good," I tell Karissa. "Thank you for sharing."

I'm putting the spoon in my mouth when I realize the guys have gone silent. I glance to the side. They are watching us.

"While Karissa and I eat our sundaes," I say, "why don't you two tell me the rest of the background information I need to understand about Bree-Ella."

"How far did you get?" Neeve asks Kaden.

Chapter Twenty-four

"I told her about my father finding the letter Bree-Ella wrote to the king. I was about ready to explain about Maldon and his bid for the throne, but I got a little distracted by trying to describe what a chronicler does and how I go about finding things."

"It's probably just as well since my father expects me to report on how this goes. Why don't you tell her about Justus II, Justus III, and Maldon? I've often wondered what that mess looked like to someone outside the family."

"All right," Kaden says, "but only if you agree to correct me if I get something wrong."

"Agreed."

Kaden sets his milkshake cup on the ground within easy reach. Then he starts to talk.

"It goes back to the reign of Justus II. His eldest son and heir, Justus III, had a brief liaison with a noble woman whose family was out of favor with the king. However, even if the family had been in good standing, the king would never have sanctioned a relationship between his son and the young woman.

"The king was looking to make an alliance with one of the northern monarchies so they could help guard Auravale's borders and thereby help protect the gold mines in the northern mountains. Nearly all the gold in Auravale comes out of those mines, and they've been raided often enough that they're a constant worry to the throne. If you remember, Kenner VI spent most of his reign waging war to protect them."

As I nod, I watch Neeve out of the corner of my eye.

He's nodding too.

"Shortly before Justus II was about to announce the marriage arrangements he'd made for his heir, one of his advisers told him about the noble woman's pregnancy. The king was furious—not just because his son had been so indiscreet, but also because his son had not been man enough to inform the king himself.

"Justus II offered to pay the woman's father a large sum of money to take her out of the kingdom until after Justus III was safely married.

"The father agreed. They did not return to Auravale until the child, a son, was eight years old. By that time, Justus III had married the woman of his father's choice and had fathered two sons and a daughter.

"The family name of the noblewoman was Darker. Her father took her illegitimate son into his home, named him Maldon Darker, and raised him with the youngest of his own children. The daughter, who had disgraced the family by bearing a bastard, was married off to a nobleman from one of the southern kingdoms and was never seen or heard from again in Auravale.

"Maldon was a different matter. He knew he was the firstborn son of Justus III. His grandfather, their relatives, and many neighbors went out of their way to remind him constantly.

"While he was a youngster, Maldon was content to live in his grandfather's home. But when Maldon reached adulthood, Justus II was an old man and close to death. Then Maldon began pressuring his grandfather to organize the other nobles to demand, when Justus III took the throne, that Maldon be recognized as the new king's firstborn and therefore his rightful heir."

"Just a minute," I say, "let me make sure I understand. Neeve's father is Justus IV and therefore the firstborn son of Justus III and his wife."

"Correct," Kaden says.

"So Maldon Darker is the half-brother of Neeve's father."

"Correct again."

"So how does all this relate to Bree-Ella Dark?"

"I'll get to that in a moment. Maldon must have been a very persuasive young man because, within months of Justus III's coronation, Maldon's grandfather led a delegation of nobles who petitioned the king and his councils to acknowledge Maldon as the new heir apparent.

"Of course, by then, Justus III had been married for many years and had fathered several children. He wasn't about to put an illegitimate son that he hardly knew above the children of his marriage.

"When he refused to name Maldon as his heir, or even acknowledge him as his son, the Darkers led a rebellion against the Crown. In other circumstances, the rebel leaders would have been executed, but Justus III was lenient toward everyone involved. I'm not sure anyone knows why."

"I've always thought it was guilt," Neeve says. "My grandfather must have known he'd wronged the noblewoman by siring a child he couldn't legally claim—and he'd wronged the child at the same time."

"Instead of death," Kaden says, "Maldon, his grandfather, many Darker relatives, some of their friends, and several of their servants were banished to an island called Hamblin Heath, which is the largest of the Natota Islands that lie off of Auravale's eastern coast. The nobles lost their titles and the Crown reclaimed their lands."

"Just a minute," I interrupt again. "I thought you were going to tell me about Bree-Ella. Her name was Dark not Darker."

"Be patient. I'm getting to that part. I just want to make sure you understand the background first."

"All right," I say. I lie down on the grass, roll onto my side, and make a pillow of my right arm. "You warned me yesterday that it was a long and complicated story. I guess you weren't joking."

"As you can imagine," Kaden resumes, "the Darkers were bitter. Hamblin Heath was an undeveloped island, and during the first year of banishment, the Darkers and their comrades had to build shelters, find fresh water, plant gardens, and raise livestock. They didn't lack for food since there has always been good fishing around the Natota Islands, but a steady diet of any one item will grow boring after a time.

"But fate is a fickle mistress. While the Darkers were digging foundations for their homes, they found a rich vein of gold. The residents of Hamblin Heath became very wealthy. Although they were still confined to the island, many Auravalians were happy to row or to fly out to the island to sell goods or to provide services for payment in gold.

"Some of the Darkers went into the business of loaning money to people from the mainland. Maldon was one of those. One day a man named Derrek Dark applied to Maldon for a loan. Derrek was the owner of a fleet of ships. He had sent them to the Eastern Islands to pick up a cargo of spices, silks, and fine linens. The ships had not returned on schedule and Derrek had bill collectors banging on his door, day and night. Derrek had several sons but only one daughter: Bree-Ella.

"Derrek was certain that his ships would return momentarily, and then he would be able to repay Maldon. Unfortunately, all but two of his ships had been sunk during a storm at sea. Derrek faced financial ruin.

"Now, when Maldon Darker was a boy, his grandfather had apprenticed him to a sorcerer named Dimneas. Maldon was magically talented—not mage-level, possibly sorcerer-level, maybe magician-level."

"How many different levels are there?" I ask.

Neeve answers, maybe to give Kaden the chance to eat some more of his milkshake. Anyway that's how Kaden uses the time.

"There are five levels of magic," Neeve says. "Everyone in our world has some magical talent. Those of us whose innate talents require no special training to develop or to control them are not counted among the five levels. The lowest level is magic-handler. The next is magic-wielder, followed by magician and then sorcerer. Mage is the fifth and highest rank. Mages almost always demonstrate their potential about the time they learn to talk.

"In your world," Neeve continues, "people often complain about the Terrible Twos, during which children begin having temper tantrums that center around their new familiarity with the word 'no.' You should see the temper tantrums that a mage-potential two-year-old can throw in our world. The only reason the fits don't have lethal consequences is because the children have limited vocabularies and undeveloped imaginations.

"As soon as toddlers throw a mage-level tantrum, the elders begin their training. By the time they're old enough to cause earthquakes and tornados, the elders have bound most of their powers. The elders gradually relax the constraints as the children acquire control. When future mages turn fourteen years old, they are assigned a mentor whose main function is to contain the youngsters' powers while they attend classes and learn how to use their gifts for good. You, Hellie, need a mentor to teach you how to handle your emotions so that no magic leaks out as it did today."

I can't think of anything to say in response.

Neeve glances over at Kaden. "Are you ready to go on with the saga of Maldon and Bree-Ella?"

"Sure." Kaden puts down his milkshake again. "The rest of what I'm going to tell you, Hellie, comes directly from the letter Bree-Ella wrote to Justus III and which my father only recently found.

"Dimneas, Maldon's mentor, had seen Bree-Ella and wanted her. She was very beautiful. Dimneas went to her father and offered a substantial sum for her. Derrek needed the money, to be sure, but he wouldn't sacrifice his daughter to get it.

"So Dimneas pressured Maldon to call in the debt that Derrek owed him. Payment had fallen due as soon his ships had docked even though there were only two of them. Under the law, if Derrek was unable to pay, Maldon could claim anything of equal value that Derrek owned.

"If Maldon would claim Bree-Ella and hand her over to him, Dimneas promised to pay whatever price Maldon asked.

"What Maldon wanted as payment was for Dimneas to kill Neeve's father, Justus IV. Maldon knew an assassination would not gain him the throne, but he at least would have revenge for his grievances.

"But Bree-Ella was a mage. It's not clear if Dimneas and Maldon were aware of it. Probably not, although they obviously sensed there was something special about her. Bree-Ella never used her powers after her initial training. She didn't have the elders bind them, but she thought they were too dangerous to be entrusted to someone as young as she was. Because she was a mage, Dimneas and Maldon couldn't keep their plot from reaching her. She saw it all in a prophetic dream."

"What did she do?" I ask.

"She ran away," Kaden says. "She came here to your world and became your progenitor."

"No," I say, shaking my head. "You've got your timetable messed up. That Bree-Ella Dark and mine can't be the same person. The earthly Bree-Ella Dark was my great-great-great grandmother. She lived and died over a hundred and fifty years ago. She couldn't be a contemporary of Neeve's father and uncle."

Kaden and Neeve exchange glances. Then they both look at Karissa.

I look at her too. "What?"

"You guys are such big cowards," Karissa says, not unkindly but with conviction.

133

Neeve takes her palm and kisses it. "We're not cowardly," he says, "just uncertain."

Karissa seems to melt when she gazes into his bright green eyes. Talk about having it bad! She raises his hand to her lips and kisses his palm. He gets the same goofy expression on his face.

I have to glance away.

When Karissa says my name, I'm almost afraid to look at her.

"Hellie," she says, "what they're nervous about telling you is that because time moves differently in our two worlds, humans and Auravalians don't grow old at the same rate. We age faster. Also, mages can play around with time, altering its course when they deem it necessary. It is possible that Bree-Ella Dark left Auravale a few years ago in their time and arrived here one hundred and fifty years ago in our time."

Involuntarily my eyes widen.

I look back and forth between her and Neeve. "But you two are going to get married. Are you going to age while he stays the same?"

"To be honest," Karissa says, "we're not exactly sure what's going to happen to us. If we planned to live full-time in this world or full-time in his, we would age at the same rate. However, if we have children, we want them to grow up to be comfortable in both places and to know both of our families. That's never happened before. Usually when humans and Auravalians marry, they must choose to live in one place or the other because of the inconvenience of traveling back and forth. This is the first time a member of the royal family has wanted to marry a human."

"I don't understand," I say. "What does being royal have to do with it?"

"Members of the royal family can pass from one world to another at will. Other people have to use portal keys, but the keys all belong to the king. They are loaned to certain families who serve the Crown, but no individual would be allowed to take a portal key out of Auravale permanently to use for his or her own purposes."

"I still don't get it," I say. "If a person can't use a key for his or her own purposes, how did Bree-Ella get here?"

"Only one of four ways that I can think of," Neeve says. "She might have had someone from the royal family take her through, she might have had someone from the royal family send her through, she might have borrowed a key and sent it back magically at the exact moment that she closed the portal, or she might have been able to create her own key."

I let that sink in for a moment.

Kaden must know this.

So if he really wants to pursue me, does that mean he's willing to spend the rest of his life on Earth or does it mean he will expect me to move to Auravale and spend the rest of my life there?

"While we're sort of on the subject," Kaden says, sounding nervous, "Hellie has unwittingly solved a mystery for us."

"What?" I ask.

But Kaden isn't looking at me. He's staring at Neeve.

"What?" Neeve says, repeating my question.

"No portal key," Kaden says, holding out his hands, palms up. "In her distress, Hellie brought me through without a key."

I have no idea why that's significant. They've told me repeatedly that I have mage-level magic. However, Neeve's mouth drops open and he stares at me like I've grown two heads.

He practically flies to his feet. "I'll be right back."

He disappears like Jerrin did. One moment he is here and the next he is gone.

Kaden looks as if he'd like to do the same thing.

He won't meet my gaze.

Chapter Twenty-five

There's no one left for me to turn to except Karissa.

My question must show because she shakes her head.

"You'll have to wait for Neeve," she says. "This is one I can't deal with."

I check the time on my cellphone. I've got less than an hour before I have to go home.

I'm starting to get antsy when Neeve, Jerrin, and another man all appear. Kaden jumps to his feet and bows from the waist.

My heart sinks.

I don't know how I pulled Kaden into our world, but it must have been the wrong thing to do.

The tension in the air is palpable.

Everyone is staring at me except Karissa, and she is focused on the new man.

I glance at him too. He must be related to Neeve and Jerrin—they look so much alike.

Another royal!

All three men are tall and fair skinned. Neeve has the lightest hair, but Jerrin's is only a shade or two darker. You'd still call him blond. The third man is brunette and obviously older than the others. He has a few wrinkles around his eyes, and there is a smattering of gray in his brown hair.

No one smiles—at least not until the new man approaches Karissa and kisses her hand. "It's good to see you again, Karissa."

"Thank you, Your Highness. May I present my friend Hellenaura Dark Powers? Hellie, this is Neeve's eldest brother and the heir apparent, Prince Skyler of Auravale."

Belatedly I start to stand.

"Please don't get up," Skyler says as he drops down beside me. "I'm very happy to meet you, Hellie."

"Thank you," I say.

Whatever rule or law or tradition I broke by bringing Kaden into this world must have been serious if Neeve felt the need to bring out the big guns. I'm close to crying from nervousness and uncertainty.

I dig my fingernails into my palms in an effort to keep the inner tears from spilling out onto my cheeks.

I can't force any more words from my mouth.

"Kaden," Skyler says, "I think your lady needs your support."

The next thing I know, Kaden is sitting on the other side of me, his arm around my waist. "There's nothing to be afraid of," he says to me gently. "They're here to help you, not to hurt you."

As I look up at Kaden, I feel all the tension flow out of me. I realize that for some reason I trust him absolutely. When did that happen?

"Why do I need help?" I ask him.

He glances over me at Skyler.

Out of the corner of my eye, I see Skyler nod.

"Unwittingly," Kaden says, "in less than a week you have performed two very powerful acts of magic. The first was when you stopped time so you could save the little girl's life. The other was when you opened a portal between our worlds and pulled me through."

"I didn't mean to do anything wrong," I say. "I'm sorry if I dragged you here against your will."

He takes my hand and kisses my palm. "You didn't drag me here against my will, Hellie. I will always want to come to you if you need me. It's just that opening a portal between worlds is usually something that even the royal family has to learn how to do in order to end up where they intend to go."

"I don't understand."

Kaden sounds infinitely patient when he answers. "Somehow you reached across time and space to a world you're unfamiliar with, found me within a country of several millions, opened a portal, and brought me here, but not just to the forest, directly to you, and not just directly to you, but to you with my arms around you.

"That was a spectacular and unprecedented use of magic, and it would have been just as spectacular and unprecedented if it had been done by a fully trained mage. Coming from an untrained girl who was raised on a world where its residents don't practice magic and don't even really believe in it, it's nearly incomprehensible. That's why Their Highnesses Skyler and Jerrin are here. Decisions about your training or your binding have to be made right now."

"Why does it take two of them?" I ask.

Prince Skyler answers. "It is protocol. If you were in Auravale, faced with the decision of accepting your powers or having them bound, you would be advised by two mages. One would point out the advantages of learning to use your powers, and the other would point out the advantages of having your powers bound. Neeve thought making you confront two mages at this time would put an unnecessary emotional strain on you. Our father sent us as the next best alternative."

If Neeve thinks facing two mages would unnerve me, they must really be scary. He can only have a vague idea about what would frighten a human, which means mages probably frighten a lot of his people too.

That's not a comforting thought.

"Before we begin," Skyler says, "have you already made a decision? Do you know what you want to do?"

I give my head a shake, remembering what Karissa said about needing good information to make good decisions.

"I don't have enough information. You want to advise me on accepting mage training as opposed to having my powers bound, but I don't even know what those terms mean. It would be like me asking you to choose between attending MIT and Oxford."

"What are MIT and Oxford?" Skyler asks.

"Exactly," I say.

He looks over at Neeve questioningly.

"They're institutions of higher learning," he answers. "I'm not sure of the differences, myself, except that MIT is in this country and Oxford is in the parent country."

"Thank you, Neeve." Then Skyler turns to me. "What information do you need in order to understand the terms?"

"I don't know—things like what should I expect from training, what will I learn to do, what kinds of resources are involved, where would I be taught, who would teach me, what is involved in having my powers bound, does it hurt, is it irreversible, what are the long-term effects—"

My cellphone alarm goes off.

When my heart stops trying to pound its way out of my chest, I tell them, "I've got to go. We'll have to finish this another time."

"No," Skyler says. "A decision must be made now, or at the least a preliminary decision. It is too dangerous for you to continue as you are."

"It's more dangerous for me not to go home on time," I say. "My mother has already bent her rules twice today. I don't want to push her over the edge."

Skyler turns away from me. "Jerrin."

"With your permission," Jerrin tells me, "I can gently modify your family's perception of the situation, but I will need access to some of your memories. With just a few—"

"No!" I exclaim. "I don't want you mucking around in my mind or the minds of my family."

Skyler and Jerrin look at Kaden.

He shakes his head. "You'll have to find another way." His arm tightens around my waist. "She is resolute."

They both nod.

I'm surprised.

They don't pressure me.

They don't argue with Kaden.

They don't ask him or Karissa to try to reason with me.

Yet, it's clear that they are still worried about what happens next.

That impresses me.

Maybe we can reach a compromise.

"Could you just put them to sleep?" I ask impulsively. "Dinner must be over by now, and they'll be relaxing."

"I could put them to sleep," Jerrin answers, "but I would still need to look into your mind long enough to locate your home and the members of your household. Although I would not need to touch any other part of your mind, I must briefly touch each of their minds to make sure they are somewhere safe so they will not be injured when sleep comes."

"All right," I say. "Go ahead." I close my eyes and wait to feel my brain being invaded. I feel nothing.

"It is done," Jerrin says. "Thank you for your trust, Hellie."

"I thank you also," Skyler says. "I will try to answer your questions now. What you can expect from training in the beginning is control. Right now you don't need to learn how to do magic. You do it instinctively. You need to learn how not to do it. The first step in your training is to be assigned a mentor to guide and protect you. He or she will give you your first lessons in control, which will teach you how to center yourself, to let go of troubling thoughts, to develop serenity, and to increase self-awareness. In time, as you master yourself and your craft, you will be given access to the resources of the Magicians Guild. That includes their library, their laboratories, their supplies and artifacts, and their membership. Naturally you will be taught at the Guild School by their faculty."

"What!" I exclaim. I shake my head emphatically. "I'm not going to Auravale to be trained. I haven't even graduated from high school yet."

Skyler and Jerrin both look at Neeve.

From their expressions I assume they're having a silent family council. It doesn't last long.

"The alternative," Jerrin says, "is having your powers bound. It takes six elders working together to block the parts of the brain that determine magic usage. It does not hurt. It is reversible for a while, but the longer the block is in place the harder it is to remove. Mage-level children have their powers bound as soon as the powers begin to manifest themselves. As the children mature, certain parts of the block are removed.

"By the time a child turns fourteen, the block should be completely gone unless the child is having trouble learning control. Even then, the greatest part of the block has been removed, and a partial block can be extended for another two years. After that, if a child has not learned control, the decision to bind his or her powers is automatic and compulsory.

"Having exceeded the age of sixteen without a binding of any kind, Hellie, you will need a strong block, and the stronger the block the shorter the amount of time it can remain in place and be removed later."

I feel frustrated.

"Still not enough information," I say.

Skyler nods tolerantly. "What else do you need?"

"It's still like trying to decide between MIT and Oxford," I assert. "I don't know anything about the good parts of magic. Most of what I've done unintentionally has been negative. I know Neeve can alter clothing and Kaden can find things and Shiane can slide down sunbeams. I suppose all of you can read minds." I point to the three brothers, since Kaden has already told me that he can't. "Other than that, all I've seen are people suddenly appearing and just as suddenly disappearing."

Without thought, I lean my head on Kaden's chest and he kisses my forehead.

I look up at him. "What do you think I should do?"

"It must be your choice," he answers. "Whatever you decide will influence the rest of your life."

Karissa, who has remained silent throughout this discussion, says, "No one has asked for my opinion, but I have one."

I sit up. "What?"

"I think the only way you'll be able to make an intelligent and informed decision is for you to have a lot more experience with magic, and I don't think you have to go to Auravale to get it." She glances around at the guys. "Speaking as an outsider, I've got to tell you that your home world is pretty darned intimidating. We humans need to be acclimated to it gradually."

"What do you suggest?" Neeve asks.

"There is one place in Shawon where Hellie could go to be around Auravalians and where she could see magic performed in a comfortable, non-threatening location."

"Brenlyn's workshop?" Neeve asks.

"Why not?" Karissa says. "It's summer vacation so there's no school to interfere. Of course, she would need a reasonable excuse for going there every day."

Neeve grins at her. "You want him to offer her a job?"

Karissa shrugs. "Since you've been practicing for the Labor Day concert with the Shawon Orchestra, you haven't been giving Brenlyn half the time you used to. I know Talitha is trying to take up the slack but—" She lets the sentence dwindle away.

Neeve addresses me. "Do you have any experience painting small objects?"

"Some," I say. "I've painted ceramics at girls' camp, and I used to make model cars and do the detailing myself instead of using the decals that came in the kits. Is that what you mean?"

"Precisely," Neeve says. "How do you think you'd like a summer job painting ceramics and miniature lead soldiers?"

"Really?" I say. "Like I would get paid, not just experience with Auravalians?"

Skyler interrupts. "If you went to the Magicians Guild School, you would receive a weekly stipend." He switches his attention to Neeve. "If Brenlyn is willing to let us use his place so a mentor could meet with Hellie for a few hours every day, the rest of the time she could help in his shop and the Guild would pay her."

"I'll see what I can arrange," Neeve says, "if Hellie is willing."

"I am." I'm trying not to grin. A real job with a real paycheck! Plus training in magic! This could turn out to be a good summer after all.

"I'm glad you're willing to give this a try, Hellie," Skyler says. "I think you are making the right decision. And you, Karissa, thank you for your suggestion. You are proving, once again, how valuable an addition you will be to our family." He gives Neeve a light punch on the arm. "How he won your heart is a mystery, but we are all grateful that he did."

We get to our feet, preparatory to going our separate ways.

Skyler nods at Jerrin, and Jerrin approaches me.

"With your permission," he says, "I can place a block on your powers. It won't be as strong as the elders would do, but it has the advantage of being temporary. It will prevent the magic from getting away from you while Neeve makes arrangements for your employment and your training."

Kaden gives my hand a little squeeze, and I find myself trusting Jerrin the same way I trust Kaden.

"All right," I say.

Jerrin places his hand on the back of my neck, captures me with his sky blue eyes, and then releases me. "That's all there is to it."

"Before all of you leave," I say, "what is the mystery that Kaden said I unintentionally solved?"

The guys turn and look away from me.

Karissa draws my attention by heaving an exaggerated sigh. "All four of you!"

Skyler looks at her sheepishly. "Admittedly, it isn't fair to ask you to do it. It's just she's a human girl and so are you, and you might handle it better than we would."

"Not in this case," Karissa says. "This has to do with your world and your history, and I'm just beginning to become familiar with them myself."

"Neeve?" Skyler asks.

"I'll try," he answers, "but it is a delicate topic."

I turn to Kaden. "Why don't you tell me? You're the one who figured it out, whatever it is."

He takes my hand and kisses my palm.

I can hardly catch my breath.

"One of the surprising things in Bree-Ella's letter to Justus III was that she was fleeing Auravale, not because she was afraid that Maldon would find a way to give her to Dimneas, but because she was pregnant and had to protect her child. She did not name the father."

Dark in the Forest: Another Modern Fairytale

"And—"

"By opening a portal to Auravale without a key, you proved yourself to be a direct descendant of the Trudimahns. There is only one member of the family who had regular contact with Bree-Ella and who could have fathered her child: Maldon."

Chapter Twenty-six

"The crazy bad guy who wanted to assassinate the king?" I shake my head. "And you think all the negative things that happen to me are just my imagination? Haven't you ever heard of heredity?"

I try to make it sound like a joke, but as the words come out of my mouth, suddenly they're not funny.

"Maybe," I say, "I'd better go home and give my mind a break. Too much information is just as bad as too little."

"How long should I wait before I rouse your family?" Jerrin asks.

"At least half an hour," I answer, "but forty-five minutes would be better."

"How can I get in touch with you," Neeve asks, "after I arrange things with Brenlyn?"

"Karissa has my phone number. Just give me a call."

"May I walk you home?" Kaden asks. "I'd like to know where you live."

"All right," I answer. "Skyler, Jerrin, it's nice to have met you. Please tell Shiane I look forward to seeing her again sometime."

"Of course," Skyler says. "Good night."

I wave and say a generalized "Bye."

Kaden and I walk from the glade side by side. When we are out of sight of the others, he takes my hand.

I don't pull away.

"Are you going to be all right?" Kaden asks.

"I hope so," I say. "I need time to think everything through."

"If you spend your days learning control with a mentor and then working for Neeve's friend, when will I be able to see you? I must see you again."

"You could always call me on the phone and ask me for a date."

He looks puzzled. "Date?"

How on earth do Auravale's teenagers get to know each other if they don't date? They can't all have arranged marriages.

"Have Neeve explain it to you."

He stops walking, so I do too.

"I wish I had better language skills," Kaden says. "What I am sensing from

143

your feelings, though, is that by using Neeve or Karissa's phone, I can call you and arrange a meeting. Is that what a date is?"

"More or less."

I start walking again. He looks as if he's not ready to move yet, but I need to get home and I don't stop. Finally he joins me.

"If I call you, then you would meet me—where? I sense not in the forest."

"If you call and ask me for a date, before we go anywhere, you will need to come to my house and meet my parents."

He looks like he just got what he wanted for Christmas. "You would let me meet your family?"

I grin at him. "Karissa told me that your people have a lot of rituals associated with relationships and how they're conducted. Dating is one of our customs, although it is too casual to be called a ritual. Part of dating, though, usually involves the boy meeting the girl's parents. In my house, it is mandatory."

"It doesn't include her meeting his family?"

"I guess that depends on the guy and his parents," I say. "Usually she meets his family before they consider anything permanent."

"Permanent?"

I'm getting embarrassed.

I don't think this is a conversation I want to have right now. "It's complicated and I don't have much time. I've got to get home. Neeve can explain it to you, or Karissa can. Or, if you want to meet in the glade tomorrow, I'll try to explain then."

"I'll see if Neeve or Karissa will explain it to me before tomorrow so we can make plans. We'll meet at noon as usual?"

"Yes."

We walk on in silence.

When we get to the hedge, I invite him through.

"It's beautiful," he says, gesturing at the landscaping.

I stand beside him and try to see it through a stranger's eyes.

Our yard is rather dazzling.

"It's as if you had an artist bring the very best of the forest here and arrange it so it still looks like the forest but better."

"This is the back of my house," I tell him, pointing. "If we go on a date, you'll need to come to the front door." I turn, intending to give him a quick little kiss, but he steps back before I can.

"I'll see you tomorrow," he says.

I'm puzzled by his abrupt departure, but I don't have time to worry about it. I sprint across the yard, unlock, open, close, and relock the backdoor as quietly as I can, and then I stand and listen. I don't hear anything except the soft sounds of the television coming from the family room.

I tiptoe around the bar that separates the kitchen from the dining room and go down a short hall. I peer into the family room. Dad is in his recliner snoring softly. Mom is lying on the couch. She shifts position.

Hoping she's not waking up yet, I slip off my shoes and run up the stairs. In record time I shuck out of my clothes and throw on a nightgown. Quickly I hang up the dress I wore to church and put my good shoes, dried mud and all, in my closet.

As I pass my desk on the way to the bathroom, I flip on my CD player. No one's going to believe I've been in my room for a significant amount of time if there's no music playing.

Of course, that's my plan—to make my folks think I've been home for hours and they just didn't notice when I came in.

I wash my face, brush my teeth, and comb out my hair.

Truth be told, I'm exhausted.

Today might not have been physically draining, but emotionally it's been a killer.

I lie down on top of my bedspread and let my mind drift away on the sweet tones of David Garrett's violin.

When I wake, someone has covered me with the afghan that is usually draped over the back of the chair in the corner. It's light outside. The clock reads 6:30.

I am wide-awake and feeling great. No way can I go back to sleep, and I don't feel like starting my chores any sooner than I have to. I put on shorts, t-shirt, socks, and my gym shoes. I grab my basketball.

This time of the morning is wonderfully invigorating. It's still cool, the air is fresh, and a breeze is coming down off the mountains.

I feel a little stiff.

I need to work out and practice more often.

As I finish my warm-up stretches, I hear Mom rattling around in the kitchen.

To get in the proper basketball frame of mind, I start by doing some fancy dribbling. Then, just for fun, I practice a few set shots from the free throw line (which is painted on the concrete). After that, I do jump shots from all different angles.

I decide to move in for a layup. I dribble until I'm almost to the basket.

Just as I'm bending at the knees for one of my super high leaps, the neighbor's cat jumps over our fence and heads straight for me.

I try to hop over the stupid thing.

I stumble instead.

Instinctively I attempt to catch myself. My knees hit the concrete first and then my right hand.

Pain!

My knees hurt like the devil and so do my hand and wrist.

I manage to get to my feet and stumble for the door.

I guess I make some kind of whimpering sound. Mom hears me and pulls the backdoor open before I get there.

Dark in the Forest: Another Modern Fairytale

I limp forward, holding my right arm next to my body with my left hand. I can feel blood slithering down my shins.

"Nathan," Mom yells.

She guides me to a chair, gets the first aid kit from under the sink, and cleans and bandages my knees.

When she reaches for my wrist, though, I pull away.

"Let me see it, Hellie," Mom says.

I shake my head. "It hurts."

Dad comes into the kitchen. As soon as he sees me, he asks, "Is it broken?"

"I don't know," Mom answers. "Hellie, you've got to let me take a look."

When she lifts my left hand away from my right, I flinch.

My right hand and wrist are covered with blood, and it's smeared all over the front of my t-shirt.

Blood from a source that isn't immediately identifiable is a red (ha ha) flag for my mother.

"I'm taking her to the ER," she says. She's still in her bathrobe and slippers. She dashes out of the room. I suppose to throw on something more appropriate.

Dad kneels down in front of me and feels my wrist and hand. He can be amazingly gentle.

"I don't think it's broken, but it's already swelling." He gets a dishtowel out of a drawer in the bar, lays it out on the counter and piles ice on it from the refrigerator freezer. He wraps it around my wrist. He gets another towel and wraps it around my hand. "I think all the blood is from your palm. It looks like you scraped it raw."

"Just so it'll match my knees," I say lightly, trying to be funny.

Dad rolls his eyes and then smiles at me.

Mom comes back dressed in jeans and a plaid shirt. She has her purse on her arm and her keys in her hand.

"Help me get her into the car," she says to Dad.

The rest of the morning goes something like this:

> arrive at ER,
> sit and wait while Mom fills out paperwork,
> sit and wait for an examination room to become available,
> feel water from melting ice soak through my t-shirt where I'm
>   holding my wrist against my stomach,
> watch wet spot on shirt grow and turn pink as melting ice
>   dilutes the blood, making it spread,
> get taken to examination room,
> sit and wait for a nurse,
> have temperature and blood pressure taken,
> answer questions about what happened,
> bite my lip instead of screaming when the nurse takes away
>   my icy dishtowel too forcefully,
> get poked and prodded,

sit and wait for the doctor,
answer more questions,
have the bandages Mom put on my knees removed,
get poked and prodded some more,
have knees re-bandaged,
have hand swabbed (Dad was right: the blood is all from
    my scraped palm [there are no protruding bones] but
    it's not just scraped raw, there's a small rock and other debris
    embedded in it),
have palm thoroughly cleaned,
have rock removed,
have palm bandaged,
get tetanus shot,
get taken to X-ray,
sit and wait until a technician comes for me,
get my wrist X-rayed in as many painful positions as the
    technician can think of,
get taken back to the examination room,
sit and wait for the doctor to return,
get assured that wrist is not broken,
am told it is badly sprained and will need to be splinted,
FINALLY get a shot for the pain,
fall asleep,
get woken up,
have wrist fitted with a removable splint,
have arm supported by a sling,
listen to doctor tell me what I can and can't do,
get printed instructions for taking care of the splint,
say goodbye to the hospital,
stop at the pharmacy,
wait in the car while Mom gets prescription filled,
arrive home,
let Mom help me out of bloody clothes and into nightgown,
have buttered toast and hot chocolate for breakfast at about 1:00,
get put to bed on the couch in the family room because Mom
    isn't sure she can get me safely up the stairs by herself,
fall asleep.

When I wake up, it's because my wrist hurts so bad.

Mom is sitting on the loveseat, which is at a right angle to the couch, watching television with the sound turned way down low.

I sit up.

I wish I hadn't.

My wrist, hand, and knees complain that they have been badly abused and plead for restraint.

Dark in the Forest: Another Modern Fairytale

"Are you hungry?" Mom asks me.

"Starved," I say. "I'm also hurting. When can I take one of those pain pills?"

"As soon as you eat something," she answers. "I made a meatloaf. Dad and Angel should be home in a few minutes, but there's no reason you should wait. I'll bring you a tray."

By the time Dad and Angel get home, I've finished eating, have taken a painkiller, and am yawning hard enough to crack my jawbones.

"Shall I help you up to your room?" Dad asks.

I shake my head.

"Would it be all right if I just stayed here? I'd like to watch a little TV before I go to sleep again."

"Sure thing," Dad says, bending over and giving me a kiss on the forehead. He hands me the TV remote.

After dinner, one by one, everyone joins me in the family room. I don't remember what we watch or when I fall asleep again.

I wake up about 2:00 in the morning.

Mom has left a dimmed lamp on in the corner.

On the coffee table I find my toothbrush, toothpaste, and floss, my CD player and a stack of my favorite CDs, a bottle of water, a snack bag containing five Ritz crackers, one pain pill, my hairbrush and comb, and my cellphone.

My slippers are on the floor.

My bathrobe is draped over the end of the couch.

I guess while I was asleep the family voted to let me take root where I am, which was very thoughtful.

First thing I do is eat the crackers and take the pain pill.

I slide my feet into my slippers.

Then with my toothbrush and related items in hand, I head for the bathroom across the hall.

Twenty minutes later I emerge feeling refreshed.

I lie back down on the couch, turn on the television, and pick up my cellphone, thinking I'll watch a little TV and play a couple of games of solitaire until I'm tired enough to go back to sleep.

When I turn on my phone, I see I have six messages.

They're all from Neeve.

The first one reads:

R u ok? Kaden is worried.

Chapter Twenty-seven

For a moment I wonder why Kaden would worry about me. Then I remember I was supposed to meet him in the woods at noon, over fourteen hours ago.

Now what?

I don't feel comfortable texting Neeve in the middle of the night.

I don't have any way of communicating directly with Kaden.

The only thing I can do is read the rest of the messages to see if they suggest anything. The next three are much like the first.

Then I get:

> Kaden knows u r home and injured.
> He's no longer worried. He's frantic.

The sixth message says:

> I got Kaden his own cellphone. His #
> is 970 555-2017. He is not going home
> till he hears from u. Please call or
> text asap.

Before I can decide what to do, my phone rings.

The caller ID reads Kaden.

I answer before it can ring a second time.

"Kaden?"

"Hellie," his voice sounds strained, "what happened? How did you get hurt?"

"I tripped over the neighbor's cat, fell, and sprained my wrist. My mother took me to the emergency room at the hospital. I was there all morning. When I got home, I was on pain medication and it put me to sleep. I'm sorry I worried you."

"I'm in your backyard. Can you come out long enough for me to see you, to assure myself that you're safe?"

"All right," I say, feeling all tingly inside as I tap *end call*.

I've got one heck of a crush on a guy I hardly know.

I put on my robe. It's lightweight nylon and matches my pale green nightie. Even though both are ankle length, I feel kind of underdressed to go outside, knowing there's a guy waiting for me.

I'm being silly, I know. I'm a lot more covered up than I would be in a bathing suit or in shorts and a tank top, and I wear those without embarrassment.

I leave the lights off as I go down the hall.

When I get to the kitchen, though, I stop.

The motion sensors should have turned on the outside lights when Kaden crossed the yard. Maybe he wasn't being literal. He must have meant that he was at the entrance to the backyard: the break in the hedge. I flip off the switch to the outside lights so I won't trip the motion detectors myself, and then I open the door.

The moonlight is almost as bright as security lights. I about jump out of my skin when I see Kaden sitting in a lawn chair at the bottom of the steps.

"Kaden," I gasp. "How—?"

In two seconds he is on the landing with his arms around me. "I didn't mean to frighten you."

I wince just a little because I'm holding my wrist against my stomach with my left hand and it's caught between his body and mine.

He pulls away quickly. "I looked up *sprained wrists* on the Internet while I waited for you to come out."

"You know how to use the Internet?"

"I do now. Neeve showed me how to access your WiFi."

I decide not to concern myself with how Neeve got our WiFi password. If his mind reading abilities include technological devices, I don't want to know. I'm having enough trouble accepting magic as a basic principle without wondering how magic and technology work together.

"Why did you look up *sprained wrists*?" I ask.

"To understand what you've been through," he says. "Are you in a lot of pain?"

"No," I say. "I've taken medication for it."

"But without the medication you would be hurting?"

"Yes."

"Will you allow me to correct that?"

"What do you mean? Correct it how?"

"My finding skills are not limited to locating lost objects. I told you I was three years into my training. What I have been learning is how to be a medical finder. I discover irregularities, such as injuries and illnesses, within the body. If the problems are simple, I can usually find the necessary curative elements in the body's chemistry and enhance them. If the problems are complex, I must

150

relay all the information I've found to a doctor.

"Based on what I learned on the Internet, I am certain I can locate the damaged ligament in your wrist and send it what it needs to heal itself. At the same time I can ease your pain by stimulating your endorphins. I believe you would be better off without taking drugs."

It never occurs to me to doubt him.

"Should I take off my cast?"

"Yes."

When I do, he has me sit on the chair he vacated earlier.

He kneels in front of me, holds my wrist on his open palms, and looks into my eyes. For several seconds I don't feel anything, but then I become aware that my wrist feels warm. The warmth moves down to my fingertips and then up to my shoulder.

It is a very pleasant warmth.

In addition, I feel my mind clear. The sluggish feeling I got from the painkiller is gone.

Kaden gets up and pulls over another lawn chair. After he sits, he takes my hand. "Do you want me to heal your scraped knees and palm?"

"I didn't tell you about those."

"I could feel the damage. It's not serious, but infection is always a concern with open wounds. It would take only a few minutes for me to help your body grow new skin over the raw areas."

I shake my head as I consider the possible consequences. "Since your people are used to magic, I suppose miraculous cures are no big deal. In my world, however, if my palm and my knees healed overnight, I'd spend the rest of my life in some laboratory while scientists tried to figure out how I did it."

He leans forward and puts a finger to his lips as if he's shushing a child. "The solution is simple," he whispers. "Don't tell the scientists."

"All right," I whisper back, "but what about my mother? She's a public information specialist. She'd probably put it in the newspapers, on Facebook and Twitter, and then sell the story to one of the major networks."

"Is she likely to check your injuries daily?"

"No," I answer after a moment's thought. "She'll probably want to change the bandages in the morning. If there's no fresh blood on them, I imagine she'll trust me to let her know if problems develop later on."

"Perfect," Kaden says. "Ordinarily my kind of healing takes only a few minutes, but I can delay it so it starts slowly and then gradually speeds up. It'll take your body a couple of days to grow the new skin, but that's still better than the normal six or seven days. Shall I do it?"

"Yes, please."

Once again he gazes into my eyes. I can feel a little tingling in my hand and knees but not the same kind of warmth I got in my wrist.

He blinks, and I know he has finished doing whatever it is that he does.

"Thank you," I tell him.

Dark in the Forest: Another Modern Fairytale

He takes my left hand, turns it over, and kisses my palm.

My heart does summersaults.

"There is something significant about that, isn't there?" I ask. "Neeve kisses Karissa's palm, and you kiss mine, but when Jerrin greeted me and Skyler greeted Karissa, they kissed the backs of our hands."

"Yes," he says, "it has a special meaning."

"What is it?"

"I'm not sure I should tell you. I don't want you to react as you did when Karissa explained the significance of fauvenell."

"I figured as much," I mutter.

"What did you figure?"

"That it's similar to fauvenell. If you tell me what it means, I promise I won't freak out. If I don't understand, I'll give you the opportunity to explain."

He kisses my palm again. "It means I love you today, I will love you tomorrow, and I will love you forever."

I remain calm. "But how can you feel that way about someone you've known for only a week?"

I like him, but I don't want to encourage him if in the end we're both going to end up hurt.

"Our people are very different from yours," Kaden answers. "Neeve has been trying to explain it to me, but I have trouble imagining that what he tells me is accurate. He says in the course of a lifetime, your people can fall in and out of love a dozen times. Is he right?"

"Not entirely," I say. "Most of us believe that finding true love is possible, but it's not always easy to identify. Sometimes we confuse it with other feelings. Those people who act like they're always falling in and out of love are probably looking for love without finding it. Love is a difficult concept for us."

"Not in my world," Kaden says. "We know that when we are born our souls are incomplete. Only by finding and uniting with the right person will each of us reach our highest potential. The recognition, the joy, and the commitment of perfectly matched souls is what we call love. It is instantaneous, and it happens only once in a lifetime. When I first saw you, my soul leaped with recognition. If you don't learn to love me, I will go back to my world and find someone whose soul is compatible with mine, and I will have a full life. But I will never reach the heights I would if you and I were together, and neither will you."

I am silent for a moment, thinking.

"What happens," I ask, "if you find someone with a compatible soul and then after you've married her, she has that instantaneous, once-in-a-lifetime recognition with someone else."

"It doesn't work that way. If we are married and have shared our first kiss, her soul will be bound to mine and mine to hers. Although I would still always love you, I would not experience the same longing that I do today. And her soul would not recognize and reach out to anyone else."

"That's the second time you've mentioned having your first kiss after you're married. Is that right? You don't kiss until you're married?"

"The kiss on the lips is what binds two souls together, so of course it must wait until after marriage. But Neeve says in your world that kissing is as casual as shaking hands. I don't understand."

"Sometimes I don't understand either," I admit.

"Have you—?" He blushes and looks away.

It doesn't take much imagination to guess what he wants to ask me.

"No," I say. "I've never had a boyfriend. I've never kissed anyone outside of my family. Do parents kiss their children in Auravale?"

"Yes," Kaden says, "but not on the lips."

I'm trying to figure out how to ask him about Justus III and his illicit relationship with the noblewoman who bore his child, and Maldon who either seduced or raped Bree-Ella, when I see a light go on upstairs in my parents' bathroom.

"Uh oh," I say. "One of my parents is up, and whoever it is will almost certainly come downstairs to check on me."

"Bye," Kaden says. "I'll call you tomorrow." Then he disappears into the night.

As I rush up the steps and into the house, I marvel at how much Kaden has changed between the time he wrote that very formal letter to me and tonight's casual farewell.

He could almost pass for human.

Chapter Twenty-eight

"You sure you're up to being alone?" Mom asks when she comes into the family room. She got up early this morning so she could cook breakfast for me. "I could take off another day of work. Heaven knows I have enough comp time."

"If you want a day off," I say, "that's up to you, but please don't waste a comp day on me. I'll probably just lie around watching TV and dozing. No big deal."

"All right," Mom says. "Call me if you need anything."

"Sure."

Within ten minutes the house is blessedly quiet.

I love my family, but sometimes it's a relief to be alone, especially on days like today when I am being less than honest, pretending I'm still in pain.

But what else can I do?

I can't tell my parents that a magical being from another world stimulated my endorphins to control my pain, fixed my sprained wrist, and sped up the healing processes in my palm and knees simply by staring into my eyes for a few seconds, can I?

Oh, and while we're on the subject, he has wings, which he can form right through his clothing and then un-form at will.

Uh huh.

Right!

My next trip to the hospital wouldn't be to the ER, it would be to the psych ward.

What my parents don't know won't hurt me.

I take off the splint.

I'm on my way upstairs to get dressed when my phone rings.

It's Kaden.

"Good morning," I say.

I sit on a step and lean against the wall.

"Good morning. How is your wrist feeling?"

"Like I never hurt it. It's amazing."

"I'll be sure to tell my master," Kaden says.

"Master?" I don't like the sound of that. It smacks of slavery.

"Those who teach us are always called master until we finish our apprenticeships."

"And then what do you call them?"

"It depends on what their names are." There is laughter in Kaden's voice. It's a wonderful sound. "May I come see you this morning?"

"Without a chaperone?"

"I thought I would bring Shiane, Neeve, and Karissa with me."

"Hmm," I say. "Is there a reason we need that many chaperones?"

"No," Kaden says. "Neeve and Shiane want to talk to you about your mage training, and Karissa is coming along for the ride." In a low aside, he asks, "Did I get that right?"

Karissa's voice in the background answers, "Perfect. You're beginning to sound like you grew up around here."

"So," Kaden says directly into the phone again, "may we come over?"

"Are you planning on walking through the woods, driving up to the front door, or just appearing in my living room?"

"It's interesting that you should ask that," Kaden says. "Part of the reason we are all coming is so Shiane and I can have our first experience riding in a car. Neeve says it can be a little unnerving at first and I should try to get used to it before you and I go on a date."

"I'm sure there's an interesting story behind that, and I look forward to hearing it, but right now I need to take a shower and get dressed. Give me an hour."

There is a slight pause before Kaden says, "That means to wait an hour before we arrive, is that correct?"

"Yes," I say.

"We will be there at approximately 9:15."

"All right. See you then."

I rush through my shower to make sure I have adequate time to fuss with my hair and makeup.

It's only after I'm dressed and trying to decide whether to wear my hair in a ponytail or let it hang loose that it occurs to me that I left the family room in a mess. I don't bother with the ponytail. I brush my hair and use a barrette on each side to sweep it back from my face.

Then I dash downstairs to fold up my blanket and stash it and my pillow in the hall closet.

I put my CD player on an end table and stack the CDs beside it. I gather up the books and magazines I asked Angel to bring down from my room, carry them over to the bookcase, and rearrange a few things so I can make room for them on a shelf. (Regardless of what I told Mom, I couldn't possibly spend an entire day staring at the TV.)

I'm just straightening the throw pillows on the couch when the doorbell rings. I don't know why I'm so nervous.

I take a deep breath and go answer the door.

"Please come in," I say.

Parked in the driveway is a brand new, shiny, cherry-red, Nissan Sentra.

Karissa leads the way—she is walking with her cane today. Neeve brings up the rear. In between them, Kaden and Shiane look a little wild-eyed.

"How was it?" I ask.

"Harrowing," Kaden says. "Humans must be extraordinarily brave to travel around in those things."

I cock my eyebrows at Neeve as I close the door.

"What did you do to them?" I ask.

He shrugs nonchalantly. "I just got the car yesterday, and I thought I might as well take it out on the highway and see how it does. Also, since Kaden and Shiane haven't seen any of Colorado except for your forest, I wanted to show them how beautiful the mountains are."

"The roads are all twisty," Shiane exclaims, "and other cars were coming at us from all directions. I had to close my eyes."

I bite my lip to keep from laughing. "I guess that means you don't have anything like cars in Auravale."

"There is no need," Kaden says. "Most of what we do is by air. When we need to transport objects too heavy for flight, we use freight wagons. Neeve says they are much like your railway trains except they run on a single track."

"We have some of those, too," I tell him. "We call them monorails."

"Monorails," Kaden repeats, adding it to his human vocabulary I suppose.

"Ours," Shiane says, "are under the control of a magician who guarantees their safety. I don't know how any of you survive a day out on those roads."

"Now that you mention it," I say, "it is kind of miraculous, especially in the winter when they're covered with ice and snow."

Kaden and Shiane both shudder.

Neeve just laughs at them.

"This way," I say, ushering them toward the family room.

Kaden and Shiane stop to take a look at the photographs in the hall.

The pictures tell the story of Angel's and my lives from birth to this year's Spring Prom.

"I can see how you became confused," Shiane says to Kaden. "On the surface they look amazingly alike, but once you got close enough to her, you couldn't have had any doubts."

"You're right, but there for a while I thought I had lost my mind or else she had lost hers."

"I wish you'd have brought me with you."

"Without your father or Skyler giving you leave?" Kaden says, shaking his head. "I was confused not stupid."

"Oh, I can handle them," Shiane says lightly.

Kaden puts his arm around her shoulders and gives her a little squeeze.

"You probably could, but I'd prefer to err on the side of caution."

I watch the interchange with interest, but Karissa and Neeve don't pay any attention. I wonder if Shiane really has her father and eldest brother wrapped around her little finger, or if maybe it's just her personality to want to be in on everything so no one takes her seriously.

When we get to the family room, Karissa and Neeve sit together on the loveseat, but Kaden and Shiane wander around looking at things.

"This is the first human dwelling I've ever been in," Shiane says to me. "Brenlyn and Talitha's place is only half a house. This room feels very comfortable, like it's a place where people can really relax." She glances at Neeve. "It feels a little like Mother's parlor, doesn't it?"

"Yes, now that you mention it," he answers, "it does."

"I'll be happy to show you the whole house later," I say, "but right now I'm curious. Kaden said you wanted to talk to me about mage training."

Shiane laughs a happy tinkling sound. "You are going to fit right into our circle. Everyone has to call me back to task because I'm—what was that new word you taught me, Karissa?"

"I said you act like a flibbertigibbet," Karissa answers, "but I also told you I didn't believe it. I still don't."

"Flibbertigibbet!" Shiane repeats. "That's a great word. I just love it."

"Well, flibbertigibbet," I say, "come sit down and tell me what I need to know about mage training."

I go sit in the middle of the couch.

Kaden sits beside me on my right, and Shiane sits on my left.

"My friend, Brenlyn," Neeve says, "has agreed to let you use his workshop in the mornings, which is when he usually goes out on business calls. Jerrin has already found you a mentor." He points to my splint, which I left on the end table beside my CD player. "Kaden said he fixed your wrist, so I assume you don't need that anymore."

"Oh, I forgot," I say, jumping up, grabbing it, and putting it back on. "I might not need it, but I've got to pretend I do for at least a week. Even then, Mom might insist on taking me back to the doctor to make sure I'm not being premature when I take it off."

"You can't wait a week to start your training," Shiane says. "The block Jerrin put on your powers will start weakening tomorrow."

"Unfortunately," I say, "my parents aren't going to believe that anyone offered me a job painting ceramics while I have a splint on my wrist."

"If someone called you on the phone to offer you a job," Kaden says, "he wouldn't know about the splint."

I pat his hand while I shake my head. "My parents know I would never accept a position under false pretenses."

"Would you have to tell your parents the job was painting ceramics?" Shiane inquires.

"They'll ask, and I'm a terrible liar, especially when I have to answer a direct question."

"Neeve," Kaden says, "I know Jerrin is the mind control expert in your family, but isn't there something you could do to—"

"Wait," I say. "We've already gone through this. I don't want anyone meddling with my family's minds."

"Don't worry, Hellie," Neeve says. "My mental touch isn't delicate enough for me to alter thoughts and beliefs without causing significant damage."

"You're all making this more difficult than it needs to be," Karissa says. "Hellie, right now Brenlyn's wife is trying to paint miniatures, mind the store, and keep house so Brenlyn can do his repair work.

"Even if your wrist was actually damaged and you couldn't paint, you could still sit out front, answer the phone, greet customers, and possibly work the cash register, which would free up Talitha so she could do other things. You wouldn't have to tell your folks more than that Brenlyn and Talitha need you to help out any way you can."

Not bad, I think, and it has the advantage of being true.

Now all I need is for Neeve to fill in the blanks so the story comes out smooth and truthful when I tell my parents. "Neeve, are you here on behalf of your friend to offer me a job?"

"Yes," Neeve says, taking my cue. "Since I am unable to put in the hours helping my friend, Brenlyn, in his shop the way I used to, I have offered to find him a substitute. When you mentioned you weren't working this summer but have had experience painting ceramics, I told Brenlyn about you.

"If you accept the position, you'll work from 8:30 a.m. until 5:00 p.m. with half an hour for lunch and a fifteen-minute break in the morning and the afternoon. You'll start out at minimum wage while you're learning. If you're good enough, he'll consider giving you a raise after a couple of weeks. He'd like you to start tomorrow, and I will be happy to pick you up and drive you over so I can introduce you."

I grin at him. "You're good. How much of that did you take from my mind?"

"A little," he admits, "but you were practically shouting your questions at me. Did I cover everything you need to know?"

"Not quite. I need to know Brenlyn's full name, the name of his business, and the address and phone number. Also, it would be a good idea for him to give me a call to confirm everything you just said. I'm sure my parents will ask if—"

My cellphone rings.

The caller ID reads Quick Fix.

"Hello?"

"Hellie, my name is Brenlyn Oaks. I'm a friend of Neeve's."

Then he repeats everything Neeve told me, plus he explains a little bit about the kind of work he does.

I make a point of telling him that I injured my wrist and have to wear a splint for at least a week. He responds by telling me almost word for word what Karissa said about how I could still help them.

"May I expect you tomorrow?" Brenlyn asks.

"Yes," I tell him. "I look forward to meeting you."

"Until then, goodbye."

Chapter Twenty-nine

"I've got to tell you," I say to Neeve, "I'm pretty uncomfortable with all this mind reading stuff, but I'll admit it speeds things up. Now that we have my employment status arranged, tell me what to expect tomorrow."

"How scared are you?" Shiane asks me.

I feel my pulse speed up. "I'm about as scared as I can be without passing out. When any of you say the word 'mage,' I feel like I'm about to be struck by lightning. I want to run and hide under my bed."

"Karissa had an idea," Neeve says. "She thought it might be easier on you if you didn't have to face a mage alone. Would it help decrease your anxiety if there were someone with you?"

"Sure it would," I answer, "but I'd feel guilty if one of you changed your schedule just to babysit me. I can tough it out somehow."

"If you have to put your energy into toughing it out," Neeve says, "you won't be able to concentrate adequately. Shiane is almost fourteen. Your mentor is willing to begin her training a few months early if her presence will help calm you."

I reach over and squeeze Shiane's hand. "That's really kind of you, but I need you to tell me the truth. Disregarding my needs, is starting early a good thing or a bad thing for you?"

"Oh, it's a good thing," Shiane says. "I'm having more and more trouble keeping the magic in, but the Magicians School can't give me my own mentor until I'm fourteen. It has something to do with their bylaws, but there is nothing that prohibits them from letting me share a mentor with someone who is the right age. Do you mind sharing?"

"I can't think of anything I'd like more."

When Mom gets home from work, I'm sitting in the family room with a TV tray, paper, and pen in front of me.

"What are you doing?" she asks.

"Practicing writing with my left hand."

"Why?"

"I have some exciting news," I answer, "but I want to announce it at dinner

160

if that's okay."

She comes over and sits down beside me. "You wouldn't like to give me a hint, would you? Exciting is such an ambiguous word since it can refer to happiness, provocation, or agitation."

I grin at her and point to my mouth with my index fingers. "Smiling. No provocation. No agitation."

"It was worth a try," she says, laughing as she stands up. "It worked when you were little."

By the time Dad and Angel are home, Mom almost has dinner ready. She's making shrimp stir-fry because it's quick and a family favorite.

As soon as we're all seated and have food on our plates, Mom says, "Hellie has some news to share."

Everyone looks at me.

"I've got a job. I start tomorrow."

Like Angel, I'm not much good at leading into things gradually.

"When did this happen?" Dad asks.

"Where and with whom?" Mom says overlapping Dad.

"How?" That's from Angel.

"I'll start at the beginning," I tell them. "Sunday when I was in the woods, I bumped into some friends."

"Does everyone around here hang out in our forest?" Dad snaps. "First this Peter Bradley friend of Angel's and now these friends of yours! Who are they?"

"Remember the Spring Concert at school?" I say. "A tall, blond guy played the violin. We all commented on how remarkable it was for someone his age to be so good."

"I remember him," Angel says. "He played at the Christmas Pageant too. He was gorgeous."

"He still is," I tell her, "and—"

"Damn it," Dad says, "do you girls always meet your male friends in the woods?"

I can't just ignore Dad's question, but there's no way I can answer it honestly considering how often I've met Kaden there. Quickly I think up a convincing cover story, one that might actually be true for all I know, but which doesn't include one single lie.

"Neeve doesn't come to the forest to meet me. His girlfriend was in a car accident a couple of years ago and has been in a wheelchair. Now she's learning how to walk again and needs to practice on a variety of surfaces. She uses a cane for balance. I didn't think you'd mind."

Dad doesn't say anything but he looks mollified.

"Sunday, they were the ones I had fast food with instead of barbequing with the family."

Mom looks as if she wants to say something, but she stops herself.

"While we were eating," I continue, "I mentioned I don't have a summer job, and Karissa—that's Neeve's girlfriend—said Neeve has been practicing so much for the Labor Day concert with the Shawon Orchestra that he hasn't been putting in the time at his job that he should. He paints ceramics and lead soldiers for the owner of Quick Fix Repair Shop. Karissa suggested that maybe I could take over Neeve's position so he can concentrate on his music.

"Neeve, Karissa, and Neeve's little sister, Shiane, came over this morning for a few minutes." I don't include Kaden. I'm not ready to try to explain him to my family. "Neeve told me that he'd given my name and phone number to his boss. They were still here when his boss called and offered me the job.

"I told him I damaged my wrist and have to wear a cast for a week or two, and he said not to worry. Right now his wife is filling in for Neeve. He said if I could answer the phone, take messages, and ring up sales tickets on the cash register, it would help them a lot. He said when my wrist is better, then I can paint too."

Dad frowns at me. "Why does a repairman need someone to paint ceramics and lead soldiers?"

"Brenlyn—that's the boss's name—said that they have a couple of showcases at the front of the shop where they display things that he makes when business is slow. He has a kiln in his workshop. Besides ceramic figurines, he makes dollhouses and miniature furniture. His wife has a greenhouse and does floral arrangements."

"Sounds like a fun place to work," Angel says, "and you're so good with your hands."

"Neeve told me the shop makes almost as much money from selling the homemade items as it makes from the repair work."

"Where is this place?" Dad asks.

"I wrote the address and phone number down for you. I'll get it after dinner. Oh, Neeve offered to pick me up in the morning and drive me to work so he can introduce me to Brenlyn and his wife."

The rest of the dinner conversation progresses predictably. After a few more questions, Mom and Dad start discussing the things that happened to them today, and I'm left to finish eating in peace.

In the morning I wake up early.

My stomach hurts.

I decide to go downstairs and have a bowl of cereal before I take my shower. I stop at the bottom of the steps because I hear my folks talking in the kitchen.

"It's just too pat for me," Dad is saying. "I think I should follow them to that shop and check it out."

"You're overreacting," Mom says. "You wouldn't follow her to work if she answered an ad in the paper and was offered a job."

"Don't you think it's a little too coincidental?"

"To me it sounds like a bit of good luck, and heaven knows Hellie deserves some. If you want to undermine her confidence, following her to work would be a good way to start."

Dad's voice is subdued when he responds. "I don't know why I feel so protective of Hellie. She's strong and smart and independent. In a lot of ways she's stronger than Angel, but I still feel like I need to pack her in bubble-wrap and store her in a closet to keep her safe."

"Yet, when I wanted to curtail her time in the forest, you fought me."

"That's another thing I don't understand," Dad says, "but I know to keep her out of the woods would wound her spirit. You were right when you said she's like my mother. There is something in the forest that feeds her soul the same way it did Mom's."

"The magic?"

"Who knows?" Dad says. "When you're feeling down, you replenish yourself by reading *Freckles* or *Girl of the Limberlost* for the hundredth time. Angel does it by surfing the Internet. I go golfing with Marv. Maybe that's the same kind of magic Hellie experiences in the forest."

"Are you going to follow her this morning?"

"No. You were right. I was overreacting and well on the way to becoming overprotective."

There's a long pause and I know Dad is kissing Mom.

"Thank you, once again," Dad says, "for keeping me on the straight and narrow."

"You're a good man, Nathan," Mom says. "The girls and I are lucky to have you."

Feeling secure and loved, I turn around and go back to my room.

Chapter Thirty

When Neeve introduces me to Brenlyn and Talitha, my first thought is that they should be a Hollywood power couple. By now I should realize that Auravalians are tall and good looking, but these two catch me off guard, especially Talitha. She is absolutely gorgeous.

She has what Grandma Powers called a waspish figure, meaning well rounded on the top and bottom with a tiny waist in between. She has masses of curly red hair down to her fanny, long legs, a movie star smile, and a flawless complexion to go with her exquisite facial features.

Brenlyn is a blue-eyed blond and the perfect handsome match for her. They are both older than Kaden and Neeve. In earthly terms, they look to be in their early thirties.

Their shop is in a square, brick house in a residential area near Shawon's only mall. There are a few other small businesses in the same neighborhood.

Shortly after the introductions, Brenlyn and Talitha excuse themselves to go make a couple of house calls.

Neeve leads me down a short hall to the back of the house where there is a huge room that is obviously Brenlyn's workshop. The walls are covered with shelves full of all the tools and hardware and supplies that a general handyman might need. There are two worktables in the middle of the floor and a kiln in the back corner.

Sitting on stools beside the larger workbench are Shiane and Jerrin.

"I'll leave you now, Hellie," Neeve says. "I'll pick you up at 5:00 and take you home."

"Thank you," I tell him.

After he goes, I glance over at Jerrin.

"No mentor?" I ask.

"Actually," Jerrin says, "there were quite a few volunteers, but after some consideration, I decided I was the best candidate. I convinced my father and the Council to let me come."

"You're a mage?" I'm surprised because I expected mages to be fifteen feet tall and to have lightning shooting out of their eyes from the way the guys

164

talked about them on Sunday.

"Yes," Jerrin says, "but we sort of play it down. I'm the first confirmed full mage the royal family has produced. Shiane will be the second."

"And Skyler?" I ask.

"He's a sorcerer," Jerrin answers, "and that's bad enough."

"I don't understand. Why is that bad?"

"The king has two councils, one of nobles and one of mages. Together they make sure the king acts within his own laws. No one wants a king who can bypass the councils' advice and start vaporizing dissenters in a fit of temper."

"Could Skyler do that?"

"He would have no problem with the Council of Nobles, but mages are stronger than sorcerers. Skyler would have to ambush the members of the Council of Mages one at a time, and he'd still need a fair amount of luck to overwhelm even a couple of them before they organized enough to bring him down."

"What about you?" I ask.

"It would depend on how much time I had to prepare, how completely I blocked my thoughts, and how quickly I acted. The Council of Mages has a couple of pre-cogs on it. If I attacked suddenly and kept the Council confused and disorganized, and if I could keep my mind blank enough that the pre-cogs didn't learn my plans, I might have a chance of defeating enough of them to make the others surrender. However, I am smart enough not to try."

I shiver. "How can your people prevent the mages from taking over?"

"They can't. Mages police themselves. That's why training starts as soon as a child begins showing mage-level skills. That's why the first lessons are always about control. And that's why it is mandatory for mage-level skills to be permanently bound if a mage-potential child hasn't learned control by the age of sixteen."

Another thought occurs to me.

"What about your father?" I ask. "He must have some pretty strong magic in his heredity or he couldn't have fathered two mages. Or don't genetics work that way in your world?"

Shaking his head slightly, Jerrin says, "It's going to be a pleasure teaching you, Hellie. Few Auravalians have made the connection between my father's powers and the inherited powers of his children. His training only went as high as magician-level, but he probably would have qualified as a mage if the Guild had retested him after he reached puberty. His powers came in late, and my grandfather concealed the truth."

I nod. "Because no one wants a king who can vaporize people?"

"That's right," Jerrin says, rewarding me with a nod and a smile. "Well, we'd better get started."

I go over and give Shiane a hug. "Thanks for being here."

She hugs me back.

Then we both turn to Jerrin.

Dark in the Forest: Another Modern Fairytale

"The first thing we're going to do," he says, "is practice relaxing. It is important that you handle magic with as much calmness of mind and body as possible. The more agitated you are, the greater the odds are that you'll lose command of your powers. I want you both to select a mat and spread it on the floor. Then take off your shoes and lie down."

I hadn't paid any attention to the diverse articles stacked on the table at Jerrin's elbow. Now I go over and look. Among a variety of other things, there are five or six mats. I can't see any differences in them except color, so I choose a blue one. Shiane picks yellow. Jerrin takes the green one.

Shiane and I spread our mats side by side. While I'm removing my shoes, I notice that Jerrin has already taken his off.

He sits down on his mat in lotus position. (That's where you sit cross-legged, but instead of your feet being under your knees, they're on top of your thighs with the soles pointing upward. Mom can do it. It makes my hips, knees, ankles, thighs and calves hurt just to watch her. I hope it's not a requirement for all mages to learn how to sit like that.)

"It's not," Jerrin says, "but you might choose to learn it later."

I stare at him. "You read my mind. Kaden told me there are rules of conduct involved with going into a person's mind, so people don't do it without permission."

"He's correct, and I apologize for not explaining. As your mentor, it is my responsibility to ensure that you don't lose control of your powers. To do this, I must be aware of you, of your thinking, and of your feelings as much as I possibly can. I am not delving into your mind. I have merely opened myself up to hear whatever you project toward me."

"Are you doing the same thing with Shiane?"

"Not quite, but similar. She has to voluntarily lower her mental shields. As a potential mage, she has been taught since she was just a few years old not to project her thoughts. Now, both of you, lie down and get comfortable so we can start."

As soon as Shiane and I have squirmed around enough to have found all of the lumps in our mats and have figured out how to avoid them, Jerrin starts talking.

"Close your eyes and clear your mind. Think of nothing."

Have you ever tried not to think about anything?

As soon as I try to clear my mind, suddenly there are a million things that pop into my head, everything from "Did I remember to brush my teeth after breakfast?" to "I wonder what time lunch is" to "What should I major in when I get to college?"

It's the most bizarre experience.

"Sometimes," Jerrin says in a soft, soothing tone, "it helps to visualize a scene that you find particularly relaxing: clouds drifting across a blue sky, sunlight reflecting on a glass-smooth pond, a beautiful flower swaying gently in a breeze. It works the best if you choose a scene that is silent: still water as opposed to a rumbling waterfall, a gentle breeze rather than a howling wind."

In my mind I picture myself on a high mountain peak. I stare at a moonless night sky where the stars are so bright against the blackness that they blind me to everything else.

I am only vaguely aware when my body relaxes and my thoughts dissolve.

The universe and I are one.

Silence.

Peace.

Nothing.

Far, far away I hear a sound.

Soft.

Gentle.

It is a voice.

Only by concentrating can I identify individual syllables.

I begin to sort out words.

"Hellie, come back to us now. Let the energy of the stars flow into you. Feel their warmth on your skin, in your muscles, in your organs, and in your mind."

I recognize the voice as Jerrin's.

He continues speaking.

"Flex your toes and your fingers. Wiggle your ankles and your wrists. Gently shift the position of your arms and legs. With every movement you will feel more and more energy gathering within your body. Rotate your shoulders. Twist at the waist. Stretch. When you feel fully alert, sit up."

It takes me a while to comply.

I was far away.

Coming back is difficult.

"Take a few deep breaths," Jerrin says. "It will help."

I do, and it does.

The extra oxygen in my blood helps clear my head.

I yawn so hard my whole body quivers.

I sit up.

I glance to the side and see that Shiane is watching me. She gives me a thumbs-up. I wonder who taught her that or if it is some kind of universal gesture of approval.

I grin at her and shrug, not knowing what the thumbs-up is for.

"How do you feel?" Jerrin asks me.

"Strange," I say. "Is it possible to feel invigorated and relaxed at the same time?"

"Yes," Jerrin says, "and sometimes that is the ideal state for a mage. In a crisis, you want your body ready to spring into action, if required, while your mind remains at peace. Do you have any idea how long you were communing with the stars?"

"A few minutes," I say. "Maybe ten."

Dark in the Forest: Another Modern Fairytale

"Over half an hour," Jerrin corrects me. "I started trying to rouse you at twenty minutes."

I frown. "Is it normal to lose time like that?"

"In the beginning," Jerrin says. "As you practice, however, you'll be able to reach that same state of relaxation without losing yourself. In fact, eventually, you will be able to evoke that sense of inner peace instantaneously while keeping your body and mind on high alert."

"I'll have to take your word on that," I say skeptically.

"Good," he says, obviously taking me literally. "Since I'm your mentor, it's important that you accept what I tell you. Now, both of you need to get up and walk around for a few minutes."

In the corner opposite the kiln is one of those water dispensers with the big bottles on top and a red spout for hot water and a blue one for cold. Next to it is a little table that holds a jar of instant coffee, a box of tea bags, a can of hot chocolate mix, powdered creamer, and a sugar shaker. Hot and cold paper cups are in tubular dispensers attached to the wall above the table.

I fill a cup with cold water and sip at it while I look out the window at Talitha's greenhouse. Splotches of bright colors, including blue and purple, are visible through lightly tinted glass, and I wonder what kinds of flowers she's growing in there.

When I finish my drink and dispose of the cup, I go back and sit down on my mat. Shiane and Jerrin are already on theirs.

"Every evening before you go to bed," Jerrin says, "you both need to practice clearing your mind and relaxing your body. Hellie, you went so easily into your starry night that I suggest you continue using it as your focus. Shiane, you need to find something more peaceful than flying through rain clouds. I could feel the little bursts of excitement every time you let a gust of wind hit you."

I can feel Shiane struggle not to overreact to the criticism. She really is a very sensitive child. Jerrin obviously knows it.

His tone becomes so soft and sweet it's almost a croon. "Shiane, it often takes several attempts to find the right focus. Hellie is more than three years older than you are, and she has obviously practiced calming herself by visualizing the stars before."

Shiane glances over at me. "Have you really?"

"Often," I say. "I learned to do it by stargazing with my grandmother. Next to wandering through the forest, stargazing was her favorite activity. We'd lie on a blanket in the backyard on the nights of the new moon and try to picture life among the stars in the perfect silence of space."

"I've never done anything like that," Shiane says. "Isn't it hard to imagine silence?"

"I don't know," I tell her. "I don't see how it could be any harder than imagining flying through rain clouds and letting the wind hit you."

She grins at me. "I guess not."

"You need to remember," Jerrin says, "that you two are not in competition. You're both here to learn. Some things will be easier and some things will be harder for each of you. I don't expect you to learn at the same rate."

He turns to the side and picks up a wooden ball. It looks like it's from an old croquet set.

"Hellie," he says, "obviously you can grab hold of a great deal of magic when you feel the need, as exhibited by your halting time and calling Kaden to you. But most magic needs to be done with a gentler touch. Shiane, I need you to help me demonstrate. Catch this without using your hands. Hellie, watch her and see if you can sense how she does it."

He tosses the ball to Shiane.

It stops before it reaches her and hovers two feet above the floor.

"Did you feel it?" Jerrin asks me.

"I sensed something," I say. "It was really quick. Will you do it again?"

For the next several minutes, Jerrin and Shiane play catch without either one of them ever making contact with the ball.

As I follow the movement with my eyes, I shake my head. They make it look so easy. I exhale loudly through my nose. I'm more than a little jealous.

How can I stop time and open portals between worlds and yet not be able to figure out how to catch a croquet ball?

"What am I supposed to be feeling?" I ask Jerrin in frustration.

"Maybe you can't sense it yet unless you need to," he says. "Catch."

He throws the ball at me overhand like a major league baseball pitcher.

Chapter Thirty-one

I don't have time to think.

I react like a batter facing a fastball.

I slam it with an imaginary bat, putting all of my strength behind the swing. To my horror, the ball sails straight for the window overlooking Talitha's greenhouse.

I close my eyes and wait for the sound of shattering glass.

It doesn't come.

When I open my eyes, the ball is suspended in the air a few inches from the window.

"We definitely need to work on your ability to handle magic with a lighter touch," Jerrin says with a laugh.

"Do you think that was funny?" I yell. "You scared me half to death. And if you'd been a split second slower stopping the ball, it would've crashed straight through the window and into Talitha's greenhouse."

I'm so angry I'm near tears.

"I'm your mentor," Jerrin says. "Do you really think I would let anything bad happen to you or through you?"

"I don't know what you'd do," I cry. Adrenaline has my nervous system revved up to the point that I want to punch something. "It looked to me like you were trying to smash the ball into my face."

"My job is to guide and protect you while you learn control," Jerrin tells me in a reassuring tone, "and that is what I will do. By throwing the ball to you unexpectedly, I hoped to help you recognize the feel of your magic. So far, all of your experiences have been instinctive. Before we can work on establishing the correct mental and emotional states, you must recognize when you are using or are about to use your powers. I certainly have no intention of teaching you to act out of fear."

No, I suppose not.

Then I am hit by a sudden revelation.

"Oh, my gosh!" I exclaim with a gasp. "I understand it now. When you talk about—"

Jerrin holds up his hand to me.

"Shiane," he says, "Hellie and I need to have a moment alone. Since I don't have an office here," he makes a sweeping gesture with his hand as he glances around the workshop, "I must ask you to give us a few minutes of privacy. Why don't you go look at Talitha's flowers?"

"You're not going to yell at her, are you?" Shiane asks. "She's human, and she's doing the best she can."

"No, I'm not going to yell at her," Jerrin says. "I caught the hint of a private thought that we need to discuss."

"All right," Shiane says.

She gets up and starts for the backdoor.

Then she pauses and turns to me. "He's really very nice, and you can trust him. But if you think you need me, you just shout. I'll come running."

I give her a reassuring smile. "I'm sure I'll be fine."

I don't know if that's true.

I'm experiencing about equal amounts of fear and curiosity.

As soon as Shiane closes the door behind her, Jerrin says, "You started to describe something you suddenly understood. Would you please complete your thought now?"

It takes me a second to recapture the moment.

"Oh," I say. "I just realized what you mean by control. When you talk about a mentor teaching control, you're not talking about controlling the *how-to* of using magic, you're talking about controlling the *when-to* of using magic.

"It didn't make any sense to me before. I couldn't understand why you would bind a toddler's powers and then release them as he gained control over them. I mean, how could he learn to use them if they're blocked? But you don't bind the magic, do you? You bind the infantile temperament that would misuse the powers. That's why mages begin working with children as soon as their powers become apparent, they're teaching impulse-control. Right?"

I don't wait for him to answer.

I'm on a roll and I plow forward.

"Your job isn't to make sure I understand the mechanics of doing magic correctly. It's to make sure I understand the ethics, the responsibilities, and the morality of doing it at all. Mage-level control isn't about being powerful enough to vaporize people, it's about being strong enough emotionally NOT to vaporize people."

"I knew you were quick," Jerrin says. "Although I will teach you the mechanics, as you call them, you're right, my main function is to make sure you will use your powers responsibly."

"That's why," I continue, "if a person hasn't learned control by the age of sixteen, the elders permanently block his powers. The assumption is, if self-control and a sense of morality haven't developed by then, they probably never will."

"Correct."

171

Dark in the Forest: Another Modern Fairytale

"But why did you send Shiane away?" I ask. "Surely she needs to understand this too."

"A mage has access to boundless quantities and varieties of magic. Each young mage must figure out for himself or herself that using that kind of power must be accompanied by total and complete acceptance of responsibility. No amount of teaching and no amount of lecturing can instill that value. It either comes from within or it doesn't come at all. Hopefully Shiane will have her own moment of insight."

I sit and consider the implications of accepting total and complete responsibility for my actions, for any of my actions.

I shudder at the thought.

The backdoor opens and Shiane comes in.

Jerrin must have called her using the family telepathy.

I'm taking a breath, but I catch myself mid-inhalation.

If I inherited the Trudimahn ability to open doorways between worlds, did I inherit their ability to read minds?

When I asked Neeve how I should greet Jerrin when we first met, was I able to speak to him because of his abilities or because of mine?

Finally, I remember to breathe.

When I glance up at Jerrin, he's grinning.

Welcome to the family, he thinks at me.

I feel a momentary panic.

I used to know who I am.

Now I'm so confused I just want to run away and hide somewhere.

You are a person of two worlds, Jerrin tells me. *It won't be easy for you because you must hide your true nature from your human family and friends in order to protect them from themselves and to protect you from those who would try to use you if they knew. But you also have an Auravalian family, and you can count on us. We will be your support.*

Shiane sits down beside me.

She leans her head on my shoulder like she did that first afternoon when she acted as chaperone so Kaden and Neeve could explain the Dark's family history to me.

"You know," she says, "being one of us isn't so bad. You'll still have your human life, it's just now you have a whole new group of people to love you."

"And a whole new set of skills to master," Jerrin says, "but you might decide that they're not so bad either."

All of a sudden I feel like I did when I admitted to myself that I made time stand still at Happy Hands Daycare Center.

I know I have power.

I know I can use it.

The croquet ball is still suspended in front of the window where Jerrin left it. I reach for it with invisible hands, pluck it from the air, and drop it gently into his lap.

"This is how I feel when I use magic," I tell him.

"Yes, it is," he agrees smilingly.

For the next little while, we play hands-free three-cornered catch.

It's fun, and surprisingly I don't fumble the ball even once.

Somehow our game of catch evolves into keep-away with Shiane in the middle. Jerrin and I sort of dance around her as we magically pass the ball back and forth. Then all of a sudden, I feel Shiane snatch up the ball right before it reaches Jerrin. She tosses it to me and darts to the side so he is now in the middle.

Of course, she and I know that Jerrin can take the ball away from us anytime he wants, but he plays along for a while.

When he decides to end the game, the ball simply disappears and then reappears on the table.

After taking another short break, we relax on the mats again.

We talk about magic.

Jerrin thinks up different scenarios that a person might encounter either here or in Auravale and asks us whether a magical or a mundane response would be the better choice in those circumstances. During the subsequent discussions, I learn a lot about what is possible and what isn't. Magic isn't always the best solution. It has limitations.

Brenlyn and Talitha come back around noon.

"See you tomorrow," Shiane says right before she and Jerrin vanish.

I feel awkward around Brenlyn and Talitha for all of five seconds.

They are exceptionally nice.

We sit outside at a picnic table in the shade of a big tree while I eat the lunch I brought with me and they munch on fresh fruits and vegetables.

At 1:00 we open the shop.

A heavy, frazzled-looking woman is waiting outside the door with a vacuum cleaner in her hand. Two children, about five and seven years old, wait in the backseat of a car with their noses pressed to the window.

Brenlyn greets the woman by name.

"What did Benny try to vacuum up this time?" he asks.

"A dead bird that the cat carried in. Do you think you can get it out?"

"Of course," Brenlyn says.

"You're a lifesaver. My husband said I absolutely cannot buy a new vacuum cleaner this year."

While Brenlyn and the woman talk, Talitha shows me how to tag an item, how to write up a receipt for the customer, and where to put anything that Brenlyn needs to get to right away.

"An appliance that contains something that could decompose and smell up the place has automatic priority," Talitha tells me.

When we return to the front of the shop, Brenlyn is just saying goodbye to the woman.

After she leaves, I ask, "Does that happen often? Clogging a vacuum cleaner with a dead bird?"

"In that family," Talitha answers, "anything is possible."

"The children are very creative," Brenlyn says. "At Easter this year, Mrs. Cline told the boys they were old enough to help her color Easter eggs, so the little guys got up early the next morning and tried coloring raw eggs with their crayons. After they broke about half a dozen, Benny decided he'd better clean up."

"Not with the vacuum cleaner!" I exclaim.

"Oh yes," Brenlyn says. "It was about the worst mess I've ever tackled. Even with magic it was a nightmare."

"So," I say, "you can't just wave your hands and magically fix something?"

"I can if it's simple enough," he answers, "but eggs are complicated. They're slippery when wet and hard when dry, which means they can ooze into all sorts of places and then solidify. When you mix them with the dirt and debris collected in an ordinary vacuum cleaner bag, you have a catastrophe. I had to remove the muck in stages."

Chapter Thirty-two

Between customers, Talitha shows me around the shop, familiarizing me with the set up and detailing the types of jobs they do.

Apparently Brenlyn prefers to work on things that he can do manually rather than magically.

He particularly enjoys fiddling with mechanical things: old-time pocket watches, grandfather clocks, antique wind-up toys, keyed or combination locks, and anything else with cogs, wheels, and/or springs.

Apparently he has quite a reputation for being able to fix anything mechanized and has had people ship items to him from around the world.

His next favorite things are electrical. He will undertake almost any challenge involving household or commercial appliances.

In addition, Talitha says, over the years he's repaired statuary, fountains, sprinkler systems, furniture, lawnmowers, book-bindings, botched do-it-yourself carpentry, and just about anything else a person can break. He'll even repair electronic devices like computers and smartphones if he's bored enough.

If he doesn't have other projects to work on, he designs new doll houses and furniture or he sculpts cottages, animals, or people and then makes plaster molds of them so he can cast new ceramic or porcelain figurines.

By the time Talitha has told me about half a dozen tough jobs that Brenlyn has conquered, I'm ready to believe he could fix a broken heart and mend a broken promise.

Talitha is demonstrating how she paints lead soldiers (which apparently Brenlyn doesn't make but gets from suppliers) when Neeve arrives to take me home.

"How did it get to be 5:00 so fast?" I exclaim.

"Time flies when you're having fun," Neeve says. (Karissa must have taught him that.)

When Neeve pulls up in front of my house, I am startled to see both of my parents sitting casually on the front porch steps with a strange car parked in the driveway.

175

Dark in the Forest: Another Modern Fairytale

As I climb out of Neeve's car, Dad approaches wearing a big smile.

Neeve gets out of the car too.

I introduce them.

As they shake hands, Dad says, "I wanted to meet you and thank you for recommending Hellie for this job. It was thoughtful."

"Not at all," Neeve says. "I was feeling guilty about not putting in the time at the shop that I should, but when this opportunity came up for me to perform with the Shawon Orchestra, I just couldn't resist. Brenlyn's been too good a friend to fire me, but he has been getting frustrated. It was a stroke of good luck for me to bump into Hellie and discover she's been looking for work."

"How was it?" Dad asks me.

"Great," I say. "Brenlyn and Talitha are so nice and they're willing to teach me so much, I almost feel like I should pay them for the privilege of working for them."

"I often felt the same way," Neeve says with a laugh. "Well, I've got to go pick up Karissa." Before he climbs back into his car, he shakes hands with my dad again. "It was nice meeting you, Mr. Powers. See you around, Hellie."

Neeve drives off.

Dad and I head for the house.

"He seems like a nice young man," Dad says.

"He is, but please tell me you didn't come home early just to check him out."

"I didn't," Dad says, "but I think it would have been rude for me just to ignore him as long as he was here."

"Why are you home early then?" I ask.

"Air conditioning went out in the Language Arts Building. When the inside temperature hit 90°, Dean Collins cancelled afternoon classes."

Dad sits on the top porch step beside Mom. I sit a couple of steps below, angled sideways so I can look up at them.

"Where's Angel?" I ask. "Do you need me to run over to the newspaper office and pick her up?"

"No," Mom says. "Peter Bradley is bringing her home." Then changing the subject, she asks me, "How do you think you're going to like working at Quick Fix?"

"I'm going to love it. I can hardly wait until I can start painting figurines. They're all originals. Brenlyn sculpts them and then makes his own molds. He's really a talented artist."

"I wonder why he bothers with the repair work then," Mom says.

"According to his wife," I tell her, "he simply enjoys it."

"I looked up the address of his shop on Google Maps," Dad says. "It's over by the mall."

"I know."

"I don't suppose Neeve plans on picking you up and bringing you home every day," Mom says with a question mark in her voice.

"No. He took me today so he could introduce me to his friends."

I can guess where this conversation is headed.

Downtown Shawon, where Mom works, is almost ten miles east of our house.

The university, where Dad works, is at the southern end of town, as is the newspaper office.

The mall and Brenlyn's workshop are both barely within the northern city limits.

"I checked the bus routes," I say, "and the closest stop to Quick Fix is at the mall, but that's okay. I'll only have to walk a few blocks. I was thinking, after I can take the splint off, I could ride my bike back and forth as long as the weather is good. Angel and I used to do it all the time."

Mom and Dad are both nodding.

"I'm glad you've given it some thought," Mom says.

"Your mom and I have been thinking about it too," Dad says. "The problem with taking the bus and then having to walk the rest of the way is that you'll have to leave early and you'll get home late—same problem with riding your bike."

"No," I cry in dismay. "Please don't tell me you want me to quit already. It's worth a little inconvenience. It's wonderful there."

Mom puts a reassuring hand on my shoulder. "We're not suggesting that you quit."

"We just thought you might prefer to drive," Dad says, nodding at the strange car in the driveway. "It's nothing fancy, but it's in good condition and I got a sweet deal on it."

He dangles a set of keys in front of my nose.

"For me?" I shriek as I try to snatch the keys from him.

"Not quite," Dad says, whisking them away and holding them just out of my reach. "It makes sense for you to drive it to and from work, but other than that, you and Angel will have to share."

"Don't we always?"

"All right," he says, handing the keys over, "go take a look."

I do.

It's a baby blue Mazda3, which is a subcompact, four years old with only 28,312 miles on it. There are a few dings, but nothing you'd notice unless you were looking for them.

"May I take it for a spin?" I ask, sitting in the driver's seat with the window down and the engine already running.

"Go ahead," Mom says, "but just once around the block. Dinner's almost ready."

When I get back, Mom and Dad are still sitting on the front steps and Angel and Peter Bradley are standing talking to them.

Peter's motorcycle is parked on the street in front of the house.

Two helmets, one silver and one pink, hang from the handlebars.

Dark in the Forest: Another Modern Fairytale

Either Peter let Angel pick out her own helmet, or he knows her tastes pretty well.

After Angel and I do some mutual squealing over our new car and she and Peter have examined it thoroughly, all five of us go in for dinner.

No one bothers mentioning to me that Peter has been invited to stay.

He and Angel sit side by side across the table from me.

He's a nice-looking guy, but nowhere near as handsome as Kaden.

He's only a few inches taller than Angel, broad in the shoulders and narrow at the hips. As he accepts and then passes the platter of lemon-pepper-seasoned rotisserie chicken, the muscles in his forearms ripple.

He has the most gorgeous tan I've ever seen, and (no disloyalty to Kaden intended) I wonder what he looks like in swimming trunks. His brown hair has reddish highlights and is thick and a bit unruly (maybe from wearing his motorcycle helmet).

I can't tell the color of his eyes except that they are light.

Halfway through the meal I feel my phone vibrate.

It's in my front pocket, and I shift position casually so I can get to it.

I hold it in my lap.

I have a text message from Kaden.

Luckily my parents are focused on Angel and Peter.

If they weren't, I'd never get away with reading Kaden's message and responding to it.

We have a "no phones at the table" rule.

I read:	Are you home yet?
I answer:	Yes. Eating dinner.
Kaden:	May I come see you later?
Me:	Any special reason?
Kaden:	I am uneasy.
Me:	It'll probably have to be after midnight.
Kaden:	Fine. Text me. I will use portal key to arrive on your back patio.

I can hardly eat.

Now I'm uneasy too.

I pick at my food until everyone else has finished.

Although this is Angel's week to do the dishes, I get up and clear the table so she and Peter can continue talking with Mom and Dad.

Angel gives me a smile of gratitude.

I smile back.

However, I'm not doing it for her.

I'm doing it to give myself an excuse not to participate in the table conversation.

I'm caught up in my own thoughts.

I want to talk to Kaden.

I need to know if his unease is like the distress I experienced on Sunday when I thought I wasn't going to see him for a whole day or if this is something more serious.

When I have the table cleared and the dishwasher running, I go to my room and make the call.

Kaden won't discuss the problem on the phone.

I want to smack him.

My parents usually go to bed right after they've watched the 10:00 news. With my door opened a crack I listen for them to come upstairs. They are discussing Angel and Peter when they go to their room at 11:00.

I delay half an hour before I text Kaden and tell him I'll meet him outside.

He's waiting for me in the moonlight when I sneak out the door.

When I see his expression, my heart stops.

"What's wrong," I ask, hurrying down the stairs.

After we're both seated, he says, "I heard the king tell my father that Maldon has fled from Auravale and that Jerrin has had a mage's forewarning. In Jerrin's vision Maldon recognized a ripple of Bree-Ella's magic and was performing dark rituals so he could follow it to her. Jerrin believes the ripples Maldon felt were the ones you caused inadvertently. He fears they are going to lead him straight to you."

"I don't understand? I'm five generations removed from Bree-Ella. Even if it was my magic that Maldon sensed, how could it feel like hers after all this time?"

Kaden takes my hands in his.

"Time isn't an issue. Your magic has come to you in a straight line from Bree-Ella, mother to daughter, just as the Dark family name has. If your magic is the same as hers, it won't matter to him that you're a completely different person."

I inhale deeply and then exhale with a loud sigh.

"I still don't get it. How can my magic be so much like hers after five generations?"

"Your world doesn't have magic-users, so her powers haven't been diluted or changed by being combined with anyone else's."

It's still doesn't make sense to me.

I'm beginning to feel frustrated.

Kaden must sense it.

He usually knows what I'm feeling.

"Pretend," he says, "that Bree-Ella left behind a beautiful red velvet cloak and that one of her direct decedents in every generation got to wear it, what condition do you think it would be in when it reached you?"

"If everyone was as hard on clothes as I am, I'd say it would be pretty shabby by the time I got it."

Dark in the Forest: Another Modern Fairytale

"Correct," he says. "Even if each woman tried to take very good care of it and only used it on special occasions, it would show some deterioration. Now imagine that Bree-Ella had the cloak sealed in a container that kept it free from sunlight, bugs, dust, and the ravages of time. If you were the first person who could open the container in five generations, what condition do you think the cloak would be in now?"

"It would be precisely as she left it."

"That's right, and that's how you need to think about the powers you got from her. Even if some of your aunts and cousins inherited magic from Bree-Ella, they would only have received bits and pieces. You're the one who got her pristine red velvet cloak, and you're the one who's wearing it. If Maldon finds you, he'll try to take it from you with or without your consent."

"With or without my consent? How can he do that?"

"There are dark spells that can be used to take control of even a mature mage. Maldon would have no trouble controlling you. You're just coming into your powers, you're still untrained, and you're here in this world where no one uses magic and where no one is qualified to protect you."

"If you're trying to scare me, you've succeeded," I say. "But maybe once Maldon learns Bree-Ella's been dead for a hundred and fifty years, he'll just leave me alone. Didn't Jerrin or Skyler or someone say in all likelihood Maldon didn't even realize she was a mage?"

"Yes," Kaden answers. "Even so, Maldon is at least a magician—and more probably a sorcerer. He would have sensed there was something special about Bree-Ella's powers, something valuable and unique that she wasn't using. He probably reasoned that if she didn't want the power, he might as well take it rather than let it sit idle."

"But maybe it isn't about power," I say. "He fathered her child. Maybe he loves her and that's why he's been looking for her."

Kaden shakes his head and tightens his hold on my hands.

"Hellie, after the Darkers were exiled to Hamlin Heath, Maldon gave himself over to evil. His wings have atrophied and fused inside his body."

"What does that mean?"

"Our wings are more than the means of getting from one place to another. They are part of our eternal souls. We nurture our wings and our souls through acts of kindness, compassion, service, and generosity, through songs and music and the appreciation of beauty, through positive thoughts, loving relationships, and the celebration of life.

"When a person gives himself over to doing evil, he can no longer nourish his soul enough to support his wings, so they wither and die. Can you imagine how a person would think and how he would behave after losing part of his soul? There would be no conscience, no internal censoring, no impulse control, no empathy, no sympathy, and no pity. In their place would be avarice, lust, conceit, anger, hatred, prejudice, vengeance, and domination."

Now I'm really frightened.

"What am I supposed to do?" I cry helplessly.

"Come to Auravale where we can protect you. The king has soldiers and mages searching for Maldon. He is accused of killing four merfolk during his escape from Hamblin Heath. When he is found he will be tried for murder, and if found guilty, he will certainly be executed. Then it will be safe for you to come home."

I am so distressed I almost miss the reference to merfolk. Do they actually exist in Auravale? When this is all over, I need to remember to ask Kaden to explain.

He turns both of my hands over and kisses my palms.

"Please, Hellie, let me take you to the king. Let him protect you."

I pull my hands gently away from his.

"I can't, Kaden. I can't just leave my family and go into hiding."

"Why not?" he demands.

"You seem to have forgotten something."

"What?"

"I have an identical twin. If Maldon's magical spell shows him what I look like, and if I'm not here, he's going to assume Angel is me. She's not a mage. She won't have any defenses."

"He'll know right away that she didn't inherit Bree-Ella's powers."

"But we look alike. What if he snatches her to use against me?"

"We'll take her with us."

"And my mother and father? And Grandma Dark? What about them? I also have three pairs of aunts and uncles and a bunch of cousins on my mother's side. Are you going to take all of us to Auravale?"

"I understand your concern for your relatives, but they don't share the same risk that you do. You're the one who's a mage. He's not going to want any of them."

"Which means he'll see them as expendable. He'll be able to use them as leverage to draw me out. How many of them do you think he'd have to torture and kill before I went to him willingly?"

The look on Kaden's face nearly rips me in half.

I can tell he is in physical pain from worrying about me. If I were the only one in danger, his agony would probably force me to go with him. But mine is not the only life at stake.

"There must be a way to keep all of you safe," he murmurs.

I nod. "It's not likely, though, is it?"

"I don't know," Kaden answers. "I imagine my father and the king are meeting with both Councils, debating the implications of the situation and considering courses of action."

"I don't know how things work in your world," I say, "but in my world Councils don't move from discussions to actions very fast."

"Our worlds are alike in that way," he admits. "Perhaps Jerrin will have more information when you meet with him for your training in the morning.

Dark in the Forest: Another Modern Fairytale

When he had his mage's forewarning, he might have learned something that will suggest a plan."

"Why don't you come with me?" I suggest. "That way you'll know what's going on and you won't have to worry about me."

"Are you sure you don't mind?"

"I'd like you to be there."

"All right. I'll meet you at Brenlyn's house in the morning."

Chapter Thirty-three

When I turn onto the street where Brenlyn's shop is, I see Kaden standing at the curb a few houses down.

I pull up next to him and open the car door.

"Climb in," I say, "I'll drive you the rest of the way."

He gets in the car but stops me before I can press on the gas pedal.

"I wanted to see you before you went in. I told you I'd go with you, but I don't think they'll let me stay. If it were just Jerrin, maybe—"

"Who else is in there?"

"Skyler. He asked Neeve and Karissa to come too, and of course Jerrin and Shiane. They're here to talk to you about Maldon and how to protect you from him."

"What makes you think they won't let you stay? They've never kept you away before."

"Neeve called to warn me. Skyler considers this a family matter."

"Whoa," I say, holding my hands up to stop him. "Didn't you go home last night?"

Looking puzzled, Kaden nods.

"Then how did Neeve call you in Auravale? Can he send his thoughts between worlds?"

"As a matter of fact," Kaden says, "he can. They all can—the royal family. But Neeve used his cellphone. He says it costs him less personal energy and is more fun."

"No, no, no," I say. "That's impossible. It takes a radio signal about fourteen minutes to travel between Earth and Mars, and they're in the same solar system."

Kaden gives me an amused but indulgent look. "You're forgetting that magic is involved. When Neeve showed Jerrin his cellphone, Jerrin took it straight to the Guild of Artificers and asked them to make a version that could be used between Earth and Auravale. It took them less than a month."

I grab my head to keep it from exploding. "I don't think I'm ready to deal with the blending of magic and technology."

Dark in the Forest: Another Modern Fairytale

Kaden takes my hands in his. "Don't worry about it. When you come to Auravale, I'll take you over to the Guild and they can explain it to you." He kisses my palm. "We got a little off subject. I was telling you why I probably wouldn't be allowed to stay with you."

"Yes, but you said Karissa's here. She's not family."

"Not yet, but she and Neeve are engaged, and even though their wedding date hasn't been set, they are perfectly matched souls and their marriage is inevitable. Besides, she's a human girl, and they might need her to help persuade you to do things their way."

All of a sudden I feel my muscles tighten up, preparing me for a fight. I don't like being manipulated, and I'm already getting angry thinking they might try.

"They don't know me very well yet," I say tensely.

"You don't know them very well yet either," Kaden replies, raising his eyebrows at me.

"I guess it's about time we get acquainted."

I put the car in gear.

I glance over at Kaden, smile, and give him a nudge with my elbow. "I'd like you to come in with me and stay. If they try to kick you out, they'll learn more about me than they want to know."

Not having expected to drive to work, I never asked Brenlyn or Talitha where I should park. There's a tree that appears to be halfway between their house and the one next door. It overhangs the street, making a nice puddle of shade. I decide to park there. That'll leave the driveway and the front curb for customers.

I don't see Neeve's car anywhere.

Maybe he and the family just opened portals and stepped through.

When Kaden and I enter the shop, I take his hand.

He shakes his head at me and gently tries to pull his hand free.

I tighten my grasp and whisper, "If we're going to take on the royals, we need to make a statement of solidarity right from the beginning." I give him a mock serious look and hold up our joined hands. "Persuasion works best when the issues are presented in multiple formats. We don't have time to print up flyers, but we can still give them a verbal and a visual message."

He looks down at me for several seconds and then grins. He keeps his voice low and his eyes beseeching. "Hellie, please, learn to love me. Life with you would be so much fun."

My heart does flip-flops. He told me he has two years of apprenticeship left before he'll be able to support a wife and family. If he keeps this up, I'll be a mass of melted putty before we can plan a wedding.

I give his hand a tug. "Let's go."

When we get to the backroom, the five people Kaden named are all seated on stools at the large worktable.

They turn in unison to face us.

They clearly didn't expect Kaden to be with me. As I glance around, I notice Karissa and Shiane trying to hide their smiles. Neither is doing a very good job of it, and I find that comforting.

Skyler stands up.

Kaden bows from the waist and I nod.

"Kaden," Skyler says, "thank you for escorting Hellie here. You may go now."

I tighten my grip on Kaden's hand. "No he can't," I say. "I've asked him to stay."

It is clear that Skyler is not used to being told no. But, except for a brief look of surprise and disapproval on his face, he keeps his cool. "We have many things to discuss," he says, "and since Kaden is not directly involved, he will probably find it rather dull. Besides, he has other duties he should attend to." His tone implies that he expects Kaden to agree and depart.

I shrug. "If he goes, I go."

Skyler appears to have used up his supply of patience and diplomacy. His face goes red and he grips the edge of the table.

Jerrin puts a hand on his shoulder. "May I, Your Highness? After all, I am her mentor."

"Yes, of course," Skyler responds with his voice strained.

Uh oh, I think. Things have gone from the casual friendliness of Sunday's "Please don't get up" to the formality of "May I, Your Highness?" and "I am her mentor."

This probably isn't going to be pretty.

"Do you know why we're all here, Hellie?" Jerrin asks.

"Yes. You think Maldon is coming after me and you want to come up with a plan to protect me."

"That's right," Jerrin says. "We have some suggestions to make and some strategies to consider. May I ask why you want Kaden to be here? Has your relationship with him become more clearly defined?"

I keep my eyes on Jerrin, but I can feel Kaden tense up. Whatever Jerrin is asking has Auravalian connotations that I don't understand. I can't tell if Kaden is angry, embarrassed, or offended. Maybe he's all three.

Step one of the manipulation: Try to make Kaden uncomfortable enough to leave voluntarily.

"My relationship with Kaden is a private matter. Thank you for asking."

"Clinging to him this way," Jerrin continues, "puts him in danger. If he is present when Maldon finds you, Maldon will not hesitate to kill him in front of you."

Step two of the manipulation: Try to make me take responsibility for Kaden's welfare.

"You're presuming," I say, "that Kaden has no resources and would be a helpless victim. I don't believe it. He is strong and smart and courageous. Combining our strengths, I think we could give Maldon a run for his money."

185

"Hellie," Jerrin says, "you are just beginning to learn about our people. You have no idea what kinds of powers are involved and the types of magic you might have to face."

Step three of the manipulation: Try to intimidate me through a direct attack.

"Give it up, Jerrin," I say. "You're not going to come up with an argument that makes me change my mind. Kaden stays or we both go."

Skyler, Neeve, and Shiane all turn to look at Jerrin. Apparently it is time for a silent family council.

Karissa gives me a sideward nod toward the back of the room. She gets up, leaves her cane behind, and takes a dozen careful steps to a stool at the smaller table.

I give Kaden's hand a squeeze, and then I join her. He remains over by the door.

"Hellie," Karissa asks quietly, "why is it so important to you to have Kaden stay?"

I glance back at the royals. They still seem intently involved in their private consultation. I decide to try to explain my reasoning to Karissa in hopes that maybe she'll back me up.

"Because," I tell Karissa in an undertone, "of all the people in this room, Kaden is the only Auravalian that I know for sure has nothing but my welfare in mind. The Trudimahns have too much history with Maldon for their motives to be simple and altruistic. There must be layers upon layers of historical, political, and familial issues involved. Kaden just wants me to be safe. He has no hidden agendas."

"But he isn't a mage," Karissa says. "He's like Neeve. He has some magical powers, as all Auravalians do, but his are not the kind that could stand up to a sorcerer."

"I realize that," I say. "But even if Kaden doesn't have the abilities of a sorcerer, he must understand their powers better than I do. He's insightful and honest. He'll explain things to me, and he'll look out for my interests. Without him here to advise me, I'm not going to trust Skyler and Jerrin's suggestions, and I'm certainly not going to agree to a course of action."

"Hellie," Karissa's voice drops below a whisper, "have you fallen in love with Kaden?"

"I don't think so." Tears form in my eyes. "But I want to. He is such a wonderful person."

"Is there anything Shiane or I can do to help you?"

When I shake my head, I realize I still have my lunch tote hanging from my shoulder. I open the front pocket and take out a tissue so I can wipe my eyes.

"Even if you and Shiane are on my side, you can't do anything to override the male trinity over there. Skyler and Jerrin are probably the two most important men in Auravale besides the king, and Neeve is the resident expert on Earth's local natives. You and Shiane can't stand up against that.

"My only real fear is that Skyler and Jerrin might take their frustrations with me out on Kaden when he goes back home. I'm sure they have the power to make his life hell, but even with that threat, I don't think they can stop Kaden from trying to protect me, even if he has to protect me from them."

"You really trust him, don't you?"

"With all my heart. Every time I see him I trust him more. I don't know much about romantic love, earthly or Auravalian, but whatever it is, I believe Kaden feels it for me. He is so kind, so attentive, so concerned, and so patient, I can't think of any justification for his actions except love."

My eyes tear up again. "I'm not worth it, you know. He's way too good for me, but—"

The next thing I know, Kaden is there with his arms wrapped around me. "Stop it," he says softly in my ear. "I can't bear to hear any more."

He cups my face with his hands and kisses my forehead.

He has tears in his eyes too.

With horror, I stare at Karissa. She told me that Neeve often acted as a relay station for her. Now I guess she has been acting as a relay station for him, and he's passed on everything he's heard to Kaden.

But when I hear Karissa gasp, I realize she wasn't in on the plot. She seems to grasp what's happened just a second or two after I do. Her eyes flash fire.

"Neeve Maynard Trudimahn," she cries out, "how could you! Now she'll never trust me, and I wanted us to be friends."

"Neeve didn't do it," Jerrin tells Karissa. "I did. I told Hellie yesterday that, as her mentor, I had to know what she's thinking and feeling. When I recognized the depth of her faith in Kaden, I felt he had the right to know as well."

"Why?" I demand. "Just to hurt him?" I put my arms around Kaden's waist and hold on tight while I continue to confront Jerrin. "You know he's had that once-in-a-lifetime recognition with me, and you know I haven't had time to develop the necessary reciprocal feelings for him."

I tip my head back so I can look up at Kaden. His cheeks are damp with tears. I reach up and wipe them away with my fingertips.

I'm really crying. I don't know when that started. "I'm sorry, Kaden. I'd cut out my tongue before I'd hurt you on purpose."

He takes my hand and kisses my palm.

"If I'm hurt," he says, "it's only because you've given me hope and I ache with impatience. I believe you'll grow to love me, Hellie. I just want it to be soon."

I turn toward Jerrin. "Why did you do that? Why not just leave us alone and let nature take its course?"

Jerrin's voice becomes very soft, almost apologetic. "Because having someone's trust, the way Kaden has yours, comes with heavy responsibilities. I needed him to understand why we will suddenly be including him in our discussions with you, and why he will be allowed to spend more time in this world. I feared he would doubt our motives, just as you do, unless he could hear you express the extent of your faith in him in your own words."

I wipe my eyes with my already soggy tissue.

"You're going to include him?" I ask.

Jerrin gives me a wry smile. "You haven't given us much of a choice, have you?"

"Maybe not," I tell him, "but you won't regret it. You'll find out for yourselves why I trust him."

Apparently Skyler has regained his composure. He appears completely calm and in control.

"Now that we have all the players identified," Skyler says, "why don't we discuss options?" He motions to Karissa, Kaden, and me. "Won't you please come join us. This table allows us all to have a little more elbow room."

When I look at Skyler, I have a startling revelation.

Step four of the manipulation: create a situation that shifts the focus of my attention from Skyler to Jerrin. If things had gone south with Jerrin, Skyler could have stepped in, offered to find me a different mentor, cast himself in the role of savior, and played on my gratitude to get me to cooperate with him. Whereas, if things had gone south with Skyler, there wouldn't have been any higher authority to step in and save the day other than the king himself.

As I sit down at the table, I try to decide if I'm going to be angry with Skyler for winning at the manipulation game.

He quickly takes my mind off the issue.

"Kaden," Skyler says, "before we start considering options, I'd like to know if you already have something in mind."

Chapter Thirty-four

"No, Your Highness," Kaden says to Skyler, "I don't. However, I think I can at least set the parameters for you. I've already suggested to Hellie that she put herself under the king's protection. She isn't willing to consider anything that will leave her sister, her parents, her grandmother, or any of her other relatives at risk. She fears that Maldon would use them as leverage against her, torturing them, to force her to submit to him."

"That's a possibility," Jerrin says. "We know Maldon enjoys causing pain."

"Kaden, are you suggesting," asks Skyler, "that we come up with a plan that protects her entire family?"

"If it can be done," Kaden replies. "As Hellie pointed out, her family has no defenses against him."

Jerrin turns his attention to Skyler. "We might be forced to take the matter to the Council of Mages. It would probably take all of us to develop a spell large enough and specific enough to cover the relevant members of her family. I assume they live in several different locations."

He gives me a sideward glance and I nod.

"We'd have to go through the Council of Nobles first," Skyler says, "to get permission to develop a spell to be used on a foreign world. Of course, Father would have to approve too."

"It would need to be a subtle spell," Neeve says. "If Maldon sensed it, he could use it as a beacon to lead him straight to her."

"I could stay here and monitor it," Shiane suggests. "If I felt him trying to use it to track her, I could misdirect him." She reaches out and touches Jerrin's arm. "I'm strong enough for that already, aren't I?"

"Yes." He puts his hand over hers. "I just hope it doesn't come to that."

"The problem," Skyler says thoughtfully, "is that the more people we involve in the matter the greater the odds are that one of Maldon's minions will hear about it."

"Which defeats the whole purpose," agrees Jerrin.

"Excuse me," I say. "I'll admit I don't understand anything about magic, but I think I have a fair grasp of violence. If I knew someone was gunning for me, the first thing I'd want to do is learn how to dodge a bullet. No matter what kind of assistance you offer me, in the end, the only person who can be with me all the time is myself."

"Which means what?" asks Jerrin.

"Teach me magical self-defense," I say. "You must have some ideas about how Maldon will try to get to me. Give me the tools I need to protect myself. You say I'm a mage and he's a sorcerer. That means I should be stronger than he is, right?"

"It would be," Jerrin says, "if you and he were both just starting out, but he's been trained as a sorcerer and he's had many years of practice doing dark magic. You need to remember that he's older than our father. It was our grandfather who exiled him, and Maldon embraced the dark arts shortly thereafter. What he lacks in power, he can make up through experience."

"Then," I say, "I suggest we get started as soon as possible. We'll need to schedule—"

"Just a moment," Skyler interrupts. "I want to make sure we're clear. If Jerrin focuses your training on self-defense and if Kaden is allowed to be with you to offer support and reassurance, are you willing to let us go ahead and make our own plans for dealing with Maldon?"

"As long as you keep me in the loop so I know what's going on, that seems reasonable to me." I look over at Kaden. "Do you see any problems with it?"

"No, it seems reasonable to me too. You will be getting what you need to feel safe, and they will be getting what they need to feel in control."

And that, I tell myself, is why I want Kaden's input. I hadn't thought forward enough to realize that what Skyler and Jerrin need right now is to feel in control—regardless of whether or not they actually are.

The way Kaden summed it up, it's win-win.

"There is one more issue that we need to consider," Skyler says. "We know that Bree-Ella brought three magical artifacts with her—artifacts that she took from the palace. In her letter to Justus III, she indicated she would return them as soon as she established herself somewhere. We don't know why she didn't.

"We know through Kaden's efforts that the items are here. It is possible that if Maldon's spells don't lead him directly to Hellie, they might lead him to the inanimate objects. Personally I've wondered why he didn't go after them long ago. What he wants is to increase his power. He could probably do it more easily if he took the power from the magical items rather than from a living person. However, if he gets close enough to sense the artifacts, he'll be close enough to sense Hellie too."

Kaden frowns. "I'm sure the stwethil-thage have two of the artifacts, perhaps all three. I hate to force them to give them up, but perhaps I can think of a way to confront and persuade them. If it's a choice between Hellie's life and their goodwill, I know which way I'll go."

"Tread lightly if you can," Skyler says. "They have performed valuable services for us in the past, and if Maldon isn't intercepted, we might need them to act as sentries in the forest."

"Yes, Your Highness," Kaden says.

"I will leave you now," Skyler says, " and go report to our father." He glances at Shiane. "It's up to Jerrin to decide if the lessons he'll be giving Hellie are appropriate for you. If he tells you to come home, you obey him without arguing."

"But Skyler—" Shiane looks up at him with big puppy-dog eyes and speaks with just a hint of a whine.

"Or I can take you home with me right now," he says firmly.

Shiane gets a pouty look on her face. "Yes, Your Highness," she says, the whine turning sarcastic.

"Shiane." With that one word Skyler somehow manages to combine an elder brother's tolerance with a bit of imperialistic warning.

"Oh, all right," she says.

"Deference," Skyler reminds her.

She smiles engagingly and bats her eyelashes at him. "As you wish, Your Highness."

"You are a little minx," he tells her. "You'd better mind your manners or when I become king I'll marry you off to some wasteland peasant."

The grin she gives him tells me that this is a frequent and empty threat.

Skyler clasps Jerrin's shoulder. "If you need me, call." Then he nods at the rest of us and vanishes.

"We'll be going, too," Neeve says. He stands, picks up Karissa's cane, and then offers her his arm. She takes it.

As they pass me, Karissa pauses a second. "Good luck," she says. "Call me if you want to talk."

"Thanks," I say.

"Kaden," Jerrin says, "if you want to stay, you're welcome, but not as an observer. You'll have to participate. Many of the basic things Hellie needs to learn will benefit you too, especially if she turns to you for guidance later."

"Thank you," Kaden says.

"Each of you needs to choose a mat so we can begin with relaxation."

As before, Shiane and I lay our mats side by side. Kaden spreads his out on the other side of me. I feel cocooned in safety.

Jerrin takes us through the same relaxation exercise as yesterday. Once again, I lose myself in the stars.

When I become aware of Jerrin's voice this time, however, he isn't trying to rouse me.

"Staying in your safe place," Jerrin says, "listen. There is a fly buzzing near the backdoor. There is a faint hum coming from the refrigerator in the kitchen. If you can hear these sounds, don't say anything, just lift up one finger." There is a pause. "Now, still in your safe place, relax even more. Breathe deeply. With each exhalation, let your muscles become heavier and heavier, almost pulling you into the floor. Now listen again. Can you hear the water dripping in the bathroom sink? Can you hear the birds in the trees outside? Open your minds to the sounds around you. Can you hear your own heartbeat?"

I never knew there were so many different sounds all happening at the same time. Our brains must automatically filter out about 90% of them or the noise would drive us crazy.

After having us listen, Jerrin has us concentrate on odors. I can smell the fruit in a bowl in the kitchen, the oily cloth on a shelf, and the flowers in a vase in Talitha and Brenlyn's bedroom.

But the most surprising and significant part of the experience for me is the delicate, lilac scent on my right, which is Shiane, the crisp spice on my left, which is Kaden, and the faint roasted nut aroma in front of me, which has to be Jerrin. I have never associated specific scents with people before. I like it.

The next part is more difficult. While staying in our safe place, Jerrin has us sit up, open our eyes, and focus on various items. Shiane and Kaden seem to have an easier time than I do. Maybe they aren't as visually reliant as humans are. With my eyes open, I completely lose touch with my inner orientation and my vision takes over.

Jerrin tells me not to get discouraged. It will become easier with practice.

Next, we get up, do some stretches, and take a short break.

Then we do a different kind of relaxation exercise: tensing and relaxing muscle groups starting with the feet.

About halfway up my body, I relax so much I fall asleep.

Jerrin wakes me up by projecting into my mind the image of a huge gong being struck by a bare chested man wielding a sledgehammer. The loud BONG ricochets in my head and scares me half to death. I practically levitate to my feet.

As soon as my heart rate and respiration return to normal, Jerrin has us try it again. I don't fall asleep, but I don't relax very much either.

When Brenlyn and Talitha come back from their house calls, I am happy to say goodbye to Jerrin and Shiane. I am less happy to say goodbye to Kaden, but I know I'll see him tomorrow morning.

Talitha starts teaching me how to paint lead soldiers, which helps me reorient to the real world by the time I go home.

The next couple of weeks are more of the same.

I ditch the wrist splint somewhere along the line. So much else is happening in my life that I probably just forgot to put it on one day. I don't remember.

Jerrin does everything he can think of to help me get in touch with what he calls "the magic center" in my mind.

I'm getting pretty good at it, but I still have struggles. Jerrin is gracious about explaining my mistakes and then letting me practice the same exercises multiple times.

When he has me do something and I lose control (like when he had me open a portal from the workshop to the glade in the forest and I took us almost all the way to Utah), Shiane or Kaden always helps me pull the power back in.

Jerrin says he decided to leave it up to them because I appear more comfortable accepting their help than his. He assures me, however, if I'm in danger of blowing myself or someone else up, he'll step in and stop me.

I feel like I'll never develop the knack of opening a portal to a specific location, but this is one skill Jerrin insists that I master.

I finally do.

After about a hundred tries, I can open a portal and end up where I want to go. Now, if Maldon threatens me with something I absolutely can't handle, I have the means of escape. I can go through a portal to safety.

There have been a couple of unexpected side effects from having Shiane and Kaden help me with control. First, Shiane's ability to keep reins on her own power is increasing. Second, Kaden is getting stronger and his range of abilities is widening.

"When things settle down," Jerrin says to him, "I think we'd better get you over to the Magicians Guild for retesting. It's possible that the Guild's philosophy is wrong and some magical skills can be taught."

"Or," Shiane says, "maybe sharing fauvenell with a mage makes a difference."

"Hmm," Jerrin says, "that's a thought." He scrutinizes Kaden for a moment. "No matter what the cause—faulty testing in the beginning, exposure to this new level of training, or falling in love with a mage—your ability to help Hellie pull in her magic when it's about to overwhelm her is at least at the magician level. As her powers increase, yours seem to also."

"It's probably just a splinter skill," Kaden says. "I don't feel any different."

"Which is another reason to have you retested," Jerrin says. "We've never had a wizard who could exert external control over a mage before."

"What's a splinter skill?" I ask.

I aim my question at Kaden, but Jerrin answers.

"It's the ability to do something at a higher level than the rest of your skill set."

"I don't get it," I say.

Before Jerrin can continue, Shiane explains. "It's like weather wizards. They know what the weather is like around the globe at any time at any location and can accurately predict it for up to a month in advance. That's a mage-level skill that not even all mages can develop. But it's the only mage-level skill the weather wizards have regardless of how much or what kind of additional training they receive."

"At least that's what we thought," Jerrin says. "Kaden may prove that assumption to be inaccurate."

"When Neeve told me about the different levels of magician," I say, "he never mentioned wizards."

"That's because wizards aren't a level of magicians," Jerrin says. "They only have one advanced skill. To qualify at the lowest level of magician, which is magic-user, you have to test with at least three distinct skills."

Dark in the Forest: Another Modern Fairytale

As Jerrin teaches me new things, I realize that part of what he calls magic is learning to use my five mundane senses in enhanced ways, like listening for sounds that are farther and farther away or focusing my eyes on something that I would ordinarily consider beyond my range of vision.

He also teaches me how not to do certain things, like not projecting my thoughts. I can keep him out of my mind now unless he pushes hard, which he has only done a couple of times to show me how it feels so I can recognize it if someone else tries. He also teaches me how not to leave foot or fingerprints on any surface. I can walk across a dirt path in the forest and handle glassware without leaving a trace. (This will particularly come in handy if I decide to turn to a life of crime.)

By the end of the summer, he says, I should be able to fade in and out of view at will, put myself into a trance, protect myself from falling under someone else's spells (except for another mage, and I should be able to protect myself from that in six or seven months), and any number of other things.

It's all very exciting.

I'm learning to trust my magical instincts.

I think I can actually learn to be a mage.

Of course, as soon as I think that, fate or God or the universe decides to throw a crisis at me to see how I handle it.

Chapter Thirty-five

"Are you sure you don't want to come with us?" Angel asks me. "There will be lots of unattached guys. Maybe you'll meet someone."

"Sorry," I say. "I'd rather stay home."

"On a Friday night?"

"It's been a long week. I just want to relax and read for a while."

"All right," Angel says. "See you later."

Now that Angel and Peter have gone public, his friends want to meet her, so a bunch of his pals are having a cookout tonight. Angel is nervous, and I'm sure she wants me along for moral support in case they don't warm up to her right away.

Her concerns are ridiculous, though, because people always like her.

Mom and Dad are going to be gone too. The mayor is having a reception for some visiting artists or musicians or something.

I will enjoy a nice quiet evening at home alone. It hasn't been easy trying to learn all about magic in the mornings and then trying to give Brenlyn and Talitha a fair afternoon's work in the shop.

When my family has gone its separate ways, I heave a sigh of relief.

I get a baggy sweatshirt out of the closet and pull it on. The nights can still get a little chilly and I don't want to have to come back and get a sweater later. Following that line of reasoning, I decide to take my lunch tote with me too. I can put some chips or crackers in it in case I have the munchies later on.

In the kitchen I fill a big plastic mug with ice and pour a can of Diet Coke over it. Into my lunch tote, I place two bottles of water, a Three Musketeers candy bar, a small bag of chips, and a snack bag full of vanilla wafers.

Then with the tote dangling from my shoulder, my Kindle tucked under my arm, and the mug full of Diet Coke in my hand, I go outside.

On the patio is a glass-topped table that mom keeps covered with a fitted, quilted pad so it won't get chipped. I put my stuff on it, pull over a lawn chair, and get comfortable.

Unless I have to take a bathroom break, I'm all set for an uninterrupted evening of listening to David Garrett play the violin while I read a Charlaine

Dark in the Forest: Another Modern Fairytale

Harris's new Aurora Teagarden mystery.

It's getting dark, but that's one nice thing about reading on my Kindle. I don't need to turn on a light.

I've read about a dozen pages when I pause, take a sip of Diet Coke, tip my head to the side, and sniff.

I smell smoke.

At first I think the neighbors must be using wood instead of charcoal in the new brick barbeque they just built.

I get up and look around.

No one in the neighborhood is burning anything that I can see, and even if it's kind of cool outside, it's still way too warm for people to use their fireplaces.

I stand on my chair and take another look.

A faint glow is visible through the trees beyond the back hedge.

My first thought is that some idiot has built a bonfire in our woods.

He'd better have dug a pit and lined it with big rocks, I tell myself, *or he'll set the entire forest ablaze.*

Then I glance again, enhancing my vision as Jerrin taught me.

I have a horrible realization.

It might have started out as a bonfire, but if so, it's out of control now.

It's spreading across the ground and licking at the trees.

Without thinking, I hop down from my chair, set my Kindle and my Diet Coke under the porch steps, hook my tote bag on my shoulder, snatch the pad off of the table, and start running.

As I crash through the hedge, I wonder what possessed me to grab my tote and the lightweight pad.

Two bottles of water won't go very far, I think, *and this fabric is too flimsy for beating out flames.*

I should have called the fire department.

I don't know if they're equipped to fight forest fires on private property, but they could have been on hand to make sure none of the houses burn if a wind comes up and blows in that direction.

My cellphone is in my pocket, but I can't stop to use it now.

The glow is getting brighter.

A puff of smoke wafts into my face.

I gag on it.

Please, please, don't let a wild breeze carry the fire toward the residential area, I pray silently.

I hear the snapping and crackling of burning wood.

When I get my first unobstructed view, I feel a cold chill scuttle up my spine even as I feel the heat on my face. Summer came early this year, and we missed the spring rains. The underbrush is dry, and as the fire creeps across it, it acts like kindling, fueling the flames so they can climb up the trunks of the tress.

I think the fire is picking up speed.

I have no way to judge how far across or how deep it is, but it looks a lot bigger now than it did when I first spied it.

Bobbing back and forth in the air in front of the flames are dozens of brightly colored flickers of light.

I simply stare at them for a moment.

I've seen them before, or at least something quite similar.

I have a flash of memory.

Before Kaden stepped out of a sunbeam and into this world, changing my concept of reality forever, I saw a grove of trees that wasn't part of our forest. A rainbow colored bird flew toward me and turned aside at the last moment. At the same time, several twinkling globes seemed to pass from that other forest into this one.

Kaden said the stwethil-thage came here to get away from the predators in their world.

Did I see some immigrants?

I believe I did.

If so, the flickers of light I see in front of the fire must be stwethil-thage. Perhaps they can only return home if they use the same portal they entered through. Perhaps they're waiting for a gap in the flames so they can get to their portal and return to Auravale.

If so, their situation is hopeless.

The entire area from the grotto to the blackberry bushes appears to be engulfed in flames.

I don't know where the stwethil-thage live, but I've always assumed they lived along the creek between the glade and the grotto. Their homes might have already been destroyed.

"Stwethil-thage," I cry out. "Come to me. I'll protect you. Hurry."

I drape the table pad over a triangular shaped bush, making what looks a little bit like a teepee.

"I'm half Auravalian, and I'm a mage. Let me help you. Come hide under the cloth. I'll keep the fire away."

Suddenly I am surrounded by bobbing lights.

Inside each is a small creature.

They have human-like oval faces with two eyes, small noses, mouths without visible lips, and pointy ears on the sides. They have two arms and two legs, but their hands have three fingers and their feet have three toes. Their heads are mostly bald, with only a strip of hair down the middle like a long Mohawk or a horse's mane. Their leathery wings look way too small to be functional, but like a bumblebee's wings, they work anyway.

They come in every color imaginable and glow with an inner light. They vary in size from about four to six inches from the tops of their heads to the bottoms of their feet.

In their own way, they're quite beautiful.

Dark in the Forest: Another Modern Fairytale

I point to the makeshift teepee.

"Hide under here. Quick." The fire is inching its way inexorably through the undergrowth toward us.

They fly around me like moths circling a bare light bulb.

"Quick," I repeat. "The fire is getting closer."

Then I have a brilliant idea.

I grab the bag of vanilla wafers out of my tote. I crush them with my hands, open the bag, and set it under the cloth.

"I brought you a treat."

After one brave little stwethil-thage darts under the pad, the rest follow.

Not knowing why I'm doing what I'm doing, I open a bottle of water and use it to draw a wet circle around the bush. I put the empty back into my tote and pull out the second bottle. I pour water into my cupped left hand, set the bottle on the ground, hold both hands above the top of the teepee, and then slap my palms together. Droplets spray into the air. As they fall, they create a dome of swirling water around the cloth-covered bush.

I pick up the half empty bottle and wonder if I can do something similar for the rest of the forest. I sense I could if I had enough water and if I had the strength, the energy, and the time to run all the way around the fire.

I don't.

However, I do have access to the stream that flows past the grotto, if I can only figure out how to use it.

I close my eyes long enough to find my safe place among the stars.

Peace and confidence enfold me.

I can do this.

Not too long ago, I watched a program on the Science Chanel about how rainstorms develop. Water evaporates, rises, cools, and condenses. Raindrops form around specks of dust. When the drops are heavy enough, they fall.

Even though I've heard that forest fires create their own weather (or is that just volcanoes), I don't think Mother Nature rushes in to save the day by pouring rain down on every wooded area that goes up in flames.

Nevertheless it just might be possible for me to create my own rainstorm. If I throw enough water from the stream into the air and pull enough cold air down from the upper atmosphere, wouldn't rain clouds form above the fire?

But how would I grasp the air to pull it down? And how would I keep atmospheric currents from ripping my storm clouds apart?

I need a better plan.

Can I use the stream like a fire hose and shoot water at the fire?

I gather my power and build a dam across the stream.

As pressure builds up, I channel the water into a hose-like shape and start spraying the ground. Splotches of grass and undergrowth stop burning for a few seconds, but the heat reignites it.

I need a lot more water, enough to surround the fire from top to bottom, and then I can dump it onto the flames and drown them all at the same time.

I draw water from the stream and start it on a circuitous route to enclose the blaze. As more water flows down the creek bed, I send it off to join the rest. The fire must be bigger than I imagined because the water seems to take forever to go all the way around and reach me again.

I keep sending water from the stream to the fire.

I become frightened. How am I doing this? I shouldn't be able to do this. I feel my confidence waver.

Then I think about all the things Jerrin has taught me.

I think about my safe place among the stars.

My body fills with renewed energy.

I will not let Great-great-great-grandfather Eugene's forest burn.

I concentrate on the task before me.

When my waterspout is as high as the tops of the trees, I try to tighten it around the flames. But the fire fights for survival like a living thing, beating against the barrier I've put around it.

My knees buckle, and I sit down on the grass with a thump.

I'm tired.

But I'm not ready to quit.

As long as I keep the stream whirling around the fire, I can keep the blaze from spreading. Eventually it'll consume all of fuel enclosed by the wall of water and burn itself out—if it doesn't burn me out first.

I'm more than tired.

I'm nearing exhaustion.

I should have called the fire department and the sheriff's office.

I can't do it now.

If I let my concentration waver even a little, the flow of water will stop, and the fire will start to grow again.

Or maybe the water has created a wide enough border around the blaze that the wet ground and foliage will act as a firebreak.

I doubt it.

I can't risk it.

I'm already exceeding my strength.

I couldn't handle a larger fire. I'll just have to hold on until the flames have burned everything inside the circle of water.

To protect the forest, I can hold on forever.

Well, if not forever, I can hold on long enough.

I might be exhausted, but I can hold on a little longer.

I can hold on another few minutes.

I can hold on, I can hold on, I can hold on.

I can't hold on.

I have to stop the fire right now before I collapse.

Like pulling the cord at the top of a duffle bag, I close the top of the cyclone.

I picture the water becoming an airtight glass dome. It solidifies, but it doesn't turn to ice. The heat doesn't melt it.

Somehow I've created something completely new out of water.

I slam my fists into the ground, creating a tiny gap under the dome, and then with one enormous inhalation I suck out the air. Magic expands my lungs to accommodate my needs.

Without oxygen the fire can't burn.

The flames start going out.

As I exhale all the air and smoke I've taken in, I start going out too.

Just before I lose consciousness, I let the dome return to its natural state. I hear the water crash to the ground.

"Hellie."

That's my name.

"Hellie."

Arms are holding me. I recognize their strong embrace. I must have called Kaden to me. I snuggle against his chest and let myself pass out again.

"Hellie."

This time the voice isn't Kaden's.

I don't recognize it.

I don't think I've ever heard it before.

Where am I?

I'm in a bed.

Not my bed.

I open my eyes.

I sense I'm in a hospital, but no hospital I've ever seen. The walls on two sides are made entirely of glass except for the metal framework.

The view outside is of a beautiful garden full of flowers that have brightly colored, oddly shaped blossoms. A few thin-trunked trees have twisted branches and ruby red leaves. The sky is blue but it's more of a turquoise than the true blue of Earth.

There's only one place I can be.

Auravale.

But how and why?

I tear my eyes away from the scenery to look for Kaden. He'll explain it to me.

A short, middle-aged man sits on a chair next to my bed.

Before I can say anything, he speaks. "Good morning, Hellie. I'm Mertley, your doctor."

"How did I get here?"

"Prince Jerrin brought you."

"Why?"

The next thing I know Jerrin is standing at the foot of my bed.

"What's the last thing you remember?" he asks.

"First," I say, "tell me what I'm doing here."

For a moment I think he's not going to answer me, but then he does. "You tried to call Kaden to you again last night, but you were so weak that if I hadn't gone with him and opened the portal, I have no idea where he might have ended up.

"You were unconscious by the time we got to you, and since the doctors in your world would not have been able to help you, I brought you here. Now I would appreciate an answer to my question. What's the last thing you remember?"

"In a minute," I say, feeling panicky. "You said *last night*. My parents must be frantic. I'll answer your questions later. Right now I need to go home and assure my parents that I'll all right. Heaven only knows what I'll tell them."

I take a deep breath.

My lungs hurt. I ignore them.

"I know," I say, thinking out loud, "I can tell them I went to watch the fire and then fell asleep in the forest after the flames miraculously went out. That would work."

"I'm sorry, Hellie," Mertley says. "You're not going anywhere for the next couple of days."

I glare at him.

"You can't keep me here against my will," I insist.

"I don't have to," he says. "Go ahead and get out of bed."

I try to sit up.

I can't.

I try to push myself up using my arms.

I can't.

I try swinging my legs off of the bed.

Again I can't.

"What have you done to me?" I demand.

"I've tried to help you recover from what you did to yourself. Have you ever heard of someone working himself to death?"

"Not really. I know horses can run themselves to death, but I don't know if it can actually happen to people."

"It can, and it almost happened last night—to you. If Jerrin hadn't brought you here, I don't think you'd have survived another hour."

I know I must look confused.

I certainly feel that way.

Mertley takes my hand. "The reason people eat and sleep is so their bodies have the means of replenishing themselves. You used up at least a week's worth of energy without refueling. I have done what I can to speed up your recovery, but you did yourself some serious damage and you need time to rejuvenate."

"But my parents—"

Jerrin stops me mid-sentence. "I know you disapprove of my tampering with the minds of your family, but in this instance I thought it was the kindest thing I could do. Your parents believe that Brenlyn and Talitha invited you to go to Seattle with them to a big Arts and Crafts Show, and you accepted. Your parents expect you home on Wednesday."

"Now," Mertley says, giving my hand a pat, "with that worry off of your mind, I hope you will relax and let your body heal."

"I'll try," I say meekly.

"I'll go arrange a meal for you," Mertley says. "You and Jerrin have that long to talk, then you'll eat and go back to sleep. Understand?"

I nod.

Chapter Thirty-six

"For the third and last time," Jerrin says impatiently, "I will ask you what the last thing is that you remember."

He looks on the verge of losing his temper, so I struggle to find an answer. My brain doesn't want to cooperate.

"The forest was on fire," I say tentatively. "The stwethil-thage couldn't get to their portal, so I had them hide and I—and I—"

Why won't my mind work?

"I did something." I stare at Jerrin. I'm really alarmed. "Are they all right? Did I keep them safe? Or did I—?"

Jerrin surprises me by smiling. "You protected them so well that they didn't feel any heat from the fire after you created the water dome. They said you told them you were half Auravalian and a mage. That's why they trusted you. Now they consider you to be one of the greatest magic practitioners of all time."

I feel my face flush with embarrassment.

"Do you remember making the water dome?"

"Sort of," I say. "I don't remember quite how I did it. I mean, I remember what I did, now that you've reminded me, but I don't remember how I knew what to do. Does that make any sense?"

"Considering the condition you were in when Kaden and I got to you, yes, it makes perfect sense. Can you remember anything else?"

"After I made the water dome, I thought maybe I could do something similar to isolate the forest fire. I remember pulling water from the stream. I tried to—I tried to—" I pause and struggle to recover the memory. I just can't. "Whatever I tried to do, it didn't work. I was tired and frustrated. I remember that part clearly. Then I punched the ground with my fists."

I look at my hands. They're bruised and scabby.

I hold them out as evidence.

"Do you remember how you finally put the fire out?"

"Did I?" I ask. "Did I really manage to put it out?"

"All but a few smoldering embers," Jerrin says. "I went back and took care of them for you. Considering what you went through, I thought you deserved that much help. But you don't remember?"

I shake my head.

"Do you remember reaching out for Kaden?"

I shake my head again.

"All right," Jerrin said. "That's enough for now. We'll talk again when you're stronger. If Mertley is going to make you eat and then go to sleep when he gets back with your dinner, I think I'd better give Kaden a few minutes with you."

"He's here?"

"Yes. I'll go get him."

I wish I could brush my teeth and comb my hair. I'm sure I look a mess. I'm glad there's no mirror.

When Kaden comes in, he looks about like I feel.

"Kaden," I exclaim, "what happened? Are you all right?"

He sits down in the chair beside my bed. As he takes my hand, I feel him trembling. He kisses my palm.

"Kaden?"

"How are you feeling?" He asks me. His voice is as weak and quivery as his hands.

"I'm fine," I answer. "Now it's your turn to answer my question."

His lips barely twitch, and I realize he's tying to smile.

Whatever happened must have been awful if he feels the need to reassure me before he can tell me what it was.

"I was meeting with the king, my father, and Princes Skyler and Jerrin when I felt your pull. Luckily Jerrin felt it at the same time and was able to recognize that you had used the last of your strength to reach me.

"He opened a portal to you." He kisses my palm again. "I thought my heart would break when I saw you. You were curled up like a child, and you were barely breathing.

"Stwethil-thage fluttered all around you, chirping with anxiety. While Jerrin talked to them to find out what happened, I held you and gave you as much strength and energy as I could. It almost wasn't enough.

"Hellie, what were you thinking? How could you risk yourself like that? When Mertley saw you, he said you were almost beyond help."

Having Kaden in the room does amazing things to my heart rate and respiration. I imagine my blood pressure has gone up too.

Suddenly, though, I'm worried about him.

"You're not sending me energy anymore, are you?"

"No," he says, "I don't have a lot to spare right now."

For the first time I notice he's dressed in pale blue pajamas that match the ones I'm wearing.

He lifts a hand to touch my face. I rub my cheek against his fingers.

"Mertley is helping you recover, too?" I ask.

"Yes, though it's really just a precautionary measure. I overexerted myself, but not to a state of complete depletion the way you did."

He gets off the chair and sits on the side of my bed.

"May I check on your condition? To relieve my mind?"

"Of course," I tell him.

I let him look into my eyes.

It takes a lot longer than it did for him to examine my sprained wrist and scraped knees. In fact he is still doing whatever it is that he does when Mertley returns carrying a tray.

"Kaden," the man snaps, "you stop that immediately. You're in no condition to do any healing."

Kaden breaks eye contact with me, but when he turns to face Mertley there is no sign of guilt in his glance. "I was only checking the damage. I had no intention of interfering with your work."

"Good. Now go back to your room, eat, and sleep. You can visit your lady after you've both napped."

"Yes, Master," Kaden says. "I'll see you later, Hellie." Then he's out the door.

"Kaden is doing his apprenticeship with you?" I ask.

"Yes," Mertley says. He sets the tray he's carrying on a little table beside the bed. "He's got quite a gift, Kaden has. I'll be glad when things settle down on your world so he can get back to his studies."

Mertley glances at the head of the bed and it rises, lifting me into a sitting position. He takes a bowl of soup from the tray and starts feeding me a spoonful at a time.

"Shouldn't you have an aide or an intern do that?" I ask. "It feels odd having a doctor feed me."

"How will I know you're getting the nourishment you need if I have someone else feed you?" Mertley asks.

"I don't know." I try to shrug but I can't.

Suddenly I'm afraid.

Jerrin, Mertley, and Kaden have all told me that I used up my energy, but I didn't realize what they meant until now. I'm as weak as a baby. Mertley is feeding me because I'm not even strong enough to hold a spoon.

I turn my questioning eyes on him.

"Just hit you, did it?" he says, meeting my gaze.

"Did I really almost kill myself putting out the fire?"

"You came closer to it than anyone I've known who still survived." He holds up the spoon, and I open my mouth obediently.

While I swallow, I have a sudden epiphany.

"Kaden used his strength to keep my heart beating and my lungs breathing while I was in the forest," I say. "You're feeding me with more than soup, aren't you? You're giving me the energy that I need to talk, to eat, and to think. Otherwise I'd be an unconscious, inert mass lying in this bed."

"Jerrin warned me that you were quick."

"Is sharing energy a normal part of Auravalian healing?"

Mertley feeds me more soup before he answers.

"When it has been necessary," he says, "I've used my energy to support my patients. You've needed more help than most, and I've had a couple of apprentices assisting me. It's been good practice for them."

"Are you—are—will you—?"

Why won't my brain work?

I am getting really frustrated, and I'm afraid I'll burst into tears soon.

"Shh," Mertley says. "The reason you're having trouble organizing your thoughts is because you're still so weak. You seem to have forgotten that the brain is one of the body's vital organs just like the heart and the lungs. Your mind is as exhausted as the rest of your body. After you sleep again, it'll be easier for you. In fact, every time you wake up, you'll notice a bit more of your mental and physical prowess has returned to you."

He holds the spoon close to my lips, and like a good little girl I open my mouth. When he has finished feeding me, he stands up, looks into my eyes, strokes my forehead, and I fall into oblivion.

For a while I seem to be in an interminable cycle of waking, eating, and sleeping. I don't see anyone except Mertley.

I don't know how long this goes on.

Then, I finally wake up and can feel a difference.

I roll over onto my side.

I can roll over, I exclaim silently.

I stretch.

Everything seems to be working. I sit up.

"Very good," Mertley says a moment later.

"Thank you. Do you happen to know how long I've been here? By Earth time, I mean?"

He makes a gesture toward the wall opposite my bed. There is now a digital clock mounted there. Besides the time, it indicates the date and the day of the week.

"Jerrin installed it," Mertley says. "He predicted that your first question would be about the date and time."

"It says Sunday morning at 11:30. Is that supposed to be the time back home?"

"That's what Jerrin told me when he hung it."

"It sure feels like I've been here longer than a day and a half."

"Time here doesn't run quite the same as it does on Earth. Since I don't travel between worlds, I don't have first hand experience with it. Jerrin or Neeve could explain the science of it to you. Do you feel like getting out of bed and enjoying some sunshine with Kaden?"

"I'd love it." I twist around and swing my legs off the bed. I stand up. Suddenly I feel lightheaded, as if I might vomit or pass out.

I sit down on the edge of the bed and lean forward until the nausea passes.

"Let's try it again," Mertley says, "but slower this time."

He goes to the far corner of the room and comes back pushing a strange looking chair. Rather than wheels, it appears to ride on casters like a laundry cart or an office chair.

"Tomorrow we'll get you on your feet so you can start walking again, but for now let's take it easy."

I accept his offered hand. It feels amazingly strong.

He supports my back with his other hand as he slowly pulls me up so I'm standing beside the chair. He helps me take two little steps, and then he holds the chair steady while I sit down.

Kaden enters the room right on cue.

He is dressed in a tan t-shirt and blue jeans.

His artificially blond hair has been parted down the middle, making the dark roots more prominent. The sides are hooked behind his ears. This is the first time I've seen him without the man bun. His hair is even longer than I imagined. I stare at him, trying to decide which hairstyle I like better on him.

After a moment's consideration, I decide I would like the way he looks even if he chose to shave his head. He is simply the most beautiful man I've ever seen. How is it possible that he's in love with me?

"Kaden," Mertley says, "you may take your lady for a walk around the gardens, but you bring her back the moment she starts to show fatigue."

"Yes, Master."

Mertley pats my shoulder. "Tell him if you get tired. I realize he is usually attuned to your feelings, but he's still recovering and might be a little slower than usual. Make it as easy on him as you can."

"I will."

A few minutes later, Kaden wheels me onto a path that winds among the most amazing plants I've ever seen. There are flowers that look as if they've been made out of crepe paper, and there are bushes with blossoms that look as if they're made of blown glass. There are clumps of decorative grass five feet tall and trees with hanging branches covered with lacy flowers that flow together and look like a bridal veil.

The colors of the foliage vary from garishly bright to delicately pastel. Yet they work harmoniously together to create a sublime, albeit surrealistic, landscape.

I'm accepting the strangeness fairly well until I see my first Auravalians winging through the air.

I start to hyperventilate.

My mind shouts that it's impossible.

My eyes tell me just the opposite.

I clearly see a dozen pre-adolescents flitting through the air on butterfly wings, playing what looks like a game of aerial tag.

I tell myself I shouldn't find the sight so disturbing.

Dark in the Forest: Another Modern Fairytale

After all, I watched Kaden's wings form.

I saw him hover mid-air.

I even let him fly me up above the forest canopy. (The use of the word *let* in the previous sentence is subjective. He didn't ask my permission before he swooped down and picked me up, but once we were in flight, he certainly had my permission not to put me down until we were solidly on the ground again.)

Nonetheless, it's hard for me to watch these kids bobbing in the air. I want to scream at them, "Get down from there before you get hurt," the same way that I might if I saw a bunch of Earth's kids climbing up a rickety, old ladder to the roof of a decrepit, rotting building.

I close my eyes.

Kaden wheels me into the shade of a big tree where there is a stone bench. He sits and turns the wheelchair so we're facing each other.

"Are you all right?" he asks.

"Just experiencing some culture shock," I answer. "Do you know what that means?"

"Yes," he answers. "Karissa explained it to me when she and Neeve came to visit you. She told me to expect it if you got to see anything other than the hospital."

"When were they here?"

"Yesterday. Mertley wouldn't let them wake you. They'll be back this afternoon or evening."

When we were first discussing the possibility of my taking mage training, Karissa mentioned that Auravale is intimidating to outsiders. That's why she suggested that I have my training in Brenlyn's workshop. I wonder what is out there beyond the hospital—besides people with wings flying around—that is so frightening.

I don't want to think about it. I change the subject.

"What's the situation with Maldon?" I ask Kaden.

"He hasn't been found, if that's what you want to know. The king has watchers posted around your forest, your home, the daycare center, your church, your high school, and Brenlyn's shop. He had Jerrin do a thorough search of the area. Those were the only places where Jerrin recognized traces of your magic."

"I've never done magic at home or at school," I exclaim.

"Just because you didn't know you were doing it at the time, that doesn't mean you didn't do it." He stands up, turns the chair around, gets behind it, and starts to push. "Do you want to see more of the gardens, or should I take you back to your room? Are you getting tired yet?"

"Actually I'm more hungry than tired," I say. "Isn't it about mealtime?"

"In your condition," he answers, "regardless of the time of day, if you feel hungry, it is mealtime for you." He stops pushing the chair and doesn't say anything for a moment.

I twist around so I can look at him. He has the slightly vacant expression he had when he was communicating long-distance with Neeve.

He glances down at me. "There will be food waiting in your room when we get back so that you can eat and then go straight to sleep."

"All right," I say, "but first I have two questions."

"I'll answer them if I can."

"You told me you can't read my mind, right?"

"That's true," he replies.

"But you talk to Neeve mind-to-mind, and just now you must have communicated with someone to request a meal for me. That means you must have some kind of telepathic skills, right?"

"Not really," Kaden answers. "When I was assigned to work on your world, I was given a spell to use if I needed to reach Neeve. He is my Auravalian contact on Earth. Mertley is Master of my apprenticeship, so I have a spell for reaching him. I let him know of your hunger, and he told me he would make the appropriate arrangements. I also have a spell for my father. Other than that, I have to use oral speech like everyone else." He smiles at me. "What is your other question?"

I'm still trying to process the concept of communication spells, and it takes me a second to remember what else I wanted to know.

"Tell me what you meant when you said the king had watchers posted all around Shawon. The people in my town are pretty close-knit. Strangers would stand out."

"They're not physically in Shawon," Kaden says. "If they were, Maldon might sense them and know something special was going on there. Watchmen are sorcerers who are skilled in precognition and farseeing."

"That means they can see the future and can view things at a great distance, right?"

"Right. The watchmen are doing everything they can to discover what Maldon's next moves will be. In the process, they're keeping vigil over your family and your town in case he figures out a way to get there that they couldn't anticipate or discover."

Chapter Thirty-seven

When we reach my room, Mertley is there with my meal. It looks as if I'm finally going to get some real food. I'm very tired of soup in its many varieties.

Mertley plumps my pillows and stacks them against the headboard. Then he lets Kaden lift me from the chair and put me in bed. Kaden kisses my palm before he leaves me. I hope he's going to eat and rest too.

My meal is on a tray that has four little legs. Mertley stands it over my lap so I can feed myself. Then he sits on the chair at my bedside to watch me eat.

On my plate is some kind of white fish in a creamy sauce plus two cooked vegetables. To the side is a little bowl of diced fruit.

Generally I am not an adventuresome eater. I prefer to have foods that I'm familiar with, at least in public. If I'm at home and I dislike something, I can spit it out, but I can't do that in front of other people.

So far, everything I've been served here has been okay, but I'm still cautious. I take a bite of fish and then one of each vegetable. They're close enough to halibut, broccoli, and carrots to satisfy my taste buds.

Now that I can feed myself, I feel silly eating while Mertley just sits there and watches me. I decide we should have some dinner conversation.

"Can you tell me about Kaden's apprenticeship?" I ask. "Or is that unethical here?"

"Apprenticeships are personal but not private. I put him back to work for a while this morning. He's gotten behind on his studies since he's been spending so much time on Earth."

There's no sense of criticism in his comment. He's just stating a fact.

"Oh," I say. "When he told me he was doing a special assignment for the king, I just assumed he was on break from his apprenticeship, like in Shawon we're out of school right now for summer vacation."

"In Auravale apprenticeships are fulltime for five years. There are breaks and vacations, of course, but usually nothing quite this extensive. Still, Kaden has a rare talent, and the king needs the best."

"Is being a finder uncommon then?" I ask.

"Finders that can locate misplaced articles or lost children are fairly common. Nearly every public facility has a finder on staff to help careless, absentminded people to reconnect with their belongings. Finders who can locate things that have been purposely hidden are scarcer, but there are still enough of them to serve where needed. Finders as versatile as Kaden, however, only come along once or twice in a generation."

"What is different about what Kaden can do?"

"Everything." Mertley points at my tray. "Eat."

I obey.

"When one of our people has a single skill that is mage level, they're usually called a wizard."

"I know," I say. "Jerrin and Kaden talked about it. Jerrin said Kaden might be a new kind of wizard because he can rein in my power when I lose control. Kaden said it was just a splinter skill."

Mertley doesn't speak. He just sits there looking thoughtful for several minutes. "I suppose Jerrin wants him to be retested at the Magician's Guild," he says at last.

"Yes," I say. "Is that bad?"

"I don't know," he answers. "Kaden is already in high demand. His abilities are not limited to finding lost or hidden objects. He can also find intangible things."

"Like what?"

Mertley gives me a little grin. "If he ever asks you a question, you might as well be honest with him, because one of the ethereal things he can do is discover the truth. The Speaker for the House of Nobles wants Kaden to serve as a criminal judge. The House member who represents Financial Institutions wants him to be an auditor. The representative of Mental Health Services wants him to be an evaluator. Kaden can find hidden agendas, broken oaths, deceptions, lies, and the solution to most mysteries. In addition, he has strong secondary powers."

"What are secondary powers?" I ask.

Looking at my plate, Mertley heaves a big sigh. "I'm distracting you from your lunch. I think we should save this conversation for later."

"No," I say, digging into the diced fruit. "I'll eat."

"You'd better," Mertley says. "You need the nourishment to heal."

I eat two spoonsful of fruit before I venture to remind him of my question. "Secondary powers?"

"Secondary powers are like the primary powers in reverse. If Kaden ever hides an object from you, don't waste your time looking for it. No one can find what a finder has hidden except another finder, and sometimes not even then. Finders also tend to be good at burying secrets, concealing the truth, engaging in thefts, and hiding themselves from discovery.

"When a finder goes bad, the only person who can catch him is a stronger finder. Kaden is this generation's most powerful finder, which is why the king sent him to recover whatever he's been looking for on your world."

"But Kaden doesn't want to just go find things, and he doesn't want to be an auditor or a judge either. He wants to make people well."

"True," Mertley says. "Medicine has been Kaden's dream ever since he was a little boy. Here at the hospital, we're all grateful he chose to accept this apprenticeship. He will be an extraordinary healer. Finders as strong as Kaden are rare, but finders who can understand the workings of both the mind and the body and can find cures for their ailments are nearly nonexistent. When Kaden finishes his apprenticeship, he will become the sixth medical finder in recorded history.

"All the physical sciences advance dramatically when a finder like Kaden reaches maturity." Mertley sighs with a look of longing on his face. "I hope I can convince him to continue working with me."

After I finish eating, before Mertley can even remove the tray, I start yawning. I'm almost asleep by the time he rearranges the pillows so I can lie down.

Soft, whispering voices wake me.

I open my eyes to see Karissa, Neeve, and Shiane in conference over by the door.

"Come on in and sit a spell," I tell them, using one of Grandma Powers' favorite sayings.

Karissa comes in and perches on the side of the bed. "I'm sorry if we woke you up. Mertley said we could visit but only if you were already awake."

"Actually," I say, "I was in that weird stage of half-consciousness when you're trying to decide whether to finish waking up or whether to go back to sleep."

"I know that stage well," Karissa says, smiling. "Going back to sleep usually wins in my battles."

Looking aggrieved, Neeve walks over to Karissa and puts a hand on her shoulder. "Apparently my mother told Shiane that if I came to Auravale to visit Hellie I had to go home and visit with her first."

Matching Neeve's expression of exasperation, Karissa says with a mock Freudian accent, "*Das alt* guilt trip ploy, *richtig*? Or *warst du tatsächlich* neglecting *deine mutter*?"

"Your German is atrocious," Neeve says, "and so is your accent."

Karissa grins at him. "I love you too."

He grins back. "Do you mind visiting with Hellie while I go home and try to convince my mother that it is not unusual for grown sons to go a week or two without seeing their parents?"

"Go on," Karissa says with a nod of her head toward the door. "I'll enjoy visiting with Hellie alone for once."

He strokes her hair and then he and Shiane leave together.

"So, you and Neeve both speak German?"

"I don't," Karissa says with a laugh. "I got a free 30-day trial of an online language course, and I chose German. I thought it was probably the most like

212

English and would be the easiest to learn. Unfortunately I don't have any natural talent with languages. But every now and then I remember a word or a phrase, so I'll toss it into a sentence.

"It drives Neeve crazy. Most Auravalians have the natural ability to pick up languages quickly and easily. However, the royal family has the gift of tongues. They have the magical ability to understand, speak, and write any language. Neeve hates listening to me butcher German."

"So what did you say to him?"

"When he said his mother insisted that he visit her before visiting with you, I said something like: *The old guilt trip ploy, right? Or have you been neglecting your mother in actuality?* Or, anyway, I think that's what I said. As Neeve pointed out, my German and my accent are both bad."

"I've taken two years of high school Spanish, and I'm afraid my Spanish is no better than your German."

For a while we chat about languages and high school and our triumphs and our failures. It's like we've been friends forever. Then Karissa brings up the fire.

"Saturday morning," Karissa says, "as soon as I heard about the fire behind your house, I tried to call you. When I couldn't get you on your cellphone, I called your home landline. Your mother answered and I talked with her for a while. She said she was relieved that you were out of town when it happened. She said they had no idea how they'd break the news to you. That was before Neeve told me what really happened. Are you going to be all right? Neeve said you almost died putting out the fire."

"I'm okay. Mertley says I'll be up and walking by tomorrow and I should be able to go home on Wednesday."

"Is there anything you need? I tried to talk Neeve into bringing you a hamburger, fries, and a Diet Coke, but he said the smell of a fried vegetable mingling with the stench of cooked animal flesh would probably cause a riot here in the hospital and might possibly lead to a few deaths."

"Wow," I say, "Neeve's mom isn't the only person in that family adept at the good old guilt trip!"

Karissa laughs. After a moment I laugh with her.

I'm not sure how we get on the topic of myths and legends, but she's comparing European and Auravalian mythology when Neeve comes back.

"The problem," Karissa says, "is that much of our mythology is based on Auravalian reality."

"What does that mean?" I ask.

She gives me a *wait a minute* look and then turns to Neeve. "Are things okay with your mother?"

"Yes." Since Karissa is still sitting on the side of my bed, Neeve settles down on the chair. "She just wanted to tell me that Rylee is pregnant and that the naming will be at Winter Solstice. She said you and I should be there."

"Rylee?" Karissa repeats, crinkling her brow. "She's your eldest, full sister,

213

right?"

"Yes," Neeve says. "She's the first child of my father by my mother."

"I'll get them all sorted out eventually," Karissa says with a smile. "Are we going to come back for the naming?"

"Would you like to?"

"Very much," she answers.

"Then we'll plan on it. What did you two talk about in my absence?"

"Lot's of stuff," Karissa answers, "but I was just now telling Hellie about part of our mythology being based on your reality. Will you explain to her about the echoes?"

"Sure." He moves the chair closer to the bed so he can take Karissa's hand before he turns to me. "All worlds that have strong magic create a kind of resonance. Sometimes the vibrations can be felt or heard by sensitive people on nearby worlds. When that happens, the people end up trying to make sense of what they've experienced. Often they do it by incorporating the events into their folktales, artwork, literature, or religious symbolism."

"For example?" I ask.

"Your people have legends about mermaids," Neeve answers. "This world actually has them."

Well, I think to myself, that answers the question I had when Kaden mentioned that Maldon had murdered some merfolk.

"And unicorns," Karissa adds. "They have real unicorns here, too, but they're not as big as horses. They're more goat-sized. And they talk. Sort of. They aren't equipped for oral speech, so they project their thoughts."

"Mermaids and unicorns," I say with a smile. "At least we adopted pleasant myths from you."

"Not all of them are pleasant," Neeve says. "We have dragons, sphinxes, and hellhounds here too. Luckily our sorcerers have been able to keep them away from the populated areas for the past eight centuries. However, the beasts are still out there."

I freeze, remembering my recurring dream. I've always assumed the hellhounds in it were symbols of evil, not living creatures.

"Is something wrong," Neeve asks with concern.

Karissa takes my hand. "You've gone pale. Do you need Mertley?"

"No," I say shakily. "It's just—Neeve, what can you tell me about hellhounds?"

"What do you want to know?"

I struggle to find the right question. I'm not sure what to ask.

"Maybe," Neeve says, "it would be easier if you start by telling me why you want to know about them."

"I'm afraid it'll sound silly."

"In my opinion," Neeve says, "nothing having to do with hellhounds will ever sound silly. They're not silly creatures."

"When I was about ten years old," I tell him, "I started having a recurring dream about being chased by hellhounds. I've always assumed it was some kind of metaphor for my evil name. It never occurred to me that they might be real, living animals somewhere."

"In your dream," he asks, "what are they like?"

"They're big, black, and have red eyes. They don't bark like dogs. They make a deep growling, howling sound that makes the hairs on the back of my neck stand up."

"Anything else?"

"They don't like water," I say without thinking. Where did that come from? In my dream they stop at the water's edge, but I've assumed it was because they lost my scent. However, now that I think about it, well-trained hunting dogs would plunge into the stream and try to pick up the scent on the other side, wouldn't they?

"My father," Karissa comments, "says that dreams are based on wishes or fears. Just because hellhounds are real on Panelda, that—"

"Panelda?" I repeat.

"That's the name of our world," Neeve says. "Auravale is one of the twenty-two kingdoms of Panelda."

"Oh," I say before looking over at Karissa. "I'm sorry. You said something about hellhounds living in Panelda and then I interrupted you."

"What I was about to say is that just because hellhounds live here that doesn't necessarily mean you were dreaming about real hellhounds. They could still just be a symbol of your fears about the possible negative effects of your name."

"The only problem with that theory," Neeve says, "is that Hellie is a mage and could, therefore, have prophetic visions. Bree-Ella did. Have you ever mentioned your recurring dream to Jerrin?"

"No," I say. "It never occurred to me that it might be anything more than a childish nightmare until you mentioned that hellhounds are real here. Do they ever bond with humans? Or, uhm, can they be trained?"

"Not trained," Neeve says, "but they can be controlled by someone with enough power. I think you'd better discuss this with Jerrin."

Karissa nods her agreement.

"All right," I say. "The first chance I get."

"I could call him for you right now," Neeve offers.

Before I can answer, a sudden yawn catches me.

"We ought to leave," Karissa says to Neeve. "She looks like she needs to go back to sleep."

"We'll stop by and check on you again before Wednesday," Neeve says. "If you haven't had the opportunity to talk to Jerrin about your recurring dream before then, I'll go get him for you. All right?"

"Sure," I say.

They leave together with their arms around each other's waists. A moment later, I glimpse them through my window.

Dark in the Forest: Another Modern Fairytale

I wonder what their lives will be like in ten years.

Before Karissa and I got on the subject of mythology, she told me that she and Neeve were both going to start attending the University in the fall. She plans to major in elementary education so she can teach grade school, and Neeve will study music education so he can teach high school orchestra and band. That way, she said, they'll be able to keep an eye on their children during the school year and they'll all have the same vacations, which they can spend in Auravale.

I really like Karissa and Neeve.

They're determined to have a good life together. In preparation, they're trying to think of all the potential problems they might face so they can come up with solutions in advance. I've got to respect that kind of insight and courage.

I'm still looking out my window when I see Kaden join them.

They stand in a little triangle, talking.

I have Kaden in profile.

Automatically I smile. Just looking at him makes me happy.

But then I'm struck by some of the things Mertley told me earlier:

He'll be an extraordinary healer. Finders as strong as Kaden are rare, but finders who can understand the workings of both the mind and the body and can find cures for their ailments are nearly nonexistent. When Kaden finishes his apprenticeship, he will become the sixth medical finder in recorded history. All the physical sciences advance dramatically when a finder like Kaden reaches maturity.

My breath catches in my throat as I consider the implications of Mertley's comments.

If Kaden stays in Auravale, within a few years he'll be a medical finder—which is so much more than just being a doctor. He'll also be in a position to make revolutionary discoveries and to help all branches of science to advance.

If he decides he doesn't want to continue in that line, he has a multitude of other choices. Mertley said he's in high demand.

But how could he make a living in Shawon, Colorado?

He couldn't practice medicine.

I'm fairly certain that the United States and Auravale don't have any reciprocal licensing agreements.

So, where does that leave us?

If Kaden and I ever got married, because of that once-in-a-lifetime love he has for me, he might be willing to try to live in Shawon, but he would have to give up his dream of becoming a doctor, a dream he's had since childhood. Or he could go through college and medical school somewhere on Earth—a long, tedious, expensive process.

He'd be in the same position with any of the other professions Mertley mentioned: he'd need a Bachelor's Degree followed by an MBA, an MSW, a J.D. or a PhD depending on what he wanted to do.

After spending five years of study and apprenticeship in Auravale, I wonder how long he'd tolerate having to start over before his love for me dwindled and was replaced by resentment.

But if living in Colorado isn't a good choice, the only other option for us would be to live in Auravale.

As much as I delight in Kaden's good qualities—and he has dozens—I don't know if I could ever love him enough to leave behind Angel, my parents, my friends, and my world to live in his. I might try, but I don't think it would take too long before the love would fail. If nothing else, I would miss Angel almost beyond bearing.

I feel tears well up in my eyes.

There isn't a solution for us the way there is for Karissa and Neeve.

Kaden chose his career and made his plans based on the certainty that he would live his life on Panelda. There's no room in his scheme of things for an alien wife who lives on an alien world.

Letting him love me is wrong.

He is a kind, affectionate, talented, generous, beautiful man.

He deserves the life Auravale can give him and that Colorado cannot.

I've got to stop this relationship before it goes any further.

As he turns a corner and walks out of sight, I realize I've fallen in love with him. I know it because my heart is breaking at the thought of letting him go.

Chapter Thirty-eight

I can't face Kaden.

He would know my feelings have changed, and it's not fair for him to learn I love him just at the moment when I realize we can't have a future together.

Summoning all my strength and courage, I swing my legs off the bed. I cautiously push myself upright and let my feet take my weight.

Hooray. I can stand unassisted.

Maybe my posture's not perfect, but it's close enough for walking.

I shuffle over to the closet. My clothes are folded neatly on a shelf—not only that, but they're also clean. As I get dressed, I'm surprised that the laundry managed to get the smoky smell out. Maybe they have a special washing wizard who takes care of odors.

I lean back against the wall as I pull on my jeans. My balance is off, but I feel stronger than I expected considering what I've been told about my condition.

Focusing on my forest, I open a portal and step through.

I stumble and fall.

My clumsiness is not caused by my diminished physical capacity.

It's just I'm too stunned to continue standing.

So much of the forest has burned that it's unrecognizable.

I thought I had put it out before it had a chance to spread very far.

No wonder I depleted my energy.

If Jerrin was being honest with me, at least I managed to save the stwethil-thage even if—my breath catches in my throat—even if I couldn't save the woods.

I sit with my legs drawn up and my chin on my knees.

I sob, flooded with guilt and sorrow.

I let Great-great-great-grandfather Eugene Powers' enchanted forest burn. This is the one place I thought I could go for safety and comfort, and now it's just charred wood and ash.

I don't know what to do.

My parents don't expect me home for another three days.

My best friends, Nadine and Karen, are still out of town.

I don't dare go to Brenlyn and Talitha. I'm sure they'd tell Neeve, and he'd haul me back to Auravale or have Jerrin come get me.

I can't turn to Karissa for the same reason.

Not only that, somewhere an evil sorcerer is looking for me to steal my powers or to force me to use them on his behalf—powers that I'm just beginning to realize are mine.

For a moment I wish my grandmother were with me, but as I look at the devastation all around me, I'm halfway glad that she's not. Seeing this would break her heart.

The only advantage would be that we could cry together.

I clamber to my feet and stumble off through the desolation.

I have no idea where I am or where I'm headed.

I'm not sure I care.

"Come," a high-pitched voice chirps beside my right ear. *"Hurry. Hurry."*

"You must hide," a similar voice twitters next to my left ear. *"We will protect you."*

Before I can even turn my head to look for the owners of the voices, a pumpkin orange stwethil-thage flies right up to my face. *"Evil comes for you. Hurry. We will hide you."*

I take a quick glance to the sides. The stwethil-thage on my right is spinach green, and the one on my left is eggplant purple.

They chirp in unison: *"Hurry, hurry, hurry."*

When they take off to the right, I totter along behind them.

Apparently my pace is unsatisfactory.

The spinach green stwethil-thage (whom I decide to think of as just plain Spinach) darts back and grabs a hunk of my hair and pulls.

The purple creature (a.k.a. Eggplant) shrieks, *"Hurry faster!"*

In the distance I hear the snarling and growling of wild animals.

Wild animals in the forest—in my burned-up forest?

"Almost too late," the pumpkin orange (now just Pumpkin) stwethil-thage yells.

We've come to the pond in the southeast section of the forest. The fire didn't touch this area. I'm glad to know something survived. I want to pause for just a split second to look around, but all three stwethil-thage grab my hair and pull.

I figure I can go with them or spend the rest of the summer partially bald.

Easy choice.

I don't know how to describe what happens next.

I follow the little creatures between two aspen trees and end up somewhere else.

I don't think we're in Auravale.

I know we're not on Earth.

I'm not sure we're on a planet at all.

Dark in the Forest: Another Modern Fairytale

It's as if we're in between worlds where matter isn't quite solid and where dreams are truer than reality.

Whatever this place is, it's lovely—full of shifting colors, sweet aromas, gentle air movements, and soft sounds, none of which is distinct.

Stwethil-thage are everywhere.

"He has the beasts with him," Pumpkin cries out. He/she/it (I have no idea how to identify gender) flies directly to the being that I assume is their leader. He (I decide this based on *pink is girls* and *blue is for boys*) is a color my grandmother called cornflower blue, which is blue with purplish undertones.

"Are you certain?" the leader asks.

"We all heard them," Eggplant and Spinach answer together.

Cornflower flies over to me and hovers a few inches from my face. *"I am sorry. We had hoped to protect you as you protected so many of us during the fire, but if the Evil One has his beasts with him, we can't hide you. He cannot sense you here, but the beasts have been trained to hunt stwethil-thage. When he cannot find you, he will have the beasts seek us, and that will lead him to you. I'm so sorry."*

"If I leave, will you be safe?"

"No. The portal gateway that our beloved Bree-Ella created for us was destroyed when the fire changed the landscape. Our magic is only strong enough to take us out of a world, but we must have a portal to enter another. The Evil One's beasts have enough magic to follow us here."

"I have only been to one place in Auravale: the hospital. It is surrounded by beautiful gardens. If I open a portal for you, will you be safe there?"

Cornflower flitters around me for a moment.

"I sense no portal key."

"I don't need one."

"A royal mage!" Cornflower exclaims.

All the stwethil-thage line up as if they're in a military formation floating in the air. As a unit they all bow their heads at me.

"I'm more like a poor relation," I say. When the leader gives me a strange look, I shrug and say, "Never mind. The important thing is I can open a portal for you."

"For us? You are not coming with us?"

"I can't. I can't leave my world unprotected."

"We will stay with you then!" Cornflower insists.

"No, please go," I say. "Having you live in this forest has brought magic into my world. When it's safe, I want you to come back and live here again. Please go now so you can return later."

I open a portal to the garden at the hospital in Auravale.

"Hurry," I tell them. "I don't want the beasts to find you."

Cornflower shoos the other stwethil-thage ahead and then touches me on the right temple. *"If you need us, think your need and we will come. You are like Bree-Ella. You can open a portal that will let us come to you on your thoughts."*

"Wait," I say, "before you go, will you please answer two questions for me?"

I'm going on gut instinct here. I'm sure I know the answer to the first question, but I can't ask the second question without some kind of preamble.

"Yes, if I can."

"The person you call the Evil One, is he Maldon Darker?"

The little creature's eyes open wide, whether with surprise or horror I can't tell.

"Yes."

"Are the three magical objects that Bree-Ella left with you safe? If Maldon can't find me, he'll try to find them."

The expression on Cornflower's face is clear this time: it is suspicion. *"Who are you? What do you know about Bree-Ella?"*

Something inside me tells me that this moment is why I was given my strange name.

"I am Hellenaura Dark Powers. Bree-Ella was my grandmother." I realize I dropped a couple of generations, but I want to keep it simple.

Cornflower whoops (which is a startling sound coming from a high pitched chirp). Gleefully he spins in the air three times. *"She told us we could only give them to a Dark who shines like a candle. When the Evil One is gone, I will give them to you. He cannot find them. She hid them well."*

"Thank you. Now go join your people while I figure out what to do about Maldon Darker."

Cornflower shoots through the portal, which then snaps shut.

I'm alone again.

What would happen if I just stayed where I am?

Cornflower said Maldon couldn't sense me here.

If Maldon doesn't detect my presence, maybe he'll go back to Auravale, or perhaps to some other world, and leave me alone for a while. It would be nice if I could finish regaining my strength before I have to confront him.

I suppose if I had a five star hotel and a good restaurant available, I might consider putting down roots. However, without food, water, and a bed, I don't suppose I'd fare very well for very long.

Besides, I can't leave Maldon roaming around our woods with his hellhounds. I need to lead them away from the residential area. The only problem is that the pond is in the widest section of the forest. I've got quite a distance to go before I reach the road that runs along the western border.

When I step back into my world, I can at least use the pond as a reference point so I know which way to run.

I start jogging.

Once I get to the road, I hope I can flag down a ride that'll take me away from Shawon. In other circumstances I might open a portal (now that I know how) to get where I want to go, but I need Maldon to follow my scent or my aura or whatever he uses to track someone. I don't want him to accidentally stumble across my family or anyone else he could use against me—which, I suppose, would be just about everybody.

Thank heavens Angel and Peter's relationship is out in the open so they don't need to meet in the woods anymore.

I hear the growling of the hellhounds.

The sound makes the hair on my arms and neck stand on end.

Even though I'm not in the best shape of my life, I take a couple of deep breaths and pretend I'm on the basketball court. I've played when I've been this tired before—and I've played well. I ease into a comfortable lope that will allow me to pace myself, keeping just enough reserve for a final sprint if needed.

As I run, I hear the hellhounds again.

They sound closer.

I don't panic.

I keep a nice even pace.

Then I top a rise and see nothing but burned out forest in front of me. I slow down.

While I was following the stwethil-thage, I couldn't help but stir up puffs of ash as I walked. I could feel it coating my nose and throat before we reached the pond.

I don't look forward to repeating the experience.

But—hmm—wouldn't the same thing happen to animals?

If the hellhounds are following my trail by scent, the ash and lingering smell of smoke might work in my favor if I can stay out of sight. I angle off to my left because there are the remnants of a cluster of trees and I want to get on the other side of them.

I feel as if I've been jogging forever.

I figure I can either sit down and rest for a moment now or I can keep going and collapse later.

I'm glad no one in the hospital fiddled around with my tote bag (I can easily imagine some overly zealous aide dumping the contents in a garbage bin and having the bag cleaned along with my clothing). Luckily, no one did that, and there is still half a bottle of water left inside.

Not too far away I see a large, squarish rock that's the right size for a stool. I sit, take a mouthful of water, swish it around for a moment, and then swallow very slowly. I do it again.

When I go to put the bottle back into the tote, I notice the corner of something silvery. After I move the bag of chips out of the way, I spy my Three Musketeer candy bar. I tear open the wrapper. It's clear that the candy has been exposed to some heat—like a forest fire—but I think it's still edible, and I'm hungry.

I nibble at the candy to make it last as long as possible. When I've eaten half, I put the rest back inside my tote, open the bag of chips, take out a couple, and eat as I run.

Doesn't this forest ever end?

Grandma and I walked all over it, and I don't remember its being this big. I come to a wide stream.

This ought to be a landmark, but all the trails are gone. I've been using the sun to keep on a straight course. Other than being west of the pond, I have no idea where I am.

The water in the stream is scummy with ash. I don't want to get my shoes wet, but even more, I don't want to get that slimy gunk all over them.

I go downstream a ways until I come to some rocks that I can use as steppingstones. I hop from one to another until I'm on the other bank.

My lungs hurt.

I've been breathing ash too long.

When I try to take a deep inhalation, it triggers a coughing fit that doubles me over.

I can't run anymore.

I don't dare stop.

As I lurch forward, I realize I'm about at the end of my strength.

Chapter Thirty-nine

The landscape begins to show more green and less char.

Ahead is a huge old lodgepole pine tree that was hardly singed by the fire. As I stumble toward it, it seems to move farther and farther away from me— a symptom of my exhaustion.

When I finally reach it, I lean against the trunk and try to catch my breath. Another coughing fit hits me.

I want to sit down and rest, but I'm afraid if I do I won't be able to get up again. I take a couple of swallows of water and then eat the last half of my candy bar.

After wandering through so much destruction, standing below branches covered in deep green pine needles is psychologically refreshing even if it doesn't actually do anything medically to revive my body.

Straining my ears, I listen for the howling and growling of pursuit. It seems as if I haven't heard the hellhounds for quite a while, but I'm sure they're still out there somewhere.

I don't hear any of the normal forest sounds either. The fire must have driven away the birds, the squirrels, the foxes, and the other natural residents, and they haven't begun to return yet.

Still, I do hear something.

I try to slow my raspy breath so I can listen harder.

Hellie, an unfamiliar deep voice calls directly into my mind. W*here are you, Hellie?*

There is a pause, and then, with the words drawn out eerily, the question is repeated. *Helllllllie? Wherrrre arrrrre yoooooooou?*

Chills skitter up my back.

I don't like it that he knows my name.

The shadows in the forest deepen.

Clouds are blanking out the sky as the sun inches toward the horizon.

I feel a bit of panic building up in my chest.

I'm not going to make it to the road before nightfall.

Now what am I supposed do?

It'll be dark soon.

Then I have two realizations at the same time.

First, I'm going to spend the night all by myself out in the open while Maldon and his hellhounds roam around looking for me.

Second, I am living my recurring dream right now.

As I make these observations, I hear the same male voice. I can't understand the words this time, but the baying and howling of the hellhounds seem to answer his call.

I clear my mind and think of nothingness.

Turning my head from left to right, I'm aware (as in my dream) that the only place I can hide where the hellhounds can't reach me is in the tree. Of course that won't keep a determined man away, but I can think about that once I'm off the ground and hidden among the branches.

Wood is one of the elemental forces that is antithetical to magic. It doesn't repel it, but it is resistant to magical influences. That might provide me with a layer of protection, not a thick layer, but any is better than none.

Keeping my mind blank, I circle the trunk looking for the low branch I know has to be here. To keep from dropping my lunch tote when I jump for the branch, I slip the strap over my head so that it slants diagonally across my chest. I shove the pouch part toward my back so it won't get in the way.

I pull the sleeves of my sweatshirt down to cover my hands in hopes that the cuffs will protect my palms from the rough bark. I won't be able to hide from the hellhounds if they scent blood.

Taking a couple of steps back, I visualize myself as light as a feather.

I lunge forward, leaping up and grasping the branch.

A tiny part of me half expects Kaden to be there to catch my wrists and pull me up. It happened once in a dream. But as Karissa told me in the hospital, some dreams are just wishes.

I dangle for a moment before I pull myself up enough to hook one arm around the branch. Then I swing a leg over. I'm really in bad shape. Ordinarily I would be able to haul myself up in one smooth movement. Now I have to push and pull, squirm and wriggle, to get the rest of my body onto the limb. I hold onto the trunk and cough some more before I start climbing. I go as high as I can.

For just a moment, I allow myself to sit motionlessly on a branch and rest. Then I close my eyes, concentrate, and erase all signs of my passage from the tree back to the stream. Water is another elemental force that is anti-magic.

Just when I'm about to modify my vision to try to catch sight of Maldon and the hellhounds, I feel a swirl of magic just inches from my body. Reaching up, I grab hold of a branch I can use to haul myself to my feet, but there's nowhere I can go and nothing I can do to prevent whatever is about to happen.

I press my back against the trunk and brace myself for the worst.

A portal opens.

Kaden steps through it.

Dark in the Forest: Another Modern Fairytale

"Sorry I'm late, but I didn't want to turn your forest into a battlefield. It took me a while to convince the king and my father to let me come alone."

I'm so glad to see him I throw my arms around him. I have tears in my eyes. "How'd you know I was hiding in a tree of all places?"

He tips my face up and kisses my forehead. "I'll always be able to find you, Hellie," he says. Then he wraps his arms around me.

"You shouldn't have come," I say. "Maldon is out there somewhere with his hellhounds."

"I know," Kaden says.

"I'm not sure how he found me, but the stwethil-thage—"

"Shh, we can talk about that later. We don't have much time. Maldon will locate you within the next few minutes."

As if Kaden's words are a signal, the hellhounds begin to grumble and growl again. They are much closer than they were, the closest they've been all evening.

"We need to switch places," Kaden says, "so I'm not in your way." He holds onto a branch that's above our heads while he steps around me.

His back is to the trunk, and I am in front of him.

"Jerrin said to tell you not to try to defeat Maldon, just try to get him away from your woods and your home."

"But I don't know how," I say.

"That's why I'm here," Kaden says. I feel his breath brush against my ear, and I shiver. He puts his hands on my shoulders to steady me.

Snarling and howling sounds come closer and closer. I enhance my vision as Jerrin taught me and get my first view of a living hellhound—correction, my first view of three living hellhounds.

Although I've seen artists' renderings in books and computer-generated images in movies, nothing can compare with the real thing.

They are enormous creatures, probably four feet at the shoulder, and shaped more like hyenas than dogs. They are completely black except for their glowing red eyes. They run with their mouths open, exposing sharp pointed teeth. When they reach the stream, they pace back and forth until they find the spot where I hopped across the water, going from from rock to rock.

The hellhounds make deep rumbling sounds and glare at the stream as if it were some kind of enemy.

A man dressed all in white and astride a gorgeous white horse rides up behind them. My first thought is: *What a cliché!*

I know he's all decked out like that to present himself as a good guy, but there is something predatory and cruel about his face that he can't conceal.

He gazes beyond the stream, and his eyes dart around for a moment.

He projects his voice, but not just into my head this time. I can hear him with my ears. When Kaden's hands tighten their grip on my shoulders, I realize he can hear him too.

"I know you're here, Hellie," Maldon shouts. "Your essence fills the forest.

I've come to take you home."

My heart freezes, but I feel compelled to respond.

"No," I call back at him.

"Don't defy me, Hellie. I can feel your fatigue. Even if you weren't weakened by your recent experiences, you wouldn't be able to resist me. Let me take you home, and I'll teach you how to use your powers. Nothing will be beyond your grasp. You'll be able to have whatever you want in this world or any other."

"No," I repeat fervently. "You can't give me what I want. I'm not going anywhere with you."

"I've come all this way to take you home. I won't leave without you."

From his pocket he takes out a strange looking talisman. It appears to be made of ivory, feathers, and green stones.

"Find your safe place," Kaden whispers in my ear, "but don't close your eyes. Stay focused on Maldon."

"I will," I whisper back.

Instead of going to the stars this time, I pull them to me. I feel their bright light and warmth filling me.

"When he holds up the charm," Kaden says, continuing to speak softly, "he'll focus his power through it and then throw it at you. Throw it right back at him."

"I don't know how," I say. "Jerrin hasn't taught me that."

"You didn't know how to stop time, but you did it anyway. Trust your instincts."

I'm scared.

I'm so scared that if Kaden weren't holding me in place, I'd probably topple—or maybe jump—from the tree out of pure panic.

"Get ready," Kaden says.

In my dream when Maldon fired his power through the charm at me, the tree burst into flames and I burned.

I remember the awful sound of my skin sizzling and crackling. I remember the pain. I remember screaming.

I was alone, and the experience was horrifying.

I didn't think anything could ever be worse.

Now I know something can be.

I have Kaden with me.

I couldn't bear to watch him burn, not Kaden.

If I can't stop Maldon, I pray I'll have enough time before the flames consume me to open a portal and shove Kaden through to safety.

Maldon holds up the talisman. It catches the last rays of sunlight, and a green beam shoots out of it straight at us.

Instinctively, as I did when Jerrin threw the croquet ball at me, I imagine an invisible bat. I swing it with all my might. It doesn't occur to me until the light deflects back at Maldon that imagining a mirror would have made more

227

sense—but it couldn't have been more effective.

His horse shies when the light rebounds at them. For a moment Maldon has the double task of preventing himself from being the victim of his own magic and keeping his horse from bucking him off.

He is briefly disoriented, and I enjoy watching him fumble around.

The moment doesn't last long.

Maldon yells at me. "So you choose to challenge me? Do not think that being Bree-Ella's child will protect you from my wrath if you continue to defy me."

I feel him doing something to manipulate the magic. The green stones on the talisman begin to glow. I guess, now that the sun has set, he has to energize the charm in a way different from before.

I feel Maldon's anger building.

He's like a little kid who is used to having his slightest demands met immediately and without question.

I think the beam of light he aimed at me a moment ago was nothing more than a warning shot. He expected to intimidate me so I'd succumb to his will on the spot. He can hardly believe he didn't succeed.

Now, he is working himself up to having a tantrum.

I can feel it.

I decide to help him along.

"You can't hurt me, Maldon," I call. "I'm sorry you felt my magic leak over into Auravale. It's given you a false impression of me. You think I'm weak, but I'm not. I'm a mage. Did you know that?"

I sense his surprise, followed by his anger increasing to rage. I remember Jerrin's telling me that magic has to be wielded with a calm mind. If it's not, people start making mistakes.

Maldon is not calm.

I decide to goad him a little more.

"I'll bet you didn't know that Bree-Ella was a mage too. That's how she remained hidden from you all these years. You couldn't control her, and you can't control me. If you turn around and leave right now, maybe I won't hurt you."

That did it!

He has completely lost control of his thoughts. In fact, he's projecting them so forcefully I can't ignore them.

I didn't know the family telepathy worked this way.

His internal monologue goes something like this:

Why is she resisting me? I'm offering to teach her everything about magic, and all I want in return is occasionally to have access to Bree-Ella's powers—and possibly hers too if she really is a mage. Even an idiot should know that's a reasonable trade.

For a moment he hesitates in his mental ramblings. Then he goes on.

Is it possible that this child really is a mage? If so, then Bree-Ella might

Connie A. Walker

have been one too. The girl feels like a perfect echo of Bree-Ella. I suppose, because of that, she'll give me as much trouble as Bree-Ella did.

He pauses again. His anger intensifies.

Why does this stupid girl want to continue living in a world that doesn't use its magic? I can offer her all of Auravale now and eventually all of Panelda as well. She ought to be down on her knees thanking me. The ungrateful wretch!

His self-discipline is draining away.

He's about ready to explode.

He's just a few seconds from unleashing everything in his arsenal in my direction.

I smile to myself.

Although I don't have younger siblings, I know what to do when a child threatens to throw a fit.

You send him to his room.

You put him in timeout.

While Maldon tries to get himself under enough control that he can obliterate me, my powers are building up in my chest. There is so much thundering magic inside of me, and it is so strong, I feel as if I'm going to split right down the middle.

Instead, I channel it.

Before Maldon knows what's happening, I open a portal, grab hold of him and his horse, pick them up, and pitch them through. Immediately after, I toss the three hellhounds through the portal too.

Before Maldon can react, I figuratively slam the door shut and lock it.

I hear a gasp from behind me.

"What did you do?" Kaden whispers, sounding stunned.

"I sent him back to Hamblin Heath. That's where he's supposed to be, isn't it?"

For several minutes Kaden doesn't say anything.

I'm beginning to think I made a mistake when Kaden finally asks me, "Did you send the hellhounds there, too?"

"Of course," I answer. "What else could I do with them?"

He takes my shoulders and spins me around so I'm facing him. He looks as if he's trying not to laugh. He hugs me so tight I can hardly breathe.

"I almost feel sorry for Maldon," Kaden says. "I'm sure he's having a rough time right now. Probably everyone on the island is."

"Why?" I say, pushing myself out of his arms. "Did I misunderstand the stories you told me? Isn't he supposed to be there?"

"Either there or in prison," Kaden says, finally giving into a few chuckles, "but I'm sure he wishes his hellhounds weren't with him."

I'm confused.

I guess it shows.

"Hellhounds aren't pets like dogs," Kaden tells me. "They're not

229

domesticated. A sorcerer has to maintain magical control of them constantly. When you sent Maldon through the portal, you broke the binding he had on the hellhounds. When you sent them through, they were free of his influence. If Maldon wasn't killed outright, I'm sure he has his hands full, trying to keep himself and his kin alive while he regains control of the beasts."

He can't hold the laughter in any longer.

It bursts out.

Maybe it is funny, and maybe I'll be able to laugh about it some day, but right now I'm having a tough time dealing with Kaden's phrase "If he wasn't killed outright."

Knowing that Maldon wanted to exploit me and probably would eventually have hurt—or maybe killed—me, I still hate the idea that I might have caused someone's death—even an evil sorcerer's.

I try to figure out how to explain my ambivalence to Kaden so I can ask him to assure me that I did the right thing.

Suddenly, I get a strange feeling in my stomach. It's like that second or two of free fall when you dive off the high board.

"What's happening?" I ask Kaden.

He puts his arms around me.

"Hold on," he says. "His Majesty is calling us to Auravale."

Chapter Forty

People who don't come from lands ruled by monarchies should receive mandatory classes in protocol, just in case, and monarchs should not have the power to pluck people who aren't their subjects out of their own worlds and drop them into the middle of their courts.

I would like to protest this peremptory summoning by His Majesty Justus IV, but since he's the ultimate authority in Auravale, there's no one to complain to. But really! Someone should have recognized the position I was being thrust into.

I have spent hours running through ankle high ash, I haven't quite recovered from inhaling a forest fire, and I've just finished doing some more magic that I didn't know I could do.

I'm exhausted.

Not only that, I haven't had a shower in heaven only knows how long. Although my clothes were laundered while I was in the hospital, they were less than formal attire even when they were clean, and they're not clean anymore. In addition, I haven't had access to a comb or a toothbrush since Jerrin brought me, unconscious, to Auravale three or four days ago.

Now, suddenly, I'm in a huge throne room with vaulted ceilings, stained glass windows, glittering gold everywhere, and elegant people dressed in fancy clothes.

The thrones are occupied by a handsome man with graying brown hair and a beautiful woman with blond cascading ringlets flowing over her shoulders.

I want to sit down on the floor and burst into tears.

Instead, I stare at the man who is responsible for my discomfort.

While I'm looking him over, I realize the room is emptying fast.

Even though he's seated, I can tell that Justus IV is at least as tall as his sons and half again as broad. He's dressed in a million-dollar suit made of burgundy brocade trimmed with golden threads and big gold buttons. Around his neck he wears a heavy gold chain that has a four-inch-diameter gold medallion hanging from it. His fingers are adorned with heavy, intricately designed gold rings. On his head is a gleaming golden crown that has peaks and gems as far around as I can see.

(Obviously he really likes gold. No wonder the mines in the northern mountains are so important.)

Despite Justus IV's elegance, his facial features are weathered and worn, as if he's had a hard time despite, or maybe because of, his station in life. He sports an attractive pointed beard that is a shade darker than his hair and has one narrow stripe of white just right of the center of his chin. His dark brown eyes stare back at me with a penetrating gaze.

"Since four of my children speak rather highly of you," he says to me, "and since the son of one of my most trusted advisors has asked for permission to court you, I thought it was about time I took a look at you." He purses his lips and shakes his head. "You are not exactly what I expected."

I'm tired and possibly not thinking straight. I answer him by saying, "Perhaps if Your Majesty had given me a bit more time to prepare after receiving your invitation, I might have arrived in better condition."

"Ah," the king says with the hint of a smile, "Shiane was right. She said I was going to like you. Of course, when I heard about the uproar you are apparently responsible for on Hamblin Heath, I was fairly certain we'd get along. Now, Kaden, I think it's time for you to present your lady officially."

Kaden bows deeply from the waist.

"Your Majesty," he says nodding at the king, "Your Highness," he says nodding at the queen, "may I please present Miss Hellenaura Dark Powers, the great-great-great-granddaughter of your former subject Bree-Ella Dark."

"Welcome to our kingdom, Hellenaura," the king says. He grins at me. (Are kings allowed to grin?) "Now, it's probably time to let you go get cleaned up."

He glances to the left where there are some deep green drapes.

"Shiane, I know you're hiding back there. Make yourself useful and show Hellenaura to the Sparrow Suite. Then tell Jacie to draw her a bath and find her something fresh to wear. She'll need a gown for dinner as well."

Shiane emerges sheepishly from behind the curtains. "I'm doing it exactly the way Jerrin told me to," she says to her father. "How can you still always know where I am?"

"Because I'm king," he says. "Keep practicing." He gives her a little shooing motion with his hand, and she comes over, beaming broadly, and gives me a quick kiss on the cheek.

"I'm so glad you're here," she says. "Come on, let me show you to your room. You might even have time to take a nap if you and Jacie can decide on your clothes fast enough."

As Shiane starts to lead me away, I look longingly over my shoulder at Kaden. We have so much to talk about.

"Kaden," the king says, "I hope you will also join us at the high table tonight."

"Thank you, Your Majesty," he says.

I stop and turn.

"Thank you, Your Majesty," I say, echoing Kaden.

Shiane babbles continuously while she leads me through double doors, across a wide foyer, and up a broad sweeping staircase. We go down the left-hand corridor and up another set of stairs. Shiane stops at the second door and pulls it open.

My first impression is *I'm not touching anything in here. Maybe there's a closet I can sit in.*

The reason for my reaction is that the room is white with a just a little pink to provide some color. Above the huge bed is a ruffled canopy, and tossed artistically on top of a white silk coverlet are about a dozen frilly white and/or pink throw pillows.

The dressing table and matching chair look so delicate that heavy breathing might knock them over. In the middle of the table is a rectangular gold tray with a lacy, pale pink doily centered on it. On the doily are a hairbrush, comb, hand mirror, and a variety of hairclips, all made of gold. On either side of the tray are a dozen crystal and gold containers, from squat little jars to thin, shapely bottles. Each one holds a colored substance, which I assume are perfumes, lotions, powders, and possibly cosmetics.

I think there is enough gold and crystal here to pay off the USA national debt.

A large oval mirror hangs on the wall.

Opposite the bed, there is a creamy white marble fireplace, and on either side of it is an overstuffed chair that appears to be upholstered in white velvet.

Centered on the mantle is a porcelain statuette of a sparrow standing on a twig, which I suppose gives the room its name.

A young woman comes through a door I haven't even had time to notice yet. Based on the fixtures I can see through the doorway behind her, I assume it's a private bathroom.

"Hellie," Shiane says, "this is Jacie. She'll take care of you. If you want or need anything, she'll get it for you. After you've had a chance to bathe and rest, if you want company, Jacie can come get me."

A second later she's out the door.

I want to go on record here and now that I am all for democracy, a classless society, and human rights regardless of gender, race, religious affiliation, country of origin, or educational status.

That said, I have to admit I thoroughly enjoy the next few hours of absolute luxury while Jacie runs my bath, scrubs my back, washes my hair, manicures my nails, picks out my clothing, and tucks me into bed.

When it is time to get dressed for dinner, she wakes me and has me put on a wraparound that's a cross between a bathrobe and a sarong. Then she uses some of the stuff in the crystal jars to soften my skin, shape my eyebrows, darken my eyelids, highlight my cheekbones, and add color to my lips.

She styles my hair by braiding the sides and then fastening them on top of my head with a clip, which she covers with a bow and a small cluster of flowers. She brushes the back of my hair and lets it hang loose.

Then she very carefully helps me into my clothing, which includes a full-length, pale green gown that Cinderella might have worn to the ball. Instead of glass slippers, though, I have white leather pumps with one-inch heels. They are so comfortable they might have been made for me.

When she finishes, I stand in front of the mirror and simply stare.

I still look like myself—but better.

I wish I had a camera with me. When I wake up tomorrow morning, I'll never believe I looked like this.

Then I spot my cellphone on a little table beside the bed.

I get it, put my arm around Jacie, tell her to smile, and take a couple of selfies. They show off the hairdo and makeup, but I want a picture of the whole effect.

I show Jacie how to take a picture.

She clicks off half a dozen before she gets a really good one.

I thank her for everything, and she blushes beautifully. I decide I need a shot of her alone. It takes a few minutes to convince her to pose for me. She stands by the window and I tap the button just before Shiane knocks on the door and then comes in without an invitation.

The rest of the evening is a bit of a blur. I use my phone to take a couple hundred pictures. Maybe later I can look them over and reconstruct the night's events.

When I see Kaden in the Auravalian equivalent of a tuxedo, my heart stops and I can't move. I thought he was beautiful in t-shirt and jeans. I was unprepared for seeing him all dressed up.

My consolation is that when he looks at me he reacts much the same way. His eyes sparkle and his cheeks dimple when he smiles at me. I had no idea he had dimples.

Skyler and Jerrin both kiss my hand and make a point of welcoming me to Auravale. I catch a brief glimpse of Neeve and Karissa at a distance, and I meet some of the other royal siblings. There seem to be several dozen.

Kaden introduces me to his parents and elder brother. They are polite if not overly warm. His mother mentions that the younger children are at home. That's when I learn Kaden has siblings other than just his older brother.

I listen to Auravalian music and observe some of their dance steps. They're enough like our own to make the differences stand out, which makes me feel a bit uncomfortable.

Oh, and sometime over the course of the evening, I eat a meal.

When things are finally winding down, Kaden suggests that we take a walk in one of the palace gardens. By now I'm feeling a little overwhelmed and am glad to get away.

We walk holding hands.

Auravale has two moons, and they are both out tonight.

The flowers, although unfamiliar, are beautiful and fragrant.

We follow a path that is outlined by a lovely flowering hedge. After a while, it opens onto a small circular area that has a fountain in the middle and a few stone benches around the edges.

We sit side by side and watch the statue of a young girl perpetually pouring water out of a pitcher into a basin that overflows, letting the water pool around her feet.

"Hellie," Kaden says, putting his arm around my waist. "Will you marry me?"

I push away from him. "Please don't, Kaden, not now."

"I know you love me," he persists. "I've been feeling it all night. I also know that you need to finish your schooling and I need to finish my apprenticeship. I'm not asking you to marry me tomorrow. I just need to know what to expect. Will you marry me?"

It takes me a few minutes to build up enough courage to answer the way I know I have to.

"No," I say, although it breaks my heart. "Mertley explained to me how rare and special your finding skills are and how many people want and need your services. You deserve to pursue your chosen career and experience all the growth and development and personal satisfaction that your profession will provide. You can't do that in Shawon, and I'm not strong enough to give up my family, my friends, and my lifestyle to live in Auravale. After tonight, I don't think we should see each other anymore."

"You're just being silly," he says, "if those are your only reasons."

I'm surprised and a little offended by his reaction. Here I am, willing to make this great personal sacrifice for his happiness, and he calls me silly.

He continues. "You talk as if two people who love each other can't find solutions to their problems. We come from different worlds. We'll face many challenges. Where we live and how we work are only two of them."

"They're big ones," I say.

"Even so, I know we can find answers that will allow us to be happy. If that's possible, will you marry me?"

"Kaden, don't. I've thought it through and I think—"

He puts his index finger up to my lips to shush me. "You thought about it alone. We can think about it together. If we come up with pleasant possibilities, will you marry me?"

He captures me with his eyes and holds me in thrall.

I want nothing more than to spend the rest of my life with him, but I could not bear to have his love turn into resentment. It would kill me. Better to let him go now than to risk the pain later.

"Hellie," Kaden says with gentle patience, "I have explained to you that I love you and I will never love another. You love me. Try to have a little faith in us."

"I want to, but—"

He puts his finger up to my lips again.

Dark in the Forest: Another Modern Fairytale

"I don't want to hear the word *but*. Believe in us together. We can find solutions to all the problems life can concoct as long as we are committed to each other and are determined to create our own happiness. So I'll ask you again. Will you marry me, Hellie?"

I'm frustrated and on the verge of losing my temper. It's not fair of him to keep making me say no.

"First," I say, letting a little of my irritation show, "tell me how we can live in Shawon so I can be near my family and you can still accomplish what you want and need to do in Auravale."

He takes my hands and kisses my palms. "That is all you need to hear?"

"Yes."

He stares up at the moons for a minute or two.

"If I can prove there's a way for us to live in Shawon and for me still to be a medical finder, then you'll be comfortable saying you'll marry me? Is that right?"

"Yes," I tell him.

He smiles at me, once again showing off his dimples. I feel my pulse pounding like the hooves of a racehorse about to win the Kentucky Derby.

I so want to be convinced it's possible.

"It is simple," Kaden says. "Neeve has explained the process to me. I will commute. We will live in Shawon, and when it is time for me to go to work, you can open a portal for me. When I have finished my shift, I will call you on your cellphone and you can open a portal so I can come home. If the time on Earth is too far out of synch with time on Panelda, which will happen from time to time, or if it is inconvenient for you to open a portal for me for any reason, I will ask a member of the royal family to do it. I'm sure Shiane would think it was fun."

"You'd really be willing to commute between worlds every day?"

"Not every day. Once I complete my apprenticeship, I will be allowed to choose my schedule. I'll only work five days out of seven, as people in your world do. You can even open portals for me to come home for lunch if that's what makes you happy. Is that a satisfactory solution?"

He kisses my palms again.

"Will you marry me, Hellie?"

What is a girl supposed to say when she's confronted by someone as determined, as persistent, as patient, as romantic, as kind, as loving, and as perfect as Kaden?

There's only one answer, and I say it.

"Yes."

Connie A. Walker was born in Blackfoot, Idaho, attended elementary school in Kansas City, Kansas, and graduated high school in Fairbanks, Alaska. She has been an insatiable reader and a compulsive writer since childhood.

She is the author of the prize-winning plays *The Light Still Burns* and *Nearly a Woman*, as well as the prize-winning children's book *Timmy and the K'nick K'nocker Ring*.

Ms. Walker has a B.A. in theatre/playwriting from Brigham Young University, plus a B.S. in psychology and an MSW from the University of Utah. She has worked as a graphic artist, a technical writer, a foster care worker, a clinical social worker, and a mental health program manager.

Regardless of what she was doing for her day job, there was never a time when she stopped writing.